Dust Off the Bones

ALSO BY PAUL HOWARTH

Only Killers and Thieves

Dust Off the Bones

A Novel

Paul Howarth

HARPER LARGE PRINT

An Imprint of HarperCollinsPublishers

DUST OFF THE BONES. Copyright © 2021 by Paul Howarth. All rights reserved. Printed in the United States of America. No part of this book may be used or reproduced in any manner whatsoever without written permission except in the case of brief quotations embodied in critical articles and reviews. For information, address HarperCollins Publishers, 195 Broadway, New York, NY 10007.

HarperCollins books may be purchased for educational, business, or sales promotional use. For information, please e-mail the Special Markets Department at SPsales@harpercollins.com.

FIRST HARPER LARGE PRINT EDITION

ISBN: 978-0-06-309056-9

Library of Congress Cataloging-in-Publication Data is available upon request.

21 22 23 24 25   LSC   10 9 8 7 6 5 4 3 2 1

To my parents, Stephen and Marion,
for making anything possible

The chief topic of the past week has been the trial of the seven black troopers for the murder of aboriginals at Irvinebank, and that of ex Sub-Inspector Nichols for being an accessory before the fact to the same. The trial of Nichols only lasted about half a day. The evidence for the Crown was of such a nature [that] the police magistrate said there was not much use going on with the case. The prisoner was discharged amid considerable applause.

—FROM "THE IRVINEBANK MURDERS,"
AN ARTICLE IN *THE QUEENSLANDER*,
FEBRUARY 7, 1885 (ABRIDGED)

Dust Off the Bones

Prologue

1885
Central Queensland, Australia

They stood on the bank of the desert crater, staring down into hell. Trampled humpies, scattered possessions, discarded weapons, severed limbs, all bogged in a churn of crimson mud; the camp had become a slaughter yard. One of the men wept openly. The other vomited on the ground. Not two days ago they had been here, in this crater, welcomed by the Kurrong people, attempting to preach to them, sharing a meal. Now that same entire community lay heaped in an enormous pyre: a knot of mangled bodies, popping, crackling, peeling as they burned. A thick smoke column rising. A smell both men would carry to their graves.

After four days' nonstop riding over a wasteland of sun-scorched scrub they reached the settled colony in the east, and the single-street outpost of Bewley perched on its frontier. Desperate and disheveled they tore into town, slid from their saddles, and scrambled along a narrow path to the courthouse, bursting through the black-tarred double doors into the cool flagstone lobby beyond.

"An outrage! A most terrible outrage!"

From his desk by the wall, the clerk looked up at the piebald-faced white man, fair skin bleached and blotted by the sun, and a properly dressed native like none they got round here. "Help you?" he called, and startled, the white man spun.

"There's been an outrage in the desert. A hundred killed! More!"

A guard wandered out from the cell block and crossed the lobby to where they stood, glaring at them, cocking and uncocking his revolver with his thumb, but before he could speak, a side door opened and out barreled Police Magistrate MacIntyre, barking, "Donnaghy, get that darkie out of here, or else throw him in the cells."

The accent was thick Scots. The guard smiled, clicked his tongue, tossed his head toward the doors.

Nobody moved. The guard cocked the revolver again, but the white man said, "Matthew, please," and reluctantly he went outside, Donnaghy following a few paces behind.

"Well now," Magistrate MacIntyre said, "what do we have here?"

"There's been an outrage in—"

"Yes, yes, I heard all that. What I mean is: who the hell are you?"

"Reverend Francis Bean, sir. That is Matthew."

"Ah, missionaries."

"Yes we are."

"I don't suppose you'd thank me for a whiskey then?"

Reverend Bean cast about the lobby. "Perhaps just some water, if I may."

The magistrate steered him toward the office. "Come through here and I'll find you some. Let's you and me have a little talk."

They sat on either side of a rosewood writing desk, MacIntyre cupping his chin in his hand, Reverend Bean fidgeting in his chair. Wiping his hands on his trousers, picking at his shirt hem; he'd soaked his chest with water, gulping it down. MacIntyre waited, expressionless, slumped over the desk, as falteringly Reverend

Bean began recounting all that had happened, all they had seen: the horror of the crater, the posse they'd encountered the day before, the tall man who'd been leading them, the one calling himself Noone.

"And how are you so sure," MacIntyre asked finally, once Reverend Bean was done, "that this group of men you claim you met were Native Police?"

"The officer admitted as much himself."

"I see." With great effort the magistrate shifted his bulk and heaved himself upright. "And did Inspector Noone tell you the nature of his work out there, I wonder?"

"He had two young white boys with him. There'd been a murder, he said."

"Exactly. Three innocents, butchered by savages in their own home. Those poor McBride brothers lost their parents, their little sister, their whole family just about. Meaning it now falls on Inspector Noone to find the culprits and bring them before the law. You don't object to justice being done in the colony, do you, Reverend Bean?"

"They can't all have been suspects, surely. There were women and children in that camp. It was obviously preplanned."

"Obvious to who? You? Yet you didn't try to stop them, or warn the Kurrong?"

Reverend Bean was aghast. "But, I couldn't have . . ."

"You did nothing. Ran away, in fact. Do I have that right?"

"There were far too many of them. We were unarmed!"

MacIntyre only shrugged.

"You don't understand. The things Noone threatened me with . . ."

"Are nothing compared to what he'll do if he learns you've been in here telling tales. Noone is not a man to be trifled with. Not if you value your life."

Reverend Bean had turned ashen. He looked suddenly unwell. Steeling himself, he said, "There is only one authority I answer to, and it is not Inspector Noone."

"Well then, make your statement. But I promise you, he will find you, and when he does no god will be able to protect you then."

The magistrate reached for one of the pens in a double holder on his desk, dipped it in the inkwell, and held it poised over his writing pad. His bushy eyebrow lifted, watching the reverend writhe, as a drop of black ink slid slowly along the gully, hung from the nib in a teardrop, then spattered on the pad.

"Forgive me Lord, I haven't the strength," Reverend Bean whispered, jumping to his feet and scurrying for the door. As his footsteps receded over the lobby flagstones, MacIntyre speared his pen into its holder and flopped back in his chair.

"If it's spiritual guidance you're in need of," the magistrate called after him, laughing, "there's a church at the end of the street!"

Outside, Matthew was sheltering in the shade of the courthouse wall. He hurried over, asked what had happened; Reverend Bean only blinked into the glare.

"Father? What did he say?"

"He'll take care of it now, Matthew." His voice distant, detached.

"Take care how?"

"We've done our duty. It's no longer our concern."

Matthew glanced at the courthouse doors. "And you believe him?"

"We have no choice. He is a man of the law, after all."

"So were them others what did it!"

"I know that," Reverend Bean said sadly. "Yes, I know they were."

They rode out of Bewley later that afternoon, heading for Mulumba, as had once been their original plan. They were washed now, and clean-shaven, and had provisions in their saddlebags; the reverend had bought a pint of rum. They were no longer talking. Hardly a word between them since. When they passed the little church at the far end of town, Matthew blessed himself dutifully and muttered a short prayer, while in sight of the cross above the doorway, Reverend Bean turned his back on the building, and hung his head in shame.

PART I

1890

Five Years Later

Chapter 1
Billy McBride

The heaving bar of the Bewley Hotel erupted at the sight of the wall-eyed musician shuffling out from behind the curtain screen, the drinkers whistling and catcalling and rising from their chairs, hurling whatever was at hand, as the young man laden with all manner of pipes and gongs parped and jangled his way to the center of the stage. Through spectacles as thick as bottle ends he gazed out at the crowd, missiles sailing by him, or in some cases finding their mark, then put his lips to the mouth organ, blew a tentative note, and by pumping a foot pedal struck a beat on his drum. He wore it like a backpack, a giant bass with FRANKIE'S TRAVELING DANCE BAND stenciled in black lettering on the dirty cream skin, one of many musical contraptions he was scaffolded in. Next came a puff on the kazoo, a ridiculous birdlike honking that drew roars of derision from the crowd. They'd been expecting Theresa and her tassels. Her name was on the chalkboard outside. Instead they'd got this strange little man wearing clackers and cowbells, clutching a ukulele, a hand-horn strapped to his knee. They heckled him all the harder. Despite everything, Frankie began to play.

From a table near the doors, farthest from the stage, Billy McBride sipped his whiskey and watched the performance steadily unravel. A chair was thrown at Frankie, glass smashed on the floor; someone had Horace, the hotelier, by his collar, demanding he get Theresa out here now. Regardless, the kid was really going for it, playing for his life so it seemed: cheeks puffing, eyes bulging, flapping his elbows and knees. A bloke took his shirt off and jumped up onstage, began imitating Theresa, fondling himself and calling her name. Frankie stalled and the man shook him. Frankie rattled like a box of spoons. "Play, you little bastard, I'm dancing!" the man yelled, to cheers from the crowd. Billy smirked and saw off his drink, rose to his feet, and started walking. He had to get the kid out of here. Only one way this would end.

Pushing his way to the stage, jostling between the men—one took exception and turned with his fist raised, only to realize who he'd be swinging at and apologetically lower it again. Billy moved past him, bounded up the stage steps, and briefly the barroom fell still. He spoke with the shirtless man, a hand on his shoulder, and obediently he rejoined the crowd. There was booing. Someone shouted for Billy to leave it alone. But now Billy had Frankie by the arm and was steering him off the stage, the drinkers reluctantly parting, a similar reluctance in Frankie too, Billy noticed, like this was a calling he couldn't leave. Billy could almost imagine him, tramping from town to town, maybe after years of watching his father perform this selfsame sorry act. Then one day the old man keels over and the act becomes Frankie's to perform, playing street corners for coppers, these dead-end drinking halls, desperately trying to better his father's legacy, or build one of his own.

Well, that much felt familiar. Billy could relate to that at least.

Out the door they stumbled, onto the lamplit verandah, down the steps to the dark dirt road. The crowd surged after them, and still Frankie was resisting— Billy had half a mind to let him go, see what became of him then. On a night just like this he'd once seen a hair cream salesman nearly mated with a dog, only for the dog to save them both by fighting harder than the man. That was what Frankie had in store for him, if he didn't get out of town.

The musician lost his footing coming down the steps, tripped and, unbalanced by his instruments, fell and landed facefirst in the dust. That brightened the mood a little. Laughter from the men spilling outside. Stuck on their cattle stations, or mustering the lonely bush, what they needed was entertainment, preferably from Theresa, but you couldn't be too choosy out here. Billy hooked Frankie by the arm then when he was partway up let him go again, to great guffaws from the crowd. Billy smiled at them. The men now egging him on. Frankie was up to his hands and knees, his bass drum wobbling—Billy gave him a kick up the backside.

"Get up," he whispered. "Get out of here. Run."

Frankie climbed to his feet and stood there dumbly, pushed his spectacles up the bridge of his nose. He squinted longingly at the hotel but Billy took hold of the drum and spun him around facing east.

"I said run, you bastard! Run!"

Another kick up the backside, harder this time, and Frankie began edging away. Billy let him get so far then set off after him, kicking him down the road, the crowd howling as the pair disappeared into the darkness at the edge of town, only the white drum skin visible, swinging back and forth, accompanied by an occasional clash of cymbals or the honk of a knee horn.

Billy returned to a grand ovation. He wasn't short of a drink all night.

Sunlight glinted in the brass fittings and upturned glasses strewn over the tables and bar, smoke and dust hanging in thick swirls. Birds chirruped outside. A carriage clattered by. Slumped in a wooden chair, Billy opened a single eyelid and squinted at the wreckage of the room. Snoring bodies on the tables, in the chairs, on the floor. Someone farted. Billy tried to move. His throat burned like hellfire and both his hands were numb. He struggled upright and glanced out of the window and wondered what had happened to his horse. Could have sworn he'd left Buck outside by the water trough, but he'd not been there when Billy had chased off that musician last night. He cupped his face with his hands and groaned into the darkness, caught the stale and deathly blowback of his breath.

"Morning."

Horace wandered through from a back room, carrying a mop and bucket; unshaven, his bald head glistening, white shirt unbuttoned to his chest. He set down his things, fetched a towel and a tray, and began clearing those tables he could get to, gathering up the glasses, wiping the surfaces down.

"What time is it?" Billy croaked.

"Seven."

"In the morning?"

"What d'you reckon?"

Billy dragged himself to standing, clutching the chair-back for support. "Some night in here last night," he said.

"There's water behind the bar if you want it."

"How about some breakfast n'all?"

"Don't bloody push it. I should be charging you lot lodging as it is."

Billy made it to the bar, flung himself against the counter, and clung on. When he had his balance he reached over and found a water pitcher, filled a glass and downed it, filled the glass again.

"Better?" Horace asked, walking over, the tray clinking in his hands.

"Getting there."

Horace unloaded the tray, watching Billy sidelong, picking his moment to speak. He had known the McBride family for years now—the father had been a touchy bugger too before he died. Now Billy had taken his place in the town and at the bar, came down from the station most rest days, and usually ended up like this. Not that Horace could blame him. The shit that young man had been through would have broken most anyone else.

"Ask you something?" Horace said.

Billy lowered his glass and looked at him. "If you want."

"Why'd you save the hide of that music man last night?"

"Saved you, more like—they'd have tore this place to the ground."

"Come off it, Billy. You didn't know him from somewhere?"

"Where the hell would I know him from? Where'd you even find him?"

Horace shrugged. "Wandered in asking if he could play. I'd have sent him packing but Theresa's got a fever from the clap."

"You should have changed the chalkboard then."

"You reckon? And get nobody in?"

"Mate," Billy said, shaking his head, "where else are we going to go?"

Horace waited to see if he'd speak again, then when he didn't said, "Suit yourself," and went back to the tables with his tray. Billy sipped his water and watched him in the long mirror, then paused and cleared his throat.

"Reminded me a bit of my brother," he said.

In the Drover's Rest roadhouse he ate a plate of sausage and eggs, with fried potatoes, bread and butter, and coffee as black as tar, then set about finding his missing horse. Buck had once been his father's, a chestnut-colored brumby he'd caught and tamed, and Billy would have been sorry to lose him, though he doubted he'd got too far. He walked along the main street, returning greetings as they came: Saturday morning, but already people were at it, happy and eager to start the day. Billy didn't know how they could stand it, this little town, their little lives. If he could have left by now he would have. Had the choice ever been his.

He found the horse in the livery stables. Jones the stableman had spotted Buck wandering and brought him inside for the night: "I fed him and brushed him for you, made sure he slept. Ride all day if he has to. No worries about that."

Billy pulled a handful of coins from his pocket. "What do I owe you?"

"Oh, no charge for you Billy-lad. Not with all what you done."

Grimly Billy looked at him. He swallowed, bit down hard. Grinning stupidly, Jones folded his hands into the bib of his overalls and shook his outsize head. Billy dropped the coins back into his pocket. "Appreciate it," he said.

A half mile out of town the native camps began: once a small smattering of humpies now almost a township in its own right. Makeshift tents and woven gunyahs, piles of salvaged scrap, people living among it, hundreds now it seemed, drifting out of the bush and settling here, arse-to-cheek with the town. They watched him pass, pausing in their chores, children breaking off their games; Billy couldn't stand to look at them. He rested his hand on the butt of his revolver, kept his head down, and rode through open scrub country toward Broken Ridge cattle station, his home for the last five years. Really there was nowhere else out here. The drought had taken it all. Little family-run smallholdings like Glendale, his father's old place, that had one by one folded or been abandoned or been swallowed by Broken Ridge. Families that for generations had tended the same patch of land had fled east without hardly a fight, and now lived in cities working in shops or on building sites or instead tended tiny hobby-farms, milking every morning, shearing the wool off a dozen dumb sheep.

Softcocks, in Billy's view. Should have stayed and ridden it out.

In his hut on the workers' compound, he stripped off his clothes and lay on the bed and slept off last night's excess, then woke feeling fresher but slicked in a thin film of sweat. Early afternoon now, the hut burning up: Billy washed himself with soap and dressed in a clean shirt and slacks. He shaved in the little mirror, careful around his beard, and combed his dark hair, though only barely, the two had never really got along. His father's sad eyes staring back at him. The lump where his brother Tommy had once broken his nose. Handsome, they generally called him, though he looked a long way older than his twenty-one years.

The broad track led straight up the hillside through a moat of barren scrub and linked the compound with the main Broken Ridge homestead. A grand white colonial mansion house with a wraparound verandah propped on wooden stilts, perching on the hillside beneath the towering sandstone escarpment that gave the station its name, overlooking its landholding, or as much as could be seen from here. The Broken Ridge empire stretched for thousands of square miles: excepting Bewley itself and those few ruined smallholdings still gamely hanging on, in one way or another almost the entire district was Sullivan land.

At the bottom of the steps Billy dismounted and

stood waiting for the native stableboy to fetch his horse. The stables were up behind the house, across a clearing; the boy was slumped on a stool outside the door. Billy whistled for him. The boy glanced up and swiped away flies, then rose and slouched into the barn. Billy stood raging. Insolent little fuck. When it became clear the boy wasn't going to return he tied Buck tight to the balustrades and left him there, in the hope he would shit on the steps.

There were voices on the verandah. Billy reached the top of the stairs and found two men sitting at an outside table, voile curtains billowing behind them through the open French doors. One Billy already knew: Wilson Drummond, Katherine's father, the man who'd first traded her to John Sullivan when she was only eighteen, then shot out here like a rat into a grain store when he'd heard the squatter had died, heirless, giving his daughter first claim on all he owned. The other man he didn't recognize. Younger, with floppy fair hair and a smooth city face; Billy could guess exactly what he was about. This would be the third such show-pony Drummond had dragged out here and tried to stud, wooed with the promise of riches and land. But then they saw what that fortune would require of them, the work, the heat, the dust, the flies, not to mention the woman they'd be marrying, who could be just as ungovernable as her land when she put her mind to it, and none had stuck it yet.

Their conversation stalled when they noticed him. Wilson Drummond set down his wineglass and stood, saying, "Billy, my boy, good to see you. Though it's not the best time, I'm afraid."

He'd never spoken so warmly to Billy before. "It's Katherine I'm here for," he replied. "She inside?"

Drummond glanced anxiously at the city boy, who was watching Billy while he drank. "Charles," Drummond said, "this is Billy McBride, the young man I was telling you about—his family had that little run to the south there. Tragic circumstances, obviously, but we're glad to still have him on board. I'm sure you'll find him very useful, being a local lad and all. Billy, this is Charles Sinclair, Katherine's fiancé."

He took his time about standing. Dabbed his lips with a napkin, folded it, set it aside, making Billy wait. Finally he ambled over with his hand outstretched, and Billy couldn't think of a way to not: he shook the hand forcefully, found it soft and damp and feminine, an urge to wipe off his own once they were done.

"A pleasure," Sinclair said. "Wilson speaks very highly of you."

"Is that right?"

Sinclair laughed, turned to the view of the hillside and the pastures far beyond. "Quite the country you have out here. I had no idea what to expect."

"It's not for everyone," Billy said.

"Well, I'm very much looking forward to becoming acquainted with it. Wilson tells me we owe you quite the debt. All this land and not a native to trouble us— almost sounds too good to be true!"

Billy glanced to the west, to the distant shadow of the ranges, to all that lay beyond, as Wilson Drummond said, "I was telling him about how you saw off those myalls after what happened with your family."

"That ain't none of his business. None of yours, neither."

A silence hung between them. Drummond said, "No, I suppose not."

"Anyway," Billy said, "we still do have it. Glendale, it's still ours."

"Sorry?"

"You said we used to have a run south of here. We still do. It's my land."

Drummond hummed doubtfully. "It's not quite that simple, Billy."

"How's that now?"

"Well, your father's lease ended when he was killed, sadly, meaning the land reverts to the agent, who holds it on my behalf. I've been through it all with the lawyers. Getting the estate ready for Charles."

Billy looked between them. His jaw creased. "On *your* behalf now, is it?"

"On behalf of the station, then."

"Which last I checked belongs to a Sullivan, which you ain't."

"It amounts to the same thing."

"It amounts to illegal dummying, did your lawyers tell you that? Only reason that agent's there in the first place is to get around the Land Acts. John told me how things work round here—I know exactly where I bloody well stand."

He marched away along the verandah, heard Charles Sinclair let out another laugh. Turning in through the front door, he brushed past the waiting houseboy, knocking him against the wall, then strode along the carpeted hallway and into the vast whitewashed atrium around which the house revolved. A broad staircase swept up to a balcony landing, the ceiling vaulted into the roof space high above, while the white-paneled ground-floor walls were inset with matching white-paneled doors, identifiable only by their little brass knobs. Billy made for the one tucked under the staircase, composed himself, knocked, and cracked it ajar.

The room that had once been John Sullivan's parlor was now the office from which his young widow ran the estate. Working at the same desk her husband had been shot over, sitting in the same chair in which he'd bled out, Katherine looked up when Billy entered, and smiled. Framed in sunlight from the window behind her, her dark ringlets tumbling, her eyes dark also, and very bright. She set down her pen in the groove and folded her hands on the desk, her bare forearms tanned golden brown. She was wearing a yellow blouse with blue and white trim, and just the very sight of her caught in Billy's chest.

"Mr. McBride," she said playfully, "I'm certainly surprised to see you."

Billy stepped forward, closed the door. "I just met your new fiancé outside."

"Oh? And what did you make of him?"

"I'm sure you'll be very happy the pair of you."

"I'm glad you approve."

"I never said I approved."

"You don't think he's suitable?"

"I think he's suitable for slapping in his smug city mouth."

She spluttered laughter. "The idea had crossed my mind too."

"Probably best coming from you then."

"We haven't quite got to that stage yet."

"Well, I'd hurry up about it. Looks like he's settling in."

"The man's only been here a few days."

"I'd have slapped the bastard the minute he first walked up them steps."

Amused, she leaned back in her chair. The leather gently creaked. She had redecorated the room since her husband's days, taken down the wall-mounted trophies, repapered in cool pastel shades. But the two wingback chairs were still there, angled in front of the desk. Billy hovered between them, fidgeting his hands.

"So then," Katherine said with mock formality, "aside from disparaging my fiancé, was there another reason for this interruption? Anything else I can do for you? Anything on your mind?"

"Aye, there is actually."

Her eyes flinched at his sincerity, but she continued, "Well, I'm sure it's very important, since you're all dressed up for the occasion. If I'm not mistaken you might even have acquainted your hair with a comb."

Billy looked at his getup. "I'd been working, so . . ."

"I'm honored. You want to tell me what this is all about?"

"Maybe after?" he said timidly, hopefully; Katherine caught the implication and the tremble in his voice, and she was up and moving, their little dance over, hurrying around the desk in a rustle of skirts, grabbing him and kissing him, pulling him against her openmouthed. Gasping, they parted, such desire in her eyes. Trailing his hand she went to the door, locked it, kissed him again. She gathered her skirts to her waist and leaned back against the desk, and they fucked then, frantically, silently, as had become their way.

It was over quickly, never lasted long, stolen moments all they had. They staggered apart and righted themselves, Billy fastening his trousers, Katherine pulling up her underwear, shrugging down her skirts, both suddenly bashful; if anything, Billy was worse. This thing between them had been at her instigation from the outset; he had never been the one in charge. Katherine laughed shyly. Billy smiled and looked away. She stepped close and he held her, kissed the top of her head.

"I missed you," she said into his chest. "Where have you been?"

"Working. Same as always."

"It's been weeks, Billy."

"I come up too often as it is."

"You don't come up often enough."

"The men'll start suspecting. Probably already do."

"I don't care. Do you?"

Billy didn't answer.

"If I made you head stockman you could come up as often as you liked."

"Headman? The bloody boy won't even stable my horse!"

"He's difficult that one. Young."

"They're all difficult."

"It wouldn't be the house staff you'd be in charge of."

"I've told you, I don't want it."

"You know what the men think of you. You're the best one for the job."

"They don't know nothing about me. Anyhow, Joe's all right."

"You've never liked him."

"He's too soft is his problem. That old cripple Morris has to go."

"The one with the knee?"

"Mm-hm."

"I heard he has nowhere else."

"Nobody has anywhere else."

"Oh, you're a coldhearted man, Billy McBride."

"Is that what you think of me now?"

"Well, it's some way of courting, asking me to throw a cripple out on his ear."

"Courting, are we? I thought you was engaged?"

"When anyone bothers to ask my opinion on the matter, they'll soon find out that I'm not."

She stepped away, unlocked the door, and Billy sat in one of the leather wingbacks, watching her move around the room. She fixed them both a whiskey, dropped a slice of lemon in each, a new fashion she'd picked up somewhere that Billy didn't care for at all. Besides, he'd had enough whiskey last night.

He took the drink anyway, thanked her; Katherine sat down opposite, smiled, and took a sip. "Seemed like you might really have something to tell me?"

"Aye, there's something." Turning the tumbler back and forth in his hands.

"Come on then, let's have it out."

He swallowed hard and looked at her. "It's time I went back to Glendale, made a proper go of the run. The paddocks are up, all it's waiting on's a mob, and there's a sale at the Lawton cattle yards the week after next."

She was watching him evenly. Another sip of her drink. "And you plan on living down there?"

"It's not far."

"No, it's not. But you're ready for that? The house?"

"It's only a house."

"Seems like you've made your mind up."

"You know it's just something I have to do."

"On your own, though?"

"I'll still get up to see you whenever I can."

"Whenever you can. So, I'm not to have any part in this venture?"

"Well, that's what we need to talk about: the terms."

Katherine inhaled and slow-blinked. "Not as a business partner, Billy, for goodness' sake. You can have whatever you need. Men, cattle, horses . . . John ruined your family, it's the least you deserve. What I'm asking is—"

"Not all of us he didn't. I'm still around."

"What I'm asking is, where do I fit in these plans?"

Billy shifted in the wingback. "Like I said, I'll get up when I can."

"Well, lucky me."

"What, then? What do you want? Aren't you getting married anyhow?"

"You know I'm not."

Katherine put her glass on a side table and came to kneel by Billy's chair. She laid a hand on his arm. "Look, I know what it means to you, turning Glendale around. But is that all you want from life? Is there really nothing else?"

Billy didn't answer her. Staring into his drink.

"I can't hold them off forever, Billy. The crows have

been circling this place since John died. I'll need a husband eventually. It shouldn't matter but it does."

"So hitch yourself to that plank out there, if it bothers you so much."

"And wouldn't that bother you?"

"'Course it bloody would."

Her hand slid free. She backed away and perched on the edge of her chair again. "Do something about it, then. You could run the two stations as one."

Already he was shaking his head. "I need to get Glendale going on its own."

"Why? Because your father couldn't? What does that prove?"

"That's just how it is."

"And how long will all this take?"

He shrugged. "Couple of years, maybe. Depends on the rains."

"A couple of *years*, Billy?"

"I'm not asking you to wait."

"So what are you asking?"

"Like you said: cattle, supplies, I might need—"

"Have you even been listening to a word I've said?"

"—a proper deed, I reckon. Your old man's out there now saying the land ain't even mine!"

Billy's anger withered under her gaze. A wall clock counted the silence until eventually Katherine stirred and said, "Well, at least now I know where I stand with you: a means to a bloody deed."

"Don't be like that now."

"How else can I be?" she said, her voice faltering. "I'm offering you everything and you're breaking my heart, and what's worse is I don't think you even know you're doing it."

She rounded the desk and sat down, picked up her pen and dipped it, her face flushed and her eyes watery, the pen trembling faintly in her hand. She spoke without looking at him: "I've work to do."

"I didn't mean it how you took it. It came out all wrong."

"I'll send word to Joe. Take whatever you need."

"Katie, please."

"I'm busy, I said."

There was a knock at the door. It opened and her father was standing there, asking, "So, what's this business that's so important? Anything I need to know?"

"Billy's moving back to Glendale, setting up on his own. We're sorry to lose him, but I think it's for the best. I've told him the land is his and we'll get him started with anything he needs. Joe can take care of the arrangements."

Wilson Drummond scowled as he processed this news, but the way Katherine had said it gave him little chance to object. She flicked her eyes to Billy then went back to her work, and for a moment Billy sat there gripping his whiskey tumbler and staring at her, before lurching to his feet and making for the door. Drummond jumped aside to let him pass, and Billy slammed the tumbler so hard on the table that the lemon slice was still bobbing long after he'd left the room.

Chapter 2
Tommy McBride

Four hundred miles south of Bewley, near the border with New South Wales, dawn filtered through the dusty bunkhouse of a sheep station called Barren Downs. Men rising groggily from their swags and cot beds, groaning and hacking, pulling on their clothes and boots. The door opened, raw sunlight breaking the gloom, as one of them stepped outside and pissed loudly against the wall. The others called him a filthy bastard. He told them to go to hell. Low laughter, muted chattering, suddenly broken by a cry from across the room. It was the new boy, Tommy McBride, tossing in his bedroll, moaning in his dreams; someone yelled for him to shut the fuck up. Irritably they went on dressing, then filed out into the morning sun, the station overseer the last to leave. A tall, wiry Tasmanian by the name of Cal Burns, he stood rolling a cigarette in the aisle. Licked it, lit it, plucked a string of loose tobacco from his lip, watching Tommy sleep. The hell he was dreaming about, Burns didn't know. Boy writhed like a whore in heat. And not for the first time, either. Burns shook his head. It had been a mistake ever setting him on. Him and his blackboy both.

"Wakey-wakey, you crazy bastard. Rise and fucking shine."

Burns tapped the ash from his cigarette over Tommy's face, nudged him with his boot cap, then outright kicked him in the gut. Tommy woke, gasping. Wrenched from the smoke-filled crater: ash swirling, boots suckered, the wounded crawling through the slurry, the dead piled into mounds. He'd heard a gunshot, felt the blood spatter on his face; now he jerked onto his elbow and looked up to find Noone laughing over him, those ghostly pale eyes, only the voice when he spoke didn't belong to Noone at all: "I thought I already warned you to cut that mad shit out."

Burns crushed his cigarette, left the bunkhouse, boots clipping the wooden boards, and steadily Tommy realized where he was. He wiped his face, relief washing through him, cast off his tangled bedroll and began dressing. Blue-eyed, fair-haired and freckled, boyish for nineteen, but the years had put a thickness in his shoulders and arms. He pulled on his boots quickly, then hurried out of the barn.

Last into breakfast, Tommy collected his oats, bread, and tea, and amid the bustle of the dining hall looked for somewhere to sit. There were no empty places. Nobody offered to make room. He knew how his dreams unsettled them; yes, they came less frequently these days, but in places like this once was often enough. Superstitious types, stockmen. As Tommy knew all too well. He managed to find a bench-end to perch on, kept his eyes down, ate his meal. He could feel the others watching him, his left hand particularly, its two missing fingers, holding his mug in an awkward, pinched grip.

"Acting like none of you's never had a bloody nightmare before."

Grumbling around him. Tommy ate his oats. At the head of the table Cal Burns stood and began doling out jobs for the day: yardwork, stockwork, repairs, errands to be run. One by one they received their instructions, gathered their breakfast things and left, until only Tommy, Burns, and a stockman called Alan Ames remained.

"McBride," Burns snapped, "you and your blackboy can finish that fencing. Most useless pair of bastards I ever hired. I want that paddock done by Sunday, understand?"

The paddock was miles of fencing, impossible in that time. Tommy shrugged and nodded, and Burns spluttered, "Look at him nodding, dumb as a bloody mule."

Ames laughed. Tommy drained his tea. Picked up his mug and bowl.

"And I don't want no cockeyed fence line on account of that gammy hand."

"Hand's fine," Tommy said, standing, a quick glance at Burns. "So's the fence."

"Bugger me, it speaks, Cal," Ames said. "Thought he was crippled *and* mute."

At the servery Tommy pocketed a hunk of leftover bread, then when he came outside found that his bedroll and clothes had been scattered throughout the yard, payback for disturbing them all last night. Sniggering, the men watched him chase his things down and ball them into a bundle that he carried to the stables, where Beau's big gray head was already hanging expectantly over the door of his stall.

"Don't," Tommy warned him. "I've took enough shit this morning as it is."

The horse nickered doubtfully. Tommy petted him

and briefly rested his brow on his neck, then saddled him, tied up the bundle, and led him back outside. A few of the men were still lingering; Tommy took off at a gallop, before they started up again.

Arthur was mounted and waiting on the track by the native workers' camp, the little village of tents and shelters in which they ate and slept: chewing on a long grass stalk, hair wild and unkempt, beard to his chest, and frail even at this distance, drowned by his baggy work clothes.

"What time d'you call this?" he hollered, when Tommy came in range.

"I was late waking."

"Oh yeah? How d'you manage that in a bunkhouse full of men?"

Tommy drew up alongside him. "Give it a rest—you ready?"

Arthur noticed the bundled clothes and bedroll. "Planning a trip?"

"Just looking after what's mine."

"Any reason?"

"Nope."

Arthur eyed him carefully. "You sure about that, Tommy?"

"I just told you, didn't I?"

Arthur turned away, blew out the grass stalk through

the gap from his missing front tooth, then set off without another word. After a moment Tommy caught him up and the two of them rode in silence, west through swaying grassland, side by side together, as it had been these past five years. Ruefully Tommy glanced across at his old friend. He might still have had a brother out there, wherever Billy was these days, but in reality Arthur was the closest thing to family that Tommy had left. But the silences between them were getting longer, and louder; Tommy hid how things still affected him, lied about his dreams. He was ashamed, was the truth of it. No doubt Arthur could tell. The old man knew him better than probably anyone—yet look how he kept his distance, how far apart they rode.

"You've not even asked where we're headed," Tommy called over, an attempt at a joke, since they'd done the same work three weeks straight.

"Mate, it's written all over your miserable face."

Their tools were where they'd left them, by the fence line, near the creek, scattered beside the final post they'd driven yesterday. Despite the many days they'd been at this, the paddock was still barely half done, a long seam of metal cutting through the grass heads where there should have been none. The thing gave Tommy shivers. Made him think of cheese wire. Of slicing something off.

"Burns says he wants it finished by Sunday."

"Wants what finished by Sunday?"

"The paddock."

Arthur laughed. "Bloke's taking the piss."

"Well, that's what he said this morning."

"He's only fucking with you, Tommy."

Better, Tommy figured, to let Arthur believe that. "Yeah," he said. "I know."

They got to work. Pacing out the next fence post, checking the alignment, marking the spot. Tommy softened the ground with the pickax while Arthur carried the post across. He stuck the point in the broken soil and asked if Tommy wanted to hit or hold first.

"Either way."

"Just choose one."

"You choose."

"Fine."

Arthur dragged the sledgehammer over, a broad snake track carved in the dirt, took off his shirt and hung it over the nearest section of wire, his body scarred and bald and lean, waited for Tommy to do the same.

"You ain't wrapping up your hands?"

"Get on with it," Tommy said, kneeling with his head lowered and arms extended, as if in prayer to the post. He waved off a fly impatiently. Arthur set his feet apart.

"Last chance. I won't spare you."

"Get on with it, I said."

Arthur sighed, hefted the sledgehammer, swung, and a shudder ran through Tommy to his boots. The hollow crack caromed across the fields, birds scattering from the red gums, sheep lifting their heads. Arthur snatched a breath and wound up another swing and Tommy bit down hard and bore it, the post nudging through his stinging hands, into the hardened earth.

Come midday they'd put in another nine fence posts and tacked between each three lengths of wire so taut they pinged. Both men now bare-skinned and glistening—quietly, Tommy had relented, wrapped his shirt around his hands. They called time on the morning and stood clicking out their backs and loosening their joints, squinting into a high hard sun. Tommy put on his shirt again, Arthur left his on the wire, and wearily they trudged across a bare earth clearing to the creek bank, sat down beneath their usual tree. Leaning against the trunk, they divvied up their food and ate in silence, then closed their eyes and dozed in the dappled sunlight, the birds chattering above them, the creek trickling by, neither noticing the pair of riders crossing the paddock behind.

Two tramlines cut through the long grass toward the fence: Cal Burns and a young stationhand. Only

Burns dismounted; the boy remained on his horse. Burns settled his hat, kicked a fence post, flicked the wire, scanned the field, noticed the shoulders protruding either side of the red gum. He walked closer, into the clearing, smiled, and said to the boy, "Watch this," then drew his revolver, cocked it, and fired a warning shot high into the air.

The crack sent Tommy scrambling. He dropped to the dirt, covered his head with both hands, eyes wide and full of fear, as Arthur swiveled and looked around the tree and told him, "It's all right, mate, it's all right. It's only Burns."

They could already hear him howling. Arthur took hold of Tommy's arm, hauled him to his feet, and led him out into the field, Tommy unsteady from the shock still, trembling, fixing Burns with a hateful glare. The overseer could not stop laughing, egging on the station-hand.

"Look at the bloody state of him! You're wetter than a waterhole, McBride!"

"Don't do nothing stupid now," Arthur whispered as they neared, shuffling into the clearing, presenting themselves in front of Burns.

"And what, are you two courting now—let go of his arm."

Arthur did so. Tommy swayed a little then straightened. His face was flushed, his jaw set, eyes boring into Burns. The overseer noticed and his own expression changed.

"I was only pulling your pizzle, boy. Take a bloody joke."

"Nothing funny about it," Tommy said. "The hell's your problem?"

"Sleeping on the job's my problem. Lucky I don't have you both flogged."

"Lunchtime, boss," Arthur said.

Burns sneered at him. "You watch your mouth, nigger. And put a fucking shirt on, you ain't in the tribe no more."

Arthur hesitated, glanced at Tommy, then slipped past Burns to the fence line, where his shirt still hung on the wire. Burns stepped close to Tommy, almost nose to nose, a smell of tobacco and tooth rot when he spoke: "Eyes on you like dinner plates—you got something more to say to me, McBride?"

The muscle on Tommy's jawline creased. Holding it all in. He'd known so many men like this over the years, most overseers were the same. The first had been the absolute worst of them—he could still taste Raymond Locke's filthy fingers digging in his mouth, trying to pinch his tongue. Locke got what was coming in the end, though. The sounds he'd made while Noone tortured him, the unearthly way he'd screamed . . .

Burns was still waiting. "No, nothing," Tommy said. They needed the money, him and Arthur, the food, the lodgings, the work. This was the first steady living they'd made in months.

"So what's with the face?"

"There was no call to shoot at us. We were only having lunch."

"I shot in the bloody air! Hell, if I'd *shot at you* you'd have known about it. Don't be so soft." Burns scowled at him. "What's wrong with you, anyway? There something not right in your head?"

He tapped the revolver against Tommy's forehead. Tommy only blinked. Glancing at Arthur, pulling his shirt on, he said, "Best be getting on, boss," through gritted teeth. "Lots more posts need putting in."

"I asked you a question. What's your problem? What's with them dreams?"

"Like I said, we'd best be getting on."

Burns's eyes narrowed. "You've always been a cocky cunt, haven't you, McBride. Thinking you're better than the rest of us. Acting like your shit don't stink."

Tommy went to move past him. Burns put a hand on his chest, his revolver hand, the gun metal warm through Tommy's shirt. A darkness was slowly consuming the overseer; it was right there in his stare. Smirking, he slopped his tongue around his mouth, stepped back, and raised the revolver, four distinct clicks of the hammer ratcheting through its gates.

"How about this? Not so cocky now, eh?"

Tommy could hardly hear him. All a blur behind the muzzle: he'd been thrust back five years, into the foothills of the Bewley ranges, far away in the north, watching Noone corral a group of natives and a pack of wild dogs, demanding that they lay down their spears; then, when they didn't obey him, leveling his gilded silver pistol at one man's forehead, just as Burns did to Tommy now, and casually blowing open his face.

Tommy lunged, knocking aside the revolver and shoving Burns so hard he fell. Incredible, how little weight there was to him, how easily he went down. No control when he landed. Limp as a sack of grain. Body first, then his head, whipping backward and smacking off the sunbaked earth with such force that it bounced like a ball.

All was still for a moment. Cal Burns didn't move. His eyes rolled so only the whites were visible and his legs began to twitch to the toes. His arms lay flaccid, his hands upturned—Tommy looked on in despair. Why had he pointed the revolver? Why had he even fallen? Why not just stumble? Why not catch himself when he hit the ground? Vaguely he was aware of movement in the paddock—Arthur running from the fence line, the young stationhand turning his horse and bolting across the fields—but now blood had begun to seep from Burns's nostril and trickle down his cheek, and although Arthur arrived, yelling "Fuck, Tommy!" and fumbling for a pulse in the overseer's neck, Tommy knew just by the look of him, and from the dozens, the hundreds, of corpses he'd seen in his short life, that he wasn't waking up. He turned away, horrified. Chalk another on his tally. Burns was as good as dead.

Chapter 3
Billy McBride

In a clearing around the back of his family's old farmhouse, Billy stood twisting his hat in his hands, staring at two bare-earth graves overgrown with weeds and buffel grass, indistinguishable from the surrounding scrub, as if the bush had swallowed them totally; only the crooked white crosses remained.

"Paddocks are up, anyhow. Drought's broke. I got rid of that dam."

He stared off into the distance, the breeze ruffling his hair and those few parts of his clothing not stuck down with sweat; behind him the rusted windmill creaked but didn't turn. It was years since he'd been down here, since that day he and Tommy had dug these holes and dropped their parents in. He should have visited more often, kept the plots clear, maybe put a fence around and got them proper headstones, or plaques with both their names.

"So I'll be heading out to Lawton soon, I reckon. Start up with a new mob."

There had been that one other time, he remembered, not long after Tommy had left, when Billy had grown tired of Katherine's pity and ridden down, intending to simply carry on with his life. Sixteen years old, newly orphaned, sitting alone at the table, lying awake in his bed, the ghosts of all he had witnessed here swirling through the night. He made it to dawn but only barely. Returned to Broken Ridge the very next day. Told Katherine to stop mothering him, there was only a couple of years between them, they were almost the same damn age. He didn't need protecting, by her or anyone—he would work for fair pay and lodgings, the same as any man, and for the last five years had done just that, waiting for Glendale's paddocks to recover, for the drought to properly break, for the *drip drip drip* of his courage to finally reach the brim.

"Well, thought I'd let you know anyhow. Plenty more work still to do."

He turned and walked beneath the windmill, past the well and the rotten log pile, around to where Buck was tethered to the front verandah rail. Billy untied him and glanced up at the house. A run-down wooden slab hut with a patchwork shingle roof; behind him a smattering of ruined outbuildings around the dust-blown yard. Mother had swept that verandah every day of her life, now dead leaves littered the deck and tumbleweed caught in the rails. The front door had blown open. It knocked against the inside wall. Billy exhaled shakily and mounted the front steps. There were so many memories. Darkness yawned within. Between the bench and doorframe was a bloodstain on the decking, and there were two others just like it inside. Billy wouldn't look at them. Wouldn't set foot inside the house. Boots nudging the threshold, he leaned in and pulled the door closed and hurried back to his horse.

Over the following weeks he withdrew from the life he'd made at Broken Ridge and began building a new one alone at Glendale. He took all Katherine had offered, ferrying feed sacks and hay bales and other supplies in the dray, and on the last day packed up his hut and said his farewells to the men, glancing at the distant homestead, imagining her up there, watching from a window or standing at the verandah rail. He'd not seen her since their argument, wasn't sure where the two of them stood. That fiancé was still sniffing around, apparently, and if she'd wanted to, Katherine could always have sent for Billy, or come down. It was all too complicated. Their fucking had once been enough for both of them, now she talked about him breaking her heart. He didn't know what else she expected. He'd always been clear about his intention of turning Glendale around.

In the empty bunkhouse he ripped down the curtain that had once separated black stockmen from white, and found Arthur's old belongings still littered around his bed. His ornaments and trinkets, a Bible, of all things—Billy took them out back and skimmed them like stones into the scrub. With his mother's old broom he swept the floor and caught the cobwebs, dust pluming in the window light and roiling in waves through the open double doors. He made up a bed at the white end of the barn and hammered nails into the coping to hang his clothes, dragged over Arthur's bookcase and filled it with trinkets of his own.

Meals he cooked outside the bunkhouse, in a firepit someone else had dug. Drifters, wandering swaggies, you got them out here sometimes. At night he'd sit in the warmth of the flames, smoking against the wall, looking at the shadow of the house in the moonlight and trying to remember happier times. The old days of his childhood, when a dozen stockmen had lived and worked here, every day a rabble of activity and, for him and Tommy, excitement and fun. Falling asleep in the bed they shared they would hear the laughter and swearing and singing under the stars, and all Billy ever wanted was to be a part of it, a man just like them.

He still sang their songs sometimes, sitting out here on his own.

With the wages he'd been putting aside over the years, Billy rode out to the saleyards at Lawton and bought himself half a small mob. The other half he'd be loaning from Broken Ridge: their cattle would graze his pastures, when they were sold he'd take a cut, and if he managed to get a calf out of any of them, that calf would be Billy's to keep. He'd agreed the deal with Joe, the headman, and had got the feeling he could have named almost any terms.

But he wouldn't accept loaned labor, not without paying a wage, and since he couldn't afford to do so had no choice but to drove the Lawton cattle back to Glendale by himself, seventy miles over rugged flatland that took him the best part of a week. Two dozen head of cows and heifers, plus a scrawny-looking bull calf. He'd not had his pick of the market, had been outbid on all but the dregs. And these were Lawton dregs, remember—most breeders only sold there when they couldn't sell anywhere else.

Under a beating sun Billy had walked the dusty pathways between the stinking pens, studying the cattle in their stalls. None was much to look at. Sunken rib cages, sagging bellies, a pained and mournful bellow. Still, some were better than others: Billy shouldered between the buyers crowding the wooden rails and tried to imagine, with the unsullied pastures he had waiting back home, what these broken beasts might become. He watched their movement, their gait, studied their coats for signs of mange; checked for eyes damp with discharge, jaws that couldn't properly chew, and those whose problems shitting were smeared on their hind legs.

All this he'd record in a little notebook, his pencil tucked behind his ear.

Some of the men he knew personally, others knew him or had heard of him, or had known his father when he was alive. Often he was stopped and his hand was shaken and he was obliged to shoot the breeze in that taciturn way all cattlemen have. Mostly they were amiable, glad to hear he was starting up again; a few commented that his father would have been proud. They asked how the young widow was faring at Broken Ridge, whether that soft city arsehole—her father— was running the place into the ground. Billy told them

Katherine was managing the station, that she was doing just fine, and they laughed until they realized it wasn't a joke. The things they said about her—he could have hit any number of them, none was fit to speak her name. But enemies were made for life out here, and enemies were the last thing Billy needed, so he shook their sweaty hands and allowed the conversation to go on: some wondered whether his brother was back yet, whether he was part of the new run, and all Billy said was that he wasn't expecting Tommy anytime soon. They'd clutch his shoulder or slap his back, then, put in mind of what had happened to them, of why Billy was on his own, would lean in and offer their sympathies, before telling him how glad they were those Kurrong bastards wouldn't be bothering him again.

"Good on ya, Billy," they whispered. "Good on ya, mate. Well done."

At which Billy, clench jawed and silent, would turn and move along.

On the crest of a rise Billy sat his horse and looked over the western pastures, watching his mongrel herd: the bedraggled stock from Lawton and the pedigrees from Broken Ridge, mingling warily, in a way cattle usually were not, as if neither fully recognized their counterparts as being of the same kind.

"Ah, they'll fatten up in a week or two. Can't but help it with all that feed."

He'd caught himself doing this recently, talking with nobody around. Not even a dog to listen to him, and Buck wasn't the listening kind. Tommy should have been here, mounted on that big gray gelding he was so fond of, sitting at Billy's side. It was all they'd ever talked about when they were boys, what they'd do when this place was theirs. Or at least they had done, before Tommy started getting ideas about himself, about a life away from Glendale.

"Yeah, well, at least I'm still here trying. I ain't running away."

Billy pulled the horse around and rode him south for home, two hours across a barren scrubland no amount of rain could cure, the soil dry and brittle, choked by dust and stones. His thoughts wandering out ahead of him, to another evening alone by the fire, another meal of stale salt beef, unless . . . there was time to go hunting before sundown, he figured, rustle up some fresh meat, maybe fill the bathtub and leave it warming, it was ages since he last washed. He could bathe while the meat was roasting, scrub his clothes after, then eat and smoke and watch the sunset, drink a little rum, raise a toast to the new cattle, to his family's run reborn.

Four loose horses were waiting for him, when he rode into the yard.

All were saddled and loaded with supplies: snuffling the weed-strewn gravel, drinking from the trough. Billy reined up and dismounted, drew and cocked his revolver, walked slowly into the yard. His gaze flitted between the buildings. His boots crunched the stones. The house door was open, as were some of the sheds, and the horses were unfamiliar: they weren't from Broken Ridge.

The men slid from behind walls and out of doorways and were converging on Billy before he even noticed they were there: two blacks, their carbines leveled at him, marching deliberately across the yard; and one white, smiling slyly, sauntering with an enormous rifle pinned behind his neck.

Billy lowered the hammer on the revolver, let it hang loose at his side.

On they came, these three men, Billy alternating between them and only now registering the pale trousers and blue tunics the two blacks wore. The white boy was dressed in tan moleskins and an ill-fitting khaki shirt, and though he was chewing tobacco looked no older than sixteen. He resembled a workhouse urchin—pug nose, narrow eyes, filthy hair, a cleft in his chin and acne pocked on his cheeks—but from their getup Billy already had a good idea who these strangers were.

The white boy was a Native Police officer. His troopers were in uniform.

And now that he'd realized, now he saw the troopers more clearly as they closed across the yard, he wondered if they weren't familiar, if he didn't know them from before, from when he and Tommy had gone after their family's killers and they had . . . and they had . . .

"Fellas!" Billy called, waving. "Good to see you! How you been?"

They were unimpressed by his bluster. Nothing in their faces at all. One on each side, fixing Billy with their carbines, while the boy rolled lazily toward him, scarecrowed by his rifle still. Desperately Billy tried to remember the troopers' names. One was older, bald-headed, a face sunken to its bones; the other bigger, younger, stronger, his left eye knotted with scars. Priest, or Bishop maybe, something to do with God?

He looked at the boy anxiously. "What you doing here? What's this about?"

As if by way of an answer a slow boot tread sounded on the house verandah, and all heads including Billy's turned: he remembered with a shiver that there had been a fourth horse. In the shadow of the porch a very tall man uncoiled himself through the open doorway and stepped up to the rail. He wore a peacock feather waistcoat with a gold watch chain and had a dark long-coat draped over one arm. With the other hand he drank from Father's favorite mug: his initials stenciled on the bottom, the only one he would ever use. Billy watched the mug rise and fall and rise again, and as it did he saw the tall man smile.

"Hello, Billy," Noone said. "Now isn't this a pleasant surprise."

Chapter 4
Tommy McBride

Arthur peeled the revolver from Burns's loose grip, then rifled through his pockets and began stripping off his boots and clothes, panting, "Grab the horses, Tommy. And that black'un too."

Tommy glanced at Burns's black stallion. Beyond, the fleeing stablehand was now a speck across the fields. "I never meant to kill him."

"He ain't dead yet, but we still have to run. We've a couple hours' start at most."

"But . . ."

On his knees, Arthur spun. "But what? What? You want to hold his hand and wait till he comes round? Either way we're fucked, mate, so get your head out your arse and help me here. Five bloody years I've been carrying you, dealing with all your horseshit;

don't you dare play possum now. Wake up, Tommy. Get that horse."

As Arthur undressed him, Burns's head flopped to one side and Tommy saw the crimson mess matted in his hair. He'd hit a rock part-buried in the dirt, the only one out here, a million-to-one chance. All he'd done was push him. Nothing more than that. It didn't matter. Death followed Tommy regardless. Shadowed him, night and day. As if years ago it had laid a hand on his shoulder and had been stalking him ever since.

He drifted in the direction of the stallion, collected him, and led him to where the others were tied in the shade. Arthur ran over, carrying a loose bundle of clothing that he stuffed into the empty saddlebags; he was already wearing Burns's boots. He fetched the long-handled shovel and a few other fencing tools and slid them under the stallion's saddle straps, then mounted up and ordered Tommy to do the same. They rode out, over a couple of miles of open grassland until they reached the rutted gravel coach track that traced the course of the Balonne River to St. George, where, on the outskirts of the little settlement, they halted by a roadside cemetery and considered the distant outline of the river crossing on the far side of town.

"We'll have to find another way across. We can't risk going through there."

Tommy wasn't listening. Studying the nearby headstones, the names and dates and descriptions: beloved father, mother, daughter, son. He wasn't any of those things, he realized. If it was him who'd died back there today, what would his inscription say? Murderer? Liar? Coward? Did he even warrant a proper grave?

One headstone near the fence read: ROBERT THOMPSON, HE ENJOYED A SIMPLE LIFE, and that phrase tolled in Tommy like a bell. A simple life—it sounded wonderful. To live and work and die in peace, to be remembered, to be mourned.

They doubled back and crossed the river out of sight of the town, then struck west through open country before joining the track again. They could follow it all the way to a place called Innamincka, Arthur explained after an hour of silent riding, of thinking his plan through, a lonely trading outpost he'd heard of, weeks away, up on the Cooper Creek, provided the track went that far. Nobody would come looking for them out there. More likely assume they'd crossed the border into New South Wales. Then from Innamincka they could trace the Cooper until it met the Birdsville Track, that fabled central stock route running north-south through the guts, now with wells and bores and camping grounds, apparently, serving the great rivers of cattle that tumbled out of Queensland onto trains waiting to whisk them directly to the south coast ports.

"We'll just follow the cattle. It'll be like old times."

Arthur smiled uneasily. He almost sounded convinced.

It would be four days' hard riding before they reached the next main town, following the ribbon of the western coach trail through sun-drenched grassland, the sky deep blue above them, thin cloud scudding like surf. Fifteen-hour days in the saddle, or as much as the horses could take, resting through the heat of the daytime, riding dusk till dawn at night. They saw nobody following. No posse on their tail. Only the occasional silhouette of some weary traveler trudging eastward, or in a spew of dust and gravel the mail coach rattling by.

They spoke very little in those early days, other than the basic business of keeping themselves alive. Arthur had Cal Burns's money clip, but there was nowhere to buy supplies, and out here both food and water were scarce. If they saw any form of settlement, the few lonely farms and hamlets dotted along the trail, they would creep from the shadows at nighttime and use whatever river, bore, or waterhole sustained the people living there, fill their flasks and water the horses, then slip away unseen.

On the second night they called time on their riding just before dawn, found a place to make camp, lit a fire. Warming themselves in silence, when suddenly Arthur said, "Look, I just can't let this lie."

"Let what lie?"

"What happened back there, how you—"

"I already told you, I never meant to kill him. He had a gun to my head!"

"Ah, you don't even know he's dead, Tommy."

"Yes, I do."

"Well, that's not what I'm saying: how you disappeared inside yourself, like you always do. Burns wasn't going to shoot you and you know it. My bet, he reminded you of something that happened from before, and that's what set you off."

Tommy didn't answer, buried his gaze in the flames.

"It's been five years, Tommy. It's time you moved on."

"Moved on? Are you serious?"

"Yeah, well, you need to hear it. We had a good thing going there, best work in years. Now look at us. This is hardly the first time, neither."

"You don't understand."

"Oh, you reckon? Listen, there's plenty buggers out

there had it just as rough as you and don't carry it with them their whole bloody lives."

Tommy shook his head. "I still see him, dream about him: Noone."

Arthur spat a thin string of saliva hissing into the flames. "Mate, I dreamed about that mission station for years after. I told you what happened to the family, remember?"

The two of them talking outside the bunkhouse, Tommy fourteen years old, glimpsing a world he could never have imagined, realizing that Arthur had a life of his own.

"'Course I do."

"Yeah, well, you were too young for the whole story back then. That place . . . there was blood and bodies everywhere, no telling who was who, and I'm picking through it all trying to figure if any of 'em's mine, the missus and the littl'uns, I never did find 'em in the end. So maybe they got took, maybe they're still alive, this was thirty ago and I still don't know. After, my head was gone, just like yours is now. Only difference is, I didn't have nobody else."

Tommy didn't know what to say to that. The fire threw out a spark.

"So don't try telling me I don't know what it's like.

But fuck it, eh, what can you do? Can't change what happened, that's for damn sure. Either forget about it or bury it or whatever else works, but quit your bloody sulking before you get us both killed."

Meekly, Tommy nodded. Staring lost into the flames.

They reached Cunnamulla late on the fourth day and camped a good distance from town, watching the lanterns burning, listening to the singing and piano music from the hotel bar, imagining the revelry and the beds awaiting the drinkers when they were done. Before dawn they looped around to the western fringe of town and once the place had come to life rode in from that direction, pretending they were traveling east, a lie they repeated to the waitress in the roadhouse, not that she seemed to care. They each had two breakfasts, courtesy of Cal Burns's money clip, and afterward headed for the livery stables along the road. A shopkeeper sweeping his doorway paused to watch them pass; Tommy touched his hat brim and, after a moment's hesitation, the man nodded in return.

Outside the stables Arthur unstrapped his battered old saddle and dumped it in Tommy's arms. "Remember what we talked about now."

"I remember."

"Just, don't tell 'em too much, all right?"

"I remember, I said."

HERMAN'S TACK & LIVERY comprised a large barn with a small tack shop annexed on one side. The shop door was already open. Hesitantly, Tommy stepped inside. An empty bare-wood counter, bits and bridles on the walls, plus a photograph of the local gun club: two dozen grim-faced riflemen scowling in a row.

Tommy dropped the saddle on the counter, called out hello, peered through the archway into the main barn, a smell of straw, shit, and tan in the air. He noticed a handbell on the counter, rang it, a voice called, "Hang on, hang on," and a moment later a bald, round-bellied man, presumably Herman, came waddling through the archway, sliding up the shoulder straps on his coveralls and fastening a button at the waist. He spread his thickly haired arms on the counter and said, "Help you?" as if Tommy had just that second walked in.

"I'm after a pack saddle, three nose bags, and a sack of grain."

"All right."

Tommy nodded at the saddle. "For this, I mean. To trade."

Herman frowned at the ragged offering then stared at Tommy a long time, taking in the unwashed clothing, the restless gaze. He flipped the saddle over, the buckles and stirrups jangling, and winced like he'd swallowed bad milk.

"Had it long, have you?"

"A while."

"I'll say. Well, she's not pretty, but I might can fix her up. I'd take this plus five pound from you—how does that sound?"

Tommy didn't haggle, terrible deal though it was. He pulled out the money clip and peeled off the notes and Herman's thick eyebrows rose. "So what are you," Herman asked, pocketing the notes in his coveralls, "just passing through?"

"Heading east, after work."

"What kind of work?"

"Sheep, cattle, anything like that."

Herman coughed and spat, like the idea offended him. "What you wanting a pack saddle for, if you're planning on stopping to work?"

Tommy's innards churned. "That's my business. Can you fetch the things?"

Herman leaned and looked past him, through the open door. "Them your horses and blackboy out there?"

"Aye."

Herman snorted. "I seen fatter corpses, he can't be

much use. And there ain't a packhorse among them—which you planning putting it on?"

"I'm not asking for advice. Can you just bring the saddle and grain?"

"Well, hell, I'm only trying to help ye."

"The saddle and grain," Tommy pleaded, his voice shaking.

Herman's eyes narrowed in a squint. "You got a name, fella?"

Fighting the urge to run, Tommy glanced over his shoulder at Arthur and felt the weight of the debt between them. He'd been right about having carried him these past five years: Tommy owed Arthur his life. And now here they were, fleeing inland, yet again because of him; they would never make it to the Cooper Creek without supplies. He dug his nails into his palms and steadied himself. Took a step toward the counter and said, "I already paid you. Either fetch my things or I will, however you prefer."

Herman held his stare a moment, then shrugged and went into the barn, Tommy leaning after him, making sure he didn't take off. When he returned, his arms laden, Tommy snatched it all off him and hurried outside, Herman watching through the doorway behind.

"We need to get out of here," Tommy whispered to Arthur.

"What happened? What did he say?"

"Nothing exactly, but still too much."

In the general store Tommy stood at the counter, his leg jigging restlessly, waiting for the shopkeeper to fill his list. A thin man in a dark waistcoat and bow tie, with a limp mustache and hair parted fastidiously to one side, he labored between the shelves and balanced the scales like he was weighing gold dust not flour.

"Can't you hurry it up there?"

"You short on time, young man?"

Tommy glanced out of the window. "Long day's ride ahead of us, that's all."

"Well, a few more minutes won't hurt."

"We're headed east," Tommy told him. "Looking for work."

"None of my business where you're going. But if it's work you're after, there's plenty round these parts, if you were inclined to stick around."

Without turning he tapped his pencil against the corkboard on the wall, and the array of job adverts pinned there, along with notices about a meeting to discuss the extension of the railroad, an upcoming racing meet, and a police poster offering a £200 reward for information leading to the capture of . . . leading to the capture of . . .

Thomas ("Tommy") McBride and the native
known as "Arthur," on charges of robbery and
murder near the town of St. George. McBride has
blond hair, blue eyes, and is approximately six
feet tall. His left hand is missing the last two
fingers and he was most recently seen dressed in
stockman's clothing, riding a (male) gray horse.
His accomplice, Arthur, is approximately five feet
nine inches tall and . . .

Tommy felt his body contracting, the blood surge hot in his veins. He had the money clip out, ready to pay, and caught the shopkeeper staring at his left hand. Their eyes met. The other man blanched. He backed away a pace then bolted from the shop, through a side door into another room. Cursing, Tommy gathered what he could of their supplies, bundling out into the street, dropping them as he ran.

"What is it?" Arthur shouted. "What's wrong?"

"A poster. Burns is dead. They're after us. Bloke knew it was me."

Along the street, in the sunshine, the slim figure of the shopkeeper emerged from an alleyway and sprinted in the direction of the courthouse, and forlornly Tommy glanced back at the open doorway and the food lying discarded in the road.

"Leave it," Arthur barked, climbing into the saddle. "Tommy—move!"

They stuck to the track for a couple of miles, driving the horses as hard as they could, before veering off through a creek so as to wipe their trail clean and striking out into open bushland. Endless country before them. No roads anymore, no towns; not even a map to show the way. With only the barest of rations they were heading into the dead heart of the continent and were doing so, God help them, entirely alone.

Chapter 5
Billy McBride

Noone balanced Father's old mug on the railing, draped the longcoat alongside, and came down the steps out of the shadows into the bright sunshine. He was exactly as Billy remembered him. Hadn't aged so much as a day. Thick black mustache, black hair parted fine as a blade, taut sunburned skin, and those eyes of his, those eyes . . . no color in them anywhere, a swirl of dead gray smoke, boring into Billy as he strode across the yard.

He closed the distance impossibly. Within seconds he was there. Billy gazing up at him, sixteen years old again, gripping the revolver, his hand trembling, boots scraping backward through the dirt. Noone extended a hand and Billy offered his revolver; the inspector frowned then took it and tossed it to the young white boy, whose high-pitched coyote laughter echoed through the yard.

"Is a handshake out of the question, between two old friends?"

Billy had disarmed himself. He flushed and accepted Noone's hand. Long bony fingers, the nails oddly clean; his grip tightened and tightened and would not yield. Billy felt his knuckles grinding. He tried to reciprocate but hadn't the strength. Finally Noone let him go and said, "Good to see you, Billy. It's been a long time."

"Aye," Billy managed, massaging his aching hand.

"Are we not welcome?"

"Them that are usually don't come armed."

Noone nodded equably. A glance and the troopers lowered their carbines. "I have a request to make of you. And some news you might be interested to hear."

"What news?"

"Let's talk inside."

"Here's fine."

"Inside, Billy."

"If you like," Billy said, shrugging, stepping toward the bunkhouse.

"The barn? We aren't animals. Come—the men will see to your horse. You remember Pope and Jarrah there. This is my new constable, Percy."

Now Billy remembered the two troopers: he'd once

seen Jarrah decapitate a man with a swing of his waddy blade; and Pope was the old witch doctor who'd butchered Tommy's hand. Neither man acknowledged him. The boy Percy dipped his head and spat messily on the ground.

Noone walked to the house, whose threshold Billy had not crossed in all these years, and waited by the door, smiling. He knew, Billy realized. The bastard knew all too well. Noone ducked through the doorway and Billy had no choice but to follow. He climbed the steps very slowly, took a breath, and went inside.

The shutters were closed, thin bars of dusty sunlight twinkling the gaudy pattern of Noone's waistcoat as he rounded the room. He dragged a hand over the table, trailing finger-marks in the dust, idly lifted the bedroom curtain and let it fall again, slow clip of his boots with each step. He brushed off Father's chair, set it back from the table and sat down, pinching his trousers as he did so, a look of rank disgust on his face.

"I was told you are living here now."

Billy was still hovering in the doorway. "On and off. Been working mostly."

"I see."

From his waistcoat pocket Noone produced a small pipe and a matchbox: he lit the pipe and got it going, his cheeks hollowing, clouds of sweet smoke filling the air, then flicked the dead match to the floor. He waved Billy forward. "Are you waiting for an invitation? It is your house, after all."

Billy edged into the room, pulled out the chair that would once have been Mary's, and lowered himself down. "So what's this news you've brung?"

Noone ignored him totally. Pulling on his pipe. "Tell me, Billy, how have things been for you? Since we last met—how have you fared?"

Billy shrugged. "There's near enough sixty head in them paddocks now."

Noone's eyebrows raised, mock-impressed. "I noticed your belongings in the barn, of course. A strange choice of accommodation for a self-made man. Still, this house must bring back memories. They don't fade, do they—much like bloodstains."

"Fuck off with you. What do you want?"

"I told you, I have a request to make. But very well, first the news I promised. Have you heard from your brother lately? Has young Tommy been in touch?"

"'Course not."

"Is it so unlikely?"

"You said you'd kill us both if we even so much as wrote."

"Ah, yes, so I did." Noone withdrew the pipe stem, exhaled, rattled it back between his teeth, and bit down. "Well, as it happens Tommy might be heading that way without my help: it seems he and your old blackboy have recently killed the overseer on a sheep station outside St. George, bounced his head off a rock so hard his brain swelled and burst like a balloon. No doubt there was provocation. Those types are always so uncouth. But the fact remains he is wanted for murder. There's already a posse out there after him, a reward for his arrest."

Noone smoked contentedly, watching Billy reel: five long years of silence, now this sudden hammer blow. His neck had roped and his jaw was set and his leg jagged up and down. He wondered if Noone was lying to him. Nothing about the story sounded right.

"How do you know it was Tommy?"

"Name, age, description—he wasn't exactly trying to hide."

"What blackboy? Not Arthur?"

"That's the one. We never did manage to catch up with him before."

Billy folded his arms. "Well, they ain't here, if that's what you're asking."

Noone chuckled. "Of course they aren't here. I had no expectation that they were. The local police, in their wisdom, have been searching over the border in New South Wales, but just a few days ago there was a sighting in Cunnamulla, meaning they are heading west, for the interior, which is actually a rather clever plan. The terrain may kill them eventually, but with a band of local officers and a few sheep shearers on their tail, it seems most unlikely they will be caught."

"Good for them then."

"Or . . ." Noone paused for another pull on the pipe. "My men and I could ride down there instead. How long would it take us to come up with them do you think?"

Billy shifted in his chair. "You can please yourself what you do."

"You aren't concerned for him?"

"This is Tommy's lookout. Nothing to do with me."

"He will hang, Billy. Unless someone shoots him first."

"What's to say you'll even find him? That bush is a bloody big place."

"Oh, you do me a disservice. But then you never were the sharper of the pair."

"What's that supposed to mean?"

Noone removed his pipe and pointed at Billy with the stem. "It means I know you. I know your brother too. Within the week I will have him, unless you agree to this trade. A favor, in return for leaving Tommy alone."

Billy said nothing. Staring at Noone. Waiting for the terms.

"There is a station a day's ride south of here, belongs to a man named Bennett—you are familiar with him, I presume?"

Billy pictured Drew Bennett shaking his hand at the Lawton stockyards. A little reluctantly, it had felt. He swallowed, and nodded his head.

"Well, it seems Mr. Bennett has taken into his possession something that rightfully belongs to me. Keeps it hidden in his barn, I believe. I am talking about the young trooper, Rabbit—you might remember him, always was a strange boy, but I expected better, I have to say."

Billy pictured the trooper, his high forehead and bulging eyes, giving Tommy water when Billy wouldn't; then later, the two of them all friendly around the canyon campfire.

"Yeah, I remember him."

"He has absconded, as our natives sometimes do. It is a common occurrence, unfortunately, but one I will not tolerate among my own men. So we must retrieve him, and for that I would like your help."

"Help how?"

"With the selector, Mr. Bennett. To ensure he stays in line."

"You don't need me for that."

"No, but he might. This is for his protection, Billy, so he doesn't go getting himself killed."

"Drew has a family. Daughters. Two sons."

"Exactly. And you will be helping them all. You see, for a man to take a runaway trooper under his wing, he must have a certain disregard for the law. Such a man, when confronted, may react unwisely to our presence on his land. There is ever greater scrutiny on us these days, Billy. Sadly, the force is not what it once was. Our numbers are down, we are unpopular with the politicians, victims of our own success in many ways. Meaning it is preferable if a bloodbath could be avoided. Wouldn't you agree?"

They sat in silence, Noone smoking, that word *bloodbath* echoing in Billy's mind. Noone frowned into the bowl of his pipe, turned it over, and with the heel of his hand knocked a wad of dead tobacco onto the floor.

"The other thing you might consider," he continued, "is what does this traitor Rabbit know? The details of your parents' murder, the dispersal we carried out afterward, on the basis of your sworn word—there are men on the coast who would drop their bowels if they learned what we did to the Kurrong, would ensure those responsible were hanged. So ask yourself: What might happen to you, Billy, or indeed your young widow on the hill up there, if the truth were ever revealed?"

Billy leaned forward in his chair, snarled, "You leave her the fuck alone," and Noone shrugged like it might yet go either way. He peered at Billy knowingly, put away his pipe and stood, brushed off his trousers, straightened his waistcoat, made for the door. "Five minutes," he said, ducking under the doorframe. There was a smashing sound outside. Billy went out after him and found Father's old mug lying shattered on the verandah boards, Noone walking toward the horses, his longcoat flaring as he whipped it on. Billy stared at the mug fragments blankly, the broken lettering of his father's name, then with his head lowered he crossed the yard to the bunkhouse and began packing his things.

Chapter 6
Henry Wells

"Mr. Wells, your closing address please."

The young lawyer nodded to the judge, rose to his feet, adjusted his robes, and solemnly regarded the jury of gray, stone-faced men, sweating in the stifling courtroom in the only suits they owned. They were butchers, blacksmiths, stevedores, mongers of all different kinds, pulled from across Brisbane and so obviously reluctant to spend even another moment listening to him.

"Judas!" came a call from the courtroom gallery, to a ripple of muted cheers.

The interruption stalled him. Henry Wells flushed and considered his notes. He could sense the defense counsel, Hugill, smirking across the aisle, as he had all through the trial. Henry was twenty years his junior, in only his second year at the bar, and, round-faced and ruddy-cheeked, looked almost cherubic in his wig.

"Gentlemen," he began, the word emerging faint and hoarse. He took a sip of water and tried again, and this time his voice rang loud and clear; he felt the jury's attention finally rouse. "Gentlemen—thank you for the time you have dedicated to this matter thus far. I know it has been trying and you are keen to go home, but this is the last you will hear from me, I promise, which I'm sure will come as something of a relief."

Henry paused after this small levity. No change in their stares. A weight of silence behind him, save the coughs and scrapes and murmurs of the crowd.

"Of course, before your duty is finished here, a verdict is required, which is a heavy burden, given the stakes. A man's life is in your hands. Believe me, I understand what I am asking of you here. A guilty verdict will doubtless mean the death penalty for the prisoner, as it must, for that is the law."

Eyes flicked to the dock and a scraggy-looking man standing hunched and manacled, one of his hands bandaged, his gaze downcast.

"But that is not your responsibility. Only the verdict is within your control. Meaning now you must ask yourselves: How are you going to make that decision? How will you carry out your duty today? By applying the law, following the evidence, the obvious difference between right and wrong; or will you dismiss such things as irrelevant when weighed against the color of a man's skin?"

Grumbles from the gallery. Henry remained unmoved.

"For that is what this case amounts to. The evidence could not be more clear. One man is dead, beaten to a pulp by another in the street. If Clarence had been white, this case would already be over, your guilty verdict rendered, the prisoner taken down. Except he wasn't white, he was Aborigine, but in all other respects the same as you or I. A husband, a father, a man. A British subject, whether you approve of that status or not, equally entitled to justice in this court. So consider, then: if it were you who had been murdered, your family left destitute, your killer on trial, what would you expect of the jurymen serving? For that is all I am asking of you.

"Because let us not kid ourselves: Mr. Brooks is a murderer. He killed Clarence in a fit of uncontrolled anger on that fateful morning in Baroo. Witnesses saw him do it. He was arrested—quite literally, gentlemen—with Clarence's blood still warm on his hands. By way of defense, Mr. Brooks has argued that he believed Clarence stole one of his pigs. Now, that has not been proven and cannot be, since Clarence is not able to answer the charge. But then he is not the one on trial here, and the theft of a pig, even if it had occurred, is really by the by: the crime is that one man beat another to death, with malice aforethought, proven beyond all possible doubt. Again, I ask you: If it were you whom Mr. Brooks had killed that day, or your brother, or your son, would you consider his actions justified?

"The events of that morning have been clearly established, so I will only briefly summarize them here. Mr. Brooks, you are aware, is the neighbor of Clarence's employer, Mr. Wood, a man of fine standing in his community and a grazier of some repute. Clarence was his farmhand and general help, and a good employee, diligent and punctual and hardworking. Now, directly abutting the Wood property is the small lot where the Brooks family has lived for generations, forever in a Wood's shadow, as it were. We have heard there is bad blood between the families. Without a trade to speak of, Mr. Brooks has recently attempted to emulate his neighbor by turning his hand to husbandry, cobbling together a pigpen and chicken coop and, incidentally, diverting Wood water and attempting to rustle a few Wood sheep.

"This is the context of the incident. Every morning and evening Clarence walked the track fronting the

Brooks place, on his way to and from work. He was noticed. On occasion, he was pelted with insults, sometimes stones, from both Mr. Brooks and his children—the impression is it had become some kind of sport. And then a pig went missing. Or so Mr. Brooks has claimed. We cannot be sure of this allegation because Mr. Brooks kept no inventory, and no pig has ever been found. But let us assume it did—what is to say it didn't simply escape? Might not the gate have been left open? Might not a fox or a dingo have got in? Is there a chance that Mr. Brooks's carpentry was not quite up to standard and the little swine simply wriggled free? We do not know. The police do not know. Sitting here today, Mr. Brooks does not know either, though at the time he decided he did. He decided that Clarence stole it. For no reason other than he was there, walking past the house every day. And perhaps because he was a native, for who else could be to blame?

"Now we come down to it. The night before the murder took place. We have heard from multiple witnesses that the prisoner spent that entire evening drinking in the Swan Hotel in Baroo and at one point regaled the bar with his story of the missing pig. He announced that Clarence had stolen it. 'That no-good nigger,' he said. Then, and I am quoting directly from the testimony of Simon Rawles here, he boasted that when next he saw Clarence: 'I'll kill the cunt, so help me God.'"

Henry lowered his notes to the table, allowed his words to hang. He could feel the discomfort in the courtroom, the atmosphere shifting, turning his way.

"Mr. Brooks drank so much that evening he never made it home, sleeping rough on the steps of the hotel. We can only imagine his mood when he was awoken early the next morning by the piercing dawn sunlight and the rumble of wagon wheels. In fact, we don't have to. Witnesses have filled in the gaps. Down from the hotel he staggered, stumbling along the road. He doused himself in water from the spigot, stole a loaf from the bakery shelves, and assaulted poor Mrs. Temple with such a barrage of lechery that she took flight along the street.

"And then Clarence arrived, walking through town on his usual route from his house to the Wood place. Multiple witnesses have testified as to what then transpired. They heard Mr. Brooks accuse Clarence of stealing the pig; an accusation Clarence denied. They saw Mr. Brooks strike him, unprovoked, in the face; they saw Clarence fall to the ground. They saw Mr. Brooks, not content with this retribution, straddle his defenseless victim and do exactly what he'd threatened the previous night, delivering a series of blows to Clarence's head so devastating that Clarence was never to wake. His face was unrecognizeable. Mr. Brooks broke one of his hands. When the constable arrived and pulled him off Clarence, he continued kicking and flailing and even spitting on the man lying dead on the ground.

"Let me just repeat that: he spat on the man he'd just killed.

"Now, the defense will no doubt argue that there is mitigation. That Mr. Brooks was under financial pressure, that he was still intoxicated, that he was somehow out of his mind. He was none of those things, gentlemen. He was a man who thought nothing of accusing a 'no-good nigger' of theft, and for whom 'killing the cunt' was not only just and reasonable but his right as a white Australian man. The law permits no such entitlement. It sees no difference between black and white. Mr. Brooks publicly stated his intention to kill Clarence then the following morning did that very thing, beating him to death with his own hands—and if that is not premeditated murder, gentlemen, then I do not know what is."

Chapter 7
Billy McBride

They rode until dusk in single file convoy, Billy behind Percy at the rear of the line, the young constable's enormous rifle slung like a longbow across his back. Every now and then he would turn and glare at Billy, not a word out of him, no clue what he was about. Billy remembered the boy Rabbit, this runaway they were going after, being just the same with Tommy, wouldn't stop staring, or sniggering, like this was all some kind of game. Which it probably was, to them: at the front of the line Noone and his two troopers trotted along happily, chatting, laughing now and then. Drew Bennett was a fucking idiot, putting his family in their path. Billy had no family of his own yet, but he had Katherine, and Glendale, and he wouldn't have risked either for anything, least of all some runaway black.

As the sun fell they made for a thin stand of brigalow stretching spidery against the gloom, dismounted in the center, and began making camp. Percy saw to the horses, the troopers gathered wood and lit a fire. Noone wandered among the trees, gazing up at the twilight, thoughtfully smoking his pipe. Billy unpacked slowly. Rummaging in his saddlebags, tying and retying the tether rope. He hadn't a container to give Buck a drink, so called over and asked Percy if he could borrow the tin when he was done.

The constable straightened and looked at him. He picked up the drinking tin and dragged the bladder bag through the dry grass and dumped both at Billy's feet. Little eyes glinting. A smirk playing on his lips. He jutted his chin at Billy and spat tobacco juice through his teeth. "Chickenshit," he said.

"What's that now?"

"Shoot a few blacks and dip your dick in the widow and reckon that makes you a man. Shit, I done fucked prettier hoors than her."

It came out of him in a torrent. Rage surged through Billy and he lunged. The boy took a quick step backward and Billy heard his name being called through the trees. He turned. Noone was standing at the edge of the camp, watching them. He tutted and shook his head. Billy seething at the young constable—he had half a foot on him and at least fifty pounds, still the boy grinned like he was begging to be hit. If it wasn't for Noone, for that rifle on his back . . . Percy caught Billy staring at it, and asked, "Want to know where I got her?"

"Fuck you."

Percy lifted the rifle over his head. "She's a Hawken. That's American. Came all this way. Longest shot in the colony, I'd wager. Here, how much do you want to put up?" Billy said nothing. Both fists clenched. Percy shrugged and told him, "I can hit a penny off a fence post at two hundred yards with this thing, or put out a fella's eyeball, take your pick. Show you tomorrow if you don't believe me, if you've a penny or an eye to spare."

Billy relaxed a little. The boy obviously wasn't right in the head. He bent and snatched up the drinking tin and tipped in some water for his horse. There was a call of *Tucker!* from the campfire, but when he straightened Percy was still beside him, running his tongue around his gums.

"I'll bet her cunny's smooth and hairless. Bet she keeps it nice and trimmed. Might be I'll pay a visit and find out for meself—how d'you like them beans?"

Billy pulled his revolver and leveled it at Percy's head but at the same time Percy switched the rifle and aimed at Billy's chest. He started laughing. A wet, yellow-toothed grin. Another shout of *Tucker!* from the campfire and Billy dropped the revolver to his side. The boy was only goading him in front of the others. It was not a fight Billy could win.

"Like I said: chickenshit." And away Percy tramped through the trees.

They sat around the fire, eating, Billy the last to join. Warily he emerged from the tree line, into the clearing, making for the space they'd left him, between Jarrah and Noone. Watching them all closely. He trusted not one. Pope sat with his long legs crossed and his bald head bent—the dome of his skull dented and ridged—nibbling on a chicken leg; Jarrah hunched moodily beside him, shoveling it all in. On the other side of the fire Percy tossed grapes into his mouth one by one, while Noone ate an apple in six enormous bites, devouring it entirely, core, pips, and all.

Billy lowered himself between them, picked up his food parcel and opened it, found chicken, bread, cheese, grapes, a couple of slices of beef.

"She really was most generous. Such an accommodating host."

Billy frowned at the comment, then noticed the napkins the food was wrapped in: green with golden trim, the same they used at Broken Ridge. Noone had mentioned Katherine back at the house, and there was all Percy had just said. He turned on Noone: "What have you done?"

"Why, nothing but pay a visit, Billy, asking after your whereabouts—I had heard you were working up there. And of course, a woman alone on a frontier property, vulnerable, it is my duty to ensure she is well. Which she was, you'll be pleased to hear. Nothing to worry about at all. I have to say, I was rather surprised to find she is engaged now, though I am sure once the poor fellow realizes what his fiancée has been up to, the condition she has got herself in, he will be far less inclined to stick around."

Billy felt himself tilting, his face burning in the flames. "What you talking about? What condition?"

"Oh, you didn't know? Now that does surprise me. For a cattle man such as yourself, I would have thought gravidity in a female would be easy enough to spot. But then, surely she should have told you—I assume the bastard is yours?"

"He spat his seed into her cunny, now she's got a babby . . . He doesn't think it's very funny, that he'll be a daddy . . ."

Percy sang it like a ditty, a nursery rhyme, then

dissolved into cackling laughter once he was done. Noone shot him a reproachful glance. The two troopers sniggered and Billy began scrambling to his feet. Again, he went for his revolver but reconsidered, pointed his finger around the circle instead.

"Shut your fucking mouths. I got done with you cunts years ago, I don't want none of this horseshit now. Drew Bennett ain't nothing to me, neither's that boy in his barn. Do what you like, see if I care, but you leave us alone, you hear me? I see any of you lot round our way again, especially this gobby little shite here, and I'll put a hole in you. To hell with it, I'm going home."

They watched his performance impassively, like bored spectators at a show. Pope picked off another morsel of chicken and put it between his teeth; Jarrah had his revolver drawn, cocked, and ready in his lap. Already Billy felt his resolve slipping. Could it possibly be true? It had been almost a month since he last saw Katherine—had it happened then, or had she already known? Had she wanted to tell him that day in her office, while he grumbled on about a deed?

"Sit down, Billy," Noone said.

He swallowed thickly. A tiny shake of the head. If he were in town or on the station he'd have hit any man who threatened him; or more likely wouldn't have had to, they wouldn't dare. But he had no authority over these men. He was powerless here, and they knew it.

"Don't you remember our deal?" Noone said. "We are already a day's ride closer to Tommy. We could continue directly from here. Or we could go back to Broken Ridge and avail ourselves of Mrs. Sullivan's hospitality again—I know my boys are more than keen. So why not give your brother a chance of making it, and leave the young widow in peace. You'll be back with her the day after tomorrow, provided everything goes to plan."

All the fight washed out of him. He looked despairingly around the circle of men. Pope had finished eating and was preparing a tobacco pipe; delicately Noone speared a grape on the end of his bowie knife and, smiling, popped it in his mouth. "You cast in your lot five years ago," he said, chewing openmouthed. "You don't really have a choice here. You're already in this up to your neck. Now sit down and eat the meal she has kindly prepared for us and stop making a fool of yourself."

Meekly he did as he was told. Legs crossed, the food parcel in his lap, every mouthful sticking in his throat. He imagined Katherine making up these parcels: her slender fingers folding the napkins, putting in the best of what she had, trembling with Noone at her shoulder . . . he should have been there to protect her, they could have done anything.

Noone produced a silver liquor flask, took a drink and passed it around. Jarrah handed it to Billy and he wiped the neck before he drank. He rolled and smoked a cigarette. The others lit their pipes. The little fire crackling between them all, tossing sparks into the night.

"They are suns, did you know that?" Noone said, gazing up at the stars. "Millions of suns, no different to our own, so distant they are but pinheads in our sky. And yet they say that some are dying, may already have done so, only their light is visible now. Meaning that at any time, like snuffing out a candle, one of those stars might simply . . . expire."

He looked at Billy expectantly. "Horseshit," was Billy's view.

"You don't believe me? Or don't understand?"

"I don't follow half the crazy things that come out your mouth."

"No, well, that doesn't surprise me at all. But consider this, if you are able: if one star can expire than so can they all, including our very own sun. The Bible claims the world was made by God's hand, but what I am talking about is the end of days, the impermanence of life here on earth. The sun may rise in the morning, or it may not, and isn't that the most thrilling thought?"

Chapter 8
Katherine Sullivan

She rode down the track to the cattle yards, and like dogs catching a scent the men paused their work and turned their heads. Bright white blouse stark against the crimson hillside, shotgun in her saddle holster, ponytail bouncing with each stride. She knew how they looked at her, what they saw: trading glances, hefting their crotches, smoothing down their hair. She would never be more than John's pretty widow to these men, her men, good only for ogling or as a punchline to their jokes.

Leaning against railings, smoking on upturned pails, kicking the dusty ground—Katherine reined up among them and asked for Joe. A young stockman came forward, Alfie Dawson, Katherine made a point of knowing their names. Someone whistled. Dawson grinned. He tipped back his hat and offered his hand to help her down.

"I'm perfectly capable, thank you, Alfie. If you could just point me in the direction of Joe."

"He's over in the barn there, miss. Be my pleasure to escort you."

A gap-toothed smile and another whistle from the men and inwardly Katherine cringed. For nearly five years she'd had to put up with this horseshit, ever since John died. Perhaps she'd been too timid in the early years, too deferential to her father; but then she was only nineteen when she was widowed, what did she know about running a cattle station then? Plucked from a circuit of needlework and gossip and dragged out to this shithole to give some rich squatter a son, it had felt like being shipped off to hell. But she got used to it. And things were much easier now John was dead. She actually had something out here, a chance of a life on her terms. Back in Melbourne she would only ever have become another somebody's wife; at least here she could do as she pleased. Though not entirely. There was her father to manage, his suitors to navigate, not that they usually stuck around long. But Charles Sinclair was still here somehow, and now Billy was gone, and in the men's eyes she'd always be nothing but a little girl.

She spurred the horse and turned so sharply that Alfie had to duck. He lost his footing and fell, howls of derision trailing Katherine to the barn. Smirking, she dismounted and walked in through the open doors, found Joe with a clipboard taking inventory along an aisle. He glanced at her then away again. Katherine waited. Outside, the cattle moaned and the men yelled, getting back to work. Sunlight spilled through the doorway. Birds sang. It wasn't all bad, she thought.

Wearily Joe lowered his clipboard and trundled along the aisle. A broad man in a flannel shirt, sleeves rolled, big arms. He wore a beard, as they all did, and in the years she'd known him his hair had thinned and peaked. Now he stood before her, evasive, wouldn't quite meet her eye.

"Hello, Joe," she said pleasantly. "How are you?"

"Help you with something, Mrs. Sullivan?"

Katherine forced a quick smile. "You've missed our last two meetings."

"Been busy here, is all."

"Even so, I still need to be kept informed."

"Of what?"

"Of everything. It's my station. I need to know what's going on."

He looked at his boots then, a kind of shrug. "Mr.

Drummond's down regular anyway. I can't be running after you too, there just ain't the time."

Katherine's eyes pinched. "What do you mean he's down regular?"

Another shrug. "I figured you knew."

She glanced at the wall then back again. "And is that also the reason the upper paddocks haven't been cleared? I told you I wanted that cattle moved."

"Mr. Drummond said not to. Said to leave 'em a bit. Said the new fella—your husband, I mean—would decide what to do about 'em soon enough."

Katherine sighed irritably. Billy thought Joe was too soft, too malleable, but there was also a sly cunning to him, Katherine knew. He wasn't stupid: he'd seen where things were headed and chosen a side.

"Charles Sinclair is a guest here and no more," she told him. "As is my father, for that matter. You report to me, Joe—surely you know that?" She looked at him imploringly, then hardened; he still wouldn't meet her eye. "So, I want those paddocks clearing, and I'll expect you next week at the house, and while we're at it I want you to let that old cripple Morris go. He's out there now, sitting on his backside smoking cigarettes on my time. You should have done it already. What use is a stockman that can hardly walk?"

Joe looked up sharply, and inside Katherine swelled.

An urge now to turn and stride out of the barn, victorious, but there was something else she needed first. Joe began worrying the edge of his clipboard and mumbling about Morris, about how long he'd been with them, how he had nowhere else to go, and Katherine couldn't help but think of Billy, holding her against him, telling her nobody did out here.

"The other thing I wanted to know," she interrupted, talking over him, "is how Billy McBride is faring on his old family run. Have you heard anything from him? Are matters concluded between us now?"

"I gave him all he wanted, like you told me to."

"And? What else?"

"How d'you mean, Mrs. Sullivan?"

"Well, have you not seen or heard from him since?"

"One of the blokes reckoned he was out at the Lawton saleyards a few weeks back, but that's all I've heard."

A pause, then Katherine said, "Right, very good. Remember about Morris. And the upper paddocks. I'll see you next week as planned."

She swiveled and marched out through the doorway, mounted up, and rode clear of the yards, whistles and catcalls as she did so; Morris finger-waved. Katherine ignored them, resisted the urge to give a finger gesture in return. She rode around the workers' compound and onto the western track, unsure of the route exactly, it had been a few years. But when she saw the barren hillside sloping up to a blue gum wood, the termite mounds and thin horse trail beaten into the dusty ground, she left the paddocks and followed it and, once through the trees, emerged onto Billy's land.

It was a long ride to the homestead, over empty rubbled scrubland, miserable grazing country and not a cow in sight. There must have been fodder somewhere, perhaps closer to the creek, but not for the first time she wondered what it was with Billy, with most men: this stubborn battle to outdo their fathers, against all logic and good sense.

Because it was such a sorry victory: the house crooked and crumbling, the inside covered in dust. There was a smashed mug on the verandah, finger marks on the table, and two of the chairs were pulled out, but otherwise no sign that Billy was living here at all. She knew the reason. The bloodstains were still visible on the floor. She crossed the yard to the bunkhouse and found a few items of his clothing scattered beside a stripped mattress—he'd left in a hurry, she realized. Gathered his blankets, packed his things. Meaning Noone had come calling like he'd threatened to, and Billy had rolled over again.

He had arrived at the house yesterday, uninvited, unannounced; the first Katherine knew, he was standing in her drawing room, impossibly tall, talking with her father and Charles. She had not seen him in half a decade but it felt much less: the unnerving way he spoke to her, so courteous and polite; that hollow stare; the warmth of his hand when they shook. His very presence set the room akilter, as if she were suddenly drunk.

"As pleasant as this is, gentlemen, I would be obliged if you would excuse us. Mrs. Sullivan and I have some urgent police business to discuss."

Amid scowls and second glances the others left the room and Katherine and Noone were alone. Katherine rang the bell and asked for tea and they sat waiting in the armchairs, facing each other, twenty feet apart. Still he felt too close. Like she couldn't breathe. He smiled and those dead eyes traced her body head to foot. She smoothed down her skirts to the ankle, but they weren't quite long enough.

"So how are you, Mrs. Sullivan? Not short of suitors, I see?"

"Very well, thank you."

"Is it official? Are you to be wed?"

"Nothing is decided. How can I help, Mr. Noone?"

The tea came and they fell silent while the housemaid poured, Katherine's gaze flicking between the girl and Noone. She served them then hurried from the room, and Katherine found she had to grip her cup tight to the saucer to stop it rattling in her hands. Once, she had amused herself by teasing him, by speaking out of turn, but she hadn't understood a thing. She'd been so naive in those days, about everything, not least this man.

"I heard Billy McBride is working for you—is that true?"

Perhaps she'd flinched at the mention of Billy's name, some twitch that had given her away, or perhaps he'd heard the gossip from the men, but when she told him that Billy was back at Glendale, starting up on his own, Noone grimaced and inclined his head a little, said, "I'm very sorry to hear that. You must miss him, I am sure."

She hadn't known how to answer him, took another sip of tea, smiling politely while Noone talked in general terms about the district, the colony, then asked quite sincerely if she'd had any trouble from the local blacks. "Good, good," he said, nodding, when she answered she had not, like this was somehow news to him, an unexpected turn of events. She couldn't read him at all, not like she could most men; there was always another meaning to everything he said. He had helped her once, after John died, going down to the compound to arrest Raymond Locke—did he assume she was now in his debt?

The state they had found Locke in afterward . . . the things Noone had done . . .

He drank his tea primly and told her about an expedition he was planning, for which apparently he needed Billy's help. And hers: Might he trouble her for some rations, whatever she could spare? Again she rang the bell and asked for food parcels to be prepared, and didn't think anything of it when Noone had said he needed five, despite there only being three men waiting when she later accompanied him outside.

"Congratulations, incidentally," Noone said as they parted, his eyes on her stomach, his tongue wetting his lips. "I wish you and the child the best of health."

Now she stood among Billy's detritus in the bunkhouse and reflexively touched her bump. Barely anything, the smallest hint of a bulge, but the signs were undeniable, no matter how hard she'd tried. Even the dates aligned. Not the last time with Billy but the time before that. Two months, then, still so early—how had Noone noticed through her housedress; how could he possibly have known?

She picked through the items on the bookcase. A deck of cards, a tobacco tin—what she knew of Billy she cared for very much but she didn't truly know him at all. There were glimpses. His tenderness, his stubbornness, his temper, his refusal to know his place . . .

but these traits were all part of the appeal. He'd grown up so fast—the suitors her father kept bringing her were boys compared to him. And now they were bound together, for better or worse, assuming the baby made it to term. She wouldn't go to the doctor. Wouldn't have anything done. If the child was God's will they would just have to accept it and make the best of things. She stepped out into the yard, still holding her stomach. It was miraculous, really, the idea of a life growing inside. A blessing. Yes, they weren't married yet, but that could be arranged, assuming Billy was willing to leave Glendale. She looked around witheringly. No child of hers would be growing up here. Suddenly she had a vision of their future together, clicking into place like lockpins: Charles Sinclair out of the picture, her father gone too, she and Billy married and living with the baby at Broken Ridge, all questions over her landholding resolved. Then just as quickly she was back in that yard, with all it still held for him, and she realized she couldn't be certain what Billy would choose. For every time he had held her, kissed her, fucked her, here was the other side to him: living in a barn like a swagman, running with people like Noone.

Chapter 9
Tommy McBride

For weeks they slogged west blindly. No river to guide them, no trail, no road; their only destination the horizon, whose features never changed. They didn't seem to have been followed. Empty country behind as well as out in front, at most a distant roo or dingo loping through the scrub, the bones of fallen creatures bleached bright white by the sun. Slow going out here. The horses struggling in the heat, water painfully scarce. They only had their canteens to store it in, having fled Cunnamulla without buying bladder bags, and were reliant on the dirty creeks and brackish pools they came across entirely by luck. The stallion fared the worst of them. Unused to hardship, and the hardscrabble terrain. He wouldn't wear the pack saddle and hated Arthur in the mount, meaning Tommy had to ride him and Beau carried their cargo, or what little of it remained. They'd gone through half their provisions already, and there was nothing out here to hunt.

Finally the scenery began changing: the soil becoming lighter, trees dotted here and there. In the distance they saw signs of a river, a steady thread of greenery weaving through the scrub, and whooping and cheering kicked the horses to a canter and raced to the nearest bank. They threw themselves in without undressing. Came up gasping and laughing like kids. They thought they'd found the Cooper Creek, no way of knowing this was the Bulloo River, hundreds of miles too far south. Drying on the bank in the sunshine, watching the horses drink, they babbled excitedly about having made it, and how they'd always known they would. Arthur did some fishing. Cooked them wrapped in river clay in the coals. It was the best damn meal they'd ever eaten: greedily they flaked the white meat off the bones, every last morsel, sucking their fingers clean, Tommy reminiscing about the first time he'd ever gone fishing, he couldn't have been much older than six. Father had taken him and Billy out to a spot called Hollow Creek, where they'd camped just the three of them, and caught more than they could eat. He'd felt like a man that day. Like he'd been given just a glimpse.

Easy to forget these happy memories—there were more if he forced himself, pushed through the veil their deaths had drawn. Mother, for no good reason, throwing an off egg at Father's head; her squeals as he chased her round the yard. That time Billy got his foot stuck in a bucket and Tommy had laughed till he cried. His earliest memory might have been the day Mary was born; he was three. Billy had been told to take the two of them off somewhere but when they'd heard Mother screaming had snuck behind the house instead. Tommy wouldn't keep quiet. Billy hushed him so loud Father heard. He broke off his pacing up and down the verandah, came round back and found them crouched beneath the sill. He'd scooped them up like they weighed nothing, carried them over to the stables, sat them on his knee. He was so strong in those days. Arms like cows' legs. He'd held them tight and promised them everything would be fine, and it was for a while, Tommy admitted—it might not have always seemed it, but their lives had been just fine.

After two days following the river they realized it couldn't be the Cooper. Its course was south-flowing, there were mountains in the west; they'd simply not ridden far enough. They crossed at a shallow point onto what looked like station land. Sheep and cattle everywhere, post-and-paling fences stretching across

the fields. Meaning somewhere out here was a homestead, with a kitchen, a store, maybe a map that would
show them where the hell they were. But such comforts
also meant people, and they couldn't risk being recognized. They were murderers, and word would almost
certainly have spread. Station gossip, a telegraph line.
They could give false names but it hardly mattered:
they couldn't change their faces, their disfigurements,
the colors of their skin.

They headed toward the hills, the first true undula-
tion in the landscape they'd seen in all this time. The
earth here softer, and golden, the grass more plentiful
and green. And there was water, the vast plains riddled
with veiny streams and waterways that from above resembled spreading fingers of mold. This was the fringe
of the Channel Country, which Arthur said was a good
sign, unaware that the Channel Country covered a
hundred thousand square miles. At least they didn't
go hungry. Sheep, calves—a meal was never far away.
Arthur butchered and cooked them and they left the
carcasses for the birds and dingos, whose kills already
littered the plains.

Still no sign of the Cooper.

"We'll find it," Arthur said.

The ranges were a line of jagged peaks and outcrops, studded with mulga and saltbush, steep downslopes strewn with boulders and buttressed by great tablet-shaped slabs, the footing sheer in places, in others riddled with scree. They climbed in a slow tacking motion, long sweeps from side to side, Tommy guiding the stallion carefully; like he'd never left the prairie the way he minced up that hill. They found a pass and followed a cutout through the ridge, walls of rock either side of them, the dull clip of hoof on stone, until the summit opened onto a wide gray plateau of almost-touching slabs, and as they made their way across it Tommy felt the stallion lurch beneath him, heard a brutal snapping sound, then a scream from the horse and it tilted, and Tommy was thrown from the saddle as it fell.

Arthur dismounted and came running. Tommy waved off his attempts to help, picking himself up gingerly, the stallion writhing beneath them, its leg in the crevice to the shin. The hoof had gone in, then the body had fallen, all the weight on that one bone. It was bent at a right angle. A thick white shard poked through the skin. Blood seeped from the wound and ran down the leg and gathered in a pool on the stone. Tommy crouched and put a hand on the horse's neck, its pulse like a wind-up drummer toy. The stallion stopped thrashing. A sudden, deathly calm. Watching Tommy fearfully with wild, wide eyes.

"Help me get his hoof out," Tommy said, shuffling into position. Behind him Arthur didn't move.

"There ain't nothing we can do, mate."

"Might be we can splint it."

"What would be the use?"

Tommy glared up at Arthur, despite knowing he was right. An injured horse out here was worse than none at all. He tugged at the foreleg anyway, felt Arthur's hand on his shoulder, shrugged it off.

"Tommy . . ."

"We can't just leave him. We need that saddle for a start."

"Here, before the pain gets any worse."

Tommy turned. Arthur was offering Cal Burns's revolver, flat in his open palm. He rose and stood looking at the gun.

"Why is this on me?"

"You were riding him. Hell, he's more your horse than mine."

Tommy looked at the horse forlornly, and at the gun in Arthur's hand. "No."

Arthur sighed. "Just . . . take a turn for once."

"What?"

"Do something, Tommy. A fish needs catching, I

catch it. We butcher a sheep, that's me too. You act like it's my fault we're here."

Five years ago, in ranges just like these, Noone had offered Tommy a gun the same way, whispering about his father, his brother, persuading him to take a life. And he'd done it, he'd buckled, the first man he'd ever killed. He could still hear the gunshot echo through the canyon, could still smell the sulfur on his skin. Arthur had no idea what he was asking. "I ain't doing it," Tommy said.

He walked away over the plateau until he reached the boulders on the far side of the rise, slipped between them out of view, and gazed at the land ahead, more of the same, the endless Channel Country, no sign of a river at all.

The gunshot made him shudder. A violent, whole-body flinch. He closed his eyes and held himself and listened to the report receding over the plains. Bracing himself. Sucking each breath through his teeth. In his mind a carousel of every shooting, every death. He scrubbed his face and scolded himself—it was only a fucking horse.

Arthur had the saddle swapped onto Beau by the time Tommy emerged from the rocks. The stallion lay dead on its side, its leg still caught in the crevice. There was a hole in its forehead. A clean shot between the ears. Arthur was crouched on the ground beside it, parceling out the remainder of their supplies—now they only had their saddlebags and what they could tie up behind. He glanced at Tommy then away again. "Here, give us a hand with these things."

"There's no river out there."

"We'll find it."

"You keep saying that, but when? Where is it? We've come far enough now anyway, why not just go south from here?"

"We talked about this. They'll be looking for us down there."

"*You* talked about it. *You* did. When do I get a say?"

"Look, I know you're upset about the horse but—"

"I'm not upset about the bloody horse. Stop treating me like a boy."

"It's you that does that, mate. Nothing to do with me."

Tommy stared at him, incredulous. "You really don't have a fucking clue."

Arthur held the stare, then in silence packed up their things. They made their way out of the hills before sundown—Tommy refused to camp there, despite the natural shelter it gave. They barely spoke in the days following, so used to each other's habits they could get by without hardly a word, such that when Tommy abruptly turned his horse to the south he did so without warning or explanation, riding off into the distance, not a backward glance. Arthur sat watching him. Weighing whether to let him go. Then he sighed and clicked his horse forward, followed on behind.

They were three days riding toward the border before they came upon the dingo fence, an immense chain-link mesh strung between thick palings and as high as any wall. They came to a halt before it, stood their horses together, scanning the fence left and right. It seemed unending. Perfectly straight, to the horizon east and west. Tommy dismounted and approached the wire mesh with his hand extended, as if it might not be real. He laced his fingers through the link and gently rattled. Dust wafted through the gaps. He tested a post but it was solid, and they'd ditched the pick and most of the other fencing tools in the hills. All they had now was the shovel, and what use was that?

For a day and a half they followed the fence line west and found not a gate or an opening; not even so much as a missing link. No choice but to abandon it, return north, heading for the Cooper and the central stock routes once again. No longer in the Channel Country. Might have been anywhere now. Desert terrain underfoot, a parched and rubbled ground, no cattle or sheep to butcher, no more little creeks and streams. They rationed their water sparingly. Made each damper loaf last two days. Sometimes they saw emu or rock wallaby or a pack of wild dogs, but the horses weren't up to hunting and they weren't yet desperate enough to eat a dog. They watched for signs of natives who might help them, but found none. Empty desert everywhere, arid gibber plains, corrugated as if a giant rib cage lay buried beneath the stony soil. No birds circling, no trees, no life at all. The wind blasting like a furnace. Dust choking their lungs, gritting their eyes, strafing their skin.

Still they persisted. What choice but to go on? Limping over the sandhills like the explorers of long ago, those men for whom these places were now named—Sturt, Burke, Strzelecki—and the many others who had died along the way. They came across reminders occasionally, harbingers of what was to come. A boot, a satchel, a rusted canteen; once, a shallow grave marked with a little cairn of stones. By a dried-up waterhole from which they wrung moisture out of mud, Tommy found a set of initials carved into a fallen tree—*APC*—and the simplicity of that message, of someone recording that they were here, moved Tommy to take out his knife and do the same. *TGM*, he wrote, Arthur looking on.

They'd been nine days in that desolate nothingness

when they felt the earth tremble beneath them and heard the unmistakable rumble of cattle on the move. They reined up and sat listening. Tommy lowered the kerchief covering his mouth. Both of them were like sandmen: gaunt, sunburned, squinting; a film of red dust like a second skin. Their lips were cracked, their cheeks hollow, it was painful just to breathe. Still, they knew the sound of a mob rushing. They'd been listening for that noise their whole lives.

"There," Tommy said, pointing to a thin dust cloud rising above the wavelike dunes. He jabbed his heels into Beau's wizened flank and despite his own condition the horse took off like he'd sensed it too. Arthur cursed and followed, Tommy by now up and over the first sand dune, no view yet but he was close. He urged Beau down the bank and up the next two dunes and when he crested the second pulled the horse up hard. There in the gully below him raged a thick flood of cattle a good few hundred strong, charging between the dunes in a great roiling cloud of red dust. At their flank a lone drover was trying desperately to keep up, snapping his stock whip again and again. Nothing was working. The drover struggled to keep his mount. Where the gully narrowed, his horse was buffeted by the mob, almost crushed against the dune. The cattle had their blood up. He'd never hold them on his own.

Arthur was still clearing the sandbank when Tommy disappeared down the other side. Traversing the slope at a gallop, spilling slides of red soil in his wake, he raced to get ahead of the mob from on high, to cut it off at the pass. If they made it out of the gully it would be hopeless; the mob would scatter and be gone. The drover hadn't seen him yet, but Tommy could hear his shouting and whipcracks over the frothing surge of the mob. The smell of them, the noise—he knew this all too well. Every year since he'd been able to ride he'd pushed his father to take him mustering, and even when he hadn't Tommy had watched with his brother as the men brought the cattle in. Down he came now, out of the sunshine, sweeping past the stampede, standing high in the saddle, his head down, his backside raised, his face lit up with joy, screaming his parched throat raw.

Now the drover noticed him. His whip fell limp in his hand.

"We'll turn them!" Tommy shouted, making a circling motion in the air. "Wait till we're out!" The drover nodded and fell away, taking a position at the mob's rear flank. By now Tommy was level with the lead bullock, its red eye glaring, spittle foaming in the corners of its mouth. He looked back for Arthur, but Arthur wasn't there: coming down the distant sandbank at a stroll. They cleared the gully and came into the open plains and Tommy began moving in, yelling at the cattle, forcing them to turn. Which they did, wheeling away to the right, the drover at their other flank, making sure they kept in line. Slowing down finally. The madness fading at last. Tommy brought the head of the column to the tail and he and the drover kept them turning like a mill wheel.

"I thought I'd bloody dreamed you," the drover panted, pulling up at Tommy's side. "Glad I didn't, anyhow. I was in the shit back there."

He was a man of around thirty, with skin tanned so dark he was barely still white, a three-month beard and blue eyes cracked like leather left too long in the sun. He wore moleskins and a filthy shirt, had two gun belts around his waist and a dark red kerchief at his throat. He took off his hat and ran a hand through light brown hair that he'd allowed to grow down to his neck. He said his name was Jack Kerrigan. "Got any water?" Tommy rasped.

Kerrigan pulled a flask from his saddlebag and Tommy drank until he coughed. Arthur joined them cautiously. Tommy motioned with the flask and Kerrigan nodded. "Don't be shy now. I got plenty back there on the mules."

Arthur drank his fill and returned it. Kerrigan

stoppered the flask, saying, "So, do I dare ask what you fellas are doing out here?"

"Looking for the Cooper Creek," Tommy replied.

"The *Cooper*? Shit-in-hell, you're about two hundred miles too far south. What you heading out that way for?"

Tommy glowered at Arthur, said, "He thought we could pick up the Birdsville Track, get ourselves into SA."

"Some tracker you've got there, mate—you're already in South Australia, probably been here about a week. You don't need the bloody Cooper . . . where's all your stuff at anyway? How are you boys still alive?"

"The other horse went lame a while back. Had to lose most of our things."

"Well, shit." Another stroke of his hair and he settled his hat back on his head. "I've seen some sorry bastards in my time but few worse than the pair of you. I thought I was lucky to have found you—I reckon it might just be the other way around."

"Where are you going?" Tommy asked.

"Marree, eventually. Or I was, until these buggers spooked. Probably a snake what did it. Took off like they'd been bloody shot."

"How far is Marree?"

"Maybe another month, give or take, depends how quick they travel, and how the track holds up. That's the Strzelecki I'm talking about, mind you. Not your Birdsville bloody Track. Shit, you boys really don't have a clue." He started chuckling then said, "Anyway, you fellas got names?"

Tommy had been waiting for this since they'd crossed those cattle stations a while back; the risk of boundary riders, of being caught. "Robert Thompson," he told him, the name off the headstone in St. George. "Or Bobby, if you like."

Kerrigan shook his hand. "Good to meet you, Bobby. What about your boy?"

After a pause Arthur said, "Arthur." They didn't shake hands, and Tommy didn't correct the reference to *boy*.

"All right. So listen, how about we work out some terms?"

"For what?"

"Well, you two are about as lost as a snowflake in spring, but you know how to handle cattle, and I could use the help. My men all quit a while back, bunch of workshy bastards that they are, got spooked by the Strez like some do. So how about you work your passage and I'll see you to Marree, or any of the stations along the way. Tucker included. Provided we can find them two mules."

Tommy glanced at Arthur. A tiny shake of his head. Tommy said, "What's to stop us just following you anyway?"

"Nothing, I suppose. Except that if you try to rob me I'll shoot you, no worries about that." He patted one of the revolvers on his gun belt. "So unless you're planning on eating rocks and dirt out there you might as well get yourselves fed. Plus I'll pay you into the bargain. Twenty-five shillings a week, same as them other cunts, and I won't ask any questions about what you're really doing out here—that sound fair?"

"Fifty," Tommy said. "Fifty a week."

"State you're in and you're bartering." Kerrigan chuckled. "You've got some nerve. All right, how about I throw in a penny a head for every one of these buggers we get loaded on the train. That's between you, mind. You can split it however you like. Or I'll point you in the direction of the Cooper and wave you both goodbye."

Tommy leaned and shook on it, Arthur watching impassively as he did. "Good," Kerrigan said as they parted. "Well, we'd best get straight to it, else we'll be hunting down them mules in the dark."

He moved his horse away, ready to begin cutting the cattle out of their wheel. "I don't like this," Arthur said.

"He's saving our lives here. Plus we're getting paid."

"We don't know nothing about this bloke."

"Neither does he. Wouldn't anyway—what did you give your real name for?"

Arthur sniffed and spat and turned his horse around. "Mate, nobody gives a shit what the blackfella's called." And he took up a position beside the mob.

Chapter 10
Billy McBride

Sunshine blanketed the homestead. A neat slab hut with well-kept storage barns and white sheets gleaming on the wash line. A barefoot woman shooed chooks while pegging out her husband's damp shirts; blond-haired children played chase through the yard. At one of the outbuildings a man was working, replacing a section of weathered boards, a delay between each hammer swing and its sound reaching the crest of the hill on which the line of five riders stood.

Billy lowered the brass telescope, handed it back to Noone.

"You will guard the family," Noone told him. "Restrain them, if you must. The rest of you to that big barn on the right there. That's where our boy will be."

Hannah Bennett was first to notice them. She dropped her peg bag and called to her husband but was muffled by his hammering and the squeals of their girls. The children halted immediately. The panic in their mother's voice. She told them to get inside the house, shouted again, and only now did Drew Bennett turn: he saw his family fleeing, saw the horses descending the hillside. He locked eyes with Hannah, a long and fearful stare. She hurried after the children. Briefly, Drew's head hung. He tossed the hammer and went into the shed and emerged with a shotgun broken over his arm. He slid in the shells as he walked to the middle of the yard, stationed himself between the riders and the house. Faces in the windows, watching him. Hannah in the crack of the door.

Drew snapped the breech face closed, set his feet apart, shouldered the shotgun, and took aim. Down the barrel he sighted them: two blacks, three whites, one tall in the saddle, his longcoat flared like wings. Drew hesitated. The shotgun sagged in his hands. One of the white men began waving madly, yelling for Drew to lower the gun, and with a jolt he noticed that the blacks were in uniform, and realized who the tall man was.

Drew glanced at his family and laid the shotgun on the ground.

Three horses swept by him, made directly for the main barn; the tall man followed them at a walk, his head twisting, watching Drew Bennett as he passed.

"Drew! Don't! Easy now—don't touch that gun!"

Drew scowled at the man shouting, dismounting his horse at a run. The face was familiar, the voice, but he couldn't quite place him here, at his property, with these men. Panting, he stopped just a few yards away, his face flushed, his hand outstretched.

"Just . . . kick the shotty over, eh?"

Drew's face unclouded. "You bring this mob to my house, Billy McBride?"

"They're only here for the boy, nothing else."

"I asked you a fucking question."

"They were coming anyway. It was them that brung me."

Drew's face twisted. "What for?"

"Drew, mate—the shotty."

He looked at the shotgun at his feet, as if wondering how it had got there. The others had dismounted and were watching from the barn.

"You know who they are?" Billy said. "Who he is? What he'll do?"

"I've an idea, aye."

"Then don't be stupid about it. Christ, it's only a black."

Drew dragged his hand over his face. He kicked the shotgun to Billy; Billy opened it and tipped out the shells. At the barn Noone gave an instruction and Percy approached the door with his pistol drawn. He tugged on the handle but it was locked. All heads turned.

Drew's voice was barely a whisper: "Lock's on the inside."

"No key," Billy yelled.

Noone dispatched Jarrah to the toolshed, and as he passed he didn't give Drew Bennett so much as a glance. Everyone waited. A hot wind whipped through the yard. The white bedsheets billowed. The house door creaked.

"I've my whole bloody family back there," Drew said.

"Which is why you have to let them do their business then leave. They only want their trooper. That's all this is about."

"I never knew he was Native Police."

"I know that, mate. I know."

Drew glared at him a long time. "I'm not your mate, you fucking dog. Your old man would be turning in his grave if he saw what you've become."

Jarrah returned with a long-handled shovel swinging nonchalantly at his side. He carried it to the barn and wedged the blade in the lock jamb and after a nod from Noone prized the doors. The wood cracked and splintered. Drew Bennett flinched at the sound. Percy and Pope had their pistols ready as Jarrah nudged the barn door open with the shovel end. Stiffly, it swung on its hinge. Noone glanced at Drew Bennett, jutted his chin, ordered Percy and the troopers inside.

"You have to stop them, Billy."

"They wouldn't listen even if I tried."

Drew had paled. He shook his head. "You don't understand."

And for a long time there was nothing. Total silence in the yard, in the barn, all eyes trained on the open door, until suddenly the silence was broken by a scream from within: a woman's scream, rent with fear.

"Who is that? Who's in there?" Billy snapped, but Drew only stared at the barn. Brief sounds of a scuffle, shouting, another scream, then the troopers emerged dragging the missing trooper Rabbit and a native woman through the door. They marched them to Noone and held them there, cowering from the sudden brightness, and from the inspector peering down.

"They're fucking animals," Drew Bennett said.

The troopers let go of their arms. The captives stood trembling in their borrowed clothes: Drew's shirt drowning Rabbit, an old dress that Hannah had loaned. Rabbit began blubbering. Hands together in prayer. He was young, perhaps Billy's age, and in that shirt looked younger still. He chopped his hands back and forth beseechingly, begging, "Marmy, please Marmy, sorry Marmy, please." Noone smiled at him, sighed; his great chest heaved. He reached out a hand and very carefully placed it on Rabbit's head, cradling his skull, and at the touch Rabbit dissolved into sobbing and a dark stain spread down the front of his leg.

"He pissed hisself!" Percy shrieked, laughing. "He pissed hisself—look here!"

Pope already had the neck cuffs. Wailing, Rabbit was put into irons. They took hold of the woman and did likewise, and it was only as she turned, as her dress tightened when her arms were pinned, that Billy realized what Drew had been talking about: a bulge in her belly; she was carrying a child.

"Oh, shit. Oh, no."

"Yeah. And you'll just stand here and watch."

The captives were chained to the back of Jarrah's horse and led to the edge of the yard. Noone and Percy remained by the barn. From the pocket of his longcoat Noone produced the silver flask they had been drinking from last night, unscrewed the lid, and saluted Drew Bennett in a toast. He took a sip and passed the flask to

Percy, who laughed and skipped along the front of the barn, dousing the wooden walls in rum. Drew lunged away from Billy. Billy was too slow to react. From the house Hannah shouted after her husband and Noone's head turned. He reached inside his longcoat. Two revolvers were reverse-holstered on his belt: he had one drawn and raised just as Billy managed to catch up with Drew and slam into him from behind.

Down the pair tumbled. Rolling through the dust. Noone slid the revolver back into his belt and fished out his matchbox instead. Drew dragged himself to his knees, Billy standing over him, arms spread, like shepherding a wantaway calf, while Hannah edged from the house into the yard. Noone struck the match and tossed it. A curtain of blue flame ripped up the barn wall and spread over the sun-parched building like a plague. Black smoke billowed. It pumped through the door and windows and up through the roof and whispered through the gaps in the walls. A hellish noise building. A roar of destruction, of death. Within a few minutes the fire had consumed the barn entirely, its redness reflected in Drew Bennett's damp eyes.

The family would watch it later. After Billy had recovered his horse and joined the others and the five of them had led their captives back over the grassy hillside, one by one they would slip timidly from the house, and would hold each other or stand alone, watching their futures burn. Their entire food store was in there. Their cattle feed and equipment, everything. They would never fully recover. When news of the fire got out, put down to a dropped branding iron, the church and their neighbors would rally round to see them through the coming months. But charity could not sustain them. Couldn't give back what they had lost. Yes, they still had their cattle, and they could rebuild, but for the rest of his life Drew Bennett would measure himself against the man he had been prior to that day and always seemed to come up short. The children became sickly. Hannah blamed the smoke. For weeks it hung over them, long after the barn had folded boxlike and collapsed into a pile of smoldering timber whose flames refused to fully die out. The fire haunted them after sunset, glowing through the windows; they saw it even when they closed their eyes. And that smell, that godawful burning, on their clothes, in their nostrils, their hair. Hannah felt terrible for having taken in the runaways—she hadn't known the boy was Native Police. Had she foreseen what would happen, that they'd be the ones punished, the night terrors and day terrors the children would endure, she would not for one second have hesitated in turning the pair away.

She should have suspected. They were so frightened and helpless, they must have been on the run. But the woman was expecting, and even Drew agreed—they had done the right thing by them, it all felt so unfair. In her weaker moments she would blame her husband, though she knew it wasn't his fault. But all she saw as she'd watched from the house was him lay down his shotgun and stand there while those men torched their barn. Yes, she had called out to stop him, she admitted as much, she was worried he would get himself shot. But Drew had always been the type who would protect them, one way or another, or so Hannah had assumed. And he hadn't. Hadn't even tried. Didn't say so much as a word. He had knelt on the ground and watched their livelihoods burn, and that was how she remembered him, from that day till their last: on his knees, in the yard, helpless. No matter how much she wished otherwise, she never looked at her husband the same way again.

For five hours they hauled the captives north, the woman flagging and falling and being yanked up by her chain, Rabbit begging in broken English for their lives. Noone simply ignored them. Eyes fixed indifferently ahead. Many times Billy readied himself to speak up on their behalf but the words withered on his tongue. It was pointless. Noone would not be swayed, and Billy would only mark himself out. He hoped that at least the woman might be spared. She hadn't done anything except fall for the wrong man.

In a nondescript patch of scrubland no different to any other, Noone called a halt and they dismounted and the pair were released from their neck chains. The woman tried to run immediately. Jarrah tripped her and dragged her back to the group; the others gathered round. Rabbit spoke to the woman tenderly. Billy had no idea what he said. Rabbit pleaded: "Is Rabbit fault, Marmy. Not she. Not she," and Billy tried to conjure some sympathy in Noone's stare, some hope for them, but the truth was there was simply nothing there at all.

"Hold him firm, the pair of you. Percy, get the gin."

Jarrah and Pope pinned Rabbit between them by his arms. Percy grabbed the woman, her hands shielding her belly, her feet shuffling backward through the dirt. She began shouting, as did Rabbit, while calmly over both of them Noone said, "I am very disappointed, Rabbit. After all I have done for you—I made you a man. You might have told me about the child, but instead you sneak out in the night like a rat. That is unacceptable. I will not allow such behavior to stand. Percy, please step aside."

Percy let go of the woman and before she even knew she was free Noone had drawn one of his revolvers and put a round directly through her hands and into her gut. She looked down at the wound, bewildered. Blood seeped between her fingers and she patted it, as if trying to keep it all in. Rabbit screamed and began thrashing but the two troopers held him fast. He looked at them imploringly. His former colleagues, his former friends—they wouldn't meet his gaze. The woman let out a wail of mourning that filled the plains, sky, and earth, then Noone abruptly silenced her with a bullet to the head.

She crumpled to the ground and lay motionless, and Noone turned to Rabbit, only upright thanks to the two troopers pinning his arms, staring at his fallen lover, his mouth agape and webbed with strands of spittle in a long and silent cry.

"Gentlemen," Noone said, "it's been a pleasure," and in one fluid motion, a quick three-beat movement as precise as a conductor's baton stroke, he shot Pope, Rabbit, and Jarrah plumb through the forehead, so swiftly they fell as one, their arms interlocked, first to their knees then pitching forward, facedown in the dirt.

Noone holstered the revolver.

"Dig the hole," he said.

That evening they camped in the same stand of brigalow as they had the previous night, sitting around the same campfire, three men instead of five. Numbly Billy stared at the empty spaces where Pope and Jarrah should have been, the low fire flickering, his food untouched in his lap. Noone and Percy chatted while they ate, like this was a normal day for them, which Billy realized it probably was. He hated the both of them, for dragging him out here, for getting him involved—all he wanted was to leave.

Noone had made him take turns on the shovel when Percy needed a spell, jamming the blade into that rocky red earth, turning out soil onto the mound. Noone smoked and watched and ambled back and forth; the bodies bled out where they lay. Flies hummed, birds waited, Billy waist-deep in the hole, mud-smeared and sweat-slicked, cupping his nose with his sleeve against the smell. One of the bodies had shat itself. He didn't know which one. Grimly he went on digging, still trying to process what he'd just seen. He couldn't explain it—murdering his own men, loyal for all these years—other than the fact Noone was fucking crazy, and treated killing like a game. But what he kept coming back to, as he dug out their grave, was the fact he'd shot the woman in her stomach first. He'd killed the baby, deliberately. He'd wanted Rabbit to see, and maybe Billy too. Again he thought of Katherine, pictured her alone in the house with Noone. Pregnant. He could have done anything, to her, to their child. And Billy wasn't there.

"Why'd you do it?" he asked now, in the moonlit clearing, a lattice of shadows from the leaves. "Why'd you kill your own men?"

Noone sighed like it was just one of those things. "I already told you, the Native Police has served its purpose, its time is almost up. Besides, it has become too difficult in the current climate to do the job properly, as one must. I do not intend being the last man standing. Percy and I are headed for a new assignment on the coast. Fun as this has been, it is time for a new challenge, and to reap the rewards of all I have sown."

Billy scoffed and said, "What sort of an answer is that?"

"Do I have to spell it out for you? I suppose I probably do. Those men, fine troopers though they were—what was I to do with them? I can hardly take them with me, so what else? Retire them? How? Where to? They are neither suited for white society, nor can they go back to their tribes; frankly I doubt their tribes even exist. Think of them like workhorses that have reached the end of their useful lives. It's kinder to simply terminate them. Makes things easier all round."

"But . . . they're not horses. They've been with you for years."

"Exactly. And consider the things they have seen, the things they know. I am to be promoted, Billy. Chief inspector, and not before time. I cannot run the risk of any scandal. There is a different sensibility on the coast. You should be thanking me, for it is your reputation as well. And besides, now you know what will happen to you and your young family if ever you decide to turn."

"Have your eye out before you opened your mouth anyway," Percy snarled at him, patting the Hawken rifle at his side.

"Come back when your balls have dropped."

"Boys, boys," Noone said, smiling. "We're all on the same side here."

When the hole was ready they'd dragged over the bodies and one by one slung them in. Echoes of his parents, of that day he and Tommy had done this exact same thing. Now it was this little shitstain Percy he crabbed to the graveside with, the boy panting and straining, barely the strength to hold his end. In they went, the four of them—five, Billy corrected himself. A tangle of limbs and bodies that at first came almost to the lip, until Percy climbed on top and like a child crushing sandcastles, set about stomping them down.

The sun was low in the west when they rode away from that place, the broken ground smoothed over and level and covered with rocks and loose grass, the only sign of what had happened here the many bloodstains on the ground, dark pools and drag marks trampled by hooves and boots, though within a few days they would be gone too, dried by the sun and buried beneath a skin of windblown dirt.

That night Billy lay awake among the brigalow, listening to the crackle of the campfire and the constant rustle of the trees. His thoughts swamped by Katherine, and their baby, if there was one, if Noone's story was real. He'd never felt anything so strongly in his life: a physical aching to get back there, twisting his insides; to be with her, protect her, to claim what was his. Tomorrow. Once Noone had said he could leave. These two fuckers lying snoring across the campfire . . . he could kill them both and be done with it, he realized. He was fully dressed, boots and all, his revolver strapped to his belt. Cast off the bedroll, jump up to his feet, two quick shots and it would be done. He'd be rid of Noone forever, the curse he'd put on Billy's life, and his brother's; if he could find him, Tommy could come home. He could bury the bodies out here and no one would ever know. He fingered the revolver restlessly. The breath surging out of him, heart hammering in his chest. He lifted his head and chanced a look, saw the outline of Noone through the flames. He was lying with his head in the crook of his arm, facing Billy, the two dark pits of his eyes, no telling if he was awake or not. Billy eased himself back down, let go of the gun, told himself it was safer not to, better to bide his time. It didn't feel any safer. All night he lay listening to Noone's breathing, unsure if he was watching, too afraid to fall asleep.

Chapter 11
Henry Wells

He'd not yet reached the doors of the courthouse when he heard his name being called, echoing over the hubbub in the grand central stairwell, its wide stone staircase spotlit by shafts of smoke-filled sunlight through the tall arched windows above.

"Mr. Wells, sir! Mr. Wells!"

Henry paused in the bustling lobby and turned to find a figure running down the stairs. A reporter, probably. Henry hadn't wanted the Clarence murder case when it was given to him, nobody did, but it was doing his profile no harm at all, both with the public and at the bar. He waited for the man to catch up—warm air teasing through the main doors behind him, the clatter of George Street trams—then noticed with a start that it wasn't a reporter at all but the judge's clerk. Henry cringed. Had he done something wrong, he wondered, said something untoward in the courtroom? Conducted himself out of turn? Perhaps he'd simply forgotten some papers, though the boy carried nothing in his hands. He slid to a halt in front of Henry, gasping every word.

"Mr. Wells, sir . . . it's . . . the jury. They're ready . . . to come back."

"But that's impossible."

"The judge told me so himself, sir. You don't know where Mr. Hugill went?"

Henry took a long time to answer. "Try the robing room," he said.

The boy scurried off. Henry couldn't move. It had barely been ten minutes—which must mean they were sending Brooks down. The evidence was so overwhelming, surely to God they couldn't be about to turn that man free. Of course they could. There was always a risk. But still, ten minutes! One man's life, and the worth of another, decided before Henry had even managed to reach the street.

Up the sunlit staircase he trudged, swirling with hope and dread. There was a scrum of people from the balcony to the courtroom—clearly word had got around. Henry pushed his way through and walked along the aisle and found Hugill already seated at the front. The defense counsel grimaced sympathetically. Henry took his seat. Waiting, while behind him the gallery filled. He hadn't lost a case so far in his short career. Surely he couldn't lose this.

The judge arrived, the prisoner was brought back in. Brooks looked ashen. A meek and cowardly stare. Henry eyeballed him but couldn't catch his gaze, then in came the jury, a sullen shuffle to their seats. The judge asked for their verdict, the foreman rose, the room held its breath.

"Not guilty."

Pandemonium in the gallery. Shouting and clapping and hats thrown in the air. The judge ordered the prisoner's fetters removed and, dumbfounded, Brooks stepped down from the dock. The jury was dismissed, the courtroom slowly emptied, Hugill patted Henry's shoulder as he passed. A man came in and began sweeping up peanut shells and orange rind from the floor, the hush of his broom on the boards, as Henry sat there numb, the only one left in the courtroom, unable to bring himself to leave.

Two bottles of wine over dinner was never going to be enough: with his hands in his pockets and collar upturned, Henry rolled between the sly-grog shops of the Frog's Hollow slums, his polished shoes sinking into the oozing mud, bypassing gambling houses, red-lit doorways and opium dens, brushing off the whores and spivs, drinking himself into a stupor until finally, long after midnight, he felt an urge for home.

It was a short walk to the boardinghouse. Henry tripped coming into the building, his laughter echoing through the empty lobby, the rug pattern blurring beneath him in the dim lantern light. He hauled himself up the stairwell, gripping the smooth wood banister, his muddied shoes scuffing stair to stair, to the first-floor landing, where he hovered by his front door before slipping his key back into his pocket with a wanton smile. What was the use in pretending? This wasn't why he'd come back—who was he even pretending for?

Along the landing he shambled, to another near-identical green door. So much of his life he had kept hidden—at least now he was beginning to admit to himself what he was. Ever since that Sunday when his father, with a stern shake of the head, had confronted him with the rumors of his deviance, his sickness, and for the first time in his life Henry had found the strength not to deny it, instead sitting straight-backed and silent as if saying, *Yes, this is me, here is your son*, the two men staring hatefully at each other while his mother clutched her chest, then his father pronouncing him banished from Sydney society like some fucking

Shakespearean king, forcing Henry to move his pupilage up here, to Brisbane, where he'd spent the last
three years trying to prove himself; or rather, to prove
that bastard wrong.

He knocked on the door and waited. Glancing down
into the lobby, over the rail. A scrabble of locks and
he jerked to attention, turned to find Jonathan standing there, a maroon robe over his pajamas, bed-tousled
hair, squinting into the dim light.

"Henry? What is it? Are you all right?"

Henry leaned against the doorframe. His speech
came mumbled and slow: "It was the Clarence murder
trial today. I lost."

"Oh, dear. I'm so sorry."

"Were you sleeping?"

"Of course, it's after two. Where have you even
been?"

Henry waved a hand, meaning *out*, and slurred,
"It was a fucking travesty. That bastard should have
swung."

"The Hollow, I'm assuming? Am I wrong?"

Henry shrugged and Jonathan grimaced; he didn't
approve of Henry's excesses. But the longer they
stood there together, Henry looking at him dolefully,
big sad bloodshot eyes, the more Jonathan's expression softened, until he held the door open and stepped

aside, saying, "Come in, before somebody sees you in this state."

Henry wobbled into the apartment. Like his own, it only comprised two rooms: a bedroom and a living room; meals were provided downstairs, and there was a shared bathroom at the end of the hall. He flopped down onto a dark-mustard-colored sofa, tipped back his head, and watched Jonathan lighting the lanterns, rekindling the stove, putting the kettle on to boil, a womanly fussing that made Henry smile.

"You know, you really should be more careful," Jonathan said. "I mean it—what if someone had recognized you?"

"Half the city is doing something. I'm hardly the only one."

"Yes, but lesser things have ruined a man. You've enough secrets as it is."

"I'm tired of keeping secrets. Let them see me for who I am."

Jonathan laughed. "You'd be run out of chambers faster than a dog chasing cats, and you most certainly would never take Silk. The only Queen's Counsel I know are respectable married men with families and children and houses in the suburbs, who keep their predilections discreet."

"Well . . ." was all Henry said, knowing he was right.

Jonathan made two cups of sweet tea and sat next to Henry on the sofa. Henry shrugged out of his coat and warily took a sip. His hand was trembling slightly. His knee bounced up and down. But the tea was warm and comforting, and steadily he calmed. He glanced across at Jonathan. "Ask how long it took them."

"How long it took whom?"

"The jury, to reach a verdict, ask me how long."

"All right—how long?"

"Ten minutes. Less. I hadn't even time to reach the courthouse door."

"It sounds like you stood no chance."

"Probably not. They called me Judas in the courtroom. And here this man beat another to death with his fists and was cheered when he was set free."

"Will you appeal?"

"They won't want me to, I am sure, but I don't see that I have any choice. It is a manifestly unsafe decision. The judge should have intervened."

"You mustn't take it personally, Henry. I'm sure you did all you could."

"But I do take it personally. And so should you. If it had been you or I killed by that man, Jonathan, or a Chinaman or an Afghan, or anyone else who doesn't fit, do you honestly think the verdict would have been any different? You've just said it yourself: we should hide like mice in our holes hoping no one will notice what we are. Nonsense. The law is the law, and all men should be equal under it, including Clarence, especially him."

He shook his head and finished his tea. Jonathan took the cup and returned it to the sideboard, perched on the sofa again. "Well, you should do something about it then. You obviously feel very strongly. Take the cases nobody else wants, force them to change."

Henry puttered his lips dismissively. "*Then* I would be ruined. I'd lose every one."

"Not necessarily."

"I have ambitions of my own, Jonathan."

"I know you do, I'm only saying—"

"Anyway, why is this on my shoulders suddenly?"

"You're angry, that's all. I'm trying to help."

"I'm angry because I lost today."

"If that's how you want to see it."

"Meaning what?"

"Meaning you're also angry because you care."

"Of course I bloody care. That verdict was a disgrace."

"I agree."

"Good."

"Good."

Henry smiled ruefully. He sank back into the sofa

and let his head fall, turned it sideways to look at his friend. Jonathan sitting primly with his knees together and hands clasped, square-shouldered in his robe, tufts of pale hair visible beneath the collar of his pajama shirt.

"Sit with me," Henry said, and Jonathan laughed.

"I am sitting with you."

"You're sitting like you're in church. Relax."

"It's late. We should both get some sleep."

"Sit, Jonathan."

Slowly, awkwardly, he did as he was told, leaning backward, his features cast in profile against the bare lamplight. He looked handsome, and even younger than he was. Henry inched sideways and lowered himself down until his head rested in Jonathan's lap. He pulled up his feet and lay with his cheek nuzzling the soft fabric of Jonathan's robe and his arm draped over his legs. He felt Jonathan's hand touch his shoulder then his fingers raking into Henry's hair. Henry moaned and arched into it, catlike; if he could, he would have purred. For a while they remained just like that, Henry listening to Jonathan's breathing and the sounds of the city outside—footsteps, a dog barking, a horse clipping by—then slowly he twisted and tipped himself over the edge of the sofa, falling clumsily to his knees. He shuffled around in front of Jonathan and parted his legs,

Jonathan saying, "No, Henry, you're drunk, or worse, and . . ." until the words trailed away. Henry untied the cord and flapped open Jonathan's robe, ran his hands over the tensed muscles of his thighs. He hooked his fingers into the pajama waistband, Jonathan raised his hips, allowed Henry to slide the trousers down. They stared at each other intently, Jonathan fully exposed now, his chest heaving, his mouth open, his eyes wild and almost scared, until Henry dipped his head and began, and Jonathan sank back on the sofa, a long breath washed out of him, and his eyes rolled slowly closed.

Chapter 12
Katherine Sullivan

In awkward silence they sat around one end of the long maple-wood dining table, eating roast rib of beef and mashed potatoes, cutlery tinkling the china plates, the room stifling from the dozens of candles Wilson Drummond had asked to be lit. The chandelier, the candelabras, the sconces on the walls—it was like eating in an oven, Katherine thought. Her father was planning something. She knew him well enough by now. Sitting on her right, at the head of the table, he wouldn't stop smiling; had even opened a special bottle of red wine. Opposite, Charles Sinclair grinned at her horribly between forkfuls of beef. The man repulsed her. His skin was too smooth, his hair too slick, his features too sharp; he reminded her of a lizard, or some buttoned-up prince in a fairy tale. And even as a girl, Katherine had always hated fairy tales.

"I went to see Joe today," she told her father, breaking the silence before one of them could. "Reminded him about the upper paddocks. Told him Morris is to be let go."

He looked up, chewing. "Has he done something? Morris?"

"The man's lame. He can't work. It's charity, us keeping him on."

"You see?" Wilson said to Charles Sinclair, pointing at her with his fork. "What did I tell you? Ruthless, when she needs to be."

"Sounds reasonable," Sinclair said. "If the man can't work."

Katherine said, "I first asked Joe to clear those paddocks two weeks ago. Apparently, you told him not to."

Her father frowned. "I think I suggested we hold off a while, that's all."

"Oh? For what reason? The cattle? The fodder? The weather, perhaps?"

"I just thought—"

"That our guest should have a say in the matter, apparently."

"Katherine, please, now is not the time. Charles? More wine?"

He slid over his glass. Wilson poured. Topped himself up too.

"This is my station," Katherine said. "You seem to have forgotten that."

"Look." Wilson took a long drink, returned his glass to the mat. "We're getting ahead of ourselves here. This is meant to be a celebration. Charles and I have some news to share . . ." She glanced across the table. Charles flashed a reptilian smile. Here it comes, she thought. "I'm delighted to say he's agreed to stay on at Broken Ridge. To marry you, that is. We were thinking a ceremony sometime in the next few weeks. Get the formalities over with. No sense messing around."

They both sat there beaming. The food caught in Katherine's throat. She forced it down and looked between the two men, settling on Charles. "And is that meant to be a proposal, Mr. Sinclair? Is this really the best you can do?"

Even in the raging candlelight, the man visibly blushed. He dabbed his lips with his napkin and hurried around the table, stammering out an apology and dropping to one knee at her side. He reached for her hand but she wouldn't give it, clasping them firmly in her lap, meaning that when he spoke his own dangled uselessly, pawing at thin air.

"I realize we haven't spoken much while I've been here . . ."

"If at all," Katherine said.

"But I've been watching you closely, and find I have become quite smitten."

Katherine rolled her eyes to her father, who gave a warning stare.

"In fact, I think you're most lovely."

"I can assure you, Mr. Sinclair, that I am not."

He laughed nervously, steadied himself, and with grave formality asked, "Katherine Sullivan, née Drummond, will you do me the honor of becoming my wife?"

She was quiet a long time, then: "You have a ring, I assume?"

He threw a panicked glance at her father. "I, uh, I didn't think it was . . . haven't really had the chance to . . ."

"There'll be a ring, Katherine. Stop torturing the poor boy."

She smoothed the creases from her napkin. "Very well. I decline."

A delicious silence followed. Katherine took a sip of wine. Savoring the flavor, and Charles Sinclair floundering beside her, and the heat of her father's stare.

"Now, now," Wilson said. "Don't be hasty. Let's discuss this at least."

"There's nothing to discuss. I do not want to marry this man."

"You're being ridiculous."

Charles piped up below her: "I vow that I will love you, care for you, honor you—"

"Oh, be quiet, man," she told him. "Have some self-respect."

"Katherine! That is enough!"

"You married me off once, Father. I won't let you do it again."

Charles struggled to his feet and stood there crestfallen. Katherine folded her napkin and laid it beside her plate. "Now, if you'll excuse me."

"Sit down!" Wilson banged a fist on the table, leaned on his elbow, and pointed at her, Charles standing dumbly at his side. "You listen to me, young lady: Charles is a fine man, the best you could ever hope for. A widow stuck out here—for all your good fortune they are hardly beating a path to your door. You think you can do this alone, playing house with the savages in the wild? This place will swallow you up, Katherine. You will find yourself run off your land, destitute, and who's going to want you then? You are not equipped for this world. You were barely equipped for

Melbourne—I only agreed to John's proposal because I knew he would make sure you were all right."

"And I suppose his money had nothing to do with it?"

"I am your father. I do not need to explain myself any more. Charles and I have reached an agreement that is more than fair. The two of you shall be married, and that is the end of it. Congratulations, Charles. Well done."

Dumbly, Charles shook his hand. Katherine sat very still in her chair. The men parted and she murmured, "I am expecting."

Wilson frowned. "Sorry? What was that?"

"I am expecting, I said."

He laughed quickly, shook his head. "Expecting what?"

"A child. I'm expecting a child. A baby."

"That's . . . impossible."

She snorted. "It really is not."

"Who's the father?" Charles demanded.

Katherine smiled at him and stood, felt their gazes slide to her midriff. "Where does your proposal stand now, Mr. Sinclair? Am I still so lovely? Will you still honor me and care for me, I wonder, while I carry another man's child?"

His mask slipped then. No longer the fairy-tale prince. His jaw clenched and his eyes burned and

Katherine gave him no chance to respond, marching around the far end of the table to the door, the candelabra guttering as she went by. Her father called out but she ignored him, pulling the door closed and exhaling shakily with the click of the latch. She stood a moment, recovering, and noticed the houseboy, Benjamin, waiting outside the room.

"Y'all right there, missus?" he asked her.

"Yes, thank you, Benjamin. I think perhaps I overate."

He looked at her evenly. His placid, weary face. She had known him longer than almost everyone else out here. Lightly she touched his arm. "Good night."

"Night, missus."

She went upstairs, suddenly exhausted. Her confession had drained her dry. She hadn't planned on telling them. Couldn't even be certain herself yet. Oh, but it was worth it. The horror in her father's face.

In her room she locked the door and dressed for bed, climbed in between the crisp, cool sheets. She sighed. Lying on her back staring up at the patterned canopy, the same view she'd endured while John grunted away on top of her; she'd always intended changing the bed but never had. Vaguely she heard raised voices downstairs, Charles and her father arguing, she'd scuppered all their plans. She closed her eyes and lay there smiling. She doubted Charles Sinclair would still be here come the morning; with any luck her father might not stick around either. Was it possible this might be the end of it? That in one fell swoop she'd rid herself of them both?

Knocking woke her. Total darkness in the room. She roused and found a broken band of light beneath the door. Another knock, a gentle but insistent tapping on the wood. "Yes?" she managed, expecting her father to answer, but instead Charles Sinclair announced himself, and the proximity of his voice there, its presence in her bedroom, jolted her upright and alert.

"What do you want?"

He took a moment to answer. His shadow shifted beneath the door. "I'm leaving tomorrow. I came to say goodbye, and to apologize for earlier."

"Both can wait until morning."

"I'll be gone at first light. Please, Katherine—I won't sleep a wink."

She sighed and climbed out of bed, spoke to him through the door: "It's my father who should be apologizing, not you."

The handle rattled. He said, "Can we at least do this face-to-face?"

"I'm hardly decent, Charles."

She thought she heard him snigger. "Put on a robe. I promise I won't peek."

Irritably, Katherine fetched her robe from the stand, flapped it around herself, cinched the belt. He'd be out there all night otherwise, she'd never get any peace. She unlocked the door and cracked it ajar, found Charles Sinclair grinning at her, fully dressed still, clutching a lantern, his face woozy and flushed with drink. He traced the length of her body, lingered on her bare feet.

"Say your piece and leave me. I'm tired. I want to go back to sleep."

His gaze settled on her face again. "Oh, but you are lovely."

"Good night, Mr. Sinclair. And goodbye."

She tried to close the door but found his foot blocking it, and in the second it took her to realize what was happening, he had forced his way into the room. He eased the door closed, then, without taking his eyes off Katherine, felt for the key, turned it, removed it, and slipped it into the breast pocket of his suit, which he patted twice with his hand.

"What the hell do you think you're doing?"

"I only want to talk. I have a proposal for you."

"I should scream this house down."

"Nobody would hear you. Your father's so drunk I

doubt he'll wake before noon, and the servants are all gone or asleep. Would you like to sit down?"

"No."

"Suit yourself."

He drifted around the room, touching things. Katherine circled back to the door. She tried the handle, tugging, but of course the lock wouldn't give. She scanned the room for a weapon, saw nothing, felt foolish for not sleeping with one to hand. He was over by the dressing table now. He dangled her rosary disdainfully then dropped it back down in the dish.

"I wouldn't have thought you particularly pious, a woman in your state."

"What do you want?"

"I already told you, I have a proposal to make."

"And I told you at dinner: I'm not interested in your proposals."

Charles smiled bitterly, placed his lantern on the dressing table, came toward her around the foot of the bed. He folded his arms. He was taller than she'd realized; broader. He tilted his head, appraising her. She clutched her robe tighter, pressed herself against the door.

"This one's a little different. Your situation . . . changes things. But first I have a question: the father, it's not a nigger, is it?"

"Of course not."

"Good. Then we are in business. I see no sign of the baby yet, meaning you are not so far along. Assuming we are married immediately, and the marriage consummated, I am willing to pass off the child as my own, provided he—or she—has no claim whatsoever on this estate. Therefore, you shall sign over all rights in the property to me, give me the station entirely, and I shall bequeath it among our other children however I see fit. I intend creating a dynasty here, of which your bastard must play no part. In return, he will live here, receive an education, be raised in the usual way, and you will keep your dignity intact. We can enjoy a very fine life together, Katherine. You might even come to care for me one day. I'm not as bad a man as you seem to think."

"No," she said coldly. "I suspect you are much worse."

"Rich, coming from a whore. You know, your father has already agreed to it. Begged me to take the child on. That's how little he thinks of you. I could have named any price."

She drew herself tall, defiant. "I'll give you my answer tomorrow."

"I bet you will."

"I deserve at least to sleep on it. Please, I'd like you to leave."

He didn't seem to be listening. Brazenly he stared at her chest. He moistened his lips and said, "Or perhaps we had best just get on with it, before I get cold feet."

Katherine bolted for the dressing room. He lunged, caught her arm, yanked her back with such force that she fell. He picked her up so easily. Shocking, his strength. He threw her on the bed and was upon her: tearing her robe open, pinning her with his weight. He shrugged off his jacket and tossed it on the floor and slobbered into her neck. He grabbed her breast through her nightdress, pinched it so hard her eyes filled. She screamed and he put his hand over her mouth, the skin soft, a smell of liquor and cigars. She felt so utterly helpless. Nothing she could do. His other hand was between her legs and he began whispering in her ear, calling her a whore, a harlot, telling her she wanted it, this was all she was good for. He would fuck the bastard out of her, he said, opening his trousers, at which Katherine dug her teeth into the flesh of his palm. He reared up and slapped her so hard she briefly lost sense of where she was, only to be brought back by the ripping of her underclothes, and the feel of him trying to force his way in. Wildly she fought him, bucking and clawing and hitting with all she had. He caught her hands but she slipped one free and raked her nails down his face, her thumb landing in the eye socket, so soft and warm and weak. She pushed. Easily it went in. Her nail, then the first knuckle, then the second to the hilt, the eyeball distending grossly, Sinclair screaming out in pain. He flung himself backward, clutching his face; Katherine scrambled off the bed. "I'm blind! I'm blind! You fucking bitch!" he was shouting, as with trembling hands she rooted in his jacket pocket for the key. She found it and was at the door when Sinclair thudded to the floor, mewling like a dying pig. She got the key in the lock finally. Her hands were shaking so hard. Out into the corridor, and as she pulled the door closed she caught a final glimpse of him writhing on the rug. She locked the door behind her, and ran.

Chapter 13
Billy McBride

Billy passed the coach on the hillside, rumbling its way down. He slowed as they crossed and saw Charles Sinclair slumped in the carriage, a bloodied white dressing over one eye. He didn't notice Billy. His head rolled side to side. Billy spurred Buck and hurried up to the house, where he found Wilson Drummond talking to Dr. Shanklin at the bottom of the front steps. Their conversation stalled when they saw him, and Billy dismounted at a run, asking, "What's happened? What's wrong?"

"None of your business," Drummond snapped. "Clear off."

"An accident, Billy," Dr. Shanklin offered. "Dealt with. No harm done."

Filthy and bloodstained, Billy stood before these

suited men like something feral that had wandered from the bush. "What accident? Is Katherine hurt?"

"She's fine," Drummond said. "But whatever this is will have to wait."

"Where is she? Inside?"

"She's sleeping," Shanklin said. "I gave her some drops."

Billy made to step between them but Drummond blocked his path. "How many times do I have to say it before I make myself clear: you're not welcome here. You've no business coming round—hell, you don't even work for us anymore. You got your bloody land back, grubbing bastard that you are, what else is there to discuss? If there's some issue with the cattle, you can speak to Joe about it; otherwise, bugger off."

Again Billy tried to pass. This time Drummond placed a hand on his shirtfront, as if to hold him there, this gray-haired city stiff with round reading glasses and a chin as weak as piss. There were so many things Billy could do to him, the man had no idea. But the longer their standoff continued, the longer Billy refused to retreat, the more the hand on his chest faltered and Drummond's stare swirled with doubt. So used to being obeyed he became powerless when he was not, and so alien to violence that the prospect clearly terrified him—Billy saw the panic building, the realization of what he'd begun.

He leaned his face closer. "Get out my fucking way."

Billy barged past him, and something in Drummond's expression changed. Slack-jawed and gormless, like he'd only just realized what Billy was doing here, why he was so concerned. Billy barked a laugh and mounted the steps, the homestead looming over him, windows glinting in the sun, and Katherine inside somewhere, carrying his child. He strode along the hall to the atrium, calling out her name, his presence huge in the still, quiet house. Upstairs, around the balcony landing, calling out again, then along the corridor toward her bedroom. A latch clicked, the door opened, and out she stepped wearing a white nightdress, holding herself with both arms. Billy halted. She'd been crying, he could tell, and immediately he guessed what had gone on. He almost went back after him. Could have caught up with that carriage in no time at all. But last night by the campfire he'd vowed to never leave her, to protect her, so instead walked forward hesitantly, as if unsure whether he dared.

"Where were you?" she asked timidly. "Where have you been?"

"Working," was all Billy could say.

"With *him*?"

"It was nothing. What happened? Are you hurt?"

"It's never nothing with that man."

"Katie, tell me."

"You first."

Billy took a long breath, his gaze on the floor. There was ten feet between them; it might as well have been ten miles.

"We went down Drew Bennett's place, he had a runaway trooper hiding in his barn. I was to mind the family, make sure nothing went wrong. And it didn't—we just took the boy and left."

"Why you, though? Why would he want your help?"

"Because Drew knows me. And the runaway was one of them from before."

"You mean . . . ?"

He nodded. "Noone threatened us, me and you, even Tommy—he knows where he is, said he'd see to it he hangs."

"He knows where Tommy is? Did he tell you?"

Billy shook his head. "He'll be lying. But that's it, that's all that happened." He waved at her. "Now it's your turn."

She touched her face reflexively, sniffed, wiped her eyes. "Charles, last night . . . well, he didn't, but he might have done. He certainly tried."

"He hurt you?"

"No, not really." A snatch of laughter. "If anything, he came off worse."

Billy stepped a pace closer, glanced at her midriff, couldn't help himself. "Is it true? Are you . . . ?"

If she was shocked she didn't show it. "Who told you? Noone?"

"He said he came here. Somehow he knew."

She let her arms fall open, looked at herself too. "Yes. I mean, I think so. God, Billy—I'm so scared."

He went to her, and held her, and she pressed herself against him, no thought about the state of his clothes. He felt her tears warm and wet on his shirtfront, the same spot where not five minutes ago her father's hand had been. He would show that bastard. Him and all the rest.

Katherine peeled away. Billy slid a filthy hand to her belly and cupped the tiny bulge, the hand dark against her bright white cotton nightdress. Billy couldn't feel anything. He'd expected maybe a pulse or kick. He looked at her doubtfully.

"Are you pleased?" Katherine said.

"Of course I'm bloody pleased. Christ, Katie—come here."

Tenderly he kissed her and again they embraced and stayed like that for a long time. The rush of their breathing, his heartbeat against her cheek, the warmth of her hands on his back. Holding on so tightly, each all the other had.

They were married three days later in Bewley's little church, in front of the whole township, it felt: people crammed into the benches and stood shoulder to shoulder along the walls. Billy wore a new suit the tailor had rushed through and Katherine was in the same gown she'd worn last time around—to hell with superstition, she wasn't waiting for a new one to be made. Not everyone thought likewise. The wedding had a whiff of scandal about it from the start. There were grumbles that the vicar had even allowed it in the church, her being a widow and all. But the marriage of a Sullivan—any Sullivan—was as close to a state occasion as the people of Bewley got, and to a local hero, no less. Nonetheless, opinion was divided on the union. Some claimed to have long suspected there was something going on between them; others correctly predicted she'd been knocked up. There were those jealous of Billy's windfall—a bride like that, plus an empire—while some could see the justice in it, what with Katherine losing her first husband and all Billy had been through as a child. Mostly they said good luck to them. Nobody in their shoes would have turned the opportunity down. You only get this one life, might as well take from it whatever you can.

And so, before the townspeople, and before God, the sun streaming through the windows as if announcing His presence there, they faced each other at the altar and made their vows, Billy slipping his mother's wedding ring onto Katherine's finger, his stomach knotting when it fit. His family should have been here with him. Tommy should have been at his side. Instead, the front pews were filled with strangers in all but name, and Billy stood up there alone. Although not any longer: from the moment Katherine arrived framed in the doorway, her father on her arm, neither was alone from now on. Later, back at the homestead, Billy would collar his new father-in-law and put him up against a wall, and warn him that if he ever showed his face at Broken Ridge again he would be taken down to the stockyards, tied to a post, and gelded like a no-good bull, Wilson Drummond's face whitening at the realization that not only had his daughter married the kind of man who would make such a threat, but also one whose reputation suggested he might actually carry it through. And he would leave then, the coward, after an awkward, perfunctory farewell, scuttling back to the city he'd come from, Billy and Katherine standing on the verandah together, watching him go.

When the ceremony was over they came down the aisle arm in arm as husband and wife. The crowd applauded, smiling faces and teary eyes, men climbing over each other to shake Billy's hand. Working their way slowly to the doors, a guard of honor already forming outside, when through the scattered bodies Billy glimpsed a very tall man at the back of the church, leaning against the wall. He hadn't taken his hat off. He smiled and touched the brim; Billy tightened his grip on Katherine's arm. Noone was politely clapping, joining in with the crowd, and though he and Billy watched each other all the way to the doors, he did not move from that position: smirking at the newlyweds, reclining against the wall.

Out they came, into the sunshine, and a showering of rice and grain. Katherine squealed as it peppered them, running to the waiting carriage and bundling inside, reeling in her dress-train. Billy fell against her on the bench. She was laughing breathlessly, her cheeks were flushed. He doubted there'd ever been a more beautiful bride. As the carriage pulled away the crowd surged after them along the street, and there were well-wishers lining the pavements either side. Some threw flowers, others simply stared; while Katherine leaned through the open window and waved to those she knew, Billy twisted to check on the church. The doors were wide open, the congregation spilling out, flowing past the giant silhouette of Noone—his hat, his longcoat—immovable among them, like a river around a stone.

"What is it?" Katherine asked, her hand on his thigh.

Billy spun. "Nothing, it's fine."

The town receded behind them, the crowd and noise died away. Katherine flopped back on the bench, sighed, looked at him and smiled.

"So that's that done," Billy said.

"My husband, the great romantic."

"All I meant was—"

"I know. I'm only teasing."

"Sounds odd you saying it: husband."

"It does, doesn't it?"

"Reckon we'll get used to it?"

She shrugged. "You can get used to anything if you give it long enough."

"Now who's being romantic?"

"Sorry. I'm just tired."

A brief silence. Billy said, "I wasn't expecting so many people."

"Nor me. You're more popular than I thought."

"They came for you. Get a look at that dress."

"Do you like it?"

"Aye."

"Shall I keep it on a while? Till tonight, maybe?"

Her eyes danced with mischief. Billy said, "If you want to."

"Do *you* want me to, though?"

"Aye."

A thump on the side of the carriage. The driver slowed. Billy sprang to the window and looked out: they were passing the native camps, and a group of boys throwing stones. The driver yelled and cursed them. Another volley of stones. One hit the back of the carriage and Katherine flinched. "Go, man!" Billy ordered. The coach pulled away with a jerk. The boys gave chase, the next stone missed, and Billy was about to sit down again when he saw by the roadside a very old man standing there in his rags, his face gummed with anger, furiously shaking a stick, shouting as the coach passed.

"Where's them Kurrong at, Billy? Where's them Kurrong gone, eh? Does she know what you did to 'em? Does she know what you done?"

Billy slammed up the window. The old man was gone. Billy retook his seat and felt Katherine watching him, fixed his stare resolutely ahead.

"What was that about?"

"How should I know?"

"You didn't know that man?"

"'Course not. How the hell would I?"

"Well, he seemed to know you."

"I don't know him, I just said."

Silence between them. The coach rumbling on. Eventually Katherine stirred and asked, "What did he mean about the Kurrong? About *what you did*?"

He looked at her sharply. "You know what we did. You were there!"

"I know what you all told me. Ran them off into the center, so you said."

"Exactly."

"And I've also heard the rumors. The same as that old man."

"So who do you believe, me or him?"

"You, if that's what you're saying." She stared at him. "Well? Is it?"

"Christ, Katie—today of all days."

"Answer me, Billy."

"You know what they're like out here. Every story's better for the telling."

"So he's wrong? They all are?"

The lie washed out of him, easy as a breath: "We went out after Joseph and got him, and that's all there is to it. There were a couple others with him but the rest . . . they buggered off into the center, and bloody good riddance too."

"And you'll swear to it?"

"Why are you so bothered about all this suddenly?"

"Because I want to know the man I just married, the father of my child. For better or worse, remember. Even this."

Billy laughed weakly. "Bit late now."

"Swear it, Billy. On our wedding day."

"I just told you . . ."

"Swear it."

"All right, for Christ's sake."

She said no more about it. Quietly, Billy stewed. Katherine adjusted her dress and turned to the window, to the continuum of sun-blushed red scrubland streaming by outside. So this is how it begins, she thought to herself. The first day of the rest of their lives.

Chapter 14
Tommy McBride

They limped into Marree like troops back from war, Tommy riding beside Jack Kerrigan at the head of the cattle train, Arthur at the back with the dogs and mules. It felt a miracle they'd actually got here; to see buildings, other people, shops, pubs, hotels. Four weeks battling their way down the Strzelecki Track, living waterhole to waterhole, or puddle to puddle most of the time. Crossing desert and salt flats, the impenetrable Cobbler Sandhills, past the wonder of Lake Blanche and the low scrubby peak of Mount Hopeless, which more than deserved its name, Jack steering them as expertly as if they'd been following road signs.

Tommy didn't need convincing, would have trusted

anything that man said. Hard going as it had been, he'd been true to his word, sharing his water and the rations off his mules; if they hadn't met the drover there was no doubt they'd both be dead. He didn't know what Arthur had been thinking, blindly bringing them west, then blaming Tommy for their troubles, like they were his fault. But this was Jack's living, he did it every year. He described it like poetry: waking with the sunrise, living off the land, the constant back-and-forth tussle with the mob. It sounded perfect to Tommy. Close to the life he'd always imagined for himself but had never quite known how to get.

They deposited the cattle into the rail yard pens and while Jack spoke with the agent, got their money, filled out forms, Tommy considered the town. He'd never seen anything like this place. As if they were no longer in Australia at all. More accurately it was two towns, a black and white side, bisected by the railway tracks. The usual fare on the white side: hotels and drink-ing holes, a post office, a general store; cattlemen and teamsters, railwaymen, women talking in shop door-ways, children running about. But across the tracks was a marketplace filled with dark-skinned men with long beards and strange toweling wrapped round their heads. They sat at tables smoking ornate contraptions and hawked their wares in an alien tongue. Tommy had never seen an Afghan before, wondered what kind of native this was. Their tents spread out over the flatland beyond, and in their cattle yards were not cattle but immense bent-necked beasts: camels, humpbacked and bandy-legged, being unloaded of their cargo in the red wash of the sun.

"You want to try riding one," Jack Kerrigan said, appearing at Tommy's side. "They take a bit of mounting, but they're not actually as uncomfortable as they look."

"Stick to the horse, I reckon."

"Very wise, young Bobby. Very wise."

He still wasn't used to it, this name he'd taken on. A few times now Jack had spoken and he'd missed it, had to pretend he was lost in thought. Arthur hadn't slipped once yet, called him Bobby from the start. On those rare occasions they'd been talking, that is, which for the most part they had not.

They stabled the horses and headed for a hotel: the best in town, Jack said. He got them three rooms with baths, ordered hot water; blacks weren't usually welcome but Jack paid up front and had a word. Years now he'd been coming here. Could hardly move for people saying hello. Tommy noticed how they greeted him, the smiles and handshakes, the winks some of the women gave. Jack introduced Tommy everywhere, like he was his new best mate, meaning people then shook Tommy's hand and clapped him on the back also, and those same women who'd winked at Jack winked at him too.

He'd never had a bath like it. Emerged a new man, reborn.

He was half-dressed and almost finished shaving when there came a gentle tapping at the door. He opened it expecting Jack, instead found Arthur standing there, his hair still damp from bathing, droplets glistening in his beard. Tommy went back to the mirror. Arthur came in and closed the door.

"Some place this, eh?" Tommy said, meaning both the hotel and town.

"We can't stay here."

"Why? What d'you mean? What's the problem?"

"They're just as likely to know us here as anywhere. We need to be heading south, Tommy. Changing your name won't do bugger all."

"How will they know us? How?"

"Well, for a start they'll have the telegraph. All it takes is that boyfriend of yours to tell 'em how we met—it's not much of a leap from there."

"He promised not to say anything."

"Stake your life on that, would you?"

"I would, actually, yeah."

Arthur rolled his eyes and turned away.

"You know," Tommy said, pointing with the straight razor, "all he's ever done is look out for us. He saved our lives back there. Paid us exactly what he said he would, even got you your own room. You'd be yon side of them tracks if it wasn't for him—wouldn't hurt to show some bloody thanks."

Arthur snorted, shook his head. "Quite the pair, aren't you."

"What's that supposed to mean?"

"It's like the last five years never happened, Tommy. Or the fourteen before that. You seem to forget where you've come from, and where you'd be without me, or does it not work that way round?"

Tommy finished with the razor. He put it down and toweled off and faced Arthur front-on, and for probably the first time ever felt he was his equal, a man. He sighed, relented a little, said, "Look, we've been through hell together these past few months, you must be feeling it the same as me. I can't head straight back out there—besides, Jack says there's more droving work if we want it, before the season ends. The pay's good, we're in the middle of nowhere, nobody'll find us out here. With money we can start a new life properly. Otherwise we'll just keep running, nothing in our pockets but sand."

Arthur shook his head. "Bloke acts like I'm his fucking boy."

"He doesn't mean nothing by it."

"Oh, you reckon?"

"What have you got against him, Arthur? What's he ever done?"

"Fellas like that, Tommy, they only want you when it suits 'em. He'll get bored soon enough and then where will you be? The state you were in when I found you . . ."

"How long are you going to keep throwing that at me? You're always telling me it's time to grow up, move on, then when I do you pull me right back down again, talking like I'm a kid, and all the shit that went on back then. It's like I can't ever forget what happened with you around."

Arthur was quiet a moment. Sadly he said, "Yeah, well, sorry for sticking by you for so long."

"Don't be like that."

"But you're staying, are you? With him?"

Tommy pulled on a shirt. "For now I am. But first, I'm going downstairs to eat a nice big steak then I plan on drinking myself under the table with Jack. I'd say you're welcome to join us but you're not. Doesn't sound like you'd want to anyhow."

They stood a long time in silence, Tommy flushed and restless, Arthur's unblinking stare. He took a breath and nodded, as if something was decided, opened the door and left the room. Tommy almost went out after him. He regretted what he'd just said. But there was a kernel of truth to it: he was sick of Arthur treating him like he was a child. At least Jack saw him simply for who he was now, unencumbered by a past he dragged behind him like an ankle chain. They had no history together, which for once was a relief. And the droving work was good work, lonely work, decent pay too, not that it mattered—Tommy could have suggested anything and Arthur would have said it was a terrible plan. Tommy had had enough of his bullshit. He snatched his money off the dresser and went downstairs.

They filled their boots with steak, beer, and whiskey, and tore up the little town, falling in with other cattlemen and drovers smashing their checks. Jack seemed to know everyone. A small place, the bush, for these men. Later, he took Tommy to the brothel, told him which was the best girl, and Tommy admitted afterward she'd been his first. Jack bought cigars, and once Tommy had recovered suggested he take another turn—second time was a charm, in Jack's view. But the girl Tommy had been with was busy with another man; drunk and besotted, Tommy barged into the room, interrupting a horse wrangler in full flow. The wrangler took exception to the intrusion and the two of them were properly brawling by the time Jack dragged Tommy away. They left the brothel laughing, Tommy yelling to the upstairs windows that he'd be back the following night, he and Jack staggering down the street together, arms round each other's shoulders, a bowlegged swaying dance. Back in the hotel they drank until Tommy passed out at the table; when he woke birds were already calling the dawn. He crawled up to his bedroom, threw himself on the bed, and slept long into the afternoon, then woke drenched in sweat and smelling faintly of piss. He cleaned himself up groggily. Tipped half a pitcher of water down his throat. When he'd changed he went along the hall, knocking on doors. Neither Jack nor Arthur answered; Tommy found Jack in the bar. He was eating a cooked chicken leg and drinking a pot of beer and looked as fresh as if last night hadn't happened at all. He laughed when he saw the state Tommy was in. Said to sit down and get something to eat. Instead Tommy went to the counter and asked the barman if he'd seen Arthur around. He looked up but went on drying the glass in his hand, said he'd seen him early that morning, heading out along the street, carrying his bag in one hand and his bedroll tucked under the other arm.

"Sorry to be the one to tell you this, friend, but word has it your blackboy skipped town."

PART II

1897

Seven Years Later

Chapter 15
Henry Wells

On the porch of a fine white Queenslander house in the north-Brisbane suburb of Spring Hill, Henry Wells stood holding the front doorknob, listening to their voices, watching their blurred outlines through the colored window glass. They hadn't noticed him, he could still leave, though he knew that he wouldn't; he never did. Every evening after work he had the same thought, yet every evening he went in. He closed his eyes briefly, turned the handle and cracked the door, and announced to his family that he was home.

Laura came to meet him, baby Audrey clinging to her hip. She kissed his cheek and, one-handed, helped him off with his coat and hung it with his hat on the stand. Supper wouldn't be long, she told him, why not enjoy a drink in the lounge—always the same routine. Dutifully he did so, sliding his feet into a pair of house slippers and pouring himself a large sherry that he threw back in one, then another that he nursed by the fire. Outside, dusk was falling, the last strains of pink in the sky. Henry watched his neighbors passing back and forth on the street, noticed a scruffy man he didn't recognize glance admiringly at the house. He liked that people did that. Liked that the house attracted looks. It was still only a stepping-stone. What he wanted— once he'd made it, once Queen's Counsel was his—was a house by the river, in Hamilton or Ascot, one of those lavish hillside mansions they were building up there. It wouldn't be long, hopefully. A couple more years at most. He would place an announcement in the newspaper, perhaps commission a photograph too, and send a copy to his father: look what I've become.

Now that would be a photograph worth paying for. The only other two Henry had wasted his money on stared back at him from the mantelpiece like a rebuke: a yellowing print of Laura's parents, taken just before they died (though from the look of them in the photograph you'd think they already had), and another of Henry and Laura on their wedding day, Laura's smile barely hidden, Henry staring petrified down the camera lens as if into the barrel of a gun.

A black-haired boy poked his head into the living room. Sipping his sherry, Henry turned. "Ah, Theo, there you are. How was your day? Are you well?"

The boy only stared at him. Eyes as dark as coals.

Henry forced a chuckle. "Very well, have it your way. We don't have to talk if you don't want to, but you can come in, no need to hide out there in the hall."

The boy shook his head determinedly and ran from the doorway. Henry sighed. Sometimes he could not believe he was his son. He spoke only to his mother. Henry doubted he'd ever even heard him laugh; for a while, he'd feared the child was mute. But it was the way Theo looked at him that was most unnerving. Like he knew everything, like he saw into Henry's soul. He tipped back the sherry and went to pour another but Laura called that supper was served. Henry set down his glass very carefully. And here we go again.

She was putting the children to bed when he pulled on his coat and wrapped around his scarf; he'd told her he was going to the club. Without calling good-bye he stepped into the cold gray evening, nearing full darkness now, and hurried through the picket gate and along the street toward the tram. He crossed the road without looking and was nearly hit by a passing carriage. The driver swore at him. Told him to open his bloody eyes. On he strode, almost running now, the excitement too much to contain; an electric tingle fizzed through him, churning his stomach, tingling down his spine. He'd suppressed it all through supper, once the idea had taken hold, now his thoughts spiraled wildly ahead: down into the city, through the streets, the lobby, up the stairs to that faded green door . . . too distracted to notice the stranger following him, the same scruffy man he'd seen earlier, admiring the house from the street.

Jonathan still lived in the boardinghouse, and for Henry coming back here always felt like coming home: now that they were over he saw those days for what they were, the happiest of his life so far. Giddily he bounded up the stone staircase, the smoothed-away divots as familiar as palm-lines, and marched along the landing to the door, where he knocked and stood waiting, straightening his tie, smoothing his hair, restlessly tapping his thighs; it had been almost a month. Music was playing inside. Sounded like Mozart: brass gave way to strings. Henry knocked again and heard laughter, footsteps approaching. The door opened and the laughter ceased.

Jonathan wore slacks and a black velvet smoking jacket and cupped a large glass of brandy in his hand. He was smiling back into the room as he opened the door; the smile faltered when he saw Henry there.

"Oh, Henry, I . . ."

Another man was with him, sitting on the sofa, watching them over the backrest. "You have company," Henry said, and Jonathan turned as if surprised.

"Yes, this is . . . this is Rupert. Will you join us? Please, come in."

Rupert saluted with his brandy glass. A ridiculous rat-faced grin.

"No, I'll leave you to it. Sorry to have disturbed."

"Henry, please." Jonathan edged out into the hall, so close they were almost touching, easing the door to. He lowered his voice: "You're being unfair."

"How?"

"He's only a friend."

"I'm sure he is."

"Well, it's not like I was expecting you—where have you even been?"

"Busy."

"And I'm supposed to sit here waiting, am I? On the off chance you grow bored of your perfect family and decide to come round?"

"Now who's being unfair?"

"You made that decision. Nobody forced you. Certainly not me."

Henry scoffed. "You really think I had a choice?"

"Yes, you did. As do we all. Your life is your own

business, you told me; well, I'm allowed my own life too. You decided your career was more important. I'm not just some rent-boy you can call on when you're bored of playing house."

Henry didn't answer. He trotted down the stairs, the cold whisper of his shoes on the stone, the music carrying faintly from above. Jonathan leaned over the railing and called to him but Henry didn't look up: out onto the front steps, where he stood sucking in the cold night air. Jonathan's door slammed, the sound echoing through the empty stairwell behind, and Henry tipped back his head and exhaled. Friends—not likely, it was obvious why that little rat-faced bastard was there. He and Jonathan had never openly discussed it, the terms of their relationship, what was allowed, but he'd always assumed they were faithful, at least. Surely Jonathan understood that Laura didn't count.

Henry paused on the street, wavering. Angry, frustrated, humiliated. He could always go to the Hollow, he thought, like in the old days, but alcohol would only numb him, wouldn't offer any kind of release. Another possibility occurred to him. That word Jonathan had used: rent-boy. He had never actually tried it but knew of a few places men like him went to meet, and there was something rather thrilling about the idea. An eye for an eye, so to speak. If he was recognized he would plead ignorance, pretend he was meeting a client or simply deny he was Henry Wells at all. He wasn't that famous anyway. Not yet.

Henry set off walking. A figure ducked out of the alleyway behind him and followed along the street.

The pub stood on the corner of two dimly lit roads and was unremarkable in every way: Henry wondered if he had the right place. From the pavement opposite he watched patrons come and go, all of them men, but there was nothing unusual about that. He crossed the road and walked beneath the awning, peering through the steamed-up windows at men drinking, smoking, playing dominoes and cards. It looked a rough establishment. Not the kind he was used to at all these days. Coarse men in coarse clothing stained and sweaty from their work. But then he wasn't used to soliciting— nothing about this felt right.

He removed his tie and scarf, rolled his shirtsleeves, roughed up his hair, and hesitated with his hand on the doorplate. Behind him a figure stood watching from the far pavement, the same spot Henry had just been. Henry pushed open the door, and went inside.

Heads turned when he entered. A noticeable pause, then the chatter resumed. He bought a beer at the bar and took a seat at a corner table, his back to the wall, a view of the whole room. He was shaking. Couldn't stop his leg from bouncing up and down. The air thick with tobacco smoke and mumbled voices, every now and then a burst of laughter, the floor sticky under his feet. Henry didn't know what to do with himself. He didn't know how this worked. Every now and then he caught someone staring, but there was nothing inviting in their expressions, and again he wondered if he'd come to the wrong place. They didn't look the type, truthfully. He would drink his beer quickly, he decided, then leave.

The door swung open and the man from the street corner walked in. He stood on the threshold, surveying the room. Short and fair-haired, his face freckled and piebald from too much sun, dressed much the same as the others in here: dirty trousers, yellowed shirt, a ragged woolen patchwork coat that fell almost to his heels. The drinkers looked him over then went back to their beers; the man's gaze found Henry and stayed there. Henry shivered. He could certainly do better than this grub. Incredulously he watched the stranger approaching and prepared to turn him down flat.

"Mr. Wells, sir? I hope you'll excuse me. Might we talk a moment, please?"

Henry was taken aback by the accent—he spoke like an English gent. At the mention of his name his thoughts turned immediately to blackmail, but there was something in the man's demeanor than didn't fit.

He looked frankly terrified. He picked furiously at his nails. Henry guessed his age at roughly forty but he may have been younger—clearly he'd led a hard life. There was an odor of filth and alcohol about him, it must have been weeks since he'd bathed. He reminded Henry of the young men he encountered when he first visited them in jail: anxious, sad, lonely, desperate for Henry's help.

"How do you know my name?" Henry asked.

"I will explain myself—please, may I sit down?"

"Why? What do you want?"

"Only to talk. And perhaps the comfort of a drink."

"Talk about what?"

"I have a crime to report, Mr. Wells. A most terrible, terrible crime."

"Then the police will be glad to hear it. Leave me alone."

"I know who you are," the man persisted. "I've seen you in court. All those trials you have won—you're not afraid of them, are you, the authorities; black or white, you are only interested in seeing that justice is done."

The praise mollified Henry. He leaned back in his chair. "Still, a crime must be reported to the police, which I am not, as you are evidently well aware."

"I can't go to the police."

"Why not?"

He glanced over both shoulders. "Because it's the police who did it."

"All right, I'll indulge you—did what?"

"Slaughtered a whole tribe of Aborigines, way out in the bush. I would guess about a hundred. Not even the children were spared."

"How on earth do you know this? Who in God's name are you?"

The man snorted bitterly. "Sadly nobody, not in His name, not anymore. But I am trying, Mr. Wells. I am trying to make amends. I was a missionary, you see, once upon a time. My name is Francis Bean and I know what happened to the Kurrong people of central Queensland because I was there, I saw it, saw them burning with my own eyes. And I did nothing except run and hide and have been hiding ever since. Until now. Now I am here to tell you the story, so that you can set matters right."

There was a long silence between them. Henry sighed and told him to sit down. Bean's face unknotted with relief and he threw himself into the other chair, knocking the table and spilling Henry's beer. Bean looked at the spillage greedily. He touched a finger to his cracked lips. "How about that drink first?" he said.

Henry bought him rum, the cheapest they had, then went back and bought another after Bean threw the first one down his neck. He nursed his own whiskey thoughtfully, turning the tumbler back and forth, making a ring pattern on the table in the pool of spilled beer.

"You said you were there. Does that mean you were involved?"

Bean shook his head, swallowing. "We were witnesses. We'd met them before and then saw the aftermath. Like I said, we ran."

"So you didn't see it happen, this . . . slaughter?"

"You doubt me, sir?"

"I am a lawyer. I believe in facts."

"If you'll just let me tell you—"

"In a minute. First I want to know what I'm dealing with here. Who is this 'we' you keep referring to?"

"Myself and my dear friend Matthew. Although not anymore."

"What does that mean? Is he dead?"

"We are no longer on speaking terms, I am sorry to say."

"Do you know where I can find him?"

"We parted ways some time ago. I have lost track of him since."

"So there's nobody else who can verify this story you're about to tell me? It's your word and nothing more?"

"They had two young brothers with them—McBride, their names were—from a town called Bewley way out west. Their family was murdered. Perhaps they're still around. There were a couple of other white men, but I never got their names."

McBride rang no bells for Henry, though it should have done. A family murdered in the outback ought to have made the press. He folded his arms doubtfully. "So it was a reprisal killing? But you said the police were involved?"

"The Native Police, yes."

"I see. Do you know which officer was in charge?"

Bean glanced at him fearfully, eyes dancing around the room. "Noone. Inspector Edmund Noone."

Henry nodded. "I've heard the name."

"He's here!" Bean hissed. "In Southport, just down the coast!"

"All right, calm down. Tell me, why are you only speaking up about this now? Why didn't you report it at the time? What do you have to gain?"

"Only to assuage my conscience, Mr. Wells. I did try to report it back then, told the local magistrate, though clearly nothing was done. Truth is, I was terrified, and weak. I had nothing with which to fortify myself . . ." He ducked his head conspiratorially. "Any chance of another drink?"

While standing at the bar, Henry glanced over his shoulder at Francis Bean fidgeting in his chair and wondered if he wasn't being played. But then it seemed a lot of trouble to go to, just to con him out of a couple of drinks. The barman brought their glasses, caught Henry staring, asked him, "That fella bothering you?"

"No, not exactly. You ever seen him before?"

"If I had I'd have slung him out on his arse. We don't like that sort here."

"What sort's that?"

"Them without money to pay."

Henry returned to the table. Bean went to pounce on his rum but Henry pulled it away. "Listen," he said. "I'm going to hear your story but there are a few conditions first. No more drinks after this one. This is your last, understand? And tomorrow, assuming I believe you, I want you to come to my chambers and we'll do all this again, but formally, a proper written record that you have signed and sworn. I am of course familiar with the Native Police. I know the kind of men they were, how they operated, but that was a long time ago; they are all but defunct these days. There might simply not be the appetite for investigating this sort of thing. So I make you no promises. I will hear you out and that is all. If I think you are lying to me I will stand up and leave and if you follow me again I'll have you arrested, are we clear?"

"Yes, sir."

"And you agree to swear a formal testimony tomorrow morning?"

"Do I have to go before a judge or anything?"

"Not yet. We can do this in chambers. Where do you live?"

Bean lowered his eyes. "There are hostels. They sometimes have beds."

"Well, there might be a way we can help you. But I want you to understand that I won't be gamed here, Mr. Bean. Now"—he slid the rum slowly across the table, Bean took it but didn't drink—"in your own time, please begin."

Chapter 16
Billy McBride

Three stockmen walked half-a-dozen docile heifers uphill from the yards and let them in through the gate of the newly built corral, its timber fence so freshly cut it gleamed in the midmorning sun. They closed the gate, found some shade beneath a nearby blue gum, and sat smoking and talking while the native stableboy brought the horses from the barn. One was Buck, Billy's aging brumby, too old now for scrub work but perfect for the corral; the other the good-natured white pony on which the children learned to ride. The stableboy tied both horses to the fence and glanced at the men beneath the tree. They shared a joke and laughed at him, spoke quietly among themselves.

Across the clearing separating the house from the

corral walked Billy and young William McBride. The boy was nearly seven years old, the eldest of two sons, with a daughter, Isobel, born in between. He had his father's coloring—the dark hair, the brooding eyes—and was dressed in almost identical clothes: a wide-brimmed hat, tan twill trousers, a freshly pressed shirt, and boots buffed till they shone. He stumbled along beside Billy, seemed to catch every divot and rock. Sulking. He didn't want to ride today. Would rather have stayed inside playing piano or reading books. Billy wouldn't hear a word of it. He prodded the boy between the shoulder blades. "Pick your feet up," he said.

At the corral Billy looped his stockwhip and catching rope over a fence post, unhitched the two horses, and handed William the pony's reins. He ignored the stableboy but waved to the men sitting smoking in the shade: "Fellas," he called, and dutifully they each raised their hands and replied with a monotone "Boss."

Billy led Buck through the gate and held it open for William but the boy stood rooted, watching the cattle through the rails. "Come on now," Billy said. "Bring him in."

"I don't want to."

"Why not? What's wrong?"

"They're too big."

"They're cows. That's the size of them. No sense learning on a calf."

"Daddy, please."

"Get in here," Billy said.

In the boy shuffled, leading the pony along. The cattle were grouped at the far end of the corral, milling dumbly, sniffing the dirt. Billy closed the gate and told William to mount up. He put the wrong foot in the stirrup. Distracted by the cattle still. His legs got in a tangle and he dropped back to the ground and Billy heard one of the men beneath the blue gum blow out a short laugh.

"Don't you lot have work to do?" he shouted over.

"Wait till you're done then bring 'em back down, we was told."

Billy nodded, adjusted his hat. He could have gone over and confronted them, insisted the men leave, but instead turned his attention back to the boy. Besides, he knew who had answered. Todd Anderson was his name. He was one of those who'd known Billy as a lowly stockman: they'd worked the scrubs together, eaten at the same table, drank around the same campfire. Now Billy was in charge, and men like Anderson resented it—he'd seen how they looked at him, the beat of hesitation before they followed a command, the little quips when they thought he was out of earshot. Billy was moving them on steadily, as he had Joe, the headman, and most others from the old regime. Todd Anderson had just bumped himself a little higher up the list.

William got into the saddle eventually. Billy swung up onto Buck. He brought the horse around and stood it next to his son; the boy couldn't have looked less comfortable if he were riding a kangaroo. He had no natural aptitude for it, Billy had seen that from the start: the very first time he lifted him onto the pony, William had screamed like he'd been scalded to the bone. Now he stared at the cattle, clutching tight to his reins.

"Right, let's get started," Billy said cheerfully, attempting to lift the mood. "First we'll just give them a little walk round, nice and steady, lead them along the fence. You stay behind them, I'll be at the side. Keep your distance. You don't want them getting spooked. Just walk your horse forward and they'll know what to do."

"What if they rush me though?"

"They won't. And if they did, I'd handle them."

"How will you?"

"You have to trust me, William, or this isn't going to work."

William didn't look comforted. He watched the

cattle like they were snakes. Billy just didn't understand him—by the same age, he could rope and shoot and ride almost as well as he could walk. Tommy was the same. Every day they'd be out there, doing some task, trying to show their father they could cope. William was the exact opposite. Didn't seem to care what Billy thought. He had tried taking him out into the station but all he did was moan. And Katherine only indulged it. There was plenty of time for all that, she said. But he would have to learn someday, and the sooner he started the easier it would come. Billy would do things differently with Thomas, he'd decided. Thank God he had another son.

"Look, stop making a bloody meal of this. Just get on with it. Come on."

Billy approached the cattle. Meekly, William did the same. Billy noticed the stableboy watching from the fence, his bare arms hanging over the railing, his head bowed, his eyes upturned. He dropped his gaze when Billy looked at him, spat out a long string of saliva, and let it dangle until it broke and hit the dirt.

The cattle were about as easy and compliant as any he could have hoped for, yet still William managed to get it wrong. He was too hesitant, too slow, kept himself too tight to the fence. Curtly Billy corrected him, once again heard the men laughing from over by the tree as William began squealing, "I'm doing it! I'm doing it!" like he'd roped the fucking moon. Billy knew what they would be thinking. Would have thought the same in their place. Making fun of the little prince.

They kept the cattle moving until William had stopped his twitching and settled himself down, though now he was too casual, his gaze wandering, wasn't paying them enough mind—if it weren't for Billy they would have scattered, or dug in, and it was obvious William neither noticed nor cared. The exercise meant nothing to him. You lost control of a mob in Billy's day, the whole family could have starved.

"All right, that'll do, now we'll try some cutting out."

This involved separating one of the heifers from the group and holding her on her own. William had never done it before but the pony knew how to cut; it was the kind of skill that wasn't always instinctive, for horses and humans both, but Billy had made sure the pony was trained before attempting to train his son.

"Can't we just stop now? I'm tired, Daddy—please?"

They'd not been at it fifteen minutes. The boy was soft as dung. "No," Billy snapped. "Pull your lip in. I'll do the first one. Watch closely now."

He singled her out easily. The other cattle moved along. Billy had the heifer pinned against the fence when all she wanted was to run. Funny how skittish a cow will get when separated from the herd. But with each dart she attempted, Billy and Buck did the same, mirroring every movement, keeping her in place.

"Right. Come up here with me. You can take a turn."

"I can't do it."

"All you do is follow her. The horse'll show you how."

The pony had its tail up, keen for a run at the cow. Billy dropped back and for a moment after the changeover neither the cow nor William moved. Watching each other closely, seeing who'd be first to flinch, and in the stillness Billy glanced over at the men watching from the tree—smoking with their hats off, enjoying the show—and at the stableboy also, a slack-jawed sneer about him, that insolent pop-eyed stare. Look! Billy wanted to shout at them. Look what he's doing now!

Suddenly the cow bolted. The pony followed suit. Leaping across to block her, then darting back again, and Billy saw William ragdoll in the saddle, and what would happen next. "Hold him, William! Hold him, bring him round!" But the boy was long past trying to control his mount: screaming, he dropped the reins and grabbed the saddle and let the pony run loose, chasing the cow, refusing to let it pass. William slid sideways, and for a long time seemed to dangle there, as Billy jumped down and ran. He wasn't quite quick enough. William cried out, and fell.

He hit the ground headfirst, breaking the fall with his hands. He rolled and Billy was over him, protecting him; he got the pony by its bridle, held it until the cow was gone, then when he let go again the pony shook himself and moved off, as if unaware anything was wrong.

Kneeling at the boy's side, Billy touched his head, body, legs, asking him, "You all right? Can you hear me? Anything broken? Let me see . . ."

William began blubbering. Billy inspected his face. There was a good-size graze on his forehead and another on his cheek; his hands had been torn up by the gravel and his shoulder hurt, he said. Billy scuffed his hair and smiled at him. "It's only a scratch. If you don't get hurt you've never tried nothing—come on now, back up, let's give it another go."

"No," William whimpered through his tears. "I don't want to."

Billy lifted him to his feet and stood with him, roughly brushed him down. He retrieved the boy's hat, straightened it out, tried to put it back on his head. William hit him. Batted his arm away. Billy heard the men laughing and felt a surge of emotion that was diffi-cult to place. Anger, embarrassment, even a little pride. "Hey now," he said quietly. "There's no need for that. It ain't my fault what just happened. You let that pony have his head."

"I don't want to ride the stupid pony."

"Well you ain't ready for a real horse yet, that's for bloody sure."

"Don't laugh at me."

"I'm not laughing. Come on, let's show this cow who's boss."

"No."

Billy touched his arm. "William."

"No, I said." Shrugging him off.

"Falling off's just a part of it. You have to get back on."

"I don't want to. I want to go home."

"Well, you ain't quitting, I'll tell you that much. Go and collect your horse."

"No."

He folded his arms and stomped his foot like some prissy schoolgirl. Billy said, "Collect your damn horse before I make you. I ain't asking again."

William only stood there. Billy felt the stares of the stableboy and the men. He put a hand on William's shoulder, attempting to steer him, but he twisted from the grip and the two of them faced off across the corral.

Billy was disgusted by him: the foppish way he held himself, the weakness that ran to his core. They may have looked alike but there was none of Billy in him, the boy was no kind of son. Even his own father, drunk and penniless, would not have stood for this behavior, wouldn't have had to, Billy would have fought like hell to get another crack at it, not to run off home. Not for the first time he wondered if the child was even his— Katherine had never been clear on the timing, and William had come out small. She'd always denied anything had happened that night with Charles Sinclair, but Billy still had his doubts.

He lunged and grabbed hold of William, pinned him by the arms, bent so they were face-to-face. William writhing, trying to kick him; Billy said, "You're making a bloody fool of yourself, and of me. Now quit acting like a baby and show me you're a proper McBride."

He shoved him gently toward the pony. Barely anything in it, but down the boy went, the dust puffing up around him as he landed in the dirt. Later, Billy would wonder if the fall had been deliberate, if William had seen Katherine watching from over by the house and thrown himself to the ground. He lay there groaning, his head buried in his arms. Billy hadn't noticed Katherine yet. "Christ," he said, sighing, trudging closer, standing over his son. He tried to rouse him. William refused to stir. His legs started flailing like he was swimming and Billy straightened, shook his head, looked up at the sky.

Behind him, at the fence line, he heard the stableboy laugh.

Billy spun and strode across the corral. Briefly the stableboy tried to control himself, to swallow his laughter and bury his gaze in the dirt, but when he saw Billy advancing, a face full of fury and his hands balled into fists, he unhooked his arms from the railing and backed away a step.

Billy snatched his stockwhip off the fence post. He vaulted the rail in one leap. Now the stableboy had his hands up, jabbering away in his own tongue—Billy could not have cared less what he said. He walked toward him folding the whip in a figure-eight motion, tightening it into a strop. The stableboy tried to run but Billy kicked his legs out and he sprawled into the dust. Billy hit him. One quick *thwack* of the strop on his temple that briefly sent him limp, then he had him by the collar and was dragging him back to the corral, yelling, "Laugh at my son, will you? Laugh at *my fucking son?*" while the stableboy grappled his wrist hopelessly, his legs cycling the ground.

The men by the gum tree were standing. Katherine, her skirts in her hand, came running from the house.

Billy threw the stableboy chest-first against the railings, stropped him again, the stableboy cowering, holding the back of his head. By now William had picked himself up and was watching from the middle of the corral, his knees pressed together, clutching one arm with the other, squirming. Billy gripped the stableboy's head, shoved it forward, snarled in his ear, "Apologize to my boy."

"Daddy . . ." William sniveled.

"Quiet!" He clamped the stableboy's jaw with his hand, saliva bubbling with each breath. "Say it," Billy told him. "Or I swear to God . . ."

The stableboy didn't answer. Or couldn't, maybe. Billy released him and stepped back a way and let out the whip to the ground.

"No!" Katherine shouted. "No, Billy, don't!"

He didn't even hear her. Lost deep inside himself now. He was sick of being disrespected—John Sullivan never had to put up with this kind of horseshit. Billy had steered the station through a crippling drought, widespread labor strikes, and a depression that had brought the colony to its knees; better than that, they had thrived. Still he met with other squatters and they sneered at him like shit on a shoe, as if marrying into it and being born into it weren't two sides of the same coin. At the same time neither did his own men fully respect him, still saw him as one of them, not the man he'd since become. Even his own son hated him. They all did, but he would show them, like he had done his whole life, starting with this insolent fucker here.

Billy drew back the whip and unleashed it and with a sharp crack the tip tore through the stableboy's shirt. The stableboy cried out and arched to the sky; a bloodstain bloomed where he'd been cut. William was wailing. Covering his face with his hands. The cattle and horses milled restlessly around him, geed up by the sound of the whip. The stableboy looked over his shoulder. Billy drew back the whip again.

Katherine slammed into him before he could get the second lashing away. She wrapped him in her arms and held him and he didn't try to fight, looking at her queerly, as if unsure who she was. They stood together, Katherine panting, the world slowly seeping back into Billy's mind: William crying; the stableboy fleeing down the hillside; the men ambling warily from the blue gum; the cattle and horses in the corral. Katherine called to William, told him it was over now, he was safe; "Get him out of there!" she yelled at the men. Two of them jumped over the railing. They picked up the boy and passed him to the other over the fence. Katherine let go of Billy and stared at him aghast.

"What the hell is wrong with you? Billy? What have you done?"

Blankly Billy looked at her. They stayed like that a long time. Then he dropped his whip and walked away without a word.

Chapter 17
Henry Wells

The train squealed into Southport station and hissed a filthy cloud of steam. The doors opened, the passengers disembarked, day-trippers mostly, mothers and their broods. It had not occurred to Henry to bring his family. They might have provided the perfect excuse. Instead he stepped down from first class alone and made his way through the bustle and noise, along the platform, through the station building, such as it was, and outdoors. A crisp winter sun greeted him. A faint whiff of salt water on the breeze. He walked along Railway Street to the park, glimpsed the pier and the beach and the sea. It was all really rather pleasant. He could see why Southport was so popular, apparently favored by the governor himself. They would come in the summer, he decided, stay for a weekend; he would find out which was the best of the hotels. It might prove useful. He could talk to the right people, his children could play with theirs, Laura could befriend their wives.

He found the little weatherboard police station and, satchel in hand, stood appraising it from the street. With its picket fence and tidy front garden, its deadheaded rosebush climbing the porch, it looked more like a holi-day cottage than a police house, and certainly too quaint and quiet for someone like Edmund Noone. The man had quite the reputation. Henry had done his research. Highly decorated for his work spanning almost two de-cades with the Native Police, a number of high-profile cases to his name, including apprehending the murderer of an outback squatter called John Sullivan . . . which just so happened to have occurred at around the same time and in roughly the same location as the massacre reported by Reverend Bean. The two couldn't be a coin-cidence. Henry was on to something, no doubt.

So what was Noone doing here, then, in this sleepy backwater retreat?

Henry walked to the gate, opened it, the hinge creaked as it swung, felt obliged to close it behind him, such was the tidiness of the place. He followed a flag-stone path between the flower beds, then noticed a man sitting smoking on the porch. He was sprawled on a bench with his legs splayed and his arms hooked over the backrest. Henry couldn't make out his face, only the white of a ragged cigarette dangling from his lips.

"Good morning. I'm looking for Chief Inspector Noone."

As he said this, Henry stepped up onto the porch and got a better look at the man. He was young, early twenties, with hooded eyes, sandy brown hair, and scar-pocked cheeks. Dressed in scruffy trousers and a loose-fitting shirt, an immense long-barreled rifle propped beside him against the bench, he certainly wasn't a police officer; he looked more like a larrikin off the streets. He drew on the cigarette, blew a smoke ring.

"He ain't here."

Through the open doorway Henry glimpsed an empty front desk and office, no sign of a clerk or constable inside. "This is the police house, isn't it? I was told this is where Mr. Noone resides?"

"Nope."

"But . . ."

"Resides means live, don't it. Ain't nobody lives in here."

He was grinning. He slopped his tongue noisily around his gums.

"Stationed, then. The chief inspector is stationed here, is he not?"

"Depends on who's asking."

"Henry Wells, attorney-at-law. And you are?"

The man spat. "I done told ye: he ain't here."

"Well, when are you expecting him back?"

"Hard to say."

He stared off into the distance, took another pull on his cigarette. Henry stood there impotently. No idea what to do next. Ordinarily he would have marched inside but this man, his rifle . . . he shifted his feet and looked about, until a voice from a back room called, "Show him in, Percy, please."

The larrikin uncrossed his ankles and leaped to his feet, scraped his cigarette dead on the arm of the bench, and tucked it behind his ear. He snatched up the rifle, barged Henry aside, went in through the open front door. Henry hesitated then followed the trail of smoldering tobacco into a pristine office bereft of people, papers, or stationery of any kind. The place looked utterly deserted. Not a working police house at all.

Through they went, along a narrow hallway to the back of the building, until they reached a door standing ajar. Percy leaned against the frame and folded his arms and rested an elbow on his rifle like a crutch. He nodded for Henry to enter. Smirking, the light now dancing in his eyes. Henry gripped the handle of his satchel all the tighter, pushed open the door and stepped into the room.

Noone was sitting behind a broad writing desk, reclining in his chair, a book open in his hand: *Nietzsche: On the Genealogy of Morality.* He placed the book facedown and stiffly turned, his posture oddly upright, as if his spine was pinned. Even sitting he was incredibly tall—over six and a half feet, Henry guessed—and wore a light gray three-piece without the jacket, a gold watch chain dangling between the waistcoat pockets. His hair was black and so precisely combed that Henry could see the tooth marks, and his mustache was black also, full but neatly trimmed. He smiled at Henry warmly. Didn't rise or offer his hand.

"Chief Inspector, I'm very grateful. Sorry to arrive like this, unannounced."

"On the contrary, Mr. Wells, you announced yourself most clearly outside."

Only now did Henry notice the man's eyes. Gray, opaque, unblinking—for a moment he even wondered if Noone was blind. Certainly that would explain how he could have heard the conversation on the porch. Henry leaned a little forward and to one side, noticed the eyes follow him, then straightened and swapped the satchel to his left hand, approached the desk with his right outstretched. Noone shook it reluctantly. A grip like a blacksmith's vise.

"Please, have a seat. Now tell me, how can I help?"

There were two wooden armchairs angled in front of the desk. Henry put his satchel on one of them, shrugged out of his coat and draped it over the back, and lowered himself into the other, saying, "A spur-of-the-moment impulse, I'm afraid. I do apologize, visiting with you uninvited, I hope you do not mind."

"That depends. What do you want?"

"Nothing," Henry said laughing. "Perhaps I'm not explaining myself very well. I happened to be in Southport this morning—looking at real estate, you understand—and when I realized you were stationed here, it occurred to me the two of us have never met. Which is a grave oversight on my part, of course, since I usually make it my business to acquaint myself with our higher-ranking officers as best I can. I find it can help immeasurably, given the line of work we are in."

Noone weighed him evenly. Henry shifted in his chair. Finally Noone clapped his hands, rose, and said, "A drink then, since it's a social visit—what's your poison, Mr. Wells?"

It was still only midmorning. Henry stuttered, "Uh . . . perhaps a whiskey?"

"Whiskey it is."

Noone fixed the drink at a side table. Henry glanced around the room. It was more like a gentleman's parlor, no indication of his position at all. On the desk were his notebook and writing things, and a pipe upturned in a golden ashtray; paintings of the seaside hung on the walls. The bookcase was filled with academic journals and legal volumes and what looked like scientific texts: Darwin, Mendel, and something foreign, possibly about history, by men called Breuer and Freud.

Noone handed him an enormous whiskey. "You're not having one?" Henry said.

"No."

He retook his seat and gestured for Henry to drink and reluctantly Henry did. All the while Noone watching him; Henry coughed as the whiskey went down.

"So," Noone said, "you're buying real estate. Whereabouts exactly?"

"Just . . . on the bluff there, along the coast. Somewhere with a sea view, it's such a lovely outlook. I have to say I was a little surprised to learn that you were stationed here. Rather a quiet post for a chief inspector, particularly one as eminent as yourself. I'll admit to being more than a little curious. Your lofty reputation rather precedes you, Mr. Noone, at least among my colleagues at the bar."

A smile twitched beneath his mustache. "Oh, it's not forever. A well-earned rest after years in the field. The commissioner and I have an arrangement. And as you say, it is a lovely little town."

"You don't miss the city then? Or the country for that matter?"

"We are building a house in Hamilton. The family will be joining me soon."

"Hamilton. Very nice."

"Yes, it is. Where are you?"

"Spring Hill." Noone grimaced and Henry added, "That's not forever, either. So, you have children?"

"Girls, both grown. Yourself?"

"A boy and a girl, still young. My wife certainly has her hands full."

"Now that does surprise me."

"Oh? How so?"

"You just don't particularly strike me as the marrying kind."

Henry didn't quite know what to make of that. He sipped his whiskey and was grateful for the pause. The conversation wasn't going how he'd intended, how he'd rehearsed it over the previous days. He got the impression that Noone was already growing bored of him. He needed to start moving things along.

"I have to ask, since I'm here, all those years you

spent in the Native Police Force, weren't they just so terribly . . . hard?"

"On the contrary, I rather enjoyed myself."

"But surely living out there, in the interior, so far from the civilized world . . . and the tasks that fell upon you, witnessing it all firsthand."

Noone shrugged, his mouth downturned. "Some are better suited to the work than others. I doubt you'd have fared quite so well."

Forcing laughter, Henry said, "No, no, I think you might be right," and drank hurriedly, more than he would have liked; already he could feel his head swimming, the heat rising into his cheeks. He leaned and placed the whiskey on the desk then remained there, bent forward, an earnest, confiding stare.

"Tell me something, Edmund, if I may be so bold: what was it really like? Did you kill as many as they say? Thousands, I have heard. Is it even possible that could be true? And rest assured I ask not as a critic but out of admiration, even wonder—through your service you have built a country, given us a land of our own."

It was as close to an accusation as he could muster. He watched Noone's reaction carefully. The man didn't so much as blink.

"I imagine your father is most ashamed of you," Noone said, his voice steady and cold. "Your accent is

Sydney, you're not from Queensland, and few in your profession would have moved north out of choice. Those nighttime proclivities you try your hardest to conceal, yet are written upon you like a tattoo; were they the real reason you left? Did you fly the nest in disgrace, I wonder, when your father discovered what you are? Was it him who caught you? Or did your mother find you fumbling with some sweaty-faced schoolboy, his hand in your trousers, yours in his? And now, what about this poor wife with her children in Spring Hill? Does she know who her husband really is, what he gets up to, where he goes? This marriage of convenience—is she aware of it, did she consent, or is the convenience all yours? Oh, I see you, Mr. Wells. I see you just as you see yourself, when you stand before the looking glass, and an ugly sight it is too. You are a fraud. Your very presence here is fraudulent. You are not buying a house in Southport. You could barely afford a beach hut, I would guess. Now, if you wish to disagree with anything I have said, I am listening. Otherwise, I suggest you leave."

Henry held Noone's gaze then straightened; all this time he'd been leaning forward, his elbow on his knee. He reached to the other chair, collected his satchel, gathered his coat, draped it over one arm. Trying hard not to hurry, to look like he was running away.

He stood and said, "Good day, Chief Inspector," then walked slowly from the room, felt Noone's gaze on his back the whole time. He didn't close the door behind him. He walked along the hall. In the front office he found Percy sitting with his boots on one of the desks, ankles crossed, cleaning his nails with a pocketknife. He smiled as Henry passed him. Neither man said a word. Out into the sunshine, beneath the rosebush on the porch, along the path into the street. He glanced behind him warily—the little house all sweetness and light—then set off to find the post office in town.

Since hearing Reverend Bean's confession, Henry had looked closely into the Native Police, that uniformed band of mercenaries marauding with impunity up and down the frontier. They were hardly a clandestine outfit—the whole colony knew what they did—but time and again blind eyes were turned. Yes, there were letters in the newspapers, and when the evidence was overwhelming or the clamor grew too loud, inquests had sometimes been held, whereupon officers were simply reprimanded, moved, or quietly retired. Henry and his clerks had been through every record they could find: despite all the evidence, the eyewitnesses, the mass graves, the charred remains, there had never been a successful criminal prosecution of a Native Police officer in relation to an Aboriginal death.

Well, Henry was going to change that. He was going to be the first.

At the post office he pulled out two envelopes from his satchel, one addressed to the colonial secretary, the other to the attorney general. He paid the postage and watched the postmaster drop them in the sack, then turned and made his way back to the station to catch the next Brisbane train.

Reverend Bean's testimony was one thing, but before taking things any further he'd wanted to get a good look at Noone. Henry had been shaken by the accuracy with which his life had been unveiled, and in such a short time; nobody had ever seen him so clearly before. But with his outburst, Noone had surely revealed himself too.

The man was guilty as hell.

As soon as the lawyer had left the building, Percy scooted in his heels and went along the hall to the open office doorway, found Noone carefully preparing a pipe. He got it going with a match, great hollows in his cheeks, then waved for Percy to come in. He offered him the matchbox. Percy plucked the cigarette stub from behind his ear, lit it, and took a seat. They sat smoking. Percy brushed ash off his thigh. He noticed the half-filled whiskey glass and took it for himself.

"I'd like you to follow that man, Percy. I believe he is up to no good. We'll find out eventually what he is planning, I suppose, but for the time being I'd like to know who he is, where he lives, where he works, what he eats, who he fucks, every little detail down to when the bastard shits. Would you do that for me, please?"

Percy nodded, drinking. "That all? You don't want nothing else done?"

"For now. There is no sense in taking unnecessary risks."

"It wouldn't be no risk to you at all. I'd be careful."

"I know you would, my boy. And I'm very grateful. But no—let's leave Henry Wells alive for the moment, until we've seen what he's going to do next."

Chapter 18
Tommy McBride

A week after Arthur had left him, as he ran errands for Jack Kerrigan in Marree, preparing for their next cattle drove, Tommy was walking past the post office when the postmaster stuck his head through the open doorway and asked if he was Bobby Thompson, and after a beat of hesitation Tommy remembered that he was. "Letter for you," the postmaster said, ducking back inside. Tommy collected the envelope and in the shade of the building found his new name and *Marree* written there in a scrawled and slanted script. He opened the flap and slid out the thin paper and, his frown lifting, a sudden churning in his gut, read his real name in the greeting, then the message underneath:

Tommy—

I hope this reaches you. I figure you're still living it up with Flash Jack in Marree. I'm headed south like I told you. I can't stay round here. Good luck on them cattle runs. I hope you're right about him. I'll write again when I get somewhere—leave word if you move on. So it'll find you. If you want to, I mean. Anyhow, take care of yourself. No hard feelings, eh?

Arthur

Tommy folded the letter and scanned the alleyway, as if expecting to find Arthur there. Every day he'd looked for him. His absence impossible to believe. But now here was confirmation: this wasn't just another fall-out, Arthur was actually gone. The finality of the letter hit Tommy like a fist: *No hard feelings, eh?* After all these years together, after all they'd been through, and done, his only true friend in the world had left him. In this place. On his own.

The postmark on the envelope said Lyndhurst, two days' quick ride south, but by now Arthur would probably have moved on and there was nothing in his note suggesting Tommy follow. He read it twice over. At least he'd said he would write again. It almost sounded like he was giving his blessing to what Tommy had planned: *Good luck on them cattle runs. I hope you're right about him.*

He looked in on the postmaster. "Hold my mail while I'm gone, will you?"

"That's the job," the man said.

Jack put a new droving plant together—horses, a horsetailer, camp cook, and stockmen—and with Tommy among their number they set out north at a lick, passing long chains of camels carrying teetering mountains of supplies, and other plants plodding in the opposite direction, as they raced for the Channel Country or the stations in the north, or sometimes out west into the Territory, where they would collect whichever mob Jack had managed to get a contract for and drove it first for supplies in Birdsville then down the infamous stock route whose name the little town shared, a grueling month-long slog back to Marree. Onto the trains with the cattle, a couple of days to rest their bones, then they were back on the hoof north again to bring the next mob down.

Tommy wondered what his father would have made of it, or Billy, or even his boyhood self, if any could have seen him now.

It was exhilarating work, but exhausting; he had never been so tired. Eighteen, nineteen hours in the saddle, dust gritting his eyeballs, so thick in his throat it hurt to breathe, droving anything up to a few thousand head over towering sandhills and barren gibber plains, through the abundance of the Cooper floodplains and the treachery of Goyder Lagoon. Nothing was predictable out here. Jack might have been familiar with all the waterholes, and the soaks and wells and bogs, but water they'd drunk and even bathed in on one trip would be gone next time they came through, and feed could disappear in a matter of days. The land followed its own rhythms. Secrets that over the years became lore. In hushed whispers drovers exchanged news with a grimace or shake of the head. Nobody really knew anything. You took your chances every time. Ah, she'll be right, they all told themselves, since what else could they say, but many times it turned out she was not. Grave markers lined the trackside. Sometimes even bodies, a party strung out one by one across the desert like dropped beads, part-covered by the drifting sand—over the years Tommy helped bury more than a few. Their follies became memorialized in the stories of how they'd died, and by the names given to each place: Misfortune Creek; Dead Man's Sandhill. It wasn't always cattlemen either. Mostly cattlemen were better prepared. The teacher who'd decided to walk all the way to Birdsville but was later found eaten by dogs. The group on their way to a race meet so desperate they slit the throats of their horses then perished having drunk too much blood. You felt their ghosts coming at you. In the great silence of the desert, on a warm breath of wind. There were times it sounded like the land itself was howling—this was a place of coochies and debil-debils, and of sandflies gnawing away at your skin. Bites that if you scratched them could get infected and blow up like boils that would later need popping, the puss leeching, a heated knife-tip in the evening campfire. It got freezing cold after sundown, during the main winter season anyway. The night watchmen shivered on their horses, the others shivered in their swags. They slept regardless: some days Tommy could have slept on his feet. He was used to riding, grew up with cattle work, but nothing quite like this. At least the heat wasn't scorching. Mild, even, in the wintertime; if you found yourself baking, you'd probably left it too late in the year. That's what did for most men. Bravado, greed, stupidity—these things got them killed. Jack had a rule that come October he wouldn't set out north again, not for any price, and so it was that Tommy found himself, at the end of that first droving season, back in Marree and at something of a loose end. Every day he called into the post office, popping his head through the door, asking

"Anything?" and growing used to the postmaster replying in the negative, until one day he looked up and grinned.

"There is, actually. Your lucky day. Here you are, young man."

It was Arthur's handwriting on the envelope. Tommy tore open the flap. The postmaster noticed and said, "A sweetheart, I'm assuming?" then, laughing, "They all say that," when Tommy replied it was just a letter from a friend.

Tommy—

Hope you got the last note. I'm a bit more settled these days. I've put the address up top there, so you can write back if you want. I don't know how long they'll keep me on for but I'm not in a hurry to leave. Work's been hard to come by—it's mostly sheep down here, and you know what I think of them. Hope you're getting along with the cattle and Flash Jack's treating you all right. Don't take shit from anyone. Be good to hear your news. Take care now.

Arthur

Tommy wrote back immediately. It tumbled out of him in a rush. The cattle droves he had been on, the places he had seen: Boulia, Bedourie, over the Territory border and out toward Alice Springs. Jack was treating him well, he told him, and despite the usual gripes and grumbles, he and the other men got along fine. He was sorry for how things had ended between them, for how he'd behaved back then, unburdening himself after months of carrying that guilt around. He missed him, and was grateful, more than he could quite bring himself to say.

Apart from the cameleers still making supply runs to the stations, Marree largely emptied during summertime, as the droving season wound up and the men returned to their families or looked for work nearer the coast. When Jack asked his plans Tommy admitted he'd never thought about it, and didn't have anywhere else to be. He might just stay in Marree, he said, shrugging; Jack told him he'd go out of his mind. "Why don't you come with me to Adelaide," he offered, then when Tommy asked what was in Adelaide he'd laughed and said, "You'll see."

They boarded the train in Marree and within a few days were on the south coast, the same journey undertaken by all that cattle they had droved, albeit with a happier end. Sitting in the carriage watching the country slip by, Tommy wearing a clean shirt and trousers, the best of all he owned. He didn't have any town clothes. Certainly none as smart as Jack: clean-shaven, his hair freshly trimmed, he wore a brown three-piece that made him look like a pimp. There was a woman down in Adelaide, he told Tommy; then later, a little shyly, admitted that one woman was actually three. He hadn't meant for it to work out that way, but you know how these things are, and it wasn't like he was married or had children or anything—not that he knew of anyway, assuming his luck had held.

Dee ran a guesthouse north of the city, which was how the two of them first met. She had short black hair and high cheekbones and greeted Jack by flinging her arms around his neck and kissing him hard on the lips, Tommy standing there awkwardly, unsure where to look. When they parted and Jack introduced him, she flashed an appraising glance and said, smirking, "Well, just wait till the girls get a look at you." He became a pet project for her: Dee gave him a room for a peppercorn rent, and while Jack was seeing to business (as he put it) she showed Tommy the town. Cleaned him up, got him a haircut, had him fitted for a suit and other new clothes. They walked arm in arm along the pavements, Dee laughing her big laugh, her head tipped back to show her apple-white neck and the damp pink of her tongue. Tommy worried about the two of them.

He was feeling things, for sure. But then he'd never had a female friend before, didn't know how these things worked. The whole city knocked him sideways: the crowds of people, the towering buildings, the traffic in the roads; even worse in the nighttime, swaying drunkenly beneath the gaslights.

In a bootleg dancehall in the back room of a pub, Dee introduced Tommy to a group of her friends, who teased him for his accent and asked for stories from the mythical north. Tommy had nothing to tell them. His stories weren't for these people, for dancehalls. He paired off with a blond girl called Sally. They spent the night together a couple of times, Tommy lying in her bed afraid to fall asleep in case he scared her with the horrors of his dreams. He didn't get them every night, but they were unpredictable to say the least, and without work to tire him out his mind roamed. He drank to keep it quiet. To knock himself out cold. He fell for Sally heavily, as a young man of his age would, and as their time in Adelaide grew shorter he began to worry about leaving her, which had Jack roaring when he heard.

"It's every woman you ever speak to, Bobby! No different to that whore!"

At Jack's instigation he opened a bank account, risky in the middle of a depression, but not as risky as carrying a rumpled stack of banknotes around. He needed some convincing. Handing over all his money like that. His father had never had one, didn't trust the banks, and it seemed way above his station in truth. But a bank account felt like something a man should have, a man of means anyway, or at least a man with aspirations beyond simply getting by. Jack had shown him such things were achievable: he led two lives, Tommy realized. One up north with the cattle and the country, another down here like some gent. That had been Tommy when he was younger: all he'd wanted was to grow up like his father, while at the same time feeling there should be more. He'd been more curious than his brother. Better at reading and numbers too. Once, he'd suggested they start at the school in Bewley, and Billy had looked at him like he'd lost his mind. Now it seemed vaguely possible that there was a life for him out there, a different life, away from all the guilt and the pain. He was unsure exactly the shape it might take, but a bank account seemed a good start, and when he came down the steps in his new suit that day, with the papers in his pocket and a lightness in his heels, he felt like he'd just sneaked a peek into his future, without knowing yet what that future held.

Still, it was a relief to leave the city. All those buildings, those crowds. He'd not realized he could miss a place like Marree but as the train rattled north and the land opened out it felt like he was going home. He went directly to the post office. He'd written Arthur from Adelaide, told him all about the city, and Sally, and everything else. It had occurred to him while he was down there that he might have tried to track Arthur down: he had the name of the station he was working on, and though it was probably still hundreds of miles away they were closer than they had been in a long time. He didn't. It felt like they were following different paths now. But when he opened the letter he found waiting for him in Marree, he allowed himself to hope those paths might cross one day, that he would see his old friend again.

Tommy—

Adelaide? Are you bloody kidding me? You'll stand out like a bald cockerel down there! I'll bet that young Sally helped you settle in some—it's good to hear you're enjoying yourself anyhow. Things are all right on the station here, even with the bloody sheep, but it won't be for long, I doubt. They've let most of the whitefellas go, now there's only the bosses and us blacks. On account of we're cheaper, see. Saving them a proper wage. But the place is for closing, I reckon, so I'll likely be on the road again. Maybe don't write for a while in case I'm not here—they're not the sort that would send on my mail. I'm pleased you're getting by though, Tommy. And don't worry about before. Nothing's ended between us. You ain't rid of me yet!

Arthur

It became the rhythm he and Jack lived by: the stock routes in the droving season, then the train down south to the coast. Tommy did some traveling. Saw the ocean for the first time in his life and it made him so queasy he had to sit down on the sand and close his eyes. It terrified him. The endless uncertainty of it all, the way the thing breathed; it felt like the earth moved under his boots. He would take up drinking almost as soon as the train landed—there was nothing else for him to do. Sally had married a blacksmith from Mile End, and for a while Tommy nursed a broken heart, until a seamstress called Jacqueline helped stitch the wound. He was nothing like himself down here. He'd left Tommy McBride in Marree. In bars and at the racetrack he was drawn into conversation with groups of other men: people seemed to find Bobby interesting, he even managed to make them laugh. If ever they asked for his story, or about the fingers missing from his hand, he would make up some bullshit tale. He got in fights sometimes. He was tall, and strong with it, the kind with whom certain men like to have a go. He held his own, mostly. Being hit didn't bother him. There was power in his swing. He felt a surge of abandon in fighting, and it surprised him, how easily violence came. More than once Jack had to drag him off a man, and Tommy would stagger away, panting, while whichever poor bastard had provoked him lay bleeding on the ground.

They were back up on the Birdsville Track, among the vicious sloping sand dunes south of the Warburton Creek, when one night around the campfire, the others all asleep, Jack poked the burning deadwood and said, "I promised not to ask when I met you, and I'm nothing if not a man of my word, but if ever you want to talk about it, I'm listening. If it would help to get it all off your chest."

Tommy frowned at him. "What you on about?"

"Mate, I've known you long enough. I can see how it's tearing you up."

"What is?"

"Whatever happened back then, over in Queensland, when you were young." Tommy dropped his eyes to the fire. A shiver against the darkness. Jack went on:

"Look, you don't have to tell me, but I've heard you dreaming, I sleep next to you every night."

"So I get nightmares—what of it?"

"Nothing, mate. Suit yourself."

"Come on, let's have it. You got something to say?"

"All right, who's Noone?"

There was a long silence between them. Tommy picked up a stone and hurled it into the night. "A copper. You ever hear of him?"

"Dunno. Don't think so."

"You'd know if you had. Well, he's what happened. Him and everything else."

"How d'you mean?"

A long breath washed out of Tommy like the breaking of a dam. "Noone was Native Police, had the district where I'm from. This one day, me and my brother went swimming at a waterhole, only when we got back we found our family killed. Shot, every one of them. Hell, they even stabbed the dogs. Our sister Mary hung on a while after but she went too in the end. They brought in Noone to catch them that did it, only he never did."

"Fucking hell, Bobby."

"Yeah." He scooped up more stones and flicked them at the ground.

"How old were you?"

"Fourteen."

"Fucking hell. And is that what you keep dreaming about? What happened to them?"

"In a way, yeah. Also him. Noone."

Jack was staring at him. "Why? What did he do?"

In the firelight Tommy glanced across at this man, Jack Kerrigan, one of the best he'd ever known. It would take so little to tell him, to unburden himself—because if not Jack, then who? "He took us . . ." he began, then stopped himself. He couldn't make himself do it, couldn't reveal himself in that way. If Jack knew who he was really, if he knew what Tommy had done . . . he shook his head by way of an answer, but it seemed Jack had already guessed.

"If he was Native Police I can imagine. Wait, you were there? You saw?"

Hesitantly, Tommy nodded.

"Fucking hell—I'll stop saying that in a minute. Your brother too?"

Bitterly, he snorted. "It was his idea in the first place."

"And this was what you were running from when I found you on the Strez?"

"Before that. Five years. Arthur got me away from there, saved me really. I didn't want to see it that way but it's true." Tommy's face twisted in the firelight. "All those people, Jack. All those people because of me."

He'd not cried in many years now, but the tears began falling and wouldn't stop. He lurched up and stumbled between the sandhills, into the empty desert beyond, fell to his knees and wept. Pain filled his body, washed out of him in gulps, and was swallowed by those immense and silent plains. He dug up the dirt and held it; dust dribbled between his fingers on the breeze. He placed his hands palms down on the earth, as if bent to the land in prayer. It had heard it all already. It knew what had been done. So much killing it had witnessed, so much blood and death and grief. Tommy straightened and sniffed and steadied himself, and finally the tears dried. The moon bright above him, the blackness peppered with stars. He wiped his face roughly on his shirtsleeve, struggled back to his feet. He could hear the mob grunting beyond the sandbar and just about see the glow of the campfire. He set off walking. When he got back to camp he found that Jack was already in his bedroll, with his head on his arm and his eyes closed, pretending to be asleep.

Tommy—
I'm in Victoria! Never even knew where the bugger
was! Turns out the only places I'm good for down

here is the Missions, which I wasn't all too happy about but the truth is I'm better suited to it than most anywhere else. There's a bunch of us to knock about with, and there's food and beds and work. Cattle now, thank Christ Almighty, which I'm not meant to say round here. It's like the rest of my life never happened, saying grace and all that horseshit, like I'm back where it all began. I'll stick it for as long as they'll have me, or until you can get down. You still thinking of coming? Bloody long way for you now. You'd like it though, I reckon. Green as a tree frog's arsehole—gets plenty bloody rain! No rush, mind, I'm only saying. Whenever you get done with them cows.

Arthur

It was their sixth season working the stock routes together when, in a pub in Urandangi, on their way north to collect another mob, Jack noticed the stranger eyeing Tommy across the room. A toothless old swaggie with straggly long hair and a beard speckled with lice, a flinty look of menace in his bloodhound eyes. Standing alone in the corner, leaning on a shelf, staring at Tommy and nursing his beer like an infant against his chest. A lively crowd in that evening. Various droving teams passing through at the same time, mingling, drinking, singing, swapping stories from the road. Tommy was playing cards at a table, the cards fanned out in his right hand, his beer glass clutched in the three fingers of his left. Laughing. Slapping the man beside him on the arm. Jack bought two beers from the barman, sidled over to the old-timer, and offered him one.

"What's this?" the stranger said, scowling.

"You don't want it, I'll drink it myself."

"I never said that, here . . ." He snatched the beer, spilling some, put the glass to his lips and drank, eyes on Jack the whole time. He lowered the glass and sighed contentedly. "Do I know ye or something, friend?"

"Might do. I've known a lot of people."

"Reckon I'd remember, generous as y'are."

"I just don't like to see a fella drinking by himself, that's all."

"Well, I'm much obliged to ye." He offered his hand. "Alan Ames."

They shook. "Jack Kerrigan. So what brings you out here, Alan Ames?"

Ames laughed like this was funny. "Might as well say it's the wind."

"Take her as she comes, is it?"

"Something like that, aye. Not by choice, mind."

"You after work then?"

"Might be. You hiring?"

"Not yet, but you never know with this lot. Anything can happen in a night."

Ames nodded. They stood drinking. Finally he said, "Here, that young blond lad playing cards over there—he's not one of yours, is he?"

"Never seen that bloke before tonight. Why?"

"Ah, nothing. I reckon I might have known him someplace, that's all."

"So go ask him."

"Not likely."

"All right then, I will."

Jack went to leave but Ames grabbed his arm. "Don't."

"There history between you or something?"

"It's him what has the history, not me." He ducked his head a little, lowered his voice. "Crazy little cunt once killed a man down in St. George, a good man, station overseer on a place called Barren Downs. I was working there when he did it. We went out looking but never caught him. Kid was madder than a one-eyed dog."

Jack sipped his beer. "You sure that's him? Bloke could be anyone."

Ames was shaking his head furiously. "Look at that hand there, the fingers he's missing. Kid had the exact same thing. Blond hair, the ages match—bit more to say for himself now by the looks of it, but that's him as I live and breathe."

"Plenty blokes I've met are missing a finger or two."

"You're not listening to me. They never caught him, I said. Even put up a reward and everything, a good few hundred it was."

"Reward? Bit old for a bounty hunter, aren't you?"

"Cheeky bastard, what d'you reckon?" Ames said, laughing. "Right place, right time, more like. 'Bout bloody time my luck changed n'all."

Jack leaned into him. "So what you thinking?"

"Dunno. I've not really worked it through yet."

"Well, it might be I've a proposition for you. Young fella like that, big with it, no disrespect but you'll struggle on your own. Unless you've got a weapon?" Ames shook his head quickly and Jack showed him the two revolvers he carried on his belt. "What say we do it together, fifty-fifty, even shares?"

Ames weighed this carefully. "Where would we take him to collect?"

"There's the police barracks in Boulia, or just hold him here and send word."

They both watched Tommy. He threw down his cards, won the hand, roaring while the other players groaned. Jack noticed the lice twist and burrow in the tangle of Ames's beard. "All right," Ames said, nodding. He spat on his hand and offered it; Jack did the same and they shook.

Jack said, "We'll get him when he goes to the dunny, catch him with his pizzle in his hand," and the old man was racked with laughter that collapsed into a cough. Jack clapped him on the shoulder while he recovered himself, then offered him another beer for the wait.

Chapter 19
Billy and Katherine McBride

A little before sunset the coach trundled up the track and halted in front of the Broken Ridge homestead. The door opened and with great effort Magistrate MacIntyre heaved himself from the carriage, which groaned and rose on its axle once he was out. He glanced at the house above him then reached back inside for an ivory-handled walking cane, told the driver he wouldn't be long. He shuffled forward, then with a grunt of displeasure planted his foot on the staircase, his cane alongside it, and slowly began to climb.

Billy was alone in what used to be the library but now doubled as his billiards room, when Hardy knocked to say the magistrate had arrived. Billy thanked him and threw down his cue and managed to fluke a ball in. He snorted. He still wasn't any good at billiards, didn't even much care for the game, but everyone seemed to be playing it these days. In the homes of other graziers, in the city clubs, billiards had a habit of cropping up. He'd felt inadequate refusing, even more so not having his own table when people visited the house. So he had ordered one from Alcocks and at great expense had it brought out, and still that fluke was the best shot he'd played all day. He stubbed out his cigar and made for the door. He wondered what MacIntyre wanted— maybe he would fancy a game.

The magistrate had collapsed his bulk into one of the drawing room armchairs and from the way he struggled to rise when Billy entered, looked like he might have wedged himself in. "Don't get up, Spencer," Billy said, striding across the room, shaking his clammy hand. He was flushed in the face, his brow was beaded, and he finished every breath with a wheeze. Billy flopped onto the sofa, hooked his ankle onto his knee. "You run here or something?" he asked.

"I swear them steps are getting steeper, Billy. It's every time I come."

"Next time we'll have a boy carry you. You want a drink? Something to eat?"

"Whiskey if you have it, maybe some cake?"

Hardy was waiting in the doorway. Billy nodded, and he left the room. Billy went to the sideboard and poured them each a whiskey, handed one to MacIntyre; they touched glasses and, smirking, Billy toasted the magistrate's health.

"So," he said, sitting down again, "what's this about?"

MacIntyre gazed admiringly around the room: the polished furniture, exotic rug, the vases, silver, gold. "Seems you're faring all right, anyhow."

"We're getting by."

"I'll say. It's been a while, Billy. Not seen you in town."

Billy shrugged. "I've a station to run, can't be spending my nights drinking in the Bewley Hotel anymore."

"Wouldn't kill you," MacIntyre said. There was a knock at the door and the girl came in with a tray bearing two slices of ginger cake topped with a dollop of thickened cream. She handed them out and had not left the room before MacIntyre tore into his portion, attacking the thing like it had done him ill. Billy set his plate on the side table and waited, MacIntyre glancing up from his gorging, crumbs and cream coating his mouth. He pointed at the cake with his fork and spluttered, "You want to get stuck into this. Best damn cake I've had in months."

Billy ignored him. "So you're missing me, is that it? That's why you came all this way?"

MacIntyre shook his head, swallowed. "It's not me

I'm telling you for. People can get an idea about a fella if he thinks he's too good for their town. Which maybe you are these days, but it doesn't hurt to show your face once in a while."

"What do I care what they think of me down there?"

"You will if you ever need them. If you wanted them to side with you, let's say. The thing about John Sullivan, Billy, heartless bastard though he really was, is that he knew how to give people the impression he cared. Wouldn't have pissed on them if they were burning, yet they treated him like a king. Donations to the church and all that horseshit, you know what I mean. It's a question of reputation, which can be worth a lot out here. More than money sometimes."

"All right," Billy said vaguely. "So . . . I'll take a trip to town."

"Good lad, good lad. Here—you planning on eating that?"

Billy handed over his plate and MacIntyre devoured that portion of cake too. He wiped his lips with a napkin, missed the corners, cream gathering like spittle, then washed it down with the whiskey and sighed. Billy braced himself.

"So, there's something else I need to talk to you about."

"I figured. Trouble?"

"Might be, aye." MacIntyre sniffed and contemplated his whiskey. "I've had a telegram from Brisbane. Colonial secretary's office, no less. Ordering me to look into what happened to your family, hold a proper inquest, and not just the murders neither—I mean what came after, with the blacks. Seems someone's kicked the nest hard enough to get a reaction on the coast, and you know what those bastards are like. Apparently there's a witness reckons he saw what went on."

"What went on with what?"

"The natives. After."

"What fucking witness?"

"There's no name yet, but I'll find out soon enough. Some lawyer's bringing him out on the train."

Billy had flushed a deep crimson. He was sitting very still. "What the hell is this, Spencer? What's going on?"

He raised his hands. "Just what I'm telling you. And I don't have a choice about it, neither. An order comes from the top like that, it'll be my neck if I don't follow it through. Like I said, someone's been stirring. Got their attention too."

"But who—" Billy checked himself. "It's not Tommy, is it? This witness?"

"What makes you ask that?"

"Because every other witness is dead."

MacIntyre sipped his whiskey, let the silence run.

Billy's gaze slid away until it was dancing about the room, flicking madly over the walls.

"Do we have anything to worry about?" MacIntyre asked.

Billy blinked and came to. "How d'you mean?"

"Well, if there is a witness, what might he have seen?"

"Nothing. Don't you already know what went on?"

"I know what was in Inspector Noone's report, and them testimonies you and your brother swore. Aside from that, I don't really want to hear another word."

Billy froze at the name. "Does he know yet? Noone?"

"I expect so. He usually does."

"About this witness, I mean—that it wasn't me who turned?"

"Ah, don't worry about that, Billy. You're both on the same side here. As am I, incidentally, or else I wouldn't have come. Besides, Edmund Noone is a different man these days: got himself a nice little posting on the coast, heading for a career in politics, so I hear."

"Will he come? For the hearing?"

MacIntyre laughed. "He'll have to! It's him it's all about!"

"I thought you said it was the murders and everything?"

"Let's just take it one step at a time, shall we? That

testimony you and your brother gave—you'll stand by it, swear to it in court?"

"'Course I bloody will."

"And what about Tommy? You heard from him at all?"

"No."

"Well, that makes it easier. The fewer the better as far as I'm concerned. Them Brisbane bastards'll be watching my every step here, I've a good idea that's what this lawyer's about. So I'm going to have to do things properly, or make it look that way at least. Which means we have to tread bloody carefully, and make sure you all have your stories straight. Might be a good idea to have a read of that testimony again, and Noone's police report, refresh your mind a bit."

"You don't think I remember it all exactly?"

"Hell, Billy, not like that. What I mean is to get the little details clear in your memory: how many natives were there, what time of day, what weapons were they carrying, that kind of thing. Plus there's the business of what came after, what you lot did—it's all in the police report, but since I'll need you to confirm under oath that you agree with what it says, you may as well have a read of it first."

"Fine."

"Look, there's really nothing to worry about. These

inquests are a formality more often than not. I just need to know that you're not planning on saying anything that's not in them papers. If there's a problem, I want to hear it now."

Billy shook his head. "No, nothing."

"Good. Because memories can be slippery as fish, in my experience. Once you have them out the water, it pays to get them good and clubbed."

Billy frowned at his meaning: What was he on about, fish? He asked, "When is this hearing anyhow?"

"Next month sometime. The exact date's not been set. I'm supposed to do some investigating beforehand"—he raised his glass, almost empty—"which in its own good way this is, and them others will all need time to travel out."

Billy's attention drifted to the French doors and the sunset glowing pink through the voiles. "It's not a girl, is it? The witness—it's not a young native girl?"

"I told you, there's no name yet. And spare me the details, I don't want to know about any girl. Just stick to what's in them papers and I'll make sure everything works out fine. Which I'm sure you'll be only too willing to thank me for, once all this is put to bed."

The old judge was grinning wantonly. He motioned for a refill, but Billy only glared. "You'd best not be threatening me here, Spencer."

"No, lad, no. Not at all. But it's like I said earlier, a man's reputation counts for a lot in these parts. The last thing I'd want is for this inquest to cause you any harm. I remember all too well how it was for your father when his luck turned—I'd hate for you to end up the same way."

"I ain't nothing like him."

"Of course not. And I'm not your enemy here, neither. All I'm asking is that if I look out for you and your family this time, which I will, then one day you'll see your way to doing the same for me and mine. I've a retirement pot that needs taking care of. All contributions gratefully received."

Billy didn't answer, didn't refill his whiskey glass. He rang the bell and without waiting for the magistrate to lever himself out of the armchair, without shaking his greasy hand, sprang to his feet and marched out of the drawing room, instructing Hardy when they crossed in the hallway to show their guest the door.

From William's bedroom window Katherine had seen the magistrate arrive at the house, then after half an hour leave again, hobbling down the steps with his walking cane, heaving himself into his carriage and trundling off along the track. He'd looked anything

but happy. Unlikely he'd brought good news. She wondered if the missing stableboy had been stupid enough
to go to the law, though surely he knew he'd get no
justice there. Or here, obviously—nobody had seen
him since the flogging in the yard. It pained her that
Billy had run him off like that. The boy had been with
them for years.

She turned from the window and checked on William, sleeping in his bed, the sheets pulled tight around
his chest. He'd not been right since. Sweating a fever
constantly, cuts to his hands and face. For three days
now he'd refused to leave his bedroom, not since it happened, save that first evening when he'd sat slumped
at the dining table with his head in his hand, pushing
his food around the plate, Billy asking in all seriousness what was wrong. He still wasn't eating properly.
Showed no interest in his piano or books. He'd been
getting the most terrible nightmares, waking petrified
and slick with sweat; last night Katherine had slept in
the room with him and had been jolted awake by his
screams. She'd sat him upright and talked to him and
he'd stared through her like she wasn't there. At least
now he was resting peacefully. Progress, of sorts. On
her way out of the room she paused, stroked his hair,
lightly smoothed down the sheets.

The maid was tidying the drawing room, collecting whiskey glasses and crumb-scattered side plates and loading them onto a tray. Of course there would have been whiskey. Not a day went by that Billy didn't drink. And always the best, the same labels John had bought. That wasn't the only similarity. The way he dressed, how he spoke sometimes, how he treated his men; her first husband had beaten his share of servants too. Billy was twenty-nine but acted forty, and despite their success moped about like a put-upon mule. He was never happy, never satisfied, and was a shadow of the man she had married: the rough-talking stockman trampling his own path through the world, taking shit from no one, particularly her father; oh, the glory of his expression when Billy had pinned him against that wall. And now look at him. Whiskey glasses and cake crumbs after a visit from the judge; that ridiculous billiards table he had bought. She noticed the ashtrays were empty. A wonder there'd not been cigars.

The maid told Katherine that Billy was outside, a wall of warm air hitting her as she opened one of the glass French doors. Out she stepped, onto the verandah, the crimson sky already sliding into dusk. Hardy hadn't lit the outside lanterns yet. Might have been leaving Billy in peace. That was another decision they had argued over: getting rid of poor Benjamin so he could bring in a white butler, but by the time Katherine had found out about it, Benjamin was gone and it was already too late.

She heard a cough from round the corner, a hock and a spit; noticed a plume of tobacco smoke drifting on the air. Slowly she walked along the front of the house and around to the side verandah, where she found Billy leaning on the railing, watching the fading sunset, the dim outline of the ranges in the faraway west. His head hung when he saw her. Another drag on his cigarette. He was smoking in that old style John had taught him: hand cupped, thumb and forefinger pinching the end. She stood alongside him, said, "So, what did he want?"

"Who?"

"I saw the carriage, Billy."

He sniffed, drew on the cigarette. "He reckons I should go to Bewley more often. Apparently they're starting to turn on me in town."

"Why?"

"I'm too up myself for their liking, Spencer says."

"Maybe he has a point." She'd said it lightly, teasing; Billy glared at her side-on. Katherine said, "And? What else?"

"There was nothing else."

She looked at him doubtfully. Billy only shrugged. On the railing beside him was a full tumbler of whiskey; he drank then offered it over, and Katherine took two sips: one that set her mouth on fire then another to put out the flames. But God, it was good whiskey. She felt the flush rising, handed back the glass.

"I thought it might have been about the stableboy. He's still not come back."

"He can please himself what he does, he ain't welcome here."

"He'd be perfectly entitled to report you," she said haughtily, and Billy laughed like this was a joke. She didn't push it. They'd already had this argument, and Billy still couldn't see what he'd done wrong. He was protecting their son, he'd insisted; wouldn't she have done the same thing? Katherine lowered her voice and told him, "William's sleeping, anyway. Let's hope he has a better night."

"Boy has a fall and you treat him like he's lost a bloody leg."

"He's still terrified, Billy. Not that you would know. Nightmares, fever—he's hardly stopped shivering since."

"He's soft as horseshit that one. Needs a good shake." She turned away and Billy protested, "Look, one day this whole place will be his to run, and those men n'all. He can't afford to stand there crying when he falls off his horse."

"He's not even seven years old. A child. None of that's his concern."

"Well it should be. The boy has it too easy. When I was his age—"

"When you were his age you could barely spell your own name, I'd bet. He's a gifted learner, Billy. Mr. Daniels told me so himself."

"Aye, and that teacher's another one could do with knowing his place."

"At least he encourages him. You humiliated William the other day. He's so desperate to please you and look what you did. You're too hard on him by far."

"And you're too soft. Filling his head with dreams."

"What dreams?"

"That learning'll get him anywhere. That books can teach him about the world. That he doesn't have to work for nothing because the work's already been done . . . that playing the bloody piano is more important than riding a horse."

"I never told him any of those things. I'm just trying to give him the kind of opportunities the two of us never had."

"The two of us? Grow up poor now, did you?"

"Billy, don't."

"What? How many nights have you gone to bed hungry in your life?"

"And how many nights were you forced to lie under a man who repulsed you? A man twice your age, grunting in your face, between your legs, and all with your own father's blessing, because since when does the woman get a say? We've both suffered, it's not a competition to see who's had it worse. All I'm saying is that William shouldn't have to—don't you agree?"

Billy was quiet a moment. He sipped his drink, mumbled, "The boy needs to learn how to become a man."

"A man like you, you mean?"

"Of course like me. You got someone else in mind?"

"You could just let him be himself."

"He's an embarrassment, a joke among the men. All of them laughing at him, even the bloody stableboy was joining in!"

She scoffed and shook her head. "Has it honestly never occurred to you that it wasn't William they were laughing at, Billy, but you?"

He turned on her so sharply that Katherine flinched, shying from a blow that never came. He hadn't hit her yet, but he could have, they were both well aware of that. God knows, the other day had proved it. There was violence in Billy, Katherine had seen it, burning right there in his eyes. She'd always believed it was a virtue, a strength. The men she had grown up around were cowards compared to him. But the way it flared up in him these days, the way he looked at her sometimes . . .

"Sorry," she said. "I didn't mean that how it sounded. Look, will you at least talk to William? Make things right?"

Billy finished his cigarette, ground it roughly on the rail. "I've more important things to be worrying about."

"More important . . . ? Such as?"

He paused and looked directly at her for the first time since she arrived, like he was only now properly seeing her, weighing something in his mind. "There's to be an inquest," he said quietly. "That's why Spencer came. He's been told to look into the killings, what went on at the house. And then afterward, when we rode out with John and them, raking over their fucking graves. He says I'll have to testify. Noone's a part of it too."

His name hung between them like a taboo. Neither had spoken of the man in years. Katherine said, "Has something happened?"

"Apparently there's some witness, I don't bloody know."

"A witness to what, though?"

The question briefly stalled him. He dismissed it, waved a hand. "Ah, it's all horseshit anyway. It's me that's the victim here, my family they killed. We don't have nothing to worry about, so Spencer says."

She remembered sitting with Tommy immediately after, right there on the front steps, talking things over, Tommy nursing his bandaged hand. *"Do you know what went on out there?"* he had asked her, and Katherine thought she already did. Clearly there'd been fighting, given the injuries they'd sustained, and since there'd not been any arrests she'd assumed at least some Kurrong must have been killed. The rest were driven into the center, or so she'd been told. The men had come home happy, anyway. John, Noone, Raymond Locke. There'd been drinks in the drawing room and a feast of a meal, though when she'd asked about the details, about what they'd done, Noone had raised his finger and silenced her like a precocious little girl.

"But . . . there must be something in it, or why have a hearing at all?"

"It's nothing. A formality. I just told you."

"You also said you're more worried about it than your own son."

He saw off the whiskey and winced, sucked in a breath through his teeth. "Yeah, well, he's a lost cause, that one. Anyway, look at me—happy as a pig in shit."

He flashed a forced grin and walked past her, along the verandah and inside. Katherine stepped up to the railing. Miles of sloping pasture before her, a tranche of ragged scrubland, the low outline of the ranges barely visible beyond. The sun had fallen below the horizon, the sky a sloughy mix of purple and gray. All was darkness out there. She had never been that far into the center, could hardly imagine it; in truth she didn't dare. A shiver passed through her and she held herself, the skin on her arms pimpling though it was anything but cold, then, still clutching herself tightly, she turned and followed her husband back into the house, for where else did she have to go?

Chapter 20
Tommy McBride

Tommy threw down his cards, collected his winnings, announced he was in need of a piss. The men gave him grief for quitting. He laughed and told them to go to hell. Weaving among the tables, a little unsteady on his feet, through the back door and across the dark yard to the outhouse, a simple shed divided into two narrow stalls. One of the doors was missing. Tommy used the other side. Humming while he did his business, closing his nose against the stench, a fly-filled fog of human waste. He buckled himself and came out gasping, only to find Jack Kerrigan and another man—some bearded old coot—waiting in the yard. He was about to warn them off the outhouse, tell them they were better pissing outside, when he noticed the revolver dangling in Jack's right hand.

"What's this? There a problem?"

"You're fucked, mate," the old fella said, smirking. "And we're about to make ourselves bloody rich."

Tommy looked at Jack, who nodded toward the stranger. "Bloke here reckons he knows you from out east, Bobby. Says you killed the overseer on some sheep station near St. George."

"I told ye, they call him Tommy: Tommy bloody McBride."

"That true?" Jack asked. "That your real name?"

Tommy's gaze slid to the ground.

"And what about this overseer?"

"I pushed him. It was an accident. He'd have shot me otherwise."

Jack looked up at the heavens and let out a deep sigh, then raised his revolver sideways to the old man's temple. He flinched and cowered away, flashing panicked glances at Jack. "Hey now, take it easy, didn't I tell you it was him?"

"You know this snake from back then, Bobby?"

In the gloom of the yard Tommy peered at him, thinking back through all those years. Barren Downs was mostly a blur to him, cut through with memories so vivid and stark they still stung. Cal Burns giving him a kicking, the faces gathered round . . . and among them this man now in front of him, beardless back then maybe, or less unkempt at least, his toothless mouth gaping, that same half-cooked look in his eyes. He'd been at the breakfast table the morning Cal Burns was killed. Alan Ames was his name.

"Yeah, I know him," Tommy said.

"See! I told ye! Wait—are yous two some kind of mates?"

"Well, shit," Jack said wearily. "I never thought it would end like this."

"End what? How d'you mean?" Tommy asked, panic rising, though surely he already knew. Unlikely as it seemed he'd been made by this man: after all this time, out here in the middle of nowhere, in front of the dunny for Christ's sake, his past had finally caught him up. He'd been a fool to assume it wouldn't, lulled into a life that couldn't last. Of all the ways it could have happened: Alan fucking Ames.

Jack said, "You're gonna have to run, mate."

"Hold up now. You ain't cutting me out of that reward money, you bastard. A deal's a fucking deal!"

"You shut your mouth before I put a hole in you. Bobby, listen—you have to leave. We don't know who else this bastard's talked to, or what he might do next."

"I ain't told no one, you're the first—"

Jack jabbed the revolver hard against Ames's skull. He yelped and stood rigid. Jack said, "Take a couple of horses and whatever supplies you need and get out of here tonight. Head west, Bobby. Stick to the trails you know best."

Tommy gawped dumbly. He didn't know any trails out west, and was this really how the two of them were going to part? A flash of hatred surged through him for this fucker, Alan Ames, who had enjoyed his every humiliation back then, and no doubt joined the posse looking to lynch him after he'd fled St. George. Now here he was, years later, trying to do it all again. Well, Tommy wouldn't let him. He'd rather take the bastard into the scrubs, shoot him and put him in the ground— nobody would find him, nobody would know. It shocked him how easily he thought it. But then, was it really so hard? He had seen it done, many times: men put down like troublesome dogs. And he could do it, he realized suddenly, if that's what it came to.

"Bobby? Did you hear me? It's time to move, mate—go!"

"What about him?"

Jack turned to look at the old swagman on the end of his revolver, Ames's attention flitting between the two of them. "Me and my new friend here are going to go inside and sink a few more beers and forget this conversation ever took place. If he likes he can join my plant for a while, assuming he ain't afraid of hard work—"

"Hell, I been working my whole goddamned life."

"—and can handle cattle as well as sheep. But, if them terms don't suit him, then I'm going to have to keep him here a while longer, and find another way of convincing the snaky bastard to keep his mouth shut."

Ames was nodding furiously. Tommy stared at Jack. He still had his right arm extended, his revolver raised; they couldn't shake hands or embrace without risking Ames getting away. Warmly, Jack smiled at him, the full Jack Kerrigan grin, and it dawned on Tommy that most likely they'd never see each other again. He would find himself looking out for him, in hotels, roadhouses, brothels, whenever he crossed a droving trail; he'd skim the obituaries half-expecting to find his name. He never did. This would be the last contact he ever had with Jack, this man who had saved his life the first time they met and one way or another had been saving it every day since.

"Thank you," he said. "For everything."

"On you go now. Take care of yourself."

"I mean it. You've been—"

"Mate, I've been standing here with my arm out for long enough as it is. Get the horses and the rest of it, and get yourself west."

Tommy nodded. A struggle to move his feet. He felt sick at the thought of leaving—he'd rather kill Ames than start his life all over again. But Jack would never allow it. He was far too principled for that. Either way, Tommy would lose him, and he'd rather keep their friendship intact.

"So long then," he said, moving past them. "Good luck with everything."

He was almost out of the yard when Jack called "Tommy!" and the shock of hearing his name after all this time, especially from Jack, made him pull up sharply and turn. Jack was looking back at him, over his shoulder, silhouetted in the shadows, his revolver extended; Tommy thought he saw the moonlight glisten in his eyes. "It's been bloody good knowing you. There aren't many out there, as you well know, but remember you're one of the good ones, eh?"

Chapter 21
Henry Wells

The coach arrived in Bewley, and like shipwrecked survivors Henry Wells and Reverend Bean staggered out of the carriage and, in the glare of the brutal sunshine, surveyed the little town. Two rows of mismatched storefronts: crooked verandahs, hand-painted signs, window stencils peeling and frayed. The townspeople silently watched them. Wind whipped dust devils along the sand-and-gravel street. A dog came sniffing by. From the verandah of the hotel opposite someone called out, "Welcome, m'lords!" and like some windup diorama the town clicked back to life again.

Henry cringed at the state of it. It was as dismal a place as he had ever seen. Already his skin was prickling in the unrelenting sun; the very air smelled like it was burning, tinged with a foul odor of shit, sweat, and slop. Beside him, Reverend Bean was pirouetting back and forth, memories assaulting him like blows— "Yes, yes, that's the courthouse, and there's the little church . . ."—the town exactly as he had described it, and so pathetic, so innocuous, given the secrets it held.

A man pushing a squeaking handcart paused and spat at their feet.

"Come on," Henry said quietly, picking up his bags and making for the hotel, Reverend Bean tripping along after him, still twisting himself in knots. He had brought no luggage, boarding the train in Brisbane with only the clothes he stood up in, and an enormous canteen of rum that he'd suckled all journey like a teat. Three trains, two coaches, four miserable days and nights—what Henry needed most, beyond a bath and a meal, was a break from Reverend Bean. The man was insufferable. As was this heat. After crossing the tablelands outside Brisbane and the arable majesty of the Darling Downs, the country had descended into a rolling hellscape of scorched red earth and incessant sun. Henry didn't know how people stood it, living out here; through the gaps between the buildings he could still make out that endless scrub, the town a tiny atoll in an ocean of desert plains. And now they too were marooned here. Christ, he thought, this better be worth it. We'd better bloody win.

One of the drinkers whistled as they came up the

hotel steps. Nobody parted to let them past. "Excuse us, please, gentlemen," Henry said, squeezing through, into the bar. They presented themselves at the counter— Henry had written ahead—and the bald publican handed over their room keys. No welcome, no pleasantries, sullenly sliding the two fobs over with a large, hairy hand.

"We will eat first, I think," Henry told him, "assuming you offer meals. An early dinner while hot water is boiled and taken up to our rooms."

Horace stared right through him. As if he'd not spoken a single word. In the long mirror Henry noticed Reverend Bean ogling the drinks shelf, and added, "Oh, and one more thing. My companion here is not to be served alcohol without my say-so. Not a drop, you understand? He has no money, not a penny to his name, and I shall not be footing his bill. If you serve him you might as well tip your liquor down the drain—do I make myself clear?"

"If you like," Horace said, glancing at the reverend, who winked at him. Henry swept up the keys. He ordered a carafe of red wine to go with the food, water for Reverend Bean, and found a table near the little raised stage at the back of the room. Quiet in here this afternoon: a man mournfully smoking, another playing dominoes alone. Henry poured the wine, Reverend Bean staring, watching every drop.

"Just one glass," he pleaded. "Something to wash down the meal."

"Water's not wet enough for you?"

"You know what I mean."

"I do," Henry said. "I have seen the very worst of you these past few days. You are an addict, Francis, you have absolutely no self-control. But I will need you at your best on the stand."

"My best," he echoed, laughing.

"Sober, then."

"I wouldn't be any use to you if I was."

"I will take my chances. It will have to suffice."

"Truthfully, Henry, I'm more likely to soil myself. I am nothing without the drink—sobriety is far from a pretty sight."

And this the man, Henry reminded himself, on whom the whole case hung. He smiled in an attempt to make light of the admission. "Well, of course you would say that. Anything to weaken my resolve."

"But you've seen me. You said so yourself. I'm in purgatory here. Please, Henry. Just to help me settle. It's been terrible these past few days."

Henry sighed and looked about. The smoking man was watching them, the other still engrossed in his dominoes. He could certainly agree with the reverend on that much, though it had felt more like damnation than purgatory to him. Baking in their train carriage, lying awake in his rickety bunk, Reverend Bean moaning and thrashing beneath him, no chance of sleep; then for two days being ceaselessly jiggered about in that coach, the reverend taken ill from withdrawal, vomiting out the window since the driver wouldn't stop. Henry could well sympathize. He'd been craving a drink himself.

"All right. Just the one glass. Help calm you down."

Reverend Bean pounced on the wine and gulped it, spilling drops on his chin and shirtfront. "Thank you," he gasped. "Truly."

Henry watched the color seep back into his cheeks. He had never met a man so contradictory. Pious yet morally bankrupt, with a strange near-childlike innocence given all he'd seen. He refilled the wineglass and noticed the reverend's gaze wander fearfully around the room. "Now what?" Henry asked.

Reverend Bean leaned closer. "What if he's already here?"

"Who?"

"*Him.*"

Henry laughed. "And? What if he is?"

"I told you what he once threatened me with."

"Twelve years ago, Francis. The man is now a harmless bureaucrat well into his middle years. You have nothing to fear there."

Henry concealed the lie with a long drink. He still hadn't shaken off his meeting with Edmund Noone, how he had somehow seen right through him; those deathly hollow eyes. Every day since the inquest was ordered he had waited for the reprisal: an anonymous letter to Laura, some thug putting him against a wall. There'd been nothing. As if Noone was only too happy to participate. Tempting to think he had the man running scared but he doubted it. Noone didn't seem the kind.

"You don't know what he's capable of," Reverend Bean was saying. "When I saw him in that desert, when I looked into those eyes . . ."

"Calm yourself, Francis. You came to me, remember, nobody forced you to do this. If you truly felt that way you would not have spoken up in the first place, or else why are we even here?"

"Isn't it obvious?"

"Well it's clearly not a crisis of conscience. You are hardly a reformed man."

Reverend Bean glanced at the wine. Henry relented, nodded, and this time Bean savored the flavor, his eyes closed. He opened them again and said, "I am dying, Mr. Wells, if you haven't noticed. I have drunk myself to an early grave. Which means that in short order I shall be standing before God attempting to justify myself, and what on earth will I say? If I do nothing, my soul is forsaken, since by then it will be too late. So I am trying. Redemption, forgiveness, these are always selfish acts. I am no different. I'm here to save myself."

Henry took a moment to process this. Indeed, it was obvious, now that he'd said it, how ill the man really was; perhaps Henry just hadn't wanted to see. He cleared his throat and asked him, "And that is worth crossing Noone for, in your eyes?"

Wearily, Reverend Bean smiled. "Like I said, I am dying—what do I have to lose?"

That night Henry lay tossing in his bedsheets, impossible to get to sleep. The sheets smelled of mildew, the mattress was misshapen, the pillow lumpen, the room was both stifling and damp. Moonlight blazed through the threadbare curtains and cast long shadows on the floor, bursts of laughter and voices coming up from the bar below. He flipped over and lay stewing. No such problems for Reverend Bean—Henry could hear him snoring through the wall. He sighed and tried to settle. Think of the case . . . think of the case. Tomorrow he would meet the magistrate, ask some questions around town; he would get a shave and haircut, and buy Reverend Bean a new suit. Off-cuts only. The cheapest and closest fit. Certain expenses might be reclaimable, others not, but this was all an investment in Henry's eyes. Any finding of impropriety against

Chief Inspector Noone, any at all—which in the circumstances should be an obscenely low bar for the
magistrate to clear—paved the way for a criminal prosecution, and that was when the real fun would begin.
They could charge him back in Brisbane, try him in
the Supreme Court, with all the pomp and ceremony,
and surely it would be Henry's case to bring. He was
the one who had been out here, laid the groundwork,
seen this place for himself. He knew the case and had
the trust of the key witness: Reverend Bean wouldn't
confide in anyone else. And he would win, goddamnit,
he would put that bastard away, the first time it had
ever been done . . . and Henry's career, his whole life,
would be transformed.

All this misery would be worth it. His very own
Trials of Hercules.

What with the snoring and the noise from downstairs and the chatter of his own thoughts, Henry didn't
hear the click of the door along the hall. He'd got his
bearings muddled: the snoring wasn't coming from
Reverend Bean's room. Instead the reverend had been
pacing, waiting for Henry to fall asleep, figured surely
he'd have dropped off by now. He closed the door gently,
padded barefoot down the stairs. He was wearing only
his trousers, and there was an uproar when people saw
him (Henry smothering himself with his pillow at the

sudden surge of noise), someone yelling was this shitty burlesque? Behind the bar Horace folded his arms until from a small slit in his waistband Reverend Bean teased out a crumpled banknote. He smoothed it on the counter and Horace reached down for a glass.

"What'll it be?" the publican asked him.

"Just give me the bottle," Reverend Bean said.

He couldn't be roused the next morning. Henry rattled the handle and banged on the door but heard coming from inside Reverend Bean's room the kind of choked apneic snoring only brought on by grog. Downstairs he thundered, found Horace clearing the bar, and snapped at him, "I told you no alcohol! He's three sheets to the wind up there!"

Horace straightened. "There a problem?"

"I warned you yesterday. Said explicitly not to serve him a drink."

"We're a hotel, mate. Serving drinks is what we do."

"But . . . he doesn't even have any money."

"Had plenty on him last night."

This stalled Henry. It didn't take him long. All this time together, sharing train carriages and sleeper berths . . . of course he had, the sneaky bastard. His anger deflated, he felt a fool. "Stolen from me, no doubt."

"None of my business where he got it."

"Please, don't indulge him anymore. I assume you know why we're here?"

"Word gets round."

"Then you know how important it is I have him dry tomorrow."

"I don't give a shit either way, mate. I just want to get paid."

Horace was making eyes at Henry and finally he caught on. He peeled a note from his money clip and handed it over. "So, we have an understanding?"

"If you like."

"Good, now, perhaps you can help me: I'll find Magistrate Spencer MacIntyre at the courthouse, I assume?"

Horace chuckled. "If he bothers going in."

"And if not?"

"The big house round the back there. Biggest one there is."

"I'm obliged to you. And what about two brothers named McBride?"

A beat before Horace answered: "Never heard of them."

"Really? Two young boys, their parents were killed?"

Horace shook his head, frowning.

"Oh, I see," Henry said brightly, warming to the game. He peeled off another note from his money clip but Horace raised a hand.

"I never heard of them, I just told you. Look, I'd best be getting on."

The barber gave him the same answer, and the waitress in the roadhouse café; people ignored his greetings but their eyes followed him constantly around town. In the tailor's he asked the proprietor how long he'd lived in Bewley and the old man told him proudly, "All my life. I was born in that back room." But when he brought up the subject of the McBride murders the man's lips tightened and he shook his head. Henry didn't push it. Clearly this was how it was going to be. For no good reason he could put his finger on, he had assumed the locals would welcome this inquest, that they'd be grateful he had come. Uncovering a hidden tragedy, rooting out injustice in their town. The idea now seemed ridiculous. At least it wasn't a jury trial.

He banged on the doors of the courthouse and stood waiting in the oppressive sun—not yet ten o'clock and already the heat was feverish and close. He dabbed his neck, knocked again, people brazenly watching from the street. Henry smiled and nodded; dumbly, they simply stared. They were a different breed out here, he was realizing. Simple-minded, truculent, docile. He had a new appreciation for Brisbane. It was the height of sophistication compared to this.

Nobody answered at the courthouse, so he followed

an alleyway around back and on a large plot behind the main street found the magistrate's house: an elegant, raised, white residence in the classic Queenslander style, not too dissimilar to his own. He climbed the steps and rang the handbell. Shortly, a maid arrived.

"Yes, good morning. Magistrate MacIntyre please."

Laughter washed through from inside. Two men, it sounded like. The maid nodded and went back there and Henry heard one of them ask irritably for his name. Of course she couldn't tell him—he'd not volunteered it and she hadn't asked—and for the first time that morning Henry felt a small flush of progress. He might need to be cannier if he was going to get anywhere here. The speaker excused himself. There was a valise on the floor inside the doorway, good leather, monogrammed. The magistrate must have been entertaining a guest. Heavy footsteps along the hallway, then the door was wrenched open and a great walrus of a man was standing before him: flush-faced, wild-haired, bloodshot eyes, wearing a fine gray morning suit expertly tailored to his bulk. He scowled at Henry and barked, "Yes? Who are you?"

"Henry Wells, sir, out from Brisbane, for the inquest."

MacIntyre shook his hand reluctantly. "So you're the lawyer," he said.

"Indeed. A pleasure, I am sure."

"Are you now. Well, you're early. Hearing's not till tomorrow."

He went to close the door but Henry blocked the way. "I thought it might be helpful for us to talk before then."

"What about?"

"Everything. You received the reverend's testimony, I take it?"

"Aye, only yesterday mind you."

"I mailed it well before we left."

"Things move slower out here, Mr. Wells, if you haven't noticed."

"My apologies. And my telegrams? You never replied."

"No, well, I'm a busy man. Until tomorrow then."

"Magistrate, please. I am at something of a loss here. There are significant gaps in my understanding of this case, matters to which the reverend cannot testify. The McBride killings, for example—I found barely any mention in the press."

"A private matter. Now if you'll excuse me."

Again he tried to close the door and again Henry stopped him, wedging his foot against the sill. MacIntyre glared at him.

"You're hardly helping yourself here."

"Sir, I have every right to—"

"You have the right to fuck-all is the truth of it. What d'you think this is?"

"The colonial secretary has authorized my full participation in—"

"Yes, yes, I got that message too. But this is my inquest, my town. As far as I'm concerned you are an observer like anyone else. And a chaperone for the witness, of course. I don't know what your agenda is here, Mr. Wells, why you are dredging this all back up, but if I were you I would watch my step."

"My agenda? To uncover the truth, surely no different from yours?"

A stillness came over the magistrate. He stepped forward and backed Henry out of the door, his little eyes burning, so close now Henry could smell his cologne, thick and woody and stale, and began jabbing a fat finger in his chest.

"I've made myself clear on the subject. Now get off my bloody porch."

He fared little better with his questions around town: nobody would talk about the Kurrong people, or what had happened to the McBrides, at most an expression of sympathy, a remorseful head-shake, before they clammed up or ushered him back outside. He didn't have to introduce himself. They all knew who he was, and what he wanted—he had the distinct impression folks had been warned off, and in the general store the little German shopkeeper all but admitted as much. After shaking hands with Henry and trying to sell him some cheese, Spruhl told him, "Billy McBride is very important man these days. Very dangerous friends."

So that's what was going on here. They weren't just reluctant, but afraid.

The doctor was at least more civil, eager for news from Brisbane, grateful for the company of another educated man, then when Henry began asking questions he sighed and his eyes glazed. "A terrible business, all that, it really was. I still wish I could have done more to help." He knew few of the details but did at least provide an address for Billy McBride: Broken Ridge cattle station, a few hours northwest of town. Henry excused himself and ran to the livery stables, where a coachman and stablehand sat smoking on stools in the stinking, hay-strewn barn. Panting, Henry asked about a ride up there. "Coach ain't running," the driver said.

Henry looked at the carriage standing ready on its chocks and the team of horses feeding in the stalls. "I'll pay you double fare," Henry offered. "Please."

"I just told ye. It ain't running."

"Triple then," he said, pointing. "The thing's right there!"

"Bloke really wants to get up to Broken Ridge," the stableman said.

"Don't blame him, Jonesy. Nice country out that way."

"Aye, nice country. Nice people too."

The stableman slid his hands into his coveralls and spat messily on the ground, and Henry sighed at the sheer hopelessness of it all. He'd been so naive. In his mind he'd imagined extracting confessions from reluctant witnesses, maybe even visiting the crater with Reverend Bean. Instead, nobody would talk to him and Reverend Bean lay drunk in his bed, the crater was weeks away, and Henry couldn't even manage to get himself up to Broken Ridge. He could try to walk, he supposed, but had no stomach for it. Heading out into that bush alone could be a death sentence. He had underestimated everything. Misread the entire situation. Meaning tomorrow he'd be walking into that courtroom with no more than he already had, plus a fire in his belly and a refusal to be cowed. It didn't feel like much but would have to be enough. He'd won other cases with less.

Through the dusty town he wandered, the sun like a blade in his back, one end to the other, toward that elusive west. "You lost, mate?" someone heckled. "Brissie's that way!" another yelled, ripples of laughter trailing him along the street. He walked past Song's

Hardware Store, where a slender young woman swept her porch with a broom, then stood at the very fringe of Bewley, looking over a country as hostile and bleak as anything on this earth. Miles of barren scrubland, that angry bloodred soil, knotty tangles of weed and grass and the arthritic skeletons of dead trees. It awed him and terrified him and made him feel very alone. He shouldn't be out here. This was no place for a man like him. He thought of Jonathan, back in Brisbane, the cozy comfort of his little flat, and even of Laura and the children, their loyalty and affection, their familiar presence in his life, and wished for home.

Along the track he drifted, toward the native camps, drawn by the outline of people moving and the smoke from cooking fires. He peered into the humpies from the safety of the road, hesitantly waved; they froze when they saw him, some hid.

"Please," Henry called, his hand extended, "I'm a lawyer, here for the inquest. I only wondered if I could talk a moment, about the Kurrong, about—"

"Fuck off with you. You bastards are all the same."

The bearded old man came at him through the fire smoke, his stick swinging wildly, beating Henry back toward the road. Fending off the blows, Henry retreated, saying, "No, please, I can help, but I need to know what happened."

"They know," the old man shouted, pointing his stick at the town. "All them bastards know—we don't want your help here." He shouldered the stick like a rifle, pointed it at Henry and, his damp eyes burning, mimicked the recoil: bang, bang, bang. Henry shuddered. The old man said, "What d'you reckon bloody happened to 'em, they just fucked off on their own?"

His stare went right through Henry. Utter fury in his face. Henry edged away, along the road, back in the direction of town, the old man watching him go. "Ask Billy McBride if you're that keen," he yelled after him. "He knows what he done."

Reverend Bean was awake when Henry got back to the hotel, and for the rest of the day Henry busied himself with the task of ironing him out straight. A haircut and shave at the barber, his suit bought and fitted, going over his testimony again. They shared a carafe of wine over dinner, to calm both their nerves, but when they retired to bed that evening Henry made the reverend hand over his room key and locked him in from the outside. "It'll all be over tomorrow," Henry assured him, through the doorjamb. "See you in the morning, Francis. Get some rest. Sleep well."

Dead of night a noise woke him: Henry Wells snatched open his eyes. He lay listening to the silence, the yips and howls from outside, and realized with a start he wasn't alone. He could hear breathing. The whisper of clothes. He lifted his head and saw a figure in the armchair at the foot of his bed, guessed it was Reverend Bean before remembering he had locked him in; he thought he'd locked himself in too. The figure shifted slightly. Only a shape in the darkness: tall, broad shoulders, no hat. His leg was jigging frantically and he was wringing something in his lap. Henry pushed himself up to sitting, leaned against the iron headboard, and for a moment the two of them sat like that, watching each other in the scant moonlight.

"Is it money you're after?" the stranger asked him. "Is that what this is about?"

"Money? What? Who are you?"

"You know who I am, you bastard. Been asking after me all over town. Don't do nothing stupid now." And he waved the revolver he was holding like a flag.

"Mr. McBride? Billy McBride?"

"Answer the bloody question."

"My name, sir, is Henry Wells and I'm a lawyer out from—"

"What I asked is why are you here?"

"For the inquest, tomorrow, when we shall—"

Billy lunged to the bedside and leveled the revolver at Henry's head. A glimpse of him in a bar of moonlight, his face twisted and snarling, dark hair and a short dark beard, before Henry clamped his eyes shut and hardly dared to breathe.

"I should shoot you and be done with it. End this circus right now."

"No, please, wait. I am here because . . . because a witness came to see me, about the Kurrong people. The colonial secretary ordered an inquest, and for me to come out—that is all, I swear."

"That was twelve bloody years ago. What you raking it all up for now?"

"I know, but the law demands . . . please, could you lower the gun?"

Footsteps, and Henry cracked open an eye. Billy returned to the armchair, hooked an ankle over his knee, lit a cigarette and exhaled. He sat there smoking, hurried little drags, while Henry trembled faintly in his bed.

"Who's the witness?" Billy asked finally.

"They didn't tell you?"

"Would I be asking if they had?"

"I'm not sure I'm at liberty to say."

"If you like, I'll put a bullet in your kneecap, see if you're at liberty then."

"Reverend Francis Bean. He was a missionary. He met you all out there."

It took Billy a moment to register, then: "The *priest?*"

"Yes, exactly. He says he saw the most terrible things."

Billy blew out smoke incredulously, crushed the cigarette on the floor. "That's who's behind all this? That fucking choirboy? Twelve years after the fact?"

"He remembers it all exactly."

"He never saw a thing!"

"He went back, saw the crater, what you did."

Billy unfolded his legs and leaned forward, elbows on his knees, wagging the barrel of the revolver at Henry Wells. "How about I tell you what *I* saw, shall I? Is that what you're wanting, to hear me confess? All right, listen up: me and my little brother, sixteen and fourteen years old, go out swimming then come home and the whole family's been shot, bastards even ran through the dogs. Our daddy's got three holes blown in him front to back, Ma's had half her head took off, our little sister Mary's bleeding out under the bed. Now, how's that for a story? What's your priest have to say about that?"

"I'm truly sorry for what happened to your family. But they should have held a proper inquest at the time, established for certain what occurred that day."

"I just told you what fucking *occurred.* I was there."

"But you were children, and it seems to me others may have used your tragedy to commit yet further crimes. In your family's name, no less. Am I right?"

"Catching the killers was a crime in your eyes?"

"Of course not. But what about the others? A hundred, I heard?"

Billy straightened and shifted, then jumped up from the chair. He paced the length of the room then back again, the revolver swinging in his hand, muttering, "You can't even prove nothing. You've no idea what went on."

"I believe I do. And that I can."

Billy stopped abruptly. "You ain't got no right . . . what's all this to you anyway? What do you stand to gain?"

"Nothing. I already told you."

"Well then, how much would it cost to make you go away?"

"It's not really a question of money."

"Try me. Or I could just as easily shoot you and bury you and nobody round here would bat an eye."

"I'm sure that's probably true, but it wouldn't do you any good."

"Do you less."

"The inquest will continue, I mean. The wheels will

still turn. This goes to the highest level in Brisbane, they won't just stop for me. In fact, they'd probably only investigate all the harder."

An exaggeration, but Henry was gambling. Billy went to the window and looked out. "So if I can't pay you, or shoot you, how do I stop this thing?"

"Work with me. Testify. Tell them what really happened. We'll put Noone behind bars, or worse. Men have hung for far less."

Billy laughed and sat down and lit another cigarette. "Have you met him?"

"I have, yes."

"And you still think he'll hang?"

"He's a man like any other, subject to the laws of this land."

"You're a fucking idiot."

"Please, Mr. McBride, all I'm asking—"

"Do you have a family yourself, Henry?"

"Of course."

"Do you want to see them dead?"

"Now just a minute, that's completely uncalled for."

Billy blew out smoke and shrugged. "He wouldn't think so. In fact, he'd probably consider it rude to let them live. Christ Almighty, the balls on you, sitting there talking like this is some game. This is my life you're toying with. And yours. Them laws might work in Brisbane but they don't count for shit out here, at least not with a man like Noone."

"Which is precisely why he must be prosecuted."

"You're not listening. You'll get nothing out of it. You're wasting your time."

"Not if you testify. I guarantee that together we would win."

"Together," Billy sneered. He stubbed out the cigarette on the arm of the chair, rose slowly to his feet, went to the door and paused with his hand on the knob. "You ain't worth the dags on my arse hairs, you dumb fucking city cunt."

He left, and a breath washed out of Henry. Scrambling from the bed, he got to the door in time to see Billy plodding down the stairs. He fumbled around on the dresser for his key, found it there alongside Reverend Bean's, and his hand shaking wildly, slid it into the lock and turned it and heard the bolt click fast.

Chapter 22
Tommy McBride

In the still and silent night he left Urandangi, leading two spare horses behind him, the bags stuffed with whatever supplies he'd managed to find. He looked back at the hotel aglow in the darkness and imagined Jack in there with Alan Ames, strong-arming him to a table, the revolver pinning him in place, then plying him with drink till he passed out. With any luck he would wake late the next morning and agree to Jack's offer of work, groggily joining the group heading north. Worst case, he'd manage to slip away and raise the alarm, breathlessly explaining how he'd caught the fugitive Tommy McBride and that he was currently fleeing west, which would also suit Tommy just fine. Now he understood Jack's meaning. He didn't know any cattle trails out west. The only trail he knew well enough to attempt on his own was the one Jack had painstakingly taught him, trip after trip, as they'd droved it together all these years: the Georgina River and Eyre's Creek down to Birdsville, then the Birdsville Track to Marree. Long hungry days in the saddle, little or nothing to eat, many of the waterholes reduced to fly-infested puddles by the drought. He sucked up the water greedily, at times so clogged with sand and grit it was easier to chew than drink. At least there was no cattle to see to. Just himself and the horses, which each day he rode as hard and far as he dared.

When finally he reached the outskirts of Marree he paused on the plains overlooking the town, the familiar outline of the buildings, the peculiar silhouettes of the camel trains. It was so tempting. Collect the latest letter from Arthur, a meal among friendly faces; he could almost taste the beer. But they knew him in Marree better than anywhere these days: they had police, and a telegraph line, and all the risks those things entailed. So he kept a safe distance, too far away to be recognized, just another anonymous rider crossing the empty plains, and stopped instead in Farina, where he was one of many weary travelers passing through. He cleaned himself up, restocked and recuperated, gave the horses a chance to do the same, then set out south again, intending to head for Adelaide; he wanted to get his money out of that bank. But the longer he rode the more risky the city felt. There were more coppers in Adelaide than anywhere, and although Jack hadn't used his full alias in front of Ames, his description could well be out there: his fair hair like a beacon, his missing fingers a red cross painted on his shirt back. That left hand of his had plagued him ever since he'd hurt it, an unshakable reminder of what he'd done. Every time he rolled a cigarette, lifted a mug, took Beau's reins in his hands, he'd feel the tug of memory, or a snapshot of that morning would flash before his eyes. The native biting his fingers; the fight with Billy that tore one loose. He had broken Billy's nose that day—did his brother get the same flashbacks, Tommy wondered, when he saw his face in the looking glass?

He decided to avoid Adelaide, for now at least. Take his time about getting down there, let the urgency (if there was any) drain from the pursuit. High in the Flinders Ranges he built a camp on a tree-stubbled hillside beneath a sandstone ridge, rigging a canvas for shade and shelter, digging a stone-lined firepit beside a fallen tree trunk against which he could lean his back. There was water at the bottom of the hillside, and sometimes he managed to catch a fish, otherwise he did well for meat by hunting rock wallabies, goannas, roos. Evenings he would climb the ridge to a lookout and sit on the slab, smoking a cigarette and watching the sunset, the golden light receding over the plains. A certain peace being up here. Nothing like the last time he ran. He was far more capable for one thing, and he trusted Jack to deal with Alan Ames. He'd come a fair old distance. Bewley to St. George, St. George to Marree, and everywhere else in between. Half a continent nearly, and still plenty out there he hadn't seen. But he understood this country better now than he ever had: it was easier if you accepted the land was king. Most whites struggled because they fought it, tried to bend it to their will, but this wasn't a place that could be tamed. Better to live within it, alongside it, on its own terms—how long had the natives lived like that, happily, before the first boats came?

Summer arrived and he had to move on; the heat became unbearable in the hills. The hunting grew scarce and the water levels fell and he worried about the horses in the sun. So out of the ranges he wandered, like some hermit leading his caravan, only to run into a pair of boundary riders as he crossed what must have been station land. They asked where he was headed; Tommy said he was looking for work, if they had any, and one of the men considered the state of him and scoffed. "Doubt it," the other told him, "but there's food and hot water if you can pay for it—the boss don't take in no strays." With a nod Tommy followed them, and that night lay soaking in the first hot bath he'd had in months.

They bred horses as well as sheep on Bluewater, as he learned the station was called, and Tommy fell in with the trainers and breakers the next morning at the corral, talking about the different breeds and their temperaments, the particular characters each had known. Again Tommy asked if there was work going, horses or sheep, he didn't mind; and again the answer came back no. But he could stay on as a dogger, the manager told him, paid by the ear plus meals and a bed, assuming he could handle a rifle and didn't mind shooting dingos. "You got a spare rifle?" Tommy asked him, and the next day he found himself riding Beau through unfamiliar pastures on the lookout for his first kill.

It didn't take long to find one. A lone male skulking through the bush, the red-brown flash of its pelt. Tommy dismounted and hushed Beau with an outstretched hand; the horse nickered and snuffled the grass. Tommy moved forward, into the trees, the dingo lost to him for now. Another memory leaped up at him: hunting with Billy as children, trespassing beyond the blue gums and onto John Sullivan's land. He shook it off but they were coming after him, more and more these days. As if these years of droving, the summers in Adelaide, the drinking and carousing with Jack, had managed to pull a blindfold over his past, and now without those things to distract him the blindfold had been ripped clean off.

He followed the dingo to a shallow creek bed, watched it sniff the water and drink, ears twitching, Tommy creeping closer through the brush. He propped himself against a tree trunk and raised the rifle. It was already loaded. Heavy in his hands, warm against his cheek. He waited. His breathing slowed. Praying for a clean shot. The dingo lifted its head quickly then bent to the water again, Tommy telling himself not yet, not yet, but if not now then when? He fired. A roar from the rifle, the kick of the recoil, and the dog keeled over on its side. Another memory hit him. Catching that group of natives and a pack of wild dogs, Raymond Locke with a spear in his shoulder, putting one of the dogs down. Tommy cried out and slapped himself hard on the side of the head, as if to knock the memories loose, lurched to his feet and went down into the creek bed. The dingo lay dead in the water. Blood trickled away in the stream. Tommy took hold of its tail and heaved it up the creek bank and here came another one: Rabbit dragging the dead kangaroo out of the sand-drift, the other troopers applauding; "Good tucker these buggers. Yum yum!"—panting, Tommy propped his rifle against a tree and hacked off the dog's ear with his knife.

He left the dingo for the flies and birds and dropped the ear into the bloodied pouch the station manager had loaned. Sick to his stomach but he had no quit in him, not anymore. He shot another four that day and with each the memories peppered him like rain. Let them come. Let them soak him to the skin. It felt like a bloodletting, like leeching a poison from his veins. He deserved it, needed it, needed to remember so he could forget. There was a perverse catharsis in hunting, in claiming each death for himself.

They let him train the horses eventually, once they realized he was more skilled at it than their own men. All kinds they bred here: stock horses and draft horses, those that would spend a life pulling coaches and buggies; even racehorses occasionally, if they had one they could stud. To the surprise of the others he was able to break the odd brumby, as his father had once done, coaxing them into obedience and watching for that change that came over them, the fear and madness fading from their eyes. And from his also: drink here was hard to come by, certainly anything stronger than beer, and somehow he didn't miss it, didn't feel the cloying need. He worked the horses until sundown, ate a meal with the others—quiet types mostly, reticent country men—then maybe read a book in the evening lying on his bed. He still had dreams occasionally. Noone laughing in the bloodied crater, Noone naked and arms-spread in the rain, Noone, Noone, Noone . . . but nobody asked him about it, nobody took the piss. They all carried demons in one form or another, or they wouldn't have been here in the first place.

He wrote to Arthur but the mail was sporadic: he never received a reply.

In early '97 he was forced to move on: drought was crippling the region, the horses would have to be sold. There wasn't the work to keep him and he had no interest in hunting dingos again. It felt time to head for Adelaide anyway. He'd been putting it off this long. There was a direct road leading down there, the men told him, the Broken Hill road, roughly a week's ride south through a hellish country of giant salt pans and desolate rubble plains, no water, no feed, he'd have to carry it all. He wouldn't have seen anything like it, they warned him gravely; Tommy smiled and said they'd be surprised.

On the fifth day out there he came across the mirage of a flotilla, a hundred white sailing boats dotted across the undulations and shimmering in the liquid haze. A township, he realized, not thirst playing tricks on his mind. The sails were canvas tents, empty, torn, unmoored, flapping loose on the wind; and here and there the skeletal frames of barns or other buildings stood like the salvaged hulls of stripped-down vessels in a shipyard. He drew closer. No movement, no sign of anyone else around. When the wind got up, the canvas rippled in a quickfire percussion; dust devils spun then disappeared. There were belongings in the tents, he noticed—a broken comb, an empty suitcase, things forgotten or left behind—and nearby each a small area had been pegged and often dug out, a warren of holes in the ground. It was a goldfield, picked dry then abandoned, the earth with nothing more to give. Carefully Tommy weaved between the claims, toward a struggling central waterhole whose feed-pipe suggested a bore. He didn't notice the heads popping up around him, like moles out of the ground, as he dismounted and led the horses to the banks of the reservoir. The water looked dirty and brackish. He walked around to the bore pipe and tried the tap to see if it turned.

"Scald you half to death if you drink it. You'll want it cooled down first."

Tommy turned with his hand on his revolver. There were four of them, standing near his horses on the other side of the waterhole, filthy scarecrow men in a bizarre assemblage of ill-fitting clothing, adorned with hats and neckerchiefs, waistcoats and bow ties. Thin as the picks and shovels they carried, beards down to their chests. Three were white, the other native; one had a rifle on a shoulder strap, and they were too near the horses to risk a gunfight. Tommy let go of the revolver, allowed his hand to hang.

"This all there is?" he called over.

"For the horses, yeah. We can't let it run or it floods. There's barrels you can get a drink from though."

"Where?"

The man squinted at him. "Y'ain't planning on robbing us are you?"

Tommy looked around. "What of?"

"Water's in that barn there," the man said, pointing with his pick. "Trade if you have anything. Save you waiting on the bore."

Tommy told them he had tobacco, flour, dried mutton, and they exchanged excited glances like Father Christmas had just come. He unhooked his bladder bags and left the horses drinking from the reservoir and cautiously followed the men to the barn. There were others here, he realized. Perhaps a dozen men in all. He spotted them standing on distant hillsides, outlined in the sun, or leaning out of their hovels with their chins resting on their arms. Some place this he'd stumbled on. He'd top up his bladder bags, maybe share a meal, then leave.

Outside the barn was a junkyard of furniture and wheelbarrows and bicycles and scrap; cash registers and bar taps and franking machines and weighing scales, all piled up or strewn loose on the ground. There were no doors on the building, only a cutout in the wall, and the roof was missing entirely—it rained so little they had no need. They led him inside, into a makeshift dwelling: there was a kitchen, a sleeping area, a rusted metal bathtub, a firepit, a blackened cooking stove. The man who'd done the talking so far showed Tommy a line of old beer kegs stacked against the wall, told him to have a try. Tommy turned one of the taps and clear water surged out. He tasted it: tepid but clean. "We got ourselves a trade, then? A meal for them bags filled?" the man asked, grinning. Tommy nodded and shook his filthy hand.

A bearded prospector wearing a flowery housedress and going by the name of Keith prepared a stew out of the mutton and a few beans, and baked two fat loaves of bread. Nobody commented on his getup. Must have always dressed that way. In from the field they dribbled, this strange community of men, jabbering excitedly about Tommy's arrival and whatever gold they'd scraped together that day. Most were white, of all kinds: German, Dutch, Australian mongrels like Tommy, plus another blackfella and two Chinese brothers, who only spoke between themselves. Tommy asked if their name was Song, the brothers from Bewley who'd gone to the goldfields and never come home. Of course it wasn't. He felt a fool for having wondered. In its heyday this place had swarmed with thousands of men, they told him, from all around the world, now this sorry handful were the only ones left. The field was all but dry, but they could just about make a living from it, and that was enough for them. Everything was communal. Sharing meant they survived. Most had tried moving on at one time or another, but this was all they knew. It wasn't much but it was something, which was better than nothing at all, and that's what awaited them out there. Rarely did anybody make it farther than Yunta, a day's walk away, before turning round and heading back here, to take up their pick again.

Tommy filled his bladder bags and left after the meal was over, as if whatever madness that afflicted these men might catch. They tried persuading him to stay longer; he should see the fun and games that went on after sundown. Music, dancing, drinking—no, he really shouldn't, Tommy already knew that much. There was a chest of women's clothing alongside a pair of fiddles and a foot drum, and he imagined Keith, and maybe the two Chinese brothers, getting dressed up in their glad rags and offering dances and maybe more—Tommy had spent enough time among lonely bushmen to imagine what might go on. He hitched the bladder bags onto his shoulder and backed out of the barn, his right hand free just in case. There was no need. The men followed him outside and waved him off like sweethearts on a train platform, and the sight of them lined up in front of the barn, big Keith in his housedress, the others like desperate vagabonds, had him chuckling all the way to Yunta, which he made by nightfall. He asked in the hotel about the goldfield. "Oh, those crazy fuckers are hell-bound," the clerk told him. "The depravity they get up to—they eat people, so I've heard. It's a wonder you got out alive."

He stabled the horses and took the train to Adelaide, looked in on Dee while he was there; she hugged him tightly and wouldn't stop touching him, as if for proof he was real. Jack had been down last summer, she told him, explained what had happened; it would make his year knowing Tommy was getting by. "Don't write him," Tommy urged, and she laughed and said she wouldn't dare, Jack wasn't one for love letters in the mail. At the little table in the guesthouse kitchen they sat eating soup and warm bread and chatting about the old times, the good times, the people they had known, Dee working herself up to asking if Jack talked about her often, if he ever discussed his plans. Drought had closed the Birdsville Track, she had read in the newspaper, most of the other stock routes too; she was hoping he might settle down.

"Maybe," Tommy offered, for what else could he say? "He thinks the world of you, Dee, honestly, but the bush is all he knows."

There were other things he would have liked to tell her. That she was as close to a partner as a man like Jack had, that he didn't see other women anymore, not even a brothel these days. From summer to summer he lived chaste as a monk then was hers for a couple of months. But to imagine him in the city, a house, a regular job . . . Jack would rather find cattle work somewhere, anywhere, Dee or no Dee, than confine himself here. Of course, he couldn't tell her any of it. None of this was his to say. Dee stirred her soup thoughtfully, a rueful smile. She asked after his own plans, he lied and said he had none, and she seemed to understand it was better for both of them if she didn't know.

At the bank, like a parent visiting a sick child in the hospital, he demanded to see his money, as if to check it was still alive. The bemused clerk tried explaining that it didn't work that way, then relented for fear of

Tommy causing a scene. He was shown into a side room, where they brought out his balance in cash— not the same crumpled banknotes he'd deposited but cleaner, newer bills. This pacified him a little. Like it was worth more, somehow. He began stuffing it all into his holdall as the flustered clerk jabbered about a letter of credit being more usual for such a large sum, but Tommy wasn't having any of that. He'd take his chances with cash. If anyone tried robbing him they'd have to kill him first, and what use would his money be then? He'd always been uneasy trusting the banks as it was, never mind walking out of here with a bloody promissory note. Up north he'd seen shinplasters that dissolved no sooner than they'd been written, men left howling over how much they were owed. So no, he was taking all his money with him, in cash, he told the bemused bank clerk.

If his plan was going to work, he would need every last penny he'd ever earned.

Chapter 23
Inquest

From across the district they came in their buggies and carriages, in the saddle and crammed into drays, a blockade of horses and vehicles choking Bewley's main street and spilling out into the scrubland beyond. A crowd jostled outside the courthouse. There wasn't room for everyone inside. Revolver in hand, Donnaghy stood guard in the doorway, ordering them all back. A decent bribe got you past him. Or if you had the right name. Reddened faces shouting, spittle flying, while throughout town people milled in the midday sunshine as if at a summer fair. There'd been a carnival atmosphere all morning: a quartet of singers, an accordion player, refreshment stalls and bunting, men let off work, children at their games. Beneath the tasseled parasols, sipping cups of flat lemonade, they mingled and swapped gossip about the proceedings, who they'd seen going in there, who looked nervous or scared, while at the very back of the crowd a small group of native men, unwelcome in the courthouse— "No blacks allowed!" Donnaghy had yelled—huddled at the mouth of an alleyway, not talking at all, their steady gazes pinned on the building's white facade.

It was shoulder to shoulder in the flagstone lobby, people squeezed in like battery hens. Some had brought crates to stand on, others climbed onto ledges or the clerk's desk, all craning for a view of the court-room through the open doors. Whispers were passed back from those in the gallery, through the lobby, and out into the crowd, embellished rumors that the parasol-carriers swallowed with their boiled sweets and lemonade.

Seats had been reserved for the witnesses and local dignitaries, such as they were in these parts, as well as for a pair of newspaper reporters who'd got wind of the inquest. One was local but the other was from the *Brisbane Post*, which when Henry Wells noticed, took him by surprise. Twisting in his chair at the front of the room—the table across from the empty jury box, the prosecutor's side—anxiously scanning the faces behind, Henry vaguely recognized him, perhaps from the courts back home. He caught the man's eye and

nodded; the reporter returned the nod with a knowing smile. Too distant for conversation—Henry would
have liked to know who'd tipped him off. Still, he was
glad to have him. He'd hoped to stir up some press interest once the inquest was over, but here they already
were. Which could only be a good thing. The scrutiny
of public opinion, a dose of outrage on the coast, all
welcome grist to his crumbling mill. Because Henry
was going to need all the help he could get: Reverend
Bean had disappeared.

He wasn't there this morning when Henry had unlocked the door onto an empty bedroom, and he wasn't
at the bar or in the restaurant downstairs. Horace
hadn't seen him. His bed was made, his suit hung on
the wall hook, nothing was out of place in the room.
The window was his only escape route. Closed but
unlocked, and a good twenty-foot drop to the ground.
Like a madman Henry scoured the town, but there
was no sign of him anywhere: panting, he asked the
townsfolk, and dumbly they shook their heads. He ran
to the church, imagined finding him on the front pew
deep in prayer. Of course, he wasn't. The benches were
deserted, the altar was bare, nothing moving save flies
and dust. Forlornly Henry checked his pocket watch.
Only a couple of hours to go. So back to the hotel he
trudged, through the gathering crowds, whispers trail-

ing him along the street, and for the next hour he sat at a table, waiting, before giving it up and heading to his room to change.

Across the aisle from Henry, seated in the very front row, were Billy and Katherine McBride: Billy in a charcoal three-piece with a gold watch chain and a fine white pinstripe running through the suit; Katherine wearing a white pleated skirt, navy suit jacket, and matching navy hat. They were not talking. Billy with his arms folded and jaw set, Katherine's hands clasped together in her lap, both stoic and silent in the bustling courtroom. When they'd entered, the crowd had hushed and parted and allowed them to pass. Billy's hand was shaken. Consoling touches on Katherine's arms and back. They'd taken their seats and there'd been a glance between Billy and Henry Wells, until Billy fixed his gaze forward and didn't look at the lawyer again.

At the stroke of two o'clock the clerk rose from his table and called the room to order and a frisson of excitement washed from the gallery to the lobby and on to those waiting outside. A pregnant silence fell. Strains of the accordion player, and of children squealing, until word reached them too and all was still. From the judge's antechamber came a burst of mirthful laughter, then the door opened and a tall figure ducked under the frame. Dressed in a black suit with a white shirt and white handkerchief, his hair meticulously parted, his mustache lifting in a smile, Chief Inspector Edmund Noone strode through the courtroom and took the aisle seat alongside Katherine, who stiffened and clenched her hands together so hard the knuckles turned white.

Noone greeted her and Billy cordially. Politely, they both replied. His name hissing like a chant through the courtroom—*Noone, Noone, Noone*—as he popped a button on his jacket and crossed his long legs at the knee.

From the same antechamber, Magistrate MacIntyre arrived, shuffling in his crumpled robes up the steps to the bench and flopping down with a sigh. The valise, Henry realized; the valise in his front hall. *EJN* were the initials. Noone was the judge's house guest. Well of course he was.

MacIntyre stacked his papers, glanced up at the crowd, perched a pair of reading spectacles on the tip of his nose. "Never been so popular," he mumbled, prompting laughter from the crowd. He peered over the rims of his spectacles at Billy, Katherine, and Noone, then his gaze slid across to Henry, sitting forward of the gallery, and far closer than he ought to have been.

"I told you yesterday, Mr. Wells, you're only an observer in my court."

Henry cleared his throat and made as if to rise, but MacIntyre waved irritably for him to keep his seat. Henry stood anyway. "Your Honor, I'd be grateful for the indulgence of a table. For my papers, you understand."

"Sir, or Magistrate, is fine here, you're not in the Supreme Court now. Very well, keep the table, but remember your place." He took a breath. "All right then, let's begin."

"Sir, if I may?"

"Did I not just make myself clear, Mr. Wells?"

"There is an urgent matter that I must bring to your attention at the outset."

"Hell, son, I've not even got the bloody thing started yet."

Henry glanced once behind him, turned dejectedly back around. "Sir, it's the witness. Reverend Bean. He's . . . not here."

Pantomime gasps in the courtroom. Billy and Katherine exchanged a frown. Beside them, his legs still crossed, Noone swiveled to the crowd, highly amused.

"What do you mean, he's not here? Where is he?"

"I don't know."

"Well, when did you last see him?"

"Last night. I even locked him in his room. But this morning . . . he was gone."

"Sink a few too many in the bar, did he? Get a little carried away?"

Sniggers from the gallery. Henry said, "On the contrary. I have kept him dry as a stone."

"Poor bastard. Well then, it seems we're somewhat buggered, since it's on his evidence this whole thing stands."

"Perhaps a brief adjournment, sir, until we can track him down?"

"And how exactly do you plan to do that, if you don't know where he went?"

"He can't have gone too far. He hasn't even a horse."

"You'd be surprised, Mr. Wells, how far a man can travel when he's running from the law. The witness was your responsibility. He's the very reason any of us is here. Why would he run if he didn't have something to hide?"

"Sir, I locked him in his bedroom, there was really nothing more I could—"

"There won't be any adjournments. I've got half the bloody district in my courtroom, men who should be working, a police chief inspector for God's sake. Poor Billy McBride is sitting there now looking pale as a bloody bedsheet and all because this reverend of yours took twelve years to pipe up about something he might or might not have seen. Wherever he is, it really makes no difference to me. We are here at the instigation of the colonial secretary, who has charged me to investigate the deaths of Edward, Elizabeth, and Mary McBride in the December of 1885, and any actions later taken against the suspected culprits and the wider Kurrong tribe by the Native Police and the officer in charge, Chief Inspector Edmund Noone. That is my duty, Mr. Wells, and I shall carry it out faithfully based on the evidence before me today. If Reverend Bean bothers to show his face I will hear him, otherwise we proceed without."

Grumbles of assent from the gallery. "You have his testimony," Henry said.

"Yes, but I don't have the man to swear to it, or to be questioned under oath." He waved a thin sheaf of papers. "This document could have been written by anybody. It's as good as worthless as far as I'm concerned."

"That is my name at the bottom, sir. He swore it in front of me."

"And what difference is that supposed to make?"

"Well, I can vouch for its veracity."

"Aye, but not its contents. Whatever he told you,

whatever you think you know, or he knows, is hearsay, irrelevant, inadmissible, as you are well aware."

Henry floundered hopelessly. He went to retake his seat, then straightened with the sudden prick of an idea. "Sir, if I may—Reverend Bean told me that he once visited with you personally. That in the aftermath of these events he came to Bewley and attempted to tell you what he had seen. Now, he might have been in shock at the time, and perhaps less coherent than in his written record—"

"Or drunk!" someone yelled, to laughter.

"—but insofar as the contents tally with what he told you face-to-face, surely his evidence can still stand. He is simply now trying to formalize what he first reported to this court all those years ago."

MacIntyre frowned heavily. "What meeting are you referring to?"

"He came here, sir. December of 1885, around the turn of the year."

"I'm afraid I don't recall, Mr. Wells."

"Sir, I can assure you—"

MacIntyre raised a hand. "Because, of course, if he had reported something as heinous back then, it would have behooved me to investigate, to have kept records, to have liaised with the parties involved. Which I did not. There are no records of any such meeting, because no meeting ever took place. I fear the reverend is proving himself most unreliable without even being here."

"And what about this time around?" Henry asked him.

"Excuse me?"

"Has this second report been taken more seriously, I wonder. Have you investigated, spoken with witnesses, visited the crater, dug in the dust for the bodies? There is plenty of other evidence available, Magistrate MacIntyre—this case does not stand or fall on Reverend Bean alone."

MacIntyre glared at him over his spectacles. His lips were puckered, his breathing rushed, his face the color of beets. "Now you listen to me, young man," he said, pointing. "You are here as a courtesy, but one that I will not hesitate to revoke. You speak to me like that again— you dare to question my integrity in my own fucking courtroom—and I will lock you up for contempt and throw away the damn key. Do I make myself clear?"

"Yes, sir."

"Good. Then sit your fat arse down and keep your mouth shut."

To jeers from the gallery, Henry did as he was told. He'd never heard language like it in a courtroom, at least not from the judge. Already he could feel the hearing slipping away and there seemed no obvious way to get it back.

"All right," MacIntyre said, taking a deep breath, lifting his eyes to the room, "unless anyone else fancies a stint in my cells, we'll proceed in whatever manner I see fit. As I have said, we are here for one reason only, which is to find out for certain what went on at the Mc-Bride place and then afterward with the Kurrong, and since there are only two men in this courtroom who can tell us about it firsthand, we might as well start with them. Chief Inspector Noone—if you would be so kind as to take the witness stand."

A hush fell over the crowd. Noone uncrossed his legs and rose to his feet and strode smoothly to the wooden witness box. The clerk brought the Bible and held it and Noone placed his hand on top, a flicker of a smirk as he gave his solemn oath. He hitched his trousers and sat down on the chair and the clerk returned to his desk.

"Chief Inspector," MacIntyre began, "may I first thank you most sincerely for your time. It is an arduous journey out from Brisbane and I'm sure you're a very busy man, but on behalf of this court and the district, we are grateful."

"You are welcome, of course. A terrible business, but I understand the need. We must do what we can to put the matter to bed and allow those affected, indeed the entire community, to move on. Such concerns are far more important than one's own personal convenience. I only wish everyone felt the same."

Noone arched an eyebrow playfully in the direction of Henry Wells. The gallery caught it, and sniggered.

"Quite," MacIntyre said, suppressing a smile. "Now, I have here your original police report from the time, which I have read again. I believe you have also had the opportunity to refresh your mind as to its contents, have you not?"

"I have."

"And are those events still familiar to you? Do you remember them well?"

"Sir, I will carry the memory of the McBride killings with me to the grave."

Katherine felt Billy jolt beside her, a sudden and violent twitch. He looked ill. Veins stood at his temples, sweat glistened his brow. She reached for his hand and he gave it, slowly unclenching his fist. He blinked and turned toward her, a pleading in his eyes, and she realized he wasn't angry but absolutely terrified.

"In that case, Chief Inspector, could I ask you to recount, in your own words, as best as you can, what you recall from that time, beginning perhaps with what you witnessed when you first arrived at the McBride murder scene."

Noone coughed and readied himself. Dead silence

in the room. "It was a couple of days afterward that I got to the house. As I recall, we were up near Jericho at the time, meaning the bodies had already been buried before I arrived. John Sullivan gave use of his men. However, the scene was still sufficiently intact to discern what had occurred: there were bloodstains on the porch and in the two bedrooms, and footprints leading out into the bush."

Billy first onto the verandah, down to his knees beside Father, sitting propped between the bench and the door. Three holes in him. Blood all over the boards. Billy's hand touches it, sticky and warm, and when he prods Father's shoulder the head rolls.

"All of which tallied with the account the brothers later gave when I met them at the Sullivan homestead. They had found their old blackboy's revolver discarded at the scene—Joseph, there had been a falling-out— and when they'd first arrived back at the property had seen a sizable group of natives fleeing west. Hence the footprints." Noone glanced at Billy. "They were remarkably clear in their recollections, given their ages and what they'd just been through."

Mother in the bedroom, half her head gone; Billy begs Tommy not to look. Trying to protect him, to somehow shoulder this all himself, though the weight is already too much to bear. He finds Mary bleeding out under the bed in their room, tries to lift her but he can't, his hands slick with blood, all his strength gone. He calls for Tommy to help him, they carry her outside, Billy's mind swirling with what to do next. His decision, his responsibility; he's head of the family now.

"So you went out after them?" MacIntyre asked. "This Joseph and whoever else?"

"We did. Myself and my troopers, plus John Sullivan, his man Locke, and the two young McBride brothers, though I knew civilians were not allowed."

"Why not?"

"It was against operational rules."

"In which case, why take them?"

Joseph's gun is not enough, Sullivan tells him; Billy will have to lie. Say he saw a mob of natives fleeing from the house, whatever gets Noone on their side. And he does so, he fabricates the whole tale, taking that burden so Tommy doesn't have to, urging him to stay out of it, and to stay behind. But he won't listen, his little brother, stubborn as he is, and in the end Noone insists it's both of them or neither, Sullivan paying him handsomely to allow the boys to come.

"Necessity. We were heading into hostile, unmapped territory in the height of summer and drought.

John Sullivan knew the region better than any man, his family had been there for generations. I believed his knowledge of waterholes and the terrain would be invaluable to the mission, and so it proved."

"And the boys?"

"They were the only ones who could identify Joseph. Naturally, I would have rather they didn't come. But it is a well-known tactic for a fugitive native to conceal himself among his own kind, much like the zebra on the African veldt—in a large group they can all look so alike. Luckily for us, the brothers knew the culprit personally. Without them, we would have had a hell of a task. As I recall, I offered to take only Billy, the eldest, so as to spare the younger brother the hardship. But they were newly orphaned and keen to stay together, understandably, so I allowed them both to come."

"Did you arm them?"

"Of course not."

"Did you allow them to participate in the attempted arrest?"

"No."

"All right. What happened next?"

"Well, after a few days of tracking, we came upon Joseph and his savages in the lowlands just before the ranges out west. The murderers were on foot and desperate, we caught them easily enough, and by the authority of Queen Victoria ordered them to lay down their spears. They refused. There was a gin with them—that is to say, an Aboriginal female—also armed, plus a pack of wild dogs; it really was quite the melee. They did not comply with my instructions. One of the blacks put a spear through Raymond Locke, missed his heart by inches, it was a wonder he survived. Of course, we retaliated. The spear thrower was shot and killed, but the others escaped into the ranges, forcing us to give chase. By now it was early evening and the light was fading, but my troopers were expert trackers and we soon found them hidden in a narrow canyon high in the hills. Again, they refused to surrender, so we had no choice but to engage. Sadly, in the fighting, all three suspects were shot and killed, including Joseph, whom Billy McBride positively identified. It was a terrible situation. I regret how it all played out. But the fact is, we attempted to arrest them on a number of occasions, then in fear for our lives had no choice but to return fire."

Billy sitting in the canyon, staring into the campfire, the two native men chained together on the ground and the woman and young girl huddled behind him on the ledge. Joseph is not among them, and somewhere deep down Billy knows he never was, probably isn't out here at all. But they have started this now, this reprisal, there is no turning back. If he and Tommy are to survive after, if they're to find a place in this world, this is a test they must pass. Suddenly Sullivan claps his hands and drags the woman to a nearby cave, urges Billy to take a turn. And he does, he follows, Tommy begging him not to go. Sullivan has his revolver pressed to her head as Billy lowers himself down. She is turned away from him, facedown on the rock, but he can feel her trembling, feel her tears. He finishes and stands and Sullivan shakes his hand and he returns to camp in a daze. Tommy will no longer look at him, something broken between them now.

Billy snatched his hand back from Katherine, cupped his nose and mouth, a long breath wobbling out of him, his eyes anguished, crazed. Katherine touched his leg lightly. He didn't seem to register she was even there. It was outrageous that they could do this, make him relive it all, and in public too. He'd never even talked to her about it. She'd not realized it still affected him as much as it obviously did.

"And what happened to the bodies?" MacIntyre asked.

"Ordinarily we would have buried them, afforded them proper Christian rites, but again our hand was forced and, terrible though it was, we had no choice but to leave the dead where they lay. They are probably still out there, God help me, were anyone inclined to go and look."

"I see. And how exactly was your hand forced, Chief Inspector?"

"Well, out of precaution I had sent a scout ahead, to see what lay beyond the hills. He returned and reported an entire tribe of natives, hundreds of them, a veritable *horde*"—gasps from the crowd—"and I knew that if we tarried we would be overrun. They must surely have heard the gunfire. Our window of escape was short. Under cover of the closing darkness, we rode for the safety of home."

No, Katherine thought, it wasn't that quick. They were gone far longer than just a few days. Tommy had been injured, he'd lost two fingers, and they'd taken some women captive, she was sure. Tommy had tried to free one, for himself, supposedly as a housegirl, and when she'd heard of the plan Katherine had been horrified.

"And that was the end of the matter? You came straight back?"

"We did. Luckily, we were not caught by the tribe. We recuperated a short while at Broken Ridge, injuries were attended to, food and drink were imbibed, a little too much by some perhaps—this was the time, as you will all no doubt remember, when Raymond Locke and John Sullivan had their fateful altercation, and I was once again forced to intervene."

Heads hung in the gallery, crosses were carved in the air. Katherine felt her chest tighten: a memory of sitting in one of the wingbacks, watching her husband die.

MacIntyre said, "Aye, a terrible tragedy, and not one we need get into today. But as far as you were concerned, Chief Inspector, that was the McBride case closed?"

"Yes, although I took no satisfaction from it. Killing suspects is never the aim. But we must remember that back then, only twelve years ago, our colony was a very different place to the one we enjoy today. The natives were still warmongering. They would fight unto the death. At any time, Joseph could have surrendered and submitted himself to the rigors of the British justice system, but he did not. He was guilty, he knew he was guilty, and would rather die than stand trial. He was a coward, ultimately: this was little more than suicide at our hands."

Silence lingered. Somber eyes watching him; much nodding of heads. Quietly, respectfully, MacIntyre asked, "You are aware, no doubt, of the allegations made by Reverend Bean, namely that the entire Kurrong tribe was killed at your hand, in some crater far out in the bush. What do you say to that?"

The sloping walls around him, littered with horse-trampled men, Billy terrified in the chaos, turning circles with his revolver, picking them off as they fled, lost in the roar of the slaughter and the drumbeat of blood in his veins.

"Pure fabrication," Noone answered quickly. "Of course, it is a difficult charge to answer when the man making it isn't here. I have not read the reverend's so-called testimony, I do not know the specifics of what he alleges. Nonetheless, I deny it, all of it—other than my lookout seeing them, we had no contact whatsoever with the larger tribe. Let me also say this. We were a group of nine only: myself and four native troopers, plus two farmers and two young boys. Nine, against how many is it alleged? Hundreds? At least half of whom would no doubt have been seasoned warriors. To anyone with even the slightest experience of combat, those are frankly laughable odds."

"I had to ask, Chief Inspector. I'm sure you understand."

Noone addressed the gallery: "I do, unfortunately, for the sad fact is, ladies and gentlemen, this is not an uncommon allegation for a Native Police officer to face,

even now, when the force is all but gone. We remain the
easiest of targets, as indeed we always were, scapegoats
for the more liberal conscience of our fellow citizens
on the coast. Over the years so much baseless rumor
and gossip has been slung that an element was bound
to stick. We acquired a reputation, through no fault of
our own. Wrongdoing—against myself or any other
officer—has hardly ever been proved, and in those few
cases when it has, our disciplinary procedures are ef-
fective and swift. But there is rarely any evidence. As
is the case today. The nature of our work exposed us to
the gravest of dangers, on your behalf, and yet now on
the whim of some madman I am forced to sit here and
justify myself over events that occurred twelve years
ago. I would remind you, Magistrate MacIntyre, and
the ladies and gentlemen of this fine town, that the only
reason I came to Bewley in the first place was that a
family had been slaughtered and two young brothers
needed my help. Which I gave, willingly, as I would
have done if it were any of your loved ones who had
been killed. The whole purpose of the Native Police was
the protection of vulnerable communities such as this,
honest hardworking families out here at the vanguard
of colonial settlement, building a life from the dust.
And we did so. We protected you. You might not have
always been aware of us, for the work went on unseen,

but now that there is peace in the colony, now that your little town is safe, I find myself in the dock answering fabricated charges about fictional crimes based on the testimony of a drunk ex-missionary who has fled. It is an unconscionable allegation. My very presence here is an affront. To the police force, to myself personally, to the lives that in service to this colony, this town, that in your own names were once lost."

Lives lost in your own name—the words landed on Billy like a stone.

Chapter 24
Inquest

Noone settled back in his chair, shrugged down his jacket, straightened his cuffs; cheeks flushed, eyes afire, scanning the bashful crowd. From the lobby there came a cry of "Hear, hear!" that was met with a smattering of applause. "Innocent!" somebody shouted, to louder cheering, and Noone's mouth twitched in a smile.

MacIntyre banged his gavel. Steadily the room calmed. "My sincere apologies, Chief Inspector, you are correct in all you say. This town does indeed owe you a debt of gratitude, and on its behalf may I thank you for your service and your candor today. Please accept our best wishes to yourself and your family. A safe journey back to the coast. You may step down."

"Surely not!"

The smile slid from Noone's face; half-risen, he lowered himself into his chair, and together with Magistrate MacIntyre glared at Henry Wells. He'd palmed the table as he said it; now he used that same hand to push himself to his feet.

"Sir, surely you cannot be about to swallow such a load of old claptrap and dismiss this witness without a proper cross-examination on the facts?"

"I have interrogated the witness, Mr. Wells. Take your seat."

"You have done no such thing. But please, if you have indeed exhausted your examination, allow me to conduct one of my own."

"Nonsense. This is my courtroom. I will decide who—"

"There are reporters here from Brisbane," Henry protested, flinging out an arm. "The colonial secretary will hear of this sham, as will the whole of Queensland. For my part, I will see to it that there is an appeal, or a judicial review, or by whatever other means ensure the proper scrutiny of the law is brought to bear on this matter, and on the conduct of this court. I will not be deterred, Magistrate MacIntyre. That much I can guarantee."

The magistrate seethed in the silence, Noone benignly watching on. Henry's hand was trembling; he clutched it firmly with the other, hoping they hadn't seen.

"I've a good mind to report you myself," MacIntyre snarled. "I don't know how they run the law courts back in Brisbane but this is not the kind of shitshow we are used to out here. Your superiors will hear of the disruption you have caused today."

"I hope so, sir. Then they'll hear my side of things too."

"Do you have any idea what you're doing, son? Have you lost your mind?"

"I am simply carrying out the duty entrusted to me. Assuming I am allowed."

Noone leaned in the witness box and said quietly to the magistrate, "Last thing any of us needs is another hearing. Why not let the boy say his piece?"

"I'm about to excuse you, Edmund."

"Ah, let's give him the rope to hang himself. What harm can it do?"

The two men stared at each other intently then MacIntyre shrugged and flapped a hand. "Fine, suit yourself, but don't say I didn't warn you. On you go then, Mr. Wells. But make sure you keep it brief."

Startled, Henry nodded. "Right, yes, well, thank

you, sir. And to you, Mr. Noone, for the opportunity to clear up just a couple of minor things."

"All that fuss for a couple of minor things?" Noone asked him, smiling pleasantly. "And it's Chief Inspector Noone, if you'd be so kind."

Henry glanced down at his papers, shuffled them a little, spreading out the pages containing his copy of Reverend Bean's testimony and the notes he had been taking while listening to Noone's version of events. He hadn't prepared a full cross-examination. That ought to have been MacIntyre's task. He'd taken himself aback by the force of his interruption, would normally never have dared threaten a judge like that. But he'd been here before: the Clarence murder trial, all those years ago, still the only one he had lost. He knew what Noone was, and what he'd done, and, after everything, could not stand to watch another blatant cover-up unfold before his eyes. Besides, how many times had he rehearsed this? How many times, as he read the dusty police reports, or the records of failed inquests, had he wished to get just one of these lying bastards before him on the stand?

He cleared his throat and looked up at the witness, his gray eyes staring playfully down. "Yes, of course, Chief Inspector—for how many years now?"

"Seven."

"And that's . . . in Brisbane? In Southport, isn't it?"

"As you well know, Mr. Wells. Or do you not recall visiting my police house just before this all began, and like some gumshoe detective attempting to deceive me into thinking you just happened to stop by? Tell me, have you bought that property in Southport yet, on the bluff overlooking the sea?"

Henry reddened uncontrollably. MacIntyre's feathery brows rose. "Not yet," Henry mumbled, before steadying himself. "All told, then, Chief Inspector, how long have you served in the Queensland Police Force?"

"Twenty-five years, give or take."

"And of those twenty-five years, how many were spent in the Native Police?"

"Perhaps mathematics isn't your strong suit: that would make eighteen."

"Ah, yes, my apologies. Still, that's quite some length of service."

"It's been my career, Mr. Wells."

"What I mean is, rarely do Native Police officers stick it for so long."

"Much like yourself, I am not so easily deterred."

"No, and you have certainly done rather well out of it. A house in Hampton, by the river, wasn't that what you told me?"

A quick laugh. "Are we here to discuss real estate now?"

"It just strikes me as curious—there can't be too many police officers living in Hampton, surely? How on earth do you supplement your wage?"

Noone turned to MacIntyre. "I didn't realize my personal affairs were on trial here, Spencer. I fear I've misjudged the boy. We're wasting our time."

"Forgive me, sir," Henry said. "Chief Inspector—"

"Because if they are," Noone interrupted, "perhaps I should be asking a few personal questions of my own. Such as, why would a respectable lawyer with a family in Spring Hill spend so much time visiting a male-only boardinghouse in the city? Why would he be seen wandering the sly-grog shops, opium dens, and brothels of the Frog's Hollow slums? Why, indeed, would he have gained for himself the reputation of one who preferred the company of men of a—how can I put this—more flowery bent?"

Uproar in the gallery. Great guffaws from the crowd. Henry shriveled at the unmasking: shoulders stooped, head bent low. He thought of the man from the *Post*, furiously scribbling his notes, and the bylines and scandal that would follow him home. He glanced up at Noone, saw him laughing, and realized the trap he'd walked into: the bastard meant to ruin him, right here in this courtroom.

Laughing along with Noone, MacIntyre said, "Were there any other questions, Mr. Wells?"

The papers blurred in front of him. The ink bled on the page. He had no choice now. He was in a fight for his reputation, his career, maybe even his life—the gallows had seen plenty of men like him. Everything in him screamed to sit down, or to snatch up his papers and run, but he couldn't, he knew that, splaying his hands on the table and forcing himself to keep his feet. He'd thrown down his cards and would have to ride it out: rip, shit, or bust.

"In those—" he began, his voice so faint and hoarse the words barely made it past his lips. He cleared his throat and swallowed. "In those eighteen years, Chief Inspector, how many arrests did you make?"

Noone was still enjoying the acclaim from the gallery, nodding and smiling at whoever was back there, and for a moment didn't realize he was being addressed.

"Sorry? Did you say something?"

"Yes, I was asking how many arrests you made in those eighteen years?"

The crowd settled finally. "In the Native Police?" Noone said.

"Exactly."

"A ridiculous question. I couldn't possibly begin to count them."

"Of Aborigines, I mean. How many Aborigines have you arrested?"

"Do you have any idea how many patrols I led, Mr. Wells?"

"Do you?"

"No. It would be well into the hundreds. More. Far too many to recall."

"And how many of those were successful, would you say? Approximately?"

"Most of them, though there are always complications now and then."

"Hundreds of successful patrols, then. And just to be clear, what do you mean when you use the word *patrol*?"

"Riding out with my troopers in pursuit of a suspect, investigating a crime, usually following some kind of depredation having been committed by the blacks."

"Depredations such as . . . ?"

Noone sighed. "Anything from unlawful assembly to attacking cattle to an outrage as heinous as that which befell the McBrides."

"And you were almost always successful, you just said?"

"I was good at my job, Mr. Wells. I still am."

"I wonder then—and since you can't recall the numbers exactly, you'll forgive me for laboring the point—why I found not a single record of an Aborigine being prosecuted following an arrest by you. Not one. After so many successful patrols, the court records should be overflowing with trials and convictions based on your good work. Yet there is nothing, at least not so far as I was able to find."

"Perhaps you just haven't looked hard enough."

"Oh, I assure you I have. As have my clerks. We have spent a great deal of time at the task. Which is why I asked the question: if these hundreds of successful patrols yielded not one single prosecution, how many arrests were actually made? You do not strike me as the kind of officer who would release a suspect without charge, having gone to the trouble of tracking him down."

"I was very thorough, Mr. Wells, as I have said."

"Quite. But can you answer the question?"

"Which was what exactly?"

"Why so few prosecutions, Chief Inspector?"

Noone shifted in his chair. "Often it was more a case of deterrence than prosecution. A warning, as it were. And of dispersing assemblages as and when."

"Dispersing, yes. And we all know what that means."

"It is a common-enough word."

"And a common-enough euphemism among Native Police officers for the massacre of Aborigines, is it not?"

Noone glanced uneasily at MacIntyre. "Of course not."

"Really? Because I have here a number of your police reports in which—"

"Keep the questions relevant, Mr. Wells," MacIntyre said. "We are only concerned with the case directly before us, not the Chief Inspector's entire career."

Henry paused, allowed Noone to stew in discomfort for a while. He was twitching impatiently, coiling like a spring. And, despite it all, Henry was beginning to enjoy himself. He was on his own stomping ground now.

"Very well then. Returning to the question of arrests . . ."

"For God's sake," Noone said.

"Given the lack of prosecutions—which is not my opinion, by the way, but recorded fact—I am curious to know, Chief Inspector, what other outcomes were you able to secure over your eighteen-year service that would have rendered these hundreds of patrols *successful*, in your own mind?"

Noone was very still for a moment. Henry forced himself to hold his gaze.

"Have you ever served in law enforcement, Henry?"

"I have not."

"The military?"

"Again, no."

"Have you ever chosen to risk your life for a purpose greater than your own?"

"Not unless standing here counts," Henry said, laughing nervously, prompting titters from the gallery behind.

"Well, let me tell you something about this country: we were not given it by the grace of God, not like they'd have you believe. By rights, none of you even ought to be here. You all, in one way or another, came on the boats. The natives whose land we are squatting on wanted nothing other than for us to leave. That is why they speared your cattle. That is why they attacked your homes. That is why, when the police come calling, they would rather fight to the death than face trial. They do not accept our laws any more than they accept our presence here. Frankly, it is a miracle I am still alive, that this town even exists. The things I have endured . . . the countless things men like me have done to keep men like you safe on these shores, and yet here you stand questioning me about arrest statistics: What the hell is this, MacIntyre?"

"It was you who insisted," the judge blustered. "I was done!"

Noone was making to leave the witness box. Henry needed to keep him there. Over the commotion in the gallery he shouted, "Then let's discuss the McBride murders, the reason we are all here. Surely you can't object to that?"

Noone settled. The muscle at his jaw creased. He took a long nasal breath and folded his arms so tightly his jacket looked ready to tear. Henry didn't wait for him to answer, pressing ahead before he could change his mind.

"You said the bodies had been buried by the time you first got to the house?"

"Yes."

"By the brothers, and you said John Sullivan gave use of his men?"

"So I was told."

"How many men?"

"I don't know."

"Enough, presumably, to help with the digging and the carrying and suchlike—would half a dozen be a reasonable estimate?"

"The man wasn't there, Mr. Wells," MacIntyre protested.

"All right. A good number of them, anyway, moving through the house, trampling all over the yard, and yet you were still able to find sufficient evidence of what had occurred and a clear set of tracks leading into the scrub?"

"As I said, I am good at my job. A damn sight better than you."

"And the brothers told you they had seen this man, Joseph?"

"Yes."

"Plus, how many natives was it?"

"It is in their testimonies."

"You don't remember? We could check the document now?"

Noone sighed. "As I recall, they said about twelve."

"Twelve? Yet when you caught up with them, there were only four?"

"I can't be expected to account for what the two brothers said. Perhaps they were mistaken. Billy Mc-Bride is sitting right there—why don't you ask him?"

"I'm sure we will, Chief Inspector. Still, twelve down to four?"

"It was dusk, they'd just found their family butchered, I think we can allow them a little leeway. For all I know, the other eight may have took off elsewhere."

"You didn't go looking for them?"

"We followed the tracks we had."

"You believed the brothers' account though?"

"I had no reason not to."

"They swore the testimonies before yourself, in fact?"

"Time was of the essence, and the bush is hardly brimming with officials authorized to take an oath. I was the only person around."

"Where did you do it?"

"At the Sullivan homestead."

"And did you write them, or did they?"

"The words are theirs. I don't recall who held the pen."

"You don't recall?"

"No. I do not." Speaking through clenched teeth.

"And then, on the basis of this trampled scene and the testimony of two young boys, you went out after the suspects, with four civilians in tow?"

"As I have already explained."

"There was a fight, all four natives were killed, including Joseph?"

"I just said so."

"In the ranges?"

"If you intend repeating back to me everything I have already said . . ."

"You believe the bodies might still be out there?"

"This is ridiculous. You're wasting my time."

"Pull your head in with your questions, Mr. Wells, or you can sit back down."

Henry turned on Magistrate MacIntyre: "Have you conducted a search for these bodies yourself, sir?"

"What's that?"

"Have you been to the ranges to look for them?"

"Well, I mean, there are others who've been out there and—"

"On your behalf, though? Specifically conducting a search?"

"Not exactly, but I've spoken to those who—"

"So, no proper search has ever been conducted in order to verify the Chief Inspector's account?"

"What's the use?" MacIntyre said, exasperated. "There'd be nothing left!"

"No search conducted. And do you recall, Chief Inspector, where exactly in the ranges this gunfight occurred?"

"I do not. It was dusk, and the ranges are a very big place."

"Indeed they are. Indeed they are. Now, as you are aware, Reverend Bean claims he encountered you half a day's ride west of there."

Noone looked about comically. "Did he? When? I never heard him."

"It's in his testimony."

"Unsworn testimony. Which I have not seen."

"Sworn before me personally. If you were good

enough for the McBride brothers, surely I will suffice for Reverend Bean?"

"I wouldn't be so certain of that."

"Are you saying, then, that you have no recollection of any meeting?"

"I am."

"Never met the man in your life?"

"Almost everyone I have met in my life is forgettable, Mr. Wells, including your good self. So I cannot be certain that your reverend has not accosted me on some street corner or pressed his hand into mine—if your intention is to scupper me with clever wordplay I am afraid I'll have to disappoint. But what I can confirm absolutely is that I did not meet Reverend Bean west of the ranges because I have never been there. We returned to Broken Ridge immediately, as I have said."

"We being"—Henry made a point of checking his notes—"yourself, your four troopers, John Sullivan, Raymond Locke, Billy and Tommy McBride. Nine in total, isn't that what you said?"

"Your mathematics are improving, Henry."

"Thank you. And where are your troopers now, Mr. Noone?"

"Retired, or killed in service. The job was equally dangerous for them."

"Liar!"

Henry stalled. All heads turned. The shout had come from the gallery, from a man standing near the back wall. The crowd parted, and Billy, twisting in his seat, let out a low, pained groan. The hair was thinning, the beard long, there were rings like bulging saddlebags under the eyes, but he recognized Drew Bennett immediately. Billy rose to his feet as Drew yelled, "I know what you done to 'em, you bastard! You killed 'em! And burned down my bloody barn!"

He was drunk. Jabbing a trembling finger, badly slurring his words. People around him began backing away until he was standing there all alone.

"Drew," Billy called. "Don't do this."

Squinting, his finger wavering as if divining who had spoken, he finally settled on Billy and said, "You ain't no different, Billy. You're just as bad as him."

"Guard!" MacIntyre began yelling. "Guard!"

"Ought we not to hear what the man has to say?" Henry asked.

"He's a drunk and a fool, anyone can see that— guard!" Finally Donnaghy managed to push through from the lobby. "Get him out of here!"

Donnaghy wrestled Drew Bennett out of the courtroom, through the crowd, and outside. Slowly the gallery settled. Billy retook his seat. Katherine was staring at him. Billy had been with Noone when he'd gone to Drew Bennett's place. Just tracking down a missing trooper, he had said. Supposedly they had found him, then left. Nothing about any killing, or burning the Bennetts' barn.

"Sir, I really think we should have heard that man."

"One interloper is bad enough, Mr. Wells. This is a courtroom, not a bloody town hall. Aren't you done yet? You don't seem to be getting anywhere and frankly I'm growing tired of hearing your voice."

"I'll press on, if I may." Henry gathered himself, tried to remember where he was going with this. "So, Chief Inspector, your troopers are at least *unaccounted for*—let us put it that way. And what of the others in the expedition: John Sullivan, Raymond Locke, Tommy McBride?"

"Am I nursemaid to all these men now?"

"It's not a difficult question. You have already explained how, shortly after the expedition, John Sullivan was killed by his headman, Raymond Locke. And then I believe you killed Locke yourself, or do I have that wrong?"

"No, that is correct."

"Care to explain?"

"The man resisted arrest. I had no choice."

"Seems a little convenient."

"Not for him."

"A lot of people die when you try to arrest them, don't they, Chief Inspector?"

"A lot of people choose to resist."

"And Tommy McBride, the younger brother, where is he?"

"The last I heard, he was a fugitive from the law, heading for New South Wales. That was about seven years ago. His brother is more likely to know."

"My point is, the only people still around with knowledge of these events are yourself and Mr. Billy McBride."

Wearily Noone said, "Hence the reason we are both here. Unlike some."

"The full details of what happened weren't released to the public, were they?"

"I wouldn't have thought so."

"Particularly the fact you took civilians with you, being contrary to police regulations—I notice you didn't mention it in your report."

"No, Mr. Wells, I did not."

"I wonder then, how it's possible that Reverend Bean in his written testimony knew all of these things exactly as you have described them. I have it here in front of me: *There were nine of them*, he says. *Noone plus four troopers, the McBride boys and two other white men—I didn't ever learn their names.* How could he possibly have known that, Chief Inspector, if he never met you out there?"

Absolute silence in the courtroom. Noone's eyes roved across the gallery then back again, boring into Henry, his chest heaving, struggling to hold himself in check.

"I have no idea," Noone said finally. "And neither do you."

"But I do know, because he told me."

Noone threw up his hands. "The man isn't even here."

"The account is inadmissible," MacIntyre added. "I've already ruled on that."

Henry ignored him, plowed ahead, reading: *"They had a young native girl with them, taken captive; she rode on the younger brother's horse."*

He looked up at Noone expectantly. "Is that a question?" Noone asked.

"You don't have anything to say about it?"

"No."

"Is it true?"

"All lies. The same as everything else."

"On the contrary, Chief Inspector, I put it to you that

you did in fact meet with Reverend Bean west of the ranges, and that you warned him most severely against ever speaking out. The poor man is still petrified to this day, which I daresay is why he's not here. Did you not threaten to remove his eyes and ears and cut out his tongue and send him wandering naked through the desert?"

"I am not even going to dignify that question with a response."

"So you don't deny it?"

MacIntyre said, "Mr. Wells, that's enough."

"Of course I bloody deny it!"

"After meeting him you rode to the Kurrong camp, didn't you?"

"No."

"Where you waited until the next morning, at dawn."

"No."

"Then you descended into that crater and slaughtered them: men, women and children, hundreds put to the sword."

"This is outrageous!"

"Before piling up the bodies and burning them, reducing an entire tribe of people to a mound of ash, and concealing your crime for all these years?"

Noone turned to MacIntyre. "You'll allow this horseshit in your courtroom?"

"You'd best answer the question, Edmund. There are reporters here."

Squirming, Noone said, "No, we did not. It is an affront to even suggest it."

"Then where are the Kurrong now?" Henry asked him, looking about. "What happened to your warmongering horde? Hundreds of them, you just told us, so where are they? Where did they all go?"

"They are an . . . an itinerant people."

"Who just happened to disappear?"

"How the hell should I know?"

"But you do know, don't you, Chief Inspector?"

"No, I . . ."

"You know, because you killed them."

"I did not. I . . ."

"You killed them and burned their bodies and left them there to rot."

"I did no such thing."

"You and your Native Police, your so-called dispersal campaigns—how many massacres have you overseen, Chief Inspector? How many people have been butchered at your command?"

"Enough!" Noone yelled, slamming his hand against

the wooden witness box as loud as a gunshot. "I do not need to sit here and listen to this!"

He rose from his seat as Magistrate MacIntyre bellowed, "Mr. Wells, I will not have the Chief Inspector spoken to in that manner in my courtroom."

"I only seek the truth, sir. A truth everyone here already knows. The whole colony is aware of what has happened on the frontier and has been happening for a hundred years. But nobody will speak of it. We close our eyes and pretend it never happened; well, the time has come to stop."

Noone fastened the button on his suit jacket but remained standing, recovered now, and huge in the little wooden box. He leaned forward and gripped the edges with his hands, knuckles like thick white burrs. He resembled a preacher in the pulpit, glaring with naked fury at Henry Wells. The crowd, cowed into silence, hung on Noone's next word. He swept a hand across his audience and summoned a voice that filled the room.

"Everybody knows it, do they? The whole colony knows the truth? Then where is your evidence, Henry? Where are your witnesses, where are the bodies, the piles and piles of the dead? Did *you* ride beyond the ranges to find them? Did *you* comb the ashes of this bonfire I'm supposed to have lit? No, I didn't think so, because the evidence does not exist. And neither are you the kind of man to get his hands dirty, are you, Henry Wells? Or at least, not in that sense of the word. No, you'd rather come in here with your theories and false testimony and besmirch me in front of this crowd. Well, I will not stand for it, and neither will they. The people of this town won't be fooled by some grubby little sodomite who is only looking to advance his own career. Have you already imagined the headlines? Was it you who invited the press? The fact is, you know nothing of policing, or of the colonies—you have not earned the right to question me. You are a parasite, men like you, feeding off this country we've created while stabbing her in the back at the same time. This man would see you ruined, ladies and gentlemen. These city dwellers telling you how and where you should live—I don't see them conducting this kind of inquisition in their own backyards. Out there on the coast they live like barbarians, as indeed does Henry Wells: without morals, without backbone, without God. What do they care about Bewley, about your struggles, about what it takes to survive out here? You are fodder to their ambition, a means to advance their agenda and little more. Mark my words, if they could, they would raze this town and return this entire district to the blacks, then retreat to their mansions and over cigars and fine brandy congratulate themselves on a job well done. They would comb through your history, as they are attempting today with mine, and throw you in the cells for ever having protected your families, your livelihoods, your town. This man buggers his way through Brisbane one back alley at a time, yet dares to come here and pour shame on you all, with that self-same condescension and hypocrisy you have always received from the coast." He pointed directly at Henry Wells. "Ladies and gentlemen, here is the long reach of government. Here is Brisbane's favorite son. Here is the authority of the old motherland that once shipped out your grandfathers and delivered them to these shores in chains, shackles you have been fighting to be free of all your lives. This man is an enemy of Australia! Do not let his conspiracy stand!"

Absolute bedlam in the courtroom. Men surged forward, pushing through the crowd, scrambling over railings and seating to get to Henry Wells. Coins and fruit were thrown at him. Something struck him on the back of the head. One man got as far as the table, screamed "Maggot!" in Henry's face and took a swing. He only just missed. Knuckles skinned Henry's chin. The man lost his balance and went tumbling and Henry ran around the table and hid on the other side. Up on the bench, Magistrate MacIntyre pounded his gavel incessantly but the noise and his yelling were drowned out by the uproar as Noone smiled to himself in satisfaction, straightened his suit, and eased himself backward, ready to step down.

The gunshot brought the room to an abrupt standstill. Vitriol was replaced by screams. From the back of the courtroom Donnaghy marched forward waving his revolver above his head. He came to the front and stood beneath the judge's bench and brandished it at the crowd, which as one pressed itself toward the back of the room.

"Any of you cunts wants it there's a bullet for you here."

MacIntyre went on beating his gavel long into the silence. Finally he let it fall still. Chest heaving, flushed and breathless, the man looked ready to expire. It took a long time until he was able to speak again, holding up his hand and wheezing, "That's enough, Donnaghy. You've put a hole in my bloody roof."

Eyes upcast to the ceiling. Sure enough: a circle of bright sunshine.

"Now listen," MacIntyre panted. "Any more of that horseshit from anyone and I'll clear this whole damn room. Get out from under that table, Mr. Wells, for God's sake. Donnaghy, go and stand next to him, anyone comes within two feet you either arrest them or shoot them, I don't really care. And not another word out of you either, Henry, or you'll meet the same end." He took a long breath and flopped back in his chair. "We only have one more witness to hear from then we can all go home. Come on up, Billy, let's get this bloody thing done."

Noone made his way down from the witness box. He and Billy crossed in the aisle. Noone gripped his arm and whispered in his ear, "Your turn now, Billy-boy, don't go fucking this up," and as Noone sat down next to Katherine she regarded him coldly then slid one seat farther along.

Chapter 25
Inquest

On leaden feet Billy trudged to the witness box: a thousand-yard shuffle, a thousand-yard stare. Katherine hardly knew him. The stooped shoulders, the bowed head, no longer her husband at all. He gripped the sides of the box as he climbed in, swore his oath so quietly she couldn't hear him, then sat down and waited, his eyes furtively flicking to her in the crowd.

"Mr. McBride—" the magistrate began, then corrected himself. "Or is *Billy* more appropriate, given we've known each other so long?"

It took Billy a while to register the question. "That's fine," he said.

"Good. Now, Billy, I'm sorry for getting you up here, and for putting you through all this, I can see just by looking at you the toll today has had. Only, when someone makes an allegation as serious as this, there's a process that must be gone through—you understand, I'm sure?"

Billy nodded.

"So let's get right to it, shall we: Were you listening when Chief Inspector Noone gave his evidence just now, concerning the events of your family's murder and the expedition that followed?"

"Yes."

"And do you agree with him, as far as you're able? Was his evidence accurate?"

A beat before he answered. "It was."

MacIntyre shuffled through his papers and held a sheet aloft. "Billy, I have here a written testimony signed by you and your brother, Tommy, dated the nineteenth of December 1885—could you take a look at it please."

He handed Billy the statement. A glance, then he gave it back.

"You recognize that document?"

"Yes."

"That's your signature on the bottom there?"

"It is."

"Have you had a chance to reread your testimony before today?"

"I have."

"And do you stand by its contents? Is there anything you'd like to correct?"

Billy cleared his throat and shifted in his chair and his voice when he spoke was feeble and meek. He was lying, Katherine knew. About all of it. She could see it right there in his face. Usually he tried to disguise his lies with bombast and bluster, most likely because they didn't bother him, he felt no guilt. This was very different, but he was lying all the same.

"Only about the number of natives," Billy said. "At the house, I mean. We thought twelve but probably there was only the four."

"So you miscounted?"

"It was dark, we was scared."

"But you are certain that you saw at least *some* natives fleeing the house, and that your former boy, Joseph, was among them?"

"Yes."

"And these were the same four natives—a woman and three men—that the chief inspector later tracked and attempted to arrest in the foothills of the western ranges, as we have just heard."

"That was them, aye."

"But they resisted? They attacked you?"

Billy nodded. "Locke got speared in his shoulder. Just like he said."

"Very well. And what about the remainder of the chief inspector's testimony, about what came next: the altercation that led to the suspects getting shot; your party not going beyond the ranges, never having met the Kurrong tribe, or for that matter Reverend Bean— this is all as you remember it too?"

"It is."

"Sir, please!" Henry Wells could no longer contain himself. Donnaghy snapped to life and raised his revolver like Henry had just let off a grenade. "You are guiding him through this entire testimony. Mr. McBride knows fine well who Reverend Bean is—he admitted as much last night."

"Last night?"

"He came to my hotel room, yes."

"Oh, aye?" MacIntyre said, eyebrows raised. "What for?"

"To discuss the case, of course."

MacIntyre turned to Billy. "That right, Billy? You visit this ponce last night?"

Gravely Billy stared at Henry, stared right through him almost. "I never seen him till this morning when I walked in this courtroom."

"It seems you are mistaken, Mr. Wells. Perhaps you are confusing him with another nighttime visitor. For a man like yourself I imagine it can be hard to keep track."

Sniggering from the gallery. Henry threw up his hands. Katherine noticed Noone smirk and roll his eyes. But Billy had disappeared last night after dinner and had not come home until late, and there'd been all sorts of messenger boys back and forth these past few days.

"Just to be clear, then," MacIntyre continued, once the gallery had settled down, "you did not witness Chief Inspector Noone or his Native Police troopers engage in any other conflict while you were out there, specifically with the Kurrong tribe?"

"Correct."

"And you were with them the whole time, until they came back?"

"Yes."

MacIntyre drew a long breath. "Right, well, I think we're done here. Thank you, Billy, you can get down."

Billy motioned uncertainly to the gallery. MacIntyre nodded and Billy stood, a weight sliding off him, rapidly blinking his eyes. He returned to his seat, Noone angling his legs for Billy to pass, and sat between him and Katherine. Noone patted his thigh kindly. Billy looked utterly lost. He groped for Katherine's hand but she wouldn't give it, holding herself tightly, stiff and straight-backed.

"I don't see the need for an adjournment," Magistrate

MacIntyre said. "We've spent long enough on this nonsense as it is. My task here today is to assess the evidence before me and determine whether there are sufficient grounds for a finding of wrongdoing by Chief Inspector Noone or by any other person or persons in relation to the murders of members of the McBride family and thereafter Aborigines belonging to the Kurrong tribe. Much of the impetus for this inquiry arose from allegations made by an individual named Reverend Francis Bean, allegations which Mr. Henry Wells assisted in bringing to light. Sadly, Reverend Bean has decided, for reasons unknown, not to appear in court today. That is most regrettable. I have of course read his written testimony, but without the witness here to swear it and to answer questions, I must take what he has said with a pinch of salt. It does not reflect well on the witness that he is unwilling to stand behind his version of events. The reliability of his evidence is therefore significantly compromised in my eyes, particularly when set against the robust rebuttals of Chief Inspector Noone and Mr. McBride. The chief inspector has been willing to appear in person to answer these most grievous of charges, and I am grateful to him for that. Despite Mr. Wells's spirited attempts to discredit him, I find Chief Inspector Noone's account most persuasive. He is correct when he notes that the colony today is much changed from how it was only twelve years ago—and mostly for the better, I might add. We all remember the depredations of the Kurrong, how they would kill our livestock, attack our citizens, how they outright refused to lay down their spears. I find it proven that four of these natives did attack and murder Edward, Elizabeth, and Mary McBride—may they rest in peace—and that it was these same four natives, including the boy known as Joseph, whom Chief Inspector Noone did attempt to apprehend near the western ranges a week or so hence. I believe him when he tells us that his patrol was set upon, and that only in defending itself were the four suspects killed. I find it utterly *unproven* that anything else did occur, and wish to make clear that any implication of violence by Chief Inspector Noone against the Kurrong is an unwarranted smear on the character of one of our finest public servants. He should not have been put through this ignominy, neither should Mr. McBride, and I shall be writing to the colonial secretary in the strongest possible terms, to request a formal apology be issued to both men, for having their valuable time wasted, their reputations jeopardized, and, in Mr. McBride's case, for having been dragged through what must have been a most trying ordeal. There is not a shred of evidence to support any of the allegations or insinuations made before this court. There are no bodies. There are no witnesses. These are as trumped-up charges as I in all my years have seen. I find that Chief Inspector Noone has committed no wrongdoing, and neither for that matter has Mr. McBride, or indeed anyone else involved at the time. If the police commissioner wishes to take action relating to the inclusion of civilians in a Native Police patrol, then that is a matter for him. My own opinion is that it is water under the bridge. As is this entire episode. The hearing is over. All are free to go. Except, that is, for you, Mr. Wells—Donnaghy, bring him to my chambers right away."

The gallery erupted in cheering and clapping that spread in a wave through the lobby to those waiting outside. Hands were shaken, hats were thrown, while at the back of the crowd the native men watching from the alleyway shook their heads in weary resignation and walked away along the street.

Old Jim on the piano, the accordion player pumping his bellows, a beat pounded out on an improvised cask drum. The hotel heaving in revelry: dancing, drinking, singing; a handful of whores circulating, demurely leading their suitors upstairs. They roared each man his own send-off. Ten minutes later, they roared him down again. And part of it all: Noone. A head taller than the mass of bodies leaping to the beat, his face sweat-lathered, his tie loose, his collar open, boots stomping the wooden boards, his dark eyes twinkling in the gathering gloom.

The door opened. Nobody paid the young man any mind. In Percy walked with his dusty longcoat and rifle that came almost to his chin. He went to the bar, ordered a beer, greedily threw it down. If Horace noticed the cuts on his knuckles, or the bloodstains on his hands and shirtfront, he gave no sign that he had. Percy propped his rifle against the counter rail and slid exhausted onto a barstool. He picked out Noone in the merrymaking; Noone went on dancing but asked a question with his eyes. Percy nodded. Noone smiled. He announced to the crowd that the drinks were on him and, laughing, was carried barward in the surge.

Chapter 26
Billy and Katherine McBride

"Damn it, Katherine, wait!"

They had traveled in different coaches, one behind the other, each stewing separately on the long ride home. Now Billy chased her up the homestead steps, Katherine running ahead of him, her skirt bunched in her hand. He caught her and grabbed her but she shrugged him off and marched inside, Billy calling, "What the hell is wrong with you? What have I even done?"

She halted in the atrium and turned on him. "What have you *done?*" she shouted as Billy advanced along the hall, her voice echoing into the vaulted roof space, filling the entire house. "How can you even ask me that? Can't you once in your life admit when you're wrong?"

Billy reached the atrium but Katherine lunged for

the nearest door, the library; she slammed it behind her but it didn't catch. Billy sighed and doggedly followed, easing open the door to find her standing on the far side of the room, holding herself and looking out of the window, a view of the hillside at the back of the house. The great jagged ridge that like a serrated guillotine had hung over them their whole lives, and the little fenced-off cemetery in which Mary was buried, and where Billy never bothered to pay his respects.

He ghosted into the room, skimmed a hand over the polished wood of the billiards table, took off his jacket and tie and slung them on the baize. He stood watching her, gripping the side cushion. She had taken her jacket off too—the bare skin of her shoulders and neck. "Katie," he said softly, noticed the little shiver when she heard. He sighed and went to the cabinet and poured himself a Scotch, glancing at the wall of books above him, spine after leather-bound spine. He doubted he'd read even one.

"It only makes things worse, you know. There's no such thing as drinking to forget. Believe me, I have tried."

She was talking to the window, her back to him still. "What?" Billy said.

She turned. "You're never without a drink. Now I know why."

"We won, if you hadn't noticed. We should be celebrating!"

"Won?" she scoffed. "I saw you in there, Billy. Guilt was on you like a rash."

Billy sipped the Scotch. "Nobody's guilty—that's the point."

"You just can't help yourself, can you?"

"Didn't you hear the magistrate?"

"I did. And I heard you too, lying through your teeth."

"I only agreed with what Noone said, it was him that—"

"It's always somebody else with you, Billy. Noone, the stableboy, even William—when are you going to take responsibility for what you've done?"

He glared at her over his whiskey. "And what's that exactly."

"You heard the lawyer. Hell, you were there!"

"So were you."

"But I wasn't, though, was I? All I know is what I was told. And I asked you, remember, on our wedding day. You swore it hadn't happened like that."

Billy blew out dismissively. "Yeah, well, that lawyer's full of shit."

"And still you're lying." She stepped closer, away from the window. "You know, all these years I've assumed it was pain that tore you up, but it's not—it's lies and shame and guilt."

Billy poured himself a refill, jaw set, eyes glazed, near-wringing the decanter's neck. "You're talking in riddles here. The magistrate just decided: they killed the family, we killed them, we didn't do nothing wrong."

"But they didn't kill them, did they. You never saw any natives at the house."

Billy paused. Whiskey dripped from the decanter lip. He set it down and drank with his back to her, his entire body clenched like a fist. "We found Joseph's gun."

"And that was enough for you, was it, to go and murder a hundred Kurrong?"

"I don't remember you having such a problem with it at the time."

The accusation stalled her. Stung, she said, "I was only a girl. I had no idea."

He started walking, pacing in front of the bookshelves. "And I was even younger than you. Anyway, why are we arguing? The inquest's over, we won, we can get on with our lives, it makes no difference now."

"It makes every difference."

"Not to me. Not to us. We're still the same people, Katie. And look at us, look where we are. We've built a fucking empire." He spread his arms to the room.

"So it was *worth* it? Shame on you, Billy McBride!"

She turned back to the window, and in the long silence that followed, Billy finished his whiskey and poured another, quickly drinking himself into a stupor, the deadening weight of the liquor, the air around him thick and full. Yet for some reason he wouldn't leave her, wouldn't walk out. He felt a need to persuade her, hear her tell him he was right. He fell into one of the fireside armchairs and sat staring at the ash in the grate, the upright clock counting the seconds, *tick-tock, tick-tock.*

Finally Katherine joined him. Lowered herself into the other armchair. Watching him coldly, she said, "You're going to tell me exactly what happened back then, Billy. The absolute truth this time, nothing altered, nothing left out."

It took a while before he could answer: "Why?"

"Because you're my husband, and I don't have the slightest idea who you are. I thought I did, but I was kidding myself. There's a hole running through you, eating you alive—I'm scared one day it'll swallow the rest of us too. Tell me, then at least there's a chance I'll understand. At the moment all I can think is the worst."

And he could feel it rising inside him, the truth,

threatening to erupt. A truth he'd been hiding from himself, even; whose every glimpse scared him to his core.

"You'll hate me."

"Maybe. But right now I can hardly stand to look at you as it is."

Billy shook his head. He needed another drink. He went to rise but Katherine put out a hand and he slumped back in the chair. "Christ, Katie, I was only sixteen."

"That doesn't change what happened."

"But it does—don't you see? First into that house, finding Daddy and Ma, Mary dying, Tommy spilling his guts on the floor. I had to *do something*. I was the one, I had to *choose*. So we came up here and John brings in Noone—it's not like I could have ever said no. Blokes like that, there's no arguing with them, then they've got you, for the rest of your life it seems. Did you see the state of Drew Bennett in that courtroom earlier? Do you know what Noone did to him?"

"Again, you were there, Billy. You talk like it wasn't you too."

He looked at her with incomprehension. How couldn't she see?

"But that's what I'm telling you. I had no choice, with any of it. I only went to the Bennett place because he threatened you and Tommy, I didn't know he would burn down their fucking barn. He shot those four blacks after like they was nothing, like they wasn't no better than dogs."

She didn't know who he was referring to—the missing troopers, maybe—but at least she had him talking. She nodded and reclined a little, waited for him to go on.

"See, that's what I'm up against, the kind of man he is. Acts like this harmless politician but there's something wrong in his head. And if I'd said what really happened in court today, I guarantee he'd be up here killing us all too."

What really happened—a prickle of fear down her spine. She tried to keep her voice even: "There's only me now, though. We aren't in any danger here."

"Aye, well, it seems like you already know anyhow, so . . ."

Though she'd known it was coming, the admission snatched the breath from her chest. The truth, after all this time. "You mean, you did it? Like they said?"

And he laughed then, somehow. Laughter riven with pain. "None of them knows the fucking half of it." Casting about the room frantically; his body had begun to shake. "Yes, we caught them others in the ranges, but there wasn't no gunfight or anything like that, just had them chained back-to-back in the camp. Locke did one on account of that spear but John said if I killed the other and . . . if I killed him and . . . I'd be a man by the morning, he said."

She asked it as gently as she could: "If you killed him and what?"

He couldn't look at her. "There was this gin they had tied up on the ledge behind. John took her to this cave and . . ."

He drifted into silence. "And what? What did you do?"

"I shot the black with Locke's revolver but it went in near his neck, bloke wouldn't die, kept reaching out, like this . . ." He mimed it, the clawing. "I couldn't get another round in to reload. Tommy had to finish the job."

"The woman, Billy."

"I had no choice, we all . . . it wasn't just me, everyone took a turn."

Revulsion surged through her, a bilious, violent lurch. She cupped her hand to her mouth and managed to keep it down, her eyes on him cold as stone.

"I ain't proud of it," Billy pleaded. "But John forced me just about."

She swallowed painfully. "Did he force Tommy too?"

"It was never the same for him, though, was it?

Tommy had me to look out for him—who did I have, Katie? Who did I have?"

She was silent a long time. "And after? The tribe?"

Billy shook his head, stared at the dead fire. "It was too late when I realized. There wasn't anything I could have done. Aye, we killed the lot of them, just like they said. But d'you want to hear the funny thing: Joseph wasn't even there!"

He began laughing wildly, breaking now and then into tears. They gathered in his eyes and fell down his cheeks and he did not wipe them away. And they were for himself, Katherine knew, not the Kurrong, not that woman in the cave. Impassively she watched him keening, his head in his hands, fingernails clawing at his hair, until abruptly he managed to stop himself and sit upright, attempting a smile as if, because it was out now, everything between them was somehow all right. He wiped his nose with the back of his hand and left a smear of blood behind, scrubbed it idly with the opposite thumb. Suddenly so calm now. So detached.

"How many? You, personally, how many did you kill?"

"Christ, I don't know. Maybe a dozen. I didn't count."

"Women? Children?"

Sniffing, still distracted by the nosebleed: "No, only the men."

"But the others did. None was spared, that lawyer said."

"That was them, not me, it was Noone and that lot wanted the Kurrong dead."

She turned away, disgusted. Couldn't stand to watch him snivel anymore. In the corner of her eye she saw him flap out his handkerchief and dab his nose, wiping away the blood, mucus, tears, all of it. Because it really was that easy for him. Wipe it all away.

"Listen, I'm sorry, all right. The whole thing was a mistake. But it's done now, isn't it. And if we hadn't, if things hadn't gone how they did, you and me wouldn't be sitting here like we are. So there, I've told you, but can we just forget about it now? There's nothing to be gained by raking over the past. And besides, there's plenty men out there have done much worse than me."

She still couldn't look at him. Facing the fireplace, her eyes distant and glazed, she took a long breath and said, "You might be right. But then isn't it all just degrees of worse? Do you know how many times I have been raped, Billy? Not the incident with Charles Sinclair, I mean actually raped like that poor woman in the cave?" He stared at her dumbly; she said, "No, neither do I. It's happened so often I've lost count. Every night John rolled himself on top of me and had his way, and I truly could do nothing about it. Not a thing. They say a husband cannot rape his wife but I'll tell you he bloody well can. You were the first man I ever chose to be with, you are the father of my children, the only man I have ever loved, and now I find out you're no better than him."

The look she gave him was withering. Like he was nothing at all.

"I already said: I wish it never happened, but it did."

"You don't though, do you—those are crocodile tears. Look what we've become, you told me, like it was all worth it in the end. Even that's a lie you tell yourself: yes, you've been a decent enough headman for the station, but this empire you lay claim to, it's still mine. How you talk now, how you dress, that ridiculous billiards table, your lord-of-the-manor act, none of it has actually been earned."

He slid from the armchair and waddled on his knees toward her; Katherine folded her arms. He cupped her knees, pawed her ankles, calves, feet, mumbling, "I'm sorry, Katie, I'm sorry. But what can I do? What can I do?"

Loud as a whipcrack the slap struck his cheek. Billy rocked back on his heels.

"Take some responsibility. Stop blubbering like a child. Make amends, somehow. Repent. All your life the only standard you've ever set yourself is your own father, which from what I can tell is a pretty low fucking bar. So do something. Be a better father, better husband, better man; why not try to be kind?"

"I will, Katie, I'll—"

"But if you mistreat our children again, Billy . . . if you dare lecture William on how to be a man, if you speak to me out of turn, if you jeopardize their futures or hurt any of us in any way, I will tell the authorities in Brisbane exactly what went on out here, the lies you told, what you did, and see to it you are prosecuted. Or better yet I'll spare us all the trouble and put a bullet in you myself."

She stood so suddenly that Billy fell backward and lay sprawled on the rug by the hearth. Katherine stepped over him and strode from the library, her footsteps echoing through the atrium then padding upstairs. Billy clambered to his feet and gazed lost around the room, staggered to the cabinet and poured another Scotch. He sat back down in the same armchair. A line had been crossed, he knew. He'd wanted so badly to get it out of him—the truth like a tumor, it had felt like he was dying today in that courtroom—but the pain of his secret was now replaced with the deep dull ache of loss. No hiding from that one. No pretending it didn't exist. He lit a cigarette and smoked in snatches, staring at the ash in the fire grate, remembering white flakes, like snow, drifting all around. And there he remained, alone in the library, in that vast and silent house, his wife locked away upstairs and not a friend in this world, as twilight fell through the window outside and darkness steadily closed.

Chapter 27
Henry Wells

The key scraping into the cell door woke Henry from a painful, fitful sleep. Huddled in his threadbare blanket on the filthy flagstone floor, he raised his head to find Donnaghy standing over him, his face in shadow from the oil lamp he held in his outstretched hand.

"Move."

Stiffly Henry struggled to his feet, dropped the blanket on the floor. He felt like he'd been assaulted, though the blows he'd feared in the night had never come. Still, his body felt bruised and uncertain, his vision was slow, his mind confused: he put a hand on the damp wall to steady himself, took a moment to catch his breath. He'd been locked in this cell since the inquest ended, late yesterday afternoon. For his own protection, apparently; MacIntyre had claimed the locals would tear him apart. A likely story, given the conditions he'd been kept in. He was being punished, and for what? Daring to speak the truth in a town filled with denial? Asking a clearly corrupt magistrate to do his job? He was now even more worried about Reverend Bean. With no money, no clothes, no supplies, he wouldn't have taken off on his own. Besides, the man was here to clear his conscience, purge his soul. He was dying, he had told Henry—after making it this far, why not testify?

Out of the cell Henry staggered. Donnaghy followed him down the narrow corridor, the light from his oil lamp flickering, the guard whistling a jaunty tune, all the way to the lobby, where, in the gray light of daybreak through the open front door, Magistrate MacIntyre was waiting with Henry's valise and briefcase at his feet.

"Sleep well?" MacIntyre asked him.

"Barely a wink."

Henry couldn't conceal his disdain. This man was no kind of judge. In any other courtroom Henry's cross-examination of Noone would have turned the hearing, yet MacIntyre had always intended him slipping the noose. Henry had so nearly had him. He'd felt it, and a lawyer knows. But then Noone had gone on his rant and swung the gallery—Henry could almost respect such skills. In another life he'd have been quite the force at the bar.

"Well, count your blessings, at least you're still alive," MacIntrye said. He glanced at the bags at his feet. "I had your things packed up and brought over, and there's a coach waiting for you outside, take you down to Charleville and the train line."

"Has Reverend Bean returned?"

"Not that I've heard."

"You haven't bothered to enquire?"

"The witness was your responsibility, Henry, not mine."

"Will you look for him, at least?"

"I doubt it," MacIntyre said, shrugging. "Where can we look? Where should we even start? My guess is he took off back to Brisbane—you're more likely to find him than we are. Either way, I hope you don't take offense when I say I'd rather not see or hear from either of you again."

"This isn't over."

"Oh, I think it is, Mr. Wells. Go on now. Godspeed."

Henry collected his bags, started for the door, then paused with his back to the two men. He wanted to say something, to have the last word. Ask the magistrate how he lived with himself, how he was able to sleep at night. There was no point. Nothing he could do or say would change anything, not in a town like this. They all lived with themselves quite comfortably here. They all managed to sleep just fine.

He arrived back in Brisbane four days later to find the story had beaten him home. Henry picked up a copy of the *Post* at the train station and stared forlornly at the front page. OUTBACK SCANDAL! screamed the headline. CITY LAWYER DISGRACED IN MISGUIDED MURDER TRIAL!

The reporter was Noone's man, he realized. Of course he fucking was.

Chapter 28
Tommy McBride

The Ebenezer bells were ringing in the tower as Tommy led his horses across the fields, toward the little white stone church fronting a hamlet of houses and barns. Somewhere he could hear voices, laughter, and the gentle sounds of work. Men handling cattle, laundry being mangled, pots clanging in the kitchen as the evening meal was prepared.

A door opened in the front wall of the church and a man stepped out. He closed the door carefully behind him and walked to meet Tommy in the clearing, and only now when the bells fell silent did Tommy wonder if they'd been for him, the stranger at their gates. He wasn't badly dressed, to be fair to him, given the distance he had come, but he had a rifle on his shoulder and a revolver on his belt, and there are some things about a person no clothes can hide. He unhooked the rifle and dropped it in the long grass, lay the revolver alongside.

"I'm not here to cause any trouble."

The man gave no acknowledgment. He halted a few yards away. He was white, wearing a simple beige collarless shirt, tan work trousers, and despite all this grass and the risk of snakes, had open leather sandals on his feet. He clasped his hands in front of him, the left cupping the right wrist, and had the faraway smile of a simpleton, the kind of smile that in Tommy's experience gets a man killed.

"Can I help you, friend?" The accent was foreign, Germanic. "Are you in need of directions? Or perhaps shelter and a meal?"

"I'm looking for someone. Name's Arthur. I think he works here."

He didn't even pretend to think about it, pursing his lips and shaking his head. "We have no man by this name on our station. I am sorry to disappoint."

"Blackfella, old, big gray beard, missing a front tooth . . ."

The man smirked. "You are describing most of them here."

"He wrote me with this address a while back. Arthur—you sure?"

"Quite sure."

"Might be he's going by a different name now."

"What is your business with this man, can I ask?"

Tommy hesitated. How to put it into words. "We're family, just about."

The stranger considered him a moment. "This letter, may I see it?"

Tommy had it in his pocket. He handed it over. The man read.

"You are Tommy?"

"Maybe, once." The man frowned at him. Tommy said, "Aye, that's me."

"Do you have any other identification?"

"Not exactly, no."

"Then perhaps you can tell me the name of the farm."

"Farm? What farm?"

"The name of the farm . . . please."

It took Tommy a moment to guess his meaning. "Glendale," he said quietly. "Glendale, it was called."

The man bent to collect Tommy's weapons then looked up grinning. "Come with me, Tommy. Arthur will be very glad that you are here."

They walked around the church into a yard, where people paused their work and conversation to get a look at who'd just arrived. Tommy scanned their faces anxiously, didn't recognize Arthur among them. His stomach was churning. It had been seven years. And despite the letters, the gradual thawing, he didn't know for sure how this would go. The priest—if that's what the German was—waved someone over to stable Tommy's horses, also handing him Tommy's guns. "We do not allow weapons to be carried here," he explained, and Tommy nodded vaguely, his attention still elsewhere. From a basket the man offered Tommy a chunk of bread and someone brought him a cup of water, both of which he accepted with thanks.

"You have traveled far, I think?" the man asked, watching him.

"You could say that," Tommy replied.

Tearing off chunks from the bread, he followed the man's directions along a path between the buildings and over a patch of grassland to the river in whose bend the mission station was built. Beautiful country down here. Tall grass everywhere, the trees improbably full and green, the air alive with unfamiliar birdsong, plus the usual parakeets. Ahead, the river was sparkling in the late afternoon sun, wide and swollen, with red gums lining its banks and sandy coves dotted here and there . . . and sitting on one of them, hunchbacked and shirtless, his legs crossed in front of him, his fishing pole in his hands, his hair a shaggy mess of black and gray and his beard its identical twin, an old man patiently waiting for a bite.

"Arthur."

Immediately he straightened. His spine unknotted, the skin slid over the ribs. He was wearing a pair of cutoff trousers tied with rope at the waist, the hardened sole of a foot poking under his leg. His only movement was breathing. The rise and fall of his chest.

Tommy took off his hat and held it. "Arthur, it's me."

Now the head turned, but slowly, little increments, his shoulders twisting around. He looked at Tommy and his eyes closed briefly; Tommy thought he heard him exhale.

Arthur stood. Dropped the fishing pole and uncoiled his legs and rose lightly and nimbly to his feet. He walked toward Tommy in an unhurried lope, a full smile spreading across his face. All the ride down here Tommy had been figuring what to say, and now that Arthur was in front of him he couldn't speak. But Christ it was good to see him again. For a long time he'd not known if he would.

They embraced and held each other so tightly Tommy could feel the warmth of Arthur's skin through his shirt. There wasn't much left of him. A body down to its bones. They parted and stood assessing each other, Arthur shaking his head.

"Well, look at you, Tommy. You're all growed up."

"And you're even older. You shrunk?"

"Nah, you're taller, I reckon. Shit, you're properly a man."

Tommy smiled bashfully. "How you been, Arthur?"

"Better now. They let you in then?"

"Asked me for a bloody password. Tougher than a bank vault, this place."

"They have this idea folks'll come and try to take us back to whatever shithole we came from. Maybe they're right. How was your journey down?"

"Long. I got made by that fucker Alan Ames."

The name meant nothing to Arthur. "And how long you stopping for?"

"A few days, maybe. Look, Arthur—"

"Only a few days?"

The hurt was obvious. Tommy raised a hand. "I need to say this. I know it was a long time ago but I'm sorry for what happened between us in Marree. I was being an idiot back then. I know that. I didn't mean to run you off."

"You never ran me off anything. Fact is, we both needed it. Maybe I shouldn't have up and left you like I did, but I figured you'd be right on your own. Hell, there ain't no hard feelings, how can there be between us? Not unless you're really only stopping here a couple of days?"

"Well, that's another thing we need to talk about. I've a plan, you see."

"A plan?" Arthur repeated, laughing. "'Course you bloody do."

"For where we're headed. Together. Unless you'd rather stick it here?"

"Mate, I'd rather stick a burning poker up my hole. I've had about as much of their praying as I can stomach. It's not through choice I'm still living here. Tell me where we're headed and I'm gone."

"South," Tommy said, smiling. "Same as we always were."

On thin wooden chairs they sat in the land office waiting room with two other men, and a receptionist who every few seconds shot a suspicious glare at Arthur as if surprised to find him still there. Arthur's leg bounced constantly, his gaze was pinned to the floor. He was already spooked by the city: the scale and opulence of Marvellous Melbourne was like nothing he had seen before. Thousands of people, the bicycles, buggies, and tram cars, rooftops touching the sky. Smoke belched from the factories and wharves west of the city and the river sat gray and low in the smog, while in the east it curved through swathes of manicured parkland, past the bowl of the famous cricket ground and out into the suburbs beyond. For this was where the money drained, from all that land, livestock, gold, all that labor put in by men like them, the wealth running off the pastures and scrubland in the north and flowing down here like a sewer.

"I'll wait outside," Arthur said, standing, but Tommy gripped his arm.

"We're doing this together, partners, fifty-fifty like we agreed."

Awkwardly Arthur retook his seat. The other men were watching him, nervous-looking characters wearing their very best suits, twisting their hats in their hands. Most likely their futures were on the line also, might have been waiting for this day their whole lives. Or maybe they owed the land man money, another month when they couldn't pay, and had now come to haggle their fate.

The office door opened and a skinny Italian with a crestfallen face skulked out with his eyes down. He walked past Tommy and Arthur—they slid in their boots—and out of the front door without a word.

"Mr. Thompson," the secretary said, nodding. "You're next."

Tommy stood, collected his holdall, waited while reluctantly Arthur rose to his feet. They walked past the reception desk and in through the still-open office door; Arthur closed it behind him, the letters running backward on the stenciled glass. "Sit down, sit down," the land man barked from behind a cluttered desk, not even a shake of hands. They sat, the land man frowning at Arthur and no doubt their attire: they were in their normal work clothes, they didn't have anything else. He was small and brown-haired and had about him a fussy, officious air. His name was Richardson, he told them, and he understood they were here about acquiring some land.

"Aye," Tommy said. "A selection. Somewhere that gets the rain."

"We get plenty of rain in Victoria, Mr. . . . ?"

"Thompson," Tommy reminded him.

"Mr. Thompson. So I'm afraid you'll have to be a little more specific than that."

"Somewhere hilly, then. Rain and hills, that's what we're after."

Richardson glanced at Arthur—that curious mention of "we"—and folded his hands on the desk. "You will need funds to set down by way of a deposit, of course. Which you have, I'm assuming, the pair of you? A letter of credit perhaps?"

He was taking the piss, Tommy realized. "I don't trust shinplasters," he said.

"Excuse me?"

Tommy stood and opened his holdall and shook out the contents onto the desk: bundles of banknotes, his entire life savings, plus the little Arthur had insisted on putting in. "That do you?" Tommy asked, and the land man flushed. Curtly, he nodded and reached behind him to a bureau, ran his finger over the handwritten labels and slid out one of the drawers to reveal a mound of tightly rolled plans. He shuffled through them until he found what he was looking for, fetched it out and went to put it on the desk but the money was still piled there. Tommy stuffed it back into his bag; Richardson unfurled the map and weighted it down.

"Now then," he said, snapping on a pair of fold-out reading spectacles, his finger tracing the map, tapping each location as he spoke. "Let me see. Here we are in Melbourne. Gippsland is less than a week's ride east. Or there is the train line, which might prove useful to you, if it's livestock you're looking to graze. There's plenty of land still available, at a very reasonable rate, and there are areas that are hilly, like you asked for. It also gets the rain. These crosses are the plots, I have another plan with more detail, a smaller scale, showing the topography and suchlike, let's see if there are any that interest you. If so, I can have my agent meet you out there and you can take a look in person for yourselves, how does all that sound?"

Tommy and Arthur glanced at each other.

"That works," Tommy said.

They stood at the top of the hillside, their backs to the gully below, looking over a plateau of rolling pasture that with a signature could be theirs. Behind them the land agent waited idly on the east-west track that bisected the gully they would also own. There was a creek at the bottom, he had told them, flowing all the way into town, while up here the ground was moist and rich, a sponge for the rainwater that fell in the faraway hills and trickled down to the creek through these fields. It was as perfect a spot for grazing as Tommy had ever seen. The cattle wouldn't know itself. They could build the first house right here where they stood, then later a second one out back somewhere so they wouldn't get on each other's nerves. Half an hour into town, Melbourne far enough away, Queensland even farther—hell, they were about as far south as the land went here, almost at the sea. Tommy could even picture the fence lines, the hedgerows and trees that would serve as natural breaking points, though he mostly planned on letting the cattle roam.

No more droving: they could take them to market on the trains. And he'd really never seen grass like it. Sink a well into this hillside, water would spout like an oil field. He had a very good feeling. By the look of him, Arthur had the same.

"Well? What do you reckon?" Tommy asked.

"I reckon she'll do us just fine."

"I was thinking one house here and another—"

"Over there by them trees."

"Exactly."

Arthur was pointing. "Paddocks, yards, stables."

"It'll take a bit of work, mind. Getting it all built."

He shook his head. "Mate, it won't feel nothing like work if it's ours."

Not since Glendale—and even then, only barely— had Tommy been able to call anywhere his own. Arthur was no different. Probably he was worse. All their lives they'd run and hid and grafted for someone else's gain, now finally here was a chance to plant their feet in the soil and say this, right here, this is mine, I have earned it, I am home.

Chapter 29
Reverend Bean

Through the dust-blown desert they ambled, one man armed with a rifle, the other a knife and spear. Hunters, though with nothing to show for it yet, chatting while they walked, laughing now and then, until one spotted the carrion birds squabbling over a carcass part-buried in the dirt. He tapped his friend on the arm, pointed with the rifle-end. Warily they approached. At the last minute the birds hopped clear and a thick blanket of flies rose into the air. The men stepped nearer and stood looking at the body lying facedown in the earth. A man, naked, chunks of him missing where he'd been gorged and pecked and gnawed. Whitefella, by the look of him, though the skin was blackened by sun and rot. The spear-carrier crouched and poked the belly with the spear tip, then between them using their weapons they rolled the body onto its back. Arms limp and heavy. The legs twisted one over the next. The head flopped toward them and they saw what was left of the face. Empty eye sockets, a swollen tongueless mouth, raw slabs of rotting flesh where the ears should have been. Ruefully they looked at him a moment until one cracked a joke and they both laughed. They moved on. The birds hopped back over and went on eating, and the flies descended again.

PART III

1906

Nine years later

Chapter 30

Katherine and Billy McBride

From her bedroom window Katherine watched the guests arriving, trundling up the track in their carriages and buggies, the Monteiths in their new motorcar, black-and-chrome, glinting in the evening sun. Bradley Monteith brought it spluttering to a halt at the bottom of the steps and waved to the gathering crowd. Off came his goggles. A cheeky honk of the horn. He leaped from the car and began parading it to the onlookers, while in the passenger seat his wife, Evelyn, sat motionless, as if dumbstruck by the drive. She too was wearing goggles, and a shawl to protect her dress, but when she removed them it was clear neither had worked: her pearl-white gown now stained with a dusty bib, a white patch from the goggles slapped across her face. She looked like a startled possum, sitting wide-eyed in the car, and when finally her husband remembered and helped her down, she swayed like a drunk on her feet. Not that Bradley noticed, turning quickly and shouting, "Isn't she a beauty!" while lovingly stroking the hood of the car.

Katherine returned to her dressing table, sat down and took up her brushes and continued powdering her eyelids and cheeks. Downstairs, a string quartet was playing; later, there would be a full band, led by someone called Frankie, goodness knows where Billy had found him. In fact she had no idea about any of this, all these people, this expense, and all on her behalf. Tomorrow she would turn forty, and for that Billy had decided a grand party must be thrown, not bothering to consult her, much as she doubted Evelyn Monteith had been consulted about that new motorcar. And yet here they were, the two of them, along with every other woman down there, caked in dust or disappointment or whatever other burden they bore, smiling prettily for their husbands, for appearances, for the bloody photographer Billy had hired. They were always expected to be somebody else's something: wife, mother, sister, widow. They were never just allowed to be themselves.

Still, it would be nice to see people, she so rarely left the station these days. Where could she go? Another trip to Bewley, the same shops, the same faces, the same smiles when she was with them, the whispered gossip once she was gone? Last year she had traveled to Melbourne for her father's funeral (only herself and the children, Billy had stayed behind), and though it had been a welcome adventure she'd felt utterly out of place. So many buildings and people, so little space. The manicured parkland of the Domain Gardens had seemed laughable, fake, people strolling with their parasols like actors on a stage. She belonged here, she'd accepted finally. The station, the bush, the nothingness—this was truly now her home.

She finished with her makeup and considered her reflection, better than when she'd started though never quite good enough. Thin lines at her eyes and mouth, the obvious signs of tiredness, the pigmentation and other marks each pregnancy had left behind. She was still considered attractive, she knew; heads still turned when she walked into a room, though how much of that was down to her status, her fine clothing, she wasn't sure. Maybe her limp drew their eyes also. Barely there anymore but she felt how it aged her, and the effort it took to keep it from her stride. Four years ago she'd been out riding and had fallen, lucky she never left the house without her shotgun or she might not have been found. The horse had spooked at something, she wasn't sure what, and she'd landed on a rock, not even a very big one, it was the angle more than anything else. A bolt of searing pain tore through her; the hip was broken, she'd later learn. Lying on the ground in agony, watching the birds cross the sky, she'd wondered if this was really it for her, if her time had come. Such an ignominy, to die like this, alone. Thoughts of the children, of Suzanna especially, she was only three years old. Then she'd remembered the shotgun. The horse now standing calmly not fifteen yards away—screaming, foaming, she had dragged herself over that hardscrabble ground and hauled on the stirrup and managed to reach the saddle holster. She lay on her back, exhausted. Fired, reloaded, fired again, kept firing until she hadn't the strength. Next thing she knew she was in bed, the doctor over her, dosed up on laudanum drops.

Billy had shot the horse right there where he found it. Took the saddle off, the bit and bridle, put a bullet straight through its head.

She went to the wardrobe, reached for the bodice of her new ballgown, held it against herself in the long mirror over her camisole. Billy had brought a dress-maker out from Brisbane for the occasion; then back again, the poor man, for a fitting once the gown was made. And it was beautiful, she had to admit. White lace with blue ruffles, silk almost too fine to touch, goodness knows how much it had cost. Heads would turn tonight, she was sure of it, then later after a few drinks there'd be hands touching her back or stroking the bare skin of her arm, the rush of their too-close breath. Repulsive, most of them, though there was a small secret part of her that enjoyed being desired. Of course, Billy still wanted her, pined for her, often painfully so, but things were more complicated there. They had reached an accommodation, was how she thought of it, a tolerance of each other, an acceptance of their shared but separate lives. She did give in to him sometimes (hence Suzanna); they were still a married couple after all. And he was trying, God love him. In his own clumsy way, and for a long time now, with both her and the children, Billy had tried his best.

Julie was waiting outside the bedroom. Katherine called her in, and together they began the rigmarole of getting her dressed. Corset, petticoat, bustle, skirt . . . on and on, pulling and tying and fastening at every stage. Her hair was pinned in a nest and finished with a thin golden tiara. She stood in the long mirror inspecting the outcome. "You look beautiful, Mrs. McBride," Julie said. And even now, sixteen years later, the name still took her a little by surprise.

Out through the door and along the corridor, her

short train whispering behind. Past Billy's bedroom, then William's and Isobel's, both away at boarding school and hardly ever home. The noise from downstairs building the closer to the atrium she came: the music and the talking, the clink of glasses, raucous laughter now and then. She thought she could hear Billy somewhere, louder than anyone, making himself heard.

At Suzanna's door she stopped and listened, heard the excited little voices inside. She turned the handle and entered, found Suzanna, Thomas, and the nanny huddled around the window, ogling the late arrivals and no doubt Bradley Monteith's car. The nanny stiffened when she noticed Katherine, tried to suppress her smile; Katherine waved that it was fine.

"Mummy, Mummy, did you see it? Did you see the motorized car?"

"It's *motor*car, not *motorized*," Thomas corrected, eleven years old and already assuming he knew it all. By now they should probably have been thinking about school for him too, but Billy was keen to keep him at home as long as he could. He had come round, belatedly, in this new century of opportunity, to the benefits a good education could bring, but Thomas was the son he'd always wanted—a horse-riding, cattle-droving replica—and although he claimed it was good for the boy to be home-tutored a while longer, to properly embed him in station life, she knew it was for Billy's benefit too. He'd be miserable without his favorite to teach and mold and tease. None of the others got a look in. Pathetic though it sounded, the boy was about as close as Billy had to a friend.

"I did see it," she told Suzanna. "And a fine machine it is too. You certainly don't get many *motorized* vehicles in our part of the world."

She raised an eyebrow at Thomas, who didn't appreciate the joke. Suzanna said, "Can we get one, Mummy? Can I ride in it . . . *please?*"

"A horse is quicker," Thomas grumbled.

"I'm sure your father is already planning it. Not too late now, you hear?"

"Yes, Mrs. McBride," the nanny said, a little curtsy and dip of the head. She had come on the boat from England, apparently, where she'd worked in some fine old country house; Lord only knew what she was doing out here. Katherine walked over and kissed both children on their heads, Thomas twisting like he'd been poked. She left the room. Pulled the door closed behind her, made her way to the landing balustrades, the crowd below revealing itself, the hats and beehive hairstyles, a constellation of shining bald heads. Happily they milled around the atrium and into the adjoining reception rooms, waiters circulating with canapés and drinks trays, the string quartet tucked under the stairs; later, when the full band played, the atrium was to become a dance floor. There were fresh flowers everywhere, tinsel hung from the chandelier, the house dolled up like Christmas—what was Billy trying to prove?

Of course, she already knew the answer. That much never changed.

One man stood out among the revelers: loitering alone by the wall, clutching his champagne flute in a fist, dressed in plain scruffy clothing and a khaki-colored jacket, he looked more like one of their stockmen in truth. Katherine thought she might have recognized him. Maybe he'd been to the house before. Light brown hair and a thick mustache, hooded eyes restlessly roving the crowd. Whenever a tray came by he snaffled as much food as he could carry, and always took a refill of champagne, throwing it back greedily, eating openmouthed. She wondered if Billy knew him. Or if somebody's coach driver had managed to sneak in unchecked.

She drifted around the balcony landing, her hand trailing the banister, and here and there heads began to turn. A fluttering in her stomach, heat rising in her cheeks; a part of her hated being the reason for all this excess.

Glasses began tinkling, rings tapping champagne flutes, as guests filtered through from the other rooms. The strings fell silent. A hush enveloped the house. Katherine paused at the turn partway down the stairs, every face now toward her, mostly strangers; a room of rich, grinning fools. And there was Billy, in the center, moving forward, the biggest fool of them all, buttoned up in his dinner suit, the waistcoat pulling at his gut. His face was flushed, his eyes wide, looked like he might already be drunk. He gazed at her warmly and hollered, "Here she is, ladies and gentlemen: my beautiful wife, the birthday girl!"

Applause and cheering. Glasses were raised. Katherine came another few steps down then halted when Billy began talking again.

"Now, you all know, I'm sure, that this party wasn't Katherine's idea. She doesn't like being the centerpiece, ridiculous as that may seem—if you have a Turner why not hang it in the middle of the wall?" Laughter. Billy paused. "But no, this evening was my idea, because I wanted to mark her birthday with the kind of occasion she deserves. A celebration in her honor, a celebration of her. We didn't have a lavish wedding. Hell, I could barely afford a suit. Sixteen years ago that was, down in Bewley's little chapel, none of you lot would have been there, I know that much. But life's been kind since then, to both of us. Not that it hasn't been bloody hard work." There was sniggering. Billy caught the implication and scolded: "I meant the station, you cheeky bastards—the station's been bloody hard work!"

As the laughter died out, Billy's expression changed. He was staring up at Katherine with an almost boyish zeal. If she didn't know him better, she might have thought him ready to cry.

"I love you," he told her earnestly, in front of all those people, those hardened cattlemen. "I'm sorry for not being around more—and for everything else. I don't know where I'd be without you. So here's to you, my Katie. Happy birthday!"

There was a momentary pause, an inhalation in the room, followed by an audible sigh. Billy raised his glass and the others joined him, to cries of *Happy Birthday!* and *To Katherine!* and *Hear Hear!* The strings began playing again while, bewildered, suspended on the staircase, Katherine could only stare. Billy had never spoken to her that way before, not in public anyway. Despite herself, despite everything, she felt a rush of warmth and gratitude that shamed her a little too. She knew what he was, what he'd done, but he was also her husband. She had stuck with him, for better or worse, and for once here was a rare *better*—what was she to make of it? Was it so wrong to be moved?

She descended the stairs, smiling bashfully, accepting well-wishes, seeking out Billy over their heads. Here he came toward her, the bodies parting, people slapping his back and shaking his hand. He was giddy in a way he hadn't been for many years. She didn't trust it. Something was very wrong.

"Do you like it?" he asked her. "It's not too much?"

"It's way too much, Billy. What the hell's going on?"

"What? It's your birthday—we're allowed to celebrate."

"All this. That speech. Why are you acting so strange?"

They were talking in whispers, smiling and nodding at the people nearby. Billy led her aside, to the wall, pausing to fetch them each a drink from a passing tray. He pressed the champagne upon her and Katherine caught a glimpse of that interloper again, watching them keenly across the room.

"That man, who is he? Over there, in the corner."

Carelessly Billy glanced over. "Don't worry about him. Listen—"

"Do you know him? Did you know he was here?"

"Yes, it's not important. Look, there's something I need to say."

She steadied herself and stared at him, at his earnest bloodshot eyes; he was, she realized, even more drunk than she'd supposed.

"We're fine now," Billy told her. "The station, there's no chance it could ever fail. We've ridden out the depression and we're drought-proof just about, there's enough good land to spread the load. Nobody out there can touch us. Kidman's not coming this far east. Everything's set for the future, Kat. For you, the children—"

Oh shit, he's dying, Katherine thought. Or he's fallen for somebody else.

"—us McBrides are made for life. Well, the rest of them are, it's you and me aren't doing so good. All the money in the world but you still can't hardly stand to look at me, and I know which I'd rather have. But it's all right, see, I've a plan to fix that too. I'm going to make things right between us, I can't tell you how yet, but I need to go away for a while. When I'm back and everything's in place you can say I'm an idiot but by then it'll be too late. Least, I hope it will be anyway. I'll explain then, and maybe you'll see I'm not that boy anymore—I love you, I just told you in front of everyone, what more's it going to take?"

"You're drunk. Have you heard yourself, Billy Mc-Bride?"

"Aye, maybe. But I mean it."

"Just like that? After all these years?"

"I've always loved you, Katie."

"I don't doubt it, in your own way. That's not what I'm talking about: How do you intend fixing everything in one fell swoop?"

Billy glanced in the direction of the stranger, but he was gone. "You're just going to have to trust me, like you once did." He raised his champagne flute and grinned at her. "Now come on, enjoy the party. It's your birthday, for Christ's sake!"

"Sir, there's a Mr. Wainwright here to see you."

Billy had been in the yard, talking to the staff about the night's arrangements, Katherine's birthday party, another grand gesture of atonement, another attempt at making things right. Not everything, maybe, but at the very least he could put on a good show for her, and for all their guests. He had quite a crowd coming. Squatters, lawmen, councilors, the great and the good from far and wide. Some had traveled days to get here. The house would be full to the brim. Now he turned at the sound of Hardy's voice, and that name he'd used: Wainwright, after all this time. Billy had presumed him the latest in a long line of frauds. A whole year had passed nearly, and not a single bloody word.

"Where is he?"

"Waiting in the atrium. Shall I show him the door?"

"No, I'll speak with him. Put him in the office. Stay till I get there. Make sure he doesn't touch anything."

Hardy nodded, went back inside. Billy finished his instructions and followed, found Hardy standing stiffly in the office doorway while Wainwright paced the room. He stopped when Billy entered. Hardy pulled the door closed. Billy walked around the desk and dropped into the leather chair with an irritated sigh. He pointed to the wingbacks and Wainwright took a seat.

"If it's more money you're after, forget it. Wasting my bloody time, the lot of you. There isn't a man out there capable of doing the job he claims."

Wainwright didn't answer. He sat with the hunched and brooding posture of most in his trade, his heavy hands together, picking the filthy nails. Light brown hair and mustache, a face that had taken a few blows. When he spoke, his voice was low and husky, like he'd breathed in too much dust.

"I'm only after what's owed. Nothing more than that."

"Owed? You thieving bastard. I've paid you too much as it is."

"The other half, I mean."

A stillness came over Billy. His anger immediately drained; he looked suddenly ill. Neither man moving. Staring each other down. Billy's mouth opened, reaching for words that wouldn't come. Finally, he managed: "You found him?"

"I did."

"He's alive?"

"He is."

"Where?"

"Gippsland, Victoria. Going by the name of Robert Thompson: Bobby's what he gets. Has a small selection on a hillside out of town. It's good land. Grazing country. He seems to be getting by."

"Alone?"

Wainwright shrugged. "He's got a darkie with him, old fella, must be some kind of boy. I never saw no woman. Seems quite fond of his dog."

Billy flopped back in his chair, his gaze sliding from Wainwright and across a thousand miles to where his brother now lived on a hillside, with a blackboy and a dog, tending his cattle and mostly alone. He could see him. He could see Tommy so clearly in his mind. He'd be mid-thirties now and healthy, Billy reckoned, handsome with that dusty fair hair.

"You saw him? Speak to him?"

"I never spoke to him, no. Didn't want to cause alarm. But I saw him plenty, from a distance, he wouldn't have known I was there."

"And how did he seem? Is he happy?"

"He was working mostly. Or sitting with his dog."

"Lonely?"

"Might be, aye."

Billy shook his head. "I need a fucking drink."

He rose and poured himself a tall whiskey, nothing for Wainwright, and sat back down behind the desk. Billy's hand was shaking. Tommy, after all this time. Wincing, he took a long pull of the whiskey, thought fuck it and tipped the whole thing down. He came up gasping. Eyes pinched, sucking in through his teeth. He set down the glass and waited while the burn subsided and the liquor swam nicely in his belly and head, then focused on Wainwright again.

"So how'd you find him?"

A shrug. "Followed the trail. He wasn't an easy man to run down."

"Could others? The police?"

"Find anyone if you look hard enough. It'd have to be worth their while."

"You bring proof?"

"Like what?"

"Anything—you could be spinning me a line."

Wainwright shifted a little in the chair, flexing his thick shoulders and neck. "I did, it would cost my reputation. And you ain't paying enough to risk that."

"But you're sure it's Tommy?"

"Now that I'll stake my name on. It's him all right."

"You know what I can do if you're lying to me?"

"I've an idea, aye."

"And you're sticking with your story?"

"It ain't a story. It's the way things is."

"Fine."

Billy leaned to the safe, opened it, counted out a stack of bills. He handed them to Wainwright, who counted them also, slowly, then folded them and slipped them into the pocket of his jacket. They sat a moment in silence until Wainwright remembered something, dipped into another of his pockets and came up with a handwritten note. "There it is all wrote down for you. His name. Directions from the town." He leaned forward and sent it fluttering across the desk. Billy picked it up and read. He wondered where *Bobby* had come from. There weren't any Robert Thompsons he knew. It was a common enough name though. Must have been thousands out there.

"We're having a party tonight. Stay for a drink and a feed."

"I don't really go to parties."

"And I'm not really asking. I want you here while I make a few enquiries."

"What enquiries?"

"I have a man in the Melbourne land office. I'll send an urgent telegram. Won't take long."

Wainwright sniffed dismissively. "I told you. It's him all right."

"Then you won't mind staying. Fill your boots with my champagne."

Billy dismissed him. Wainwright skulked from the room. Hardy came in soon afterward and Billy told him to watch their guest: he wasn't to leave the station until Billy said he could. Billy picked up the piece of paper and reread it. The words seemed magical on the page. A few simple ink scrawls and within them a whole world. Tommy. It had been twenty-one years. Apart longer than they were together—the thought stopped Billy cold. It seemed only weeks ago they had embraced and said their final goodbye. But now here he was: a grazier, in the green hills of Victoria, where they got the rain. Billy shook his head, and smiled.

"If either of you talks, if Billy leaves, or Tommy returns, if there's so much as a letter in the mail, I will kill the both of you and your families and anyone else you hold dear. There will be no warning. One day you

will simply look upon my face and know what the other has done."

Noone. Well, fuck him. Billy wasn't scared of that cunt now. He'd been a boy, sixteen years old, when out there in the atrium Noone had laid down those terms; sixteen and trembling like a beat dog. Now Billy owned the atrium, and the house around it, the entire district, while Noone was some pencil-pushing civil servant, commissioner of police for whatever that was worth, sitting around in dusty guildhalls, wearing wigs and smoking cigars. And he was old, the fucker, he was an old man these days—Billy had done some digging too. Big house on the river, a wife and two grown-up girls, moving in all the right society circles and with far too much to lose. What did Noone care about Billy and Tommy now? About threats made two decades ago? Billy was not some young pup he could frighten anymore—he would wager his own influence stretched just as far as Noone's, you only had to look at who was coming tonight. The real power in Queensland lay not in the city but in those who owned the land. The people Billy had in his pocket, the favors he could call in. Christ, he could only imagine what it would feel like to ruin him, to bring that bastard down. Let him feel powerless for a change; your life on another man's whim. And he could do it, he was suddenly realizing; he'd always had the means. But he hadn't been strong enough. He hadn't dared. Not now. Now he had the strength, the power, the wealth: Billy could ride out any scandal far easier than Noone. Because Noone was a politician, and politicians are men of straw: light a fire under them and see how quickly they burn. With him gone Tommy would be safe, Billy could fix it for his brother to come home. And if he did this, if he was able to pull it off, Katherine might find a way to forgive him, they could have a real marriage again.

He was seeing it so clearly: redemption, at last.

All he had to do was confess.

Chapter 31
Tommy McBride

B irds chirruped softly as Tommy rose and swiveled to the edge of the bed; the rapid-fire cackle of a kookaburra's cry. Carefully he slid the bedsheet back over Emily, protecting her modesty, and her body from the early morning chill, let his hand rest on her shoulder, cupping the slender bone. She lay on her front, her head turned away from him, blond hair spread over the pillow, naked beneath the sheet. Tommy was naked also. They'd slept however they fell. He stood and padded quietly from the bedroom, eased the door to behind him, stopped short of closing it fully on account of the hinges' creak. Into the living room, where he found his trousers and pulled them on, then the kitchen, the coffeepot, the stove. He rolled a cigarette while the water was boiling. Their dinner plates were still on the table. Tommy tucked the cigarette behind his ear and tidied them away, scraped the leftovers into a bowl and put the plates in the washtub for later. He poured his coffee. Steaming in the cool dawn air. Juggling the mug and bowl of leftovers, he opened the door and found Tess waiting on the back verandah, her black-and-white head cocked toward him, like she'd heard them last night and known.

"Don't look at me like that, you cheeky bugger. Come and have a feed."

He stepped out, set down the bowl, and lit the cigarette while she tucked in. Prime beef steak and fried potatoes, she had a good right to be keen. Tommy sipped his coffee. Looking out over the backyard with its fowl house and veggie patch, its dunny and wash station, into the paddocks beyond. Some cattle were near the fence line, grazing peacefully on feed as green and rich as the day he'd first come—somehow he still didn't trust it, assumed it couldn't last. He drew deeply on the cigarette, exhaled through his nose, blue eyes narrowed in their customary squint. His face was lightly stubbled, gray and gold, red in places, he didn't ever grow a full beard. Broad in the chest and shoulders, work-thick sunburned arms, his torso dusted in freckles and wispy fair hair. He scratched his chest and yawned heavily, tossed the coffee dregs. With the cigarette between his lips he unbuckled his trousers to piss off the steps, then reconsidered after a glance at the house. She was probably still sleeping, but what if she saw him? He dropped his cigarette in the bucket, then, holding up his trousers, waddled awkwardly down the steps and barefoot across the yard to the dunny instead.

Tess glanced up curiously, wondering at this change in routine.

Sure enough, he left the outhouse to find Emily waiting on the back porch, wrapped in a bedsheet, her hair loosely tied, blond strands falling about her face. Tommy stalled at the sight of her, draped all in white and framed by the house in the pale morning light. How had he got so lucky? How hadn't that luck run out yet? Once, she'd been married to the fat baker in town; the day his heart gave out was the day Tommy's fortunes really changed. And Emily's—they should never have been together in the first place. Tommy was almost waiting for her to realize the same thing about him. Good job she'd not caught him earlier, pissing off the steps.

"Morning," Emily said, smiling. Tommy began walking again.

"Morning."

"You should have woke me."

"You were sleeping." He came up the steps and

kissed her. Soft lips, her breath sleep-warm, the tanned and freckled skin of her bare shoulders. "I made coffee if you want one. Or tea, however you like."

"I have to be getting back, Bobby. I've the shop to open. I'm already late."

He looked down shyly. "You know you don't have to."

"It's not about having to. I want to. The bakery's my life, my living."

"What I meant was it doesn't have to be, I—"

She touched his face tenderly. He didn't go on. There were things he wanted to tell her, ask her, there had been for a long time now. He was worried he might spoil something between them. That she might not feel the same.

"I know what you meant. Maybe one day. But that shop means a lot to me too, and I'm good at it, or I would be if you weren't always making me late."

"I'll take you down then."

"I can walk."

"Be quicker if we rode."

"All right, but we'd best hurry up about it."

"Before anyone's awake to see us, you mean."

"Well, you aren't exactly respectable. And me a widow and everything . . ."

They smiled at each other, at her teasing. Tommy never knew when she was being serious, when he should worry, or take offense, and that playfulness she had about her, that unpredictability, set off butterflies. The simplest word could send him spinning. He'd never experienced anything like it in his life.

Inside, Emily gathered up her scattered clothes and took them into the bedroom to get dressed. Tommy found a shirt and a pair of socks, sniffed both, figured they would do, pulled them on. He tidied up a little, collecting their wineglasses, emptying the ashtray. He was always tidying when she visited. Before Emily, he'd lived like any other bloke. Now all his books were lined up neatly on the sideboard, his old *Queenslander* journals were in a tall pile by the fire. For years those journals had been like a millstone, Tommy scouring the pages for news from home. Now he was working his way through them a little differently: a couple of pages a night got his fire going just fine.

He sat down in the armchair and waited. Furtive glances at the bedroom door. Through the gap he could see her moving, her shadow playing over the wall. He could already feel her leaving, the absence of her in the house. There'd been one other brief relationship before this—Anne, they'd not been right from the start—and since then he'd made his peace with being alone. He'd never figured he deserved true happiness, not in that way, content to count the other blessings in his life. But now, with Emily, it was like he could touch it: a life together, the two of them, maybe children, a proper family—Christ, he didn't dare.

He never woke up screaming, those mornings she was here.

After dropping Emily in town, Tommy ate a quick breakfast then with Tess by his side rode out on Lady, to Arthur's place, north across the undulating fields, the three of them loping along together, comfortable in their routine. Lady was good for him that way. Her easy, unhurried gait. She was a hazel-colored mare and only the second horse he'd had since Beau died; the first had been a mistake, another dun-gray gelding he'd hoped would be just like his old mate. No horse could have been. Beau was a true one-off. He'd died not long after they'd got here, like he'd been waiting to see Tommy right. Those thousands of miles he'd carried him: all over Queensland, from Bewley to St. George; the long slog into the center then the stock routes year on year; south through the ranges and goldfields, then across into Victoria and finally here, until one day he simply lay down like he was knackered, and died. Tommy had wept when he found him, held tight to the cooling flank, then in the days following had toiled to dig a grave big enough, now a lonely little marker in a copse of sapling trees. He'd mourned that horse far longer than he should have— what would his father have said?—but was now quite taken with Lady, they'd been together almost six years. He liked her steady temperament. Just riding her kept him calm.

They'd built the second house about a mile away from the first, put some distance between them, just in case. Arthur hadn't wanted to be too near the track anyway, the risk of inviting trouble, he knew how folks could be. He'd been right about that, the locals had never accepted him, not once they'd learned he wasn't just Tommy's boy. Arthur didn't care, instead contenting himself back here, with his work, his land, with Rosie; especially so with her.

Arthur's horse was already saddled and hitched to the verandah rail; as soon as Tommy came within sight of the windows the front door opened and there he was, hobbling down the steps, shouting, "You're late. What time d'you call this?"

Tommy chuckled. He rode up to the house. Arthur was as thin and wizened as he'd always been, his hair and beard fully gray, but his spirit remained un- dimmed. He walked bandy-legged, like he was forever saddle-sore, his joints twisted and gnarled like roots. It took him a few attempts to get into the saddle. Tommy knew better than to help. He also knew what it meant to Arthur, the two of them still doing this, working together every day.

Rosie came out with their food parcels. She was short and plump and healthy, with hair braided tight to her head. Down the steps, eyes alight with affection, she handed a parcel to each man. "It's not much but it'll keep you living—I've a stew on for supper that'll fill you both to the gills. Morning, Bobby-love, how you been?"

"Ah, can't complain. Not like this old bugger, mind. Not even got a hello."

"Should bloody sack you," Arthur grumbled. "Nearer lunchtime just about."

Rosie rolled her eyes. "He's ten minutes late if anything, quit flapping your gums." She turned to Tommy. "Will you be over for supper tonight, love?"

He thought of Emily. They rarely saw each other two nights running, as if not wanting to push their luck. Or arouse suspicion, though everyone in town already knew, Emily far more concerned with appearances than Tommy had ever been. But then she had to spend her days among them, depended on their custom in the bakery—everything would be so much easier if she just came and lived up here.

"Aye, that'd be lovely. Looking forward to the stew."

They rode away together, Tess following at their heels. Trotting lightly over open country, into the pastures beyond. Flat grassland up here, rolling green plains, occasional trees and hedgerows, not a clump of spinifex or scrub grass in view.

"She came by again, I take it," Arthur said, once they were clear of the house.

"Might have done, aye."

"No might have done about it."

"Why d'you say that?"

"Rode in late and smiling, that's why."

Tommy laughed. The two of them side by side together, like it had always been. "She had the shop to open, the ovens to get on. I rode her down this morning. Might have said some things I shouldn't."

Arthur looked at him sharply. "You stupid bugger. What did you say?"

"Not like that. Just got a bit ahead of myself. Talking about her moving in."

"And? What did she make of it?"

"Said one day, maybe. She won't let go of the shop."

"Well, don't ask her to. Then you'd be making her choose."

"So how the hell do I get her out here?"

"Let her do it on her own terms. Shit, Tommy, buy her a horse so she can ride to and fro, then she could keep the shop on too."

"I'm talking about marrying her, Arthur."

"Why can't she do both?"

"Get married and still work?"

"Now there's a thought," Arthur said.

They spent all that day in the fields with the cattle. Arthur tired in the early afternoon and Tommy left him dozing beneath a tree, woke him up two hours later; Arthur denied he'd been asleep. At day's end they rode back home then separated, each to his own place, Tommy calling out to make sure Rosie saved him some stew. He stabled Lady, gave himself a wash, found a clean shirt, and slung it on. There was still a little wine left from last night, so he poured himself a glass and rolled a cigarette and took them onto the front veran- dah to watch the sunset. Tess wandered around the side of the house and hopped up onto the deck, lay down at his feet on the boards. Tommy lit his cigarette. He sipped the dark red wine. The gully falling away be- neath him, the birds flocking for the trees, the chaos of their twilight dance. He felt dangerously on the cusp of something. As if teetering on an edge. Happiness, contentment, love . . . these weren't words he'd ever recognized, or certainly not for many years, hadn't thought it possible they could apply to him, yet here they were. It scared the shit out of him, honestly. The risk of having something unwarranted, something he might then lose. But he couldn't stop his thoughts from spiraling, plans fluttering over him like falling leaves. Emily living up here, the house painted and prettied-up with all her things. She could keep the bakery, like Arthur suggested, ride there and back every day. And if they ever had children, well, maybe then she might decide to give it up. Or not. She might not have to, if she could find a caretaker to run the place for a wage. Tommy could help pay for it. He had plenty of money—their cattle sold more than well. Then, when she was ready, she could take the shop back again, and on those days when things were difficult with the children maybe Rosie could lend a hand.

Dreamily he watched the sky purple as the sun slid from view. The birds took their roosts and fell silent, settling down for the night.

Chapter 32
Billy McBride

Billy took the train to Brisbane: private coach to Charleville then first class all the way, dining cars and single-sleeper carriages, he didn't like to share. At Roma Street station he hailed a buggy and told the driver to take him to the Bellevue Hotel, only a short trip down George Street but he wasn't inclined to walk. Po-faced, he watched the city trundle by. He'd visited often enough by now. Some of the architecture was impressive, he supposed—the courthouse, the new treasury building, the land office and suchlike—but think of the money it had cost to build them, and to what end? That was the thing with cities: everything was on the surface, no substance, no return. They built these things out of vanity: a bunch of monied old boys putting their pizzles on display.

They reached the Bellevue quickly, Billy climbed down, a bellboy came to take his bags. He was traveling with just a small suitcase but let the boy carry it anyway, Billy marching ahead of him into the hotel. A curved three-story corner building, with ornate cast-iron balustrades encircling the two upper floors, the Bellevue sat adjacent to the immense grandeur of Parliament House, opposite the famous Queensland Club, and looked out over the ornamental parkland of the Botanic Gardens, the river just beyond. Billy noticed none of it. Not even a glance. Ignoring the doorman's greeting, he walked through the lobby to the desk.

"Mr. McBride," the clerk said, smiling. "So nice to see you again."

"Is my room ready?"

"Of course, sir. Will you be needing anything after your journey? Refreshments? Laundry? A bath?"

"Aye, a bath. Hot. I'll eat in the restaurant after. A table by the window."

"Very good, sir. There's a bell in your room, just give it a pull and—"

"I know how the bloody bell works."

"Of course. My apologies. James will take you up."

"There is one other thing, actually." Billy leaned forward a little, lowered his voice. "I need an address for an old friend of mine, a lawyer by the name of Henry

Wells. It's been a while since I saw him, I thought I might drop in. His office, ideally. Whatever you can find."

"I'll get right on it. I'm sure it won't take long. Please, enjoy your stay."

Billy lay in the perfumed bathwater, soaking the journey from his bones, then unpacked and dressed, put his travel clothes in for laundering, and ate alone in the restaurant downstairs. He was one of only a few diners. Midafternoon, most tables empty: a man sipping tea and reading a newspaper, two women giddily drinking champagne. Billy ordered steak and stared out the window, chewing. Watching the crowds shuffle by. From a back room somewhere there came bursts of raucous laughter, the sounds of glasses clinking, voices competing to be heard. Billy asked the waiter what was happening and was told it was the members' bar.

"It's a hotel—what members?"

"Of parliament, sir. From next door. They're finished for the day."

Billy checked the wall clock, scowling. It was just after three o'clock. Workshy bastards. No wonder nothing in government ever got done.

He was crossing the lobby again when the desk clerk called to him: "A message for you, Mr. McBride." Then, quietly: "That address you asked me for."

Billy took the folded sheet of paper, glanced at it, tucked the note away. "Thanks," he said, swiveling on his heels and making for the main doors. He didn't hear the clerk say "My pleasure, sir," or see him scurry away into a side office as soon as Billy's back was turned.

If Henry Wells's name wasn't on the little brass door-plate, Billy would have assumed he'd been given the wrong address. The office was in a run-down back-street somewhere in Fortitude Valley, halfway along a row of boarded-up shopfronts, dilapidated tenements, piss-stained doorways, and rat-infested rubbish piles, and might once have been a tailor's workshop judging by the faded lettering on the sign. There was shouting coming from the tenements, an argument; somewhere a door slammed. Billy checked the street in both directions, cupped his hands to the filthy window and peered inside, saw a little seating area and empty reception desk, light coming from the office behind. Billy tried the door and opened it. A bell tinkled overhead. He stepped into the waiting area and a voice called, "Just a moment! Please take a seat!"

Billy didn't bother. The tiny chairs looked more suited to a schoolroom. Instead he browsed the framed certificates hanging on the walls, and the spines of ancient law books on the shelves. He picked up an old magazine from the coffee table and dropped it again. There were no papers on the reception desk, he noticed, no stationery; a dusty film coated the plain, unvarnished wood.

"Sorry about that," Henry Wells announced, bursting through the office door. "I'm afraid my secretary is sick at the moment and I'm just so flat out with—"

He pulled up short when he recognized the visitor, flushing suddenly, shock then anger in his face. Other than being a little heavier, Billy had not changed much these past nine years, though for Henry age had not been so kind. He was bald now, an auburn crown, and his once cherubic plumpness had turned emphatically to jowl. His eyes were dark and bloodshot behind his little round spectacles, and his suit looked years-old and threadbare, the cuffs fraying, patches sewn onto the elbows.

"Billy McBride. What the hell are you doing here?"

"I wondered if we could have a talk."

Bitterly, Henry snorted. "And what could we possibly have to discuss?"

"Well I wouldn't be here about the bloody weather now, would I?"

Henry weighed him carefully. "You're changing your story?"

A shrug. "Might be, aye."

"Now? After all these years?"

"If you ain't interested, I could go find someone else."

"There is nobody else. You know that. Nobody would touch that case, not after what happened to me. I should have been King's Counsel by now, running my own set, but look at me: look what that bastard did!"

He held out his arms to the office, his life. Billy said, "Noone put you here?"

"Of course, Noone—who else?" He nodded at Billy's suit, his pocket watch, the obvious trappings of his wealth. "Seems you've fared a little better. All that blood money feathering your nest."

"Hey now, I never had nothing to do with your troubles."

"You had everything to do with them. You lied through your teeth!"

"For my own protection. That wasn't about you."

A burst of laughter from Henry. He looked about in disbelief. "He doesn't even deny it! As if perjury isn't a crime!" He pointed at Billy. "If you'd told the truth, if you'd contradicted Noone, we'd have had him hanged by now, and my career would have been made. Do you know how long it took chambers to get rid of me? Two days! I'd been with them since my pupilage and they dropped me like a bad penny. I lost my career, my marriage, my children—I'm a pariah in this city thanks to you."

After a moment Billy said, "I thought you chased the fellas anyhow?"

"Excuse me?"

"I didn't figure you were married, I mean."

"Well, if there is a silver lining, perhaps that is it. Work might be in the sewer but I am perfectly happy at home. Not that I suspect you actually care."

He seemed to have blown himself out a bit. Billy said, "Is there somewhere we can talk, out of view of the street?"

Henry took a long breath then led him into the office, an airless little room drowning under the sea of paper that spilled from every surface and covered most of the floor. "Just clear off those files there," he told Billy, pointing to a chair, while he edged round the other side. "So," Henry said, flopping down, as warily Billy took a seat, "what's with this sudden change of heart?"

"I need to know if I can trust you first."

"You've already admitted lying under oath. It's a little late for that."

"Just answer the bloody question."

"I don't . . . what are you even asking here?"

"If I tell you, if we do anything, it's on my terms, understand?"

Henry straightened a little, his attention piqued. "All right. Go on."

"What you just said, about me lying, it being a crime—is that right?"

"I'm afraid so, yes."

"Meaning what exactly?"

"Well, you could be prosecuted for perjury, but I suppose it would depend."

"On what?"

"On whether a deal could be struck first."

Billy pointed at him. "That's what I'm getting at: What kind of deal?"

"Again, it would depend on what the perjurer has to say." He noticed Billy's irritation, explained, "I'm not trying to be circuitous here. It really does boil down to a *quid pro quo*. But for you, for something like this, let's say you were to retract your earlier testimony and blow this thing wide open, help root out Noone and all the rest—assuming we have support, politically—then I'd expect immunity from prosecution wouldn't be out of the question."

"And you could arrange that?"

"I could certainly try. Anonymously, of course. Until the terms are agreed."

"It wouldn't just be for me, neither. Katherine, Tommy . . . all of us involved."

"My God, how many of you were there?"

Laughing, Billy said, "The whole fucking country knows what went on back then. But the only ones I'm bothered about taking care of are my own."

"That sounds reasonable enough. You were all children, I suppose."

"Would I have to go to court again?"

"I'd imagine so, in one form or another. Actually, I'm thinking we might be better off doing something extra-judiciously. Royal Commission, Parliamentary Enquiry, that sort of thing."

"And how long would all that take to set up?"

"Probably months, certainly weeks. I'd want to be discreet."

"But you know people?"

"Not as many as I used to, admittedly, but there is someone, yes. I have a friend high up in the attorney general's office. I will see if he can help."

"Do you trust him?"

"With my life." Henry leaned forward, elbows crinkling the papers spread over the desk. "Listen, Billy, our personal history aside, there is nothing I want more in this world than to get another crack at Edmund Noone. I see him parading around the city and I had him, the bastard, I had him and he wriggled free."

"You ain't scared of him then?"

"The man has already ruined me. What more could he do?"

Billy sat there contemplating a tea-stained document on the cluttered desk, and when he spoke his eyes never moved: "Well, I might as well just say it. We did it. We killed them. Exactly like that priest of yours said."

"All of them?"

"Aye, other than the gins Noone kept to sell."

Henry fell back in his chair, as if blown there. "And the bodies?"

"Burned."

"Have you been back?"

"What do you think?"

"But could you find it? Do you know where the crater is?"

"Probably, aye."

"So you could take me there?"

Billy sighed, nodding. "If I have to."

"Because I've learned my lesson, Billy. If we're to win this time, we'll need more than just your word. Bodies, preferably. I'll bring a photographer. Are there any other witnesses we could try to find?"

"What happened to your priest?"

"He disappeared. I never heard from him again. In fact, I always wondered if you'd had something to do with that, the night you came to my room."

Billy shook his head. "Not me."

"So there's nobody else?" Henry said. "Your brother, perhaps?"

"No. Tommy's not involved, neither's Katherine. You get them immunity but they're kept out of it, understand?"

"Fine. But in that case we'll need every last shred of evidence we can get."

"Well, there's something else they might be interested in. His troopers, them that were with us at the time, Noone shot all three of them, plus a pregnant gin. I seen him do it, same day he burned down Drew Bennett's barn. Helped dig the hole myself."

"Bennett? The man from the inquest?"

Billy nodded. "He might be willing to talk about it, I don't know."

Henry was watching him gravely. "Quite the team, you and Noone. Is there anything else?"

"Isn't this enough?"

"Assuming we can prove any of it, yes."

"I doubt we'll find them troopers, mind. Middle of nowhere it was."

Henry paused. "Can I ask, has something happened? Why are you doing this now?"

"You look at your life . . ." Billy began, then faltered. The words felt all wrong in his mouth. "I've done all right for myself, Henry. Better than all right. Everything I ever wanted, I've got it, but it's like it's hollow somehow, empty underneath."

"Ah, I see."

"Don't you fucking judge me."

"No judgment here. Your conscience is your own business. Lord knows, I've had enough trouble with mine."

Billy waved a hand. "Hell, at least you tried."

"Not about that. I know fine well I tried. Of course, if I had my time again I would do things very differently. I was overconfident back then, naive."

"Here's to second chances all round then."

They shared the silence a little more comfortably. Henry asked, "How long are you in town?"

"Till tomorrow. I've business down south for a couple of days, then I'll be coming back through on the way home. Does that give you enough time?"

"I can make some initial enquiries, certainly. Get a feel for how it lies."

"Good."

"Perhaps I should travel with you. To Bewley. Strike while the iron's hot."

"To see the crater?"

"Exactly. And talk to this man Bennett about the rest."

"Bit soon for all that, isn't it?"

"The authorities will want to know what we have before signing off on any deal. Like I said, your word alone won't be enough."

"Yeah, well, I'll think about it. Don't book your ticket yet."

Billy scraped back the chair and stood. They shook hands. He paused in the office a moment but could think of nothing more to say, so he left. Through the little reception area and out into the alley; the bell didn't ring when he opened the front door. A dull thudding sound—Billy scowled up at it then pulled the door closed, dodging a rodent that came scrabbling over the cobbled ground. Christ, he hated cities. He buried his hands in his pockets, and walked on.

Chapter 33
Police Sergeant Percy

They had a telephone at the Bellevue, in the office behind the front desk. The clerk watched Billy leave through the main doors, climb into a waiting buggy, pull away. He picked up the telephone and dialed. When the call was connected he gave his name and said, "Our mutual friend from the country is in town again. He's attending a meeting currently. I have the details." There was no reply from the other end. A click, and the line went dead. The clerk returned the earpiece to the cradle and set down the telephone, went out and resumed his post. Within ten minutes, Percy had arrived.

Into the lobby he skulked, chin tucked, head down, a furtive stoop to his shoulders, eyes roving all corners of the room. The doorman went to challenge him, hesitated; Percy walked directly to the desk. He stared at the clerk in silence until the clerk began to squirm. Pockmarked cheeks, that dimple in his chin—he still looked young for a man in his thirties, but the eyes were black and firm.

"Where is he?"

The clerk plucked a note from his waistcoat and handed it over. Percy read it, expressionless, folded the note, and slipped it into his trouser pocket. He was wearing a brown suit with a cream-colored shirt, no waistcoat, no tie.

"When did he leave?"

"Right before I telephoned. He'd only just walked out the door."

Percy held out a calloused hand. "Room key."

"I really don't think I should—"

"Key."

A long blink then the clerk reached under the counter and placed a key in Percy's hand. He told him the room number. Percy took the stairs. He found the door and unlocked it, turned the handle, slipped inside, locked it again once he was in. He moved through the room slowly. Not touching anything, barely making a sound, smooth soles whispering over the carpet pile. Shirts and a suit hung in the wardrobe, a small suitcase stored below. Percy checked the suit pockets then picked up the suitcase and laid it open on the bed, found a small stack of travel documents tucked into the lid. Onward train tickets to Melbourne, departing tomorrow; a name and address on a handwritten note. Percy read it all very carefully, memorizing every detail, then he restacked the papers and returned them to the case. He put the suitcase back in the wardrobe, cracked the door and checked the corridor, then slid out of the room.

In Fortitude Valley he walked casually through the slums and alleyways, like a man who very much belonged. Hands in his pockets, side-stepping vendors and grifters, carriages, horseshit, dogs, he found the street the clerk had given him, then the law office of Henry Wells. He stood outside the window, considering. The waiting room was empty but there was light farther inside. There'd be an alleyway or yard behind the building, but he wasn't sure he had time; Billy might even have left by now. He tried the door and found it unlocked, felt the resistance of the bell above, the clapper lying inert on the rim. Percy snaked his hand up through the gap, took hold of the clapper, and with a sharp yank, broke it off. He dropped it into his pocket, eased open the door, leaving it ajar as he crossed the little waiting room and stood pressed against the office wall, listening to the conversation inside.

"*How long are you in town?*"

"*Till tomorrow. I've business down south for a couple of days, then I'll be coming back through on the way home. Does that give you enough time?*"

"*I can make some initial enquiries, certainly. Get a feel for how it lies.*"

"*Good.*"

"*Perhaps I should travel with you. To Bewley. Strike while the iron's hot.*"

"*To see the crater?*"

"*Exactly. And talk to this man Bennett about the rest.*"

"*Bit soon for all that, isn't it?*"

"*The authorities will want to know what we have before signing off on any deal. Like I said, your word alone won't be enough.*"

"*Yeah, well, I'll think about it. Don't book your ticket yet.*"

A chair scraping, sounds of movement; Percy hurried around the reception desk and back outside, the bell thudding dully as he closed the front door. He found a corner to hide behind and moments later watched Billy McBride—older since he last saw him, heavier, looked to have put on some weight—step out of the law office, glance up at the broken bell, put his hands in his pockets, and walk away along the street.

Percy didn't bother following. He already knew what Billy had planned.

In a box at His Majesty's Theatre on Queen Street, Police Commissioner Edmund Noone sat with his wife, Cassandra, and their two daughters and their husbands, watching an evening performance of *La Bohème*. The men were dressed formally in dinner suits, the women were expensively, elaborately frocked. Five rapt faces fixated on the stage, while Noone's gray gaze wandered the stalls. He was intolerably bored. All this warbling about poverty and love. He shifted in his chair—the thing had been going for hours—and Cassandra reached for his hand, gripped it so tight her nails dug into his skin. Evidently something had happened. It seemed someone was dying onstage. A woman lay in bed while a man wailed over her; idly Noone patted his wife's hand, hoping this might mean they were nearing the end.

"There there," he whispered softly. "There there."

The curtain fell finally. An eruption of applause from below. People began standing, including his family; Noone felt obliged to do the same. He didn't applaud. One of his sons-in-law whooped and shouted "Bravo!" Noone glowered at him and he stopped. He disliked both of his daughters' husbands. In their way they were perfectly suitable, of course—came from the right families, with the right prospects, careers in politics and law—but when they'd asked his permission for marriage it had been mostly apathy he had felt. But then, the girls had to marry eventually, so why not these two dolts? Truthfully, any suitor that presented himself would have been as unsatisfactory as the next.

He leaned close to Cassandra, eyeing the exit door behind. "I'll see you outside," he told her, and she glanced at him reproachfully, her hands still a blur of applause; the actors were now taking their curtain call. Noone didn't care whether she approved or not. He found these social occasions utterly stultifying. Rise and fall, clap and cheer, shake hands, kiss cheeks, the banality of the conversations he endured. As he'd already done during each intermission, he would now be expected to mingle in the bar, talking to all the right men. He was so thoroughly sick of it, the mundanity— yesterday he had opened a new police station, cutting the ribbon like some trumped-up mayor. And Noone couldn't stand the mayor of Brisbane. Never had a welder risen so far.

He left the box, waved away the startled usher, and

stood on the balcony overlooking the foyer. Waiters and bellboys scurrying, preparing for the end of the show . . . and Percy down there waiting for him, leaning against a pillar near the doors. Noone straightened. A shiver of excitement down his spine. With a lightness belying his age he skipped down the curved staircase to the ground floor. The years had not diminished him. In fact he looked very much the same. No gray in his hair or mustache, few lines creasing his skin. He strode across the foyer to Percy. "My boy," he said. "Thank God."

"You ain't enjoying the show then?"

"I've been to better funerals. Tell me, what's happened?"

"Billy McBride's in town again. Staying at the Bellevue."

"Another milkmaids' convention, is it? A symposium on castration techniques?"

"He's just been to Henry Wells's office. I seen him there myself. They was talking about the lawyer going out to Bewley, visiting the crater, talking to that cunt Bennett, after cutting some deal here with the high-up law."

Noone's face hardened. Hollow eyes staring down. "When?"

"Not yet. Billy's headed to Melbourne first. Wells says he'll make enquiries, they'll meet up when he's back."

Noone inhaled deeply, his chest swelling, his nostrils flared. The smile when it came was wicked. "Oh dear, Billy-boy. What have you done?"

Chapter 34
Tommy McBride

Tommy leaned casually against the bakery counter, waiting for Emily to finish for the day. Wrapping up the leftovers, wiping round with a cloth, an easy economy in her movement, she'd done it so many times. She was wearing a plain white dress and a flour-stained brown apron and her hair was tied up in a bun. Rosy-cheeked from the bread ovens, and all those customers, hour after hour on her feet. Tommy smiled absently. Tired after another day in the fields, lost in the rhythm of her work. It was dark outside, for three-thirty. Thick clouds threatening rain.

"Stop it," Emily said, glancing up at him.

"Stop what?"

"Looking at me like that. I'm trying to work."

"I'm only looking."

She paused. "No you're not. You're thinking. I can hear the wheels turn."

"You've not even given me an answer. Are you coming back or not?"

"I said maybe. Let me get finished up here first."

"It's been ages."

She laughed. "It's been two days."

"Well, it looks like we're in for a soaking if you don't hurry up deciding."

"You go. I'll walk up if the weather holds."

"We could eat them two leftover pies if you fancy. Take them off your hands."

She smirked at him. "You've only ever wanted me for my pies."

"Now come on, that's not fair. Bread, pasties—you know I ain't choosy." She laughed again, couldn't help herself. Tommy said, "Is that a yes, then?"

She took up wiping. "I think you hear what you want to hear."

"I haven't heard a no."

"Oh, for goodness' sake, there's just no arguing with you, is there. All right, give me ten minutes. Meet me round the back."

Tommy slapped the counter victoriously. "I'll be at the pub."

He crossed the road to Mickey's, the rusted, iron-

roofed shack that served as the town's only watering hole, pushed open the door and weaved among
the empty tables to the bar. Few drinkers in at this
hour: by six o'clock you'd be lucky to find a seat, the
room filled with laughter and swearing and smoke so
thick you could hardly breathe. Tommy greeted the
men in there. They nodded and mumbled his name.
He pulled out a stool and sat down beside Jim Collier at the bar; Mick standing behind it, slab-faced
and white-haired, tattoos on his thick folded arms.
He poured Tommy a beer without him ordering, set
it foaming on the mat.

"What's got you so bloody cheerful for a change."

Tommy drank the beer in one and passed it back for
a refill. "Smiling's allowed in here now, is it not?"

"Unusual, that's all. You're about the miserablest
bugger I know."

"Been over the bakery, I reckon," Collier piped up
beside him. "Never mind smiling, I'd be crowing all
over town if that was me."

Tommy nursed the second beer. "Which is why you
ain't married, Jim."

Mick smirked. Collier sat there frowning. Mick
said, "Busy day, then, Bobby? Saw you had a visitor out
your way?"

Tommy paused, lowered the glass. "What visitor?"

"Wasn't he coming to see you, then? Tall fella, kind of fancy-looking?"

"I was working," Tommy said, his voice tightening. "I've not been back to the house, came straight off the fields. When was this?"

"Hard to say, I mean—"

"When, Mick?"

"A couple of hours ago. Y'all right there, Bobby? You've gone pale."

His gaze roamed the bar and the dusty shelves behind. He teetered from the stool to his feet. "Tall, did you say? Did he have a longcoat on?"

"I wasn't paying much attention to what he was wearing, like."

"Did he have a fucking longcoat or not?"

"I seen him," one of the other drinkers said, and Tommy spun. "Long dark coat on him, aye. Like a rain slicker almost."

"How tall was he?"

The man shrugged.

"How tall?"

"How should I know? He was on a bloody horse!"

Despairingly Tommy reached above his head. "Like this? Seven foot almost?"

"I wouldn't quite go that far. More like your own height, maybe."

Tommy lurched forward, knocking the stool; it clattered loudly on the floor. He left the pub without paying. Staggering to the door then outside, where the first fat raindrops had just begun to fall, peppering his shoulders and carving little craters in the sandy road. Tommy stood there trembling head to toe. It could have been anyone, might not have been going to his house, the track followed the creek for miles beyond. He glanced in that direction. He didn't even have a gun. He'd got comfortable, careless, and now a man had come to see him, tall, wearing a longcoat. He should leave, he thought suddenly. Ride off and lose himself and start all over again. Lady was across the road, tied to the rail, it would be so easy, but . . . the bakery now in darkness, Emily waiting round back, Arthur and Rosie, even Tess, this little life he'd so tentatively built. He couldn't leave them. He closed his eyes, cupped his face, groaned. He wasn't that boy who'd run from Noone, from Burns, from everyone; all his life he had run. Not this time. Not again. If this was what it had come to, he decided, he would face it, take his chances, even if it meant the end.

Around the back of the bakery he found Emily sheltering beneath the canopy, against the wall. She had changed her dress and lost the apron, and stood clutching a little overnight bag in her hand. In the other she held the two leftover pies he had wanted, wrapped in a clean white towel, and the sight of her holding them, smiling at him, nearly broke Tommy's brittle heart. "Thought you'd forgotten all about me," she began teasing, then stopped when she saw his face. "Bobby? What is it? What's wrong?"

"You can't come to the house. Stay upstairs, keep the door locked. I'll come and get you. Wait here."

"Get me when?"

"Tonight, tomorrow, when I know it's safe."

"Safe? You're scaring me now—what's happened?"

He shook his head, slick with rain. "Just . . . please, Emily, do what I ask."

"Not unless you tell me what's going on."

Tommy looked up at the sky, the clouds full, heavy, pillowy-gray; blinking raindrops from his eyes. "There might be a bloke come looking for me. I just need to see what he's about."

There was something in her stare that changed then, like she'd always suspected this moment would come. She'd asked about his past, his childhood; he'd assumed she believed the answers he gave. Maybe not, he now realized. Maybe she just felt enough for him that she'd decided to leave it alone.

"It could be anyone," she said hopefully. "Cattle business, maybe?"

"Maybe."

"But you don't think so."

"I'm not sure."

"Because you already know who this man might be."

He nodded.

"And you're afraid of him? Is that what this is?"

Yes, but it stung hearing her say it. "I just need to go and check."

"And then you'll come back and tell me?"

"I will."

"When, exactly?"

"I don't know. As soon as I can."

She swiped her cheek. It wasn't rain she was brushing away. Tommy reached out to touch her but she swatted his hand. "You come back to me, you hear? You come back to me, Bobby, understand?"

Meekly he nodded. They came together and kissed, hard and desperate. As if trying to tell each other all those things they hadn't yet said. As if it was their last.

Tommy pulled away but Emily moved with him, reluctant to let go.

Chapter 35
Henry Wells

"But did he at least say he would consider it?" Henry called into the dining room, washing his hands in the kitchen sink. "Once I have all the evidence in place?"

Jonathan was lighting candles, pouring wine, their food already served and steaming on the plates. "Yes, I think so. I don't really see how he could refuse."

Henry came through, drying his hands on a tea towel, which he balled and dropped on the table as he sat down. Jonathan looked at him reproachfully. Henry smirked and rolled his eyes, moved the towel onto a spare chair. Jonathan sat down beside him, they touched glasses and drank, but before they could begin eating, the doorbell rang.

"Are you expecting anyone?" Jonathan asked.

"Of course not." Henry nodded at the wall clock. "Look at the time."

Sighing, Jonathan rose, brushing off Henry's protests, touching his shoulder as he passed. Henry watched him fondly. He still got a kick from them doing this, living together, their little domestic routines. To the world they acted chaste and respectable: gentleman companions in the vein of Herbert and Bramston, their famous counterparts in town. The neighbors seemed to have accepted them anyway. No doubt their ages helped. As did their professions: Jonathan now held a senior position in the attorney general's office, and a disgraced barrister was still a barrister all the same. It also helped that they were very discreet.

Henry sipped his wine and ogled Jonathan walking along the hall: the slender triangle of his body, the buttocks tight and round. He was one of those annoying people who kept the weight off, no matter what he ate, and had hardly changed since they'd first met. A little gray at the temples, a couple of crow's feet, but his face had taken on a kinder, softer quality, and the eyes were still keen and full of life. Henry cringed at the disparity; he didn't enjoy looking in the mirror these days. The ordeal he had gone through, his public shaming, had robbed him of the best years of his life. Almost broke him, truth be told. He worried that Jonathan would see it. Yes, he had stood by him, had rescued him in fact, but his fear was that whatever magic had brought them together would evaporate as mysteriously as it once came. He still considered himself lucky. And luck was a fickle friend.

From where Henry was sitting he couldn't see the front door. He heard Jonathan's footsteps slowing, the familiar click of the latch, the handle as it turned, then a brief exchange of voices, low and muffled, Henry couldn't make out the words. Soon Jonathan was returning along the corridor, must have given the visitor the shortest of shrifts.

"Who was it?" Henry called, but already he could see in Jonathan's expression that something was very wrong. His face was ashen. Clear panic in his eyes. Henry half-rose in his chair and saw a tall figure behind him, enormous in the narrow hall, his longcoat flaring as he moved. Henry's legs buckled. Clinging to the table edge.

"Hello again, Henry," Noone said pleasantly. "May I?"

He swept toward the corner armchair; Henry wondered if he meant to sit down. Instead, Noone snatched up one of the scatter cushions, brought it back to where Jonathan cowered by the wall, and planted it into his face. Jonathan flailed helplessly. The cushion smothered his cries. Noone pinned him there with one hand while with the other he drew a gleaming silver revolver from inside his longcoat. He wedged it under Jonathan's jaw and fired, the muffled shot no louder than a dropped book. Henry tried to scream but couldn't. A noise that withered to barely a whimper, then died. Still, it was enough for Noone to notice: he spun and pistol-whipped Henry before he had the chance to cry out again.

Henry awoke to find himself gagged and hog-tied, bent over the table and lashed tightly in place with a rope, Noone sitting in Jonathan's chair beside him, eating his meal, drinking his wine. There was a ghastly red clawlike smear on the wall behind him, the blood running thickly like paint, matted with clumps of that puppy-soft hair. Henry retched against the tea towel stuffed in his mouth, tears falling hot on his cheeks.

Noone ate the meal patiently, delicately, like he wasn't even there.

When his plate was clear, Noone sighed and straightened his cutlery, dabbed his lips and sipped the wine. He glanced at Henry. Smiling faintly, he leaned back in his chair, and Henry got a look at Jonathan's body, slumped and lifeless against the wall, and the black revolver that had been placed in his open palm. He thrashed against his bindings hopelessly, then with a sudden chill of horror fell still. He was naked below the waist, he realized. His trousers and underwear were down.

"You know, I have rather missed this," Noone said. "I so rarely get to enjoy myself these days. I am actually rather grateful. The chance may not arise again."

He sipped Jonathan's wine contentedly. Henry moaned into his gag.

"None of us can change our nature. I have known what I am my whole life, Henry, as I suspect have you. Lying with men while you were married, living here in sin, even taking up your little case against me when you already knew the risks. You are as selfish an individual as I have ever met. Bravo, I must say."

Noone drained the wine, stood, tucked in the chair.

"A great deal has been written about it, actually, I don't know if you are aware. Fatalism, determinism, nihilism, and of course predestination, for what that is worth: Why would this, why would anything we do, be any concern of God's?"

Henry raged unintelligibly. Noone inclined his head. "You have a point to make on the subject? Some thoughts on Nietzsche, perhaps?" He took hold of the gag and paused. "If you scream I will cut out your tongue."

"Jonathan was innocent," Henry gasped. "He wasn't even involved."

"No? Had you not already co-opted him into your little scheme?"

"But he'd done nothing. All his life, he'd done nothing wrong."

Henry began sobbing. Noone puttered his lips. "How disappointing, Henry. You blather like a child. This is not my doing. The blame here is all yours. You knew what might happen but thought you could get away with it, and so here we are. Honestly, I thought you had more sense than to go in with a bullheaded imbecile like Billy McBride. What is it with you people? Did you really think I would not come?"

He prized open Henry's mouth and stuffed the towel back in.

"I thought about poisoning you, both of you, a fatal dose of moonshine liquor, or even opium, since I know you're prone to excess. It must look accidental, you see. But then the last thing I want is for you to enjoy this, Henry, to drift away happily into a calm and blissful sleep. So I reconsidered, and asked myself: What other deviance, what other vice, does Henry Wells have?"

He smoothed his hair carefully, flicked out his longcoat, unhooked a polished foot-long police truncheon from its belt loop and thwacked it hard against his palm, at which Henry began struggling wildly like a chained and muzzled dog.

"They will assume your paramour did it. Sodom, exposed. Then, unable to live with himself, your friend takes his life with that little pistol there; a rather neat explanation, don't you think? I will make sure the papers have all the juicy details—imagine your father's reaction when he reads the story in the press!"

Chapter 36
Tommy McBride

Tommy dismounted short of the house and, hidden by the hedgerow, led Lady up the hillside through the rain. Lashing down now, his shirt soaked through, water running off his hat brim and trickling in little rivulets down the sand-and-pebble road. The pitch of the roof peeled into view, then the gate posts, the path, the corner of the verandah . . . and an unfamiliar horse tied to the balustrades. Tommy froze. Inching through the swirling mud. He peeked around the hedgerow and saw in the gloom a hunched figure smoking on his front steps, tall, broad, dark-haired, wearing a longcoat that pooled at his heels. As he smoked, he cast irritated glances around the front yard; Tommy couldn't make out his face. But there was something in his manner-isms, in how he held himself, the inverted grip on the cigarette, that sent the memories tumbling, his entire past cascading down. All the air emptied out of him in a gasp.

That was his brother up there. Billy, at last.

Tess jumped down from the verandah and came bounding along the path. Startled, Billy looked up. He saw Tommy, flicked away his cigarette, rose stiffly to his feet, reached for his hat, squared it on his head, and trudged down the steps into the rain, while Tommy stood rooted on the track, clutching Lady's bridle, Tess happily circling his legs. Billy waved at him, then when he got no response impatiently opened his arms. Tommy's head hung. He'd never walked so slowly up his own path before, halted ten yards away. It felt close enough. Billy grinning stupidly through the rain: dark eyes, dark beard, crooked nose, the threat of a chin. The resemblance to Father was chilling. He was Ned McBride in a good year.

"Hello, brother," Billy said.

He took off his hat and stepped forward, swallowed Tommy in an embrace, Tommy standing rigid in his arms, paralyzed by the contact, the enormity of it, and by the little details too: he was taller now, he realized; the flowery whiff of Billy's cologne. Billy kissed him roughly on the cheek. The intimacy felt obscene. They parted and Billy was frowning. He put on his hat again.

"Hell, Tommy, will you say something? I'm stood here like a limp dick!"

But what could he say? What, after all this time? It was unreal he was even standing here—over the years Tommy had imagined their reunion so often, the things he would yell at him, the blows he would land, but now that Billy was in front of him it had the quality of a dream.

"I traveled a week to see you. It's been twenty bloody years!"

"Twenty-one," Tommy corrected, his voice near-drowned by the rain.

"There you go now, that wasn't so hard."

That grin again—it sickened Tommy, a glimpse of who his brother was now. He knew him. Knew exactly the kind of man he would be. He was Billy at his worst back when they were children, full of cocksure arrogance, treating everything like a game. Daring Tommy to do whatever he wouldn't, mocking him if he refused, then afterward, when it went wrong, when someone got hurt or they got in trouble, laughing off the consequences, no fucking worries mate.

"Is that it then?" Billy asked him. "You don't got nothing else to say?"

"How . . . ?" Tommy began, then faltered. He slicked water from his face. "How did you find me?"

"I hired a man. More than one. Took them long enough, but here I am."

"But . . . why?"

"What sort of a question's that?"

"What are you doing here, Billy?"

"Shit, I wanted to see you. Figured maybe you felt the same. If you like I can head back to Queensland, try you in another twenty years' time?"

They stared at each other through the rainstorm, all trace of the grin gone. Two men, brothers once, taking the measure of each other again.

"Stables are this way," Tommy told him, leading Lady up the hill.

In silence they saw to their horses, furtive glances back and forth between the stalls. Billy seemed a little rusty. Looked like it had been a while. When Tommy had finished he leaned on the partition, watching him struggle. "Hell," Billy grumbled, "this ain't even my damn horse."

On the back verandah Billy slid off his coat and hung it on a peg beside their hats, a puddle collecting on the boards below. They peeled off their boots and stood them in pairs against the wall: Billy's knee-highs, glossy leather, alongside Tommy's mud-caked work boots. His trousers were twill, his shirt was fine cotton, the silk lining of his coat likely cost about as much as Tommy's house.

"Nice little place," Billy said, looking the yard over. "Land any good?"

"Wouldn't have bought it if it wasn't."

"Bought, not leased?"

Tommy paused with a hand on the door. "That so hard to believe?"

They went inside. Tommy lit the stove while Billy rubbed the raindrops from his hair and appraised the little room. "So what's the acreage?" he asked.

"Enough."

"Just the cattle? No sheep?"

"No sheep. Tea do you?"

"Appreciate it." He idled while he was waiting, fingering the books on the dresser, the few ornaments on the shelves. Tommy could guess what he thought of the house, of him. Billy said, "I don't run sheep no more neither. Too much bloody work, what with the droughts we get up our way, and the dogs."

Tommy stalled and looked at him. "You're still at Glendale?"

"I was." He coughed, suddenly bashful. "Actually, me and Katherine Sullivan are married now. Shit, Tommy, I'm co-owner of Broken Ridge!"

Billy stood there beaming. Proud as a baboon's arse. Bitterly Tommy smirked and put the kettle on to boil. "The new John Sullivan. Just like you always wanted."

"It ain't like that."

"It's exactly like that. Right down to your fucking boots."

"Hey now."

"We were never good enough for you, Billy. You grew up ashamed."

That silenced him. Tommy patted himself dry with a towel, then when the water was boiled made the tea. He cleared space at the table, shoving aside the papers and crockery, the ashtray and dirty cups, and set their mugs opposite each other, though neither moved to sit down.

"It's not what you think," Billy said. "I never meant for things to work out how they did. Truth is, I didn't want it, the estate, not at first anyway. She'd have likely married someone else if William hadn't come along."

"Seems you're making the best of it, anyhow."

"Is it my money you're most jealous of, little brother, or my wife?"

"Jealous? Do you have any idea the shit I've been through? By rights I should probably be dead, and there's you moaning about making your fortune, not a hair out of place. Sitting up there on Sullivan's throne, wearing his clothes, fucking his wife . . . hell, you even talk like him almost. That man was behind everything, Billy—he knew damn well there were never any natives at the house that day. You knew it too."

The hurt on Billy's face was obvious. Quietly, he said, "We found Joseph's gun."

Tommy sighed. "The gun proves nothing. It never did. All those people we killed—how is that still all right in your mind?"

"It was only Joseph I went after. The rest was up to them."

"But Joseph wasn't there! And Sullivan, Noone, they already knew he wouldn't be—they used us, you more than anyone, as an excuse to slaughter the Kurrong. And we let them. Went with them. If you can't see that you're even stupider than I thought."

Billy stood there, his face flushed and knotted with doubt. He scraped out a chair and flopped into it. "Yeah, well, I ain't done with that cunt yet."

Tommy shook his head. Billy hadn't changed. Reluctantly he sat down. Watching his brother sip the steaming tea, returning his stare over the rim. Billy pulled a cigarette tin from his pocket, popped the lid, offered the tin across.

"I heard you like a smoke nowadays. So my man said anyway."

Tommy paused then took one. "What else did he tell you?"

"That you're fond of your dog," Billy said, tapping his own cigarette on the tabletop, turning it over and pinching it between his lips. "And you've a blackboy here, no woman . . ." He glanced around the room. "Which seems about right to me."

Tommy smoked with his arms folded, holding himself across the chest. "You'd better not have told anyone else."

"'Course not."

"He can't find me, Billy."

"Who you on about now?"

"You know who I'm bloody on about. He said it wasn't allowed. This."

Tommy waved a hand between the pair of them. Billy sighed. "Ah, Noone's not interested in you no more. If he'd wanted to find you he could have. He knew you killed that overseer down in St. George. Told me all about it too."

Dread crippled him. He couldn't move. The cigarette at his lips, his mug gripped in his hand, picturing the two of them, Noone and Billy, laughing in John Sullivan's old parlor, drinking whiskey and sharing the news. Of course Billy would be in with him. Of course he would, the dog.

"This was a good while back, mind you. Long story short, one of his troopers had took off, Possum or Wombat or whatever the fuck he was called."

"Rabbit," Tommy whispered, his bat-like face rearing to mind.

"That's the fella. Anyhow, you remember Drew Bennett, Daddy knew him, has that little place to the south there; the stupid bugger let the boy hide in his barn. Noone said unless I helped bring him in he'd ride out and track you down. He guessed where you were headed, everything. I saved you from him, Tommy, can't you see?"

So Noone had spared him, had let him get away. It shocked Tommy to realize that he'd meant so little; that he'd been running from a man who didn't care.

"The point is," Billy said, sliding the ashtray closer, crushing his cigarette, lighting another, "if Noone didn't give a shit back then, he sure as hell doesn't now. And things are different, I'm a rich man these days, I ain't scared of him. Keeping us apart all this time, treating me like his lapdog . . . he wants something, he whistles, like he did with that trial. It wasn't me they were after, but he roped me in as well."

Blinking, Tommy tuned in again. "What trial?"

"You didn't read about it? Thing was all over the Brisbane papers."

"I don't exactly follow the northern news."

"There was this inquest, back in ninety-seven, into the killings, and all what came after. Remember that priest we stumbled on out there, well, he hired this city lawyer, name of Henry Wells, who stirred up all sorts of trouble on the coast. They did the trial in Bewley, though, the whole thing was rigged. Noone walked. So did I, not that I should have been there in the first place—we were the victims after all."

"They put *Noone* on trial?"

"In a manner of speaking, aye. 'Course, he fed them a load of horseshit, which I had to back up, and that priest never made it to the courthouse, they must have got to him before."

A creeping fear rose in Tommy. There was something in how Billy was talking, that smirk in his eyes. *I ain't done with that cunt yet*, he had said, and Tommy had dismissed it. But there was more to this than just sharing a tale.

"Why are you telling me all this?"

"I thought you might be interested. Among other things."

"What other things? What have you done, Billy?"

"Nothing yet," Billy said, exhaling. "But I plan to. Noone needs paying back. I met with that same lawyer in Brisbane just now, he's going to cut us a deal. Immunity, including for you. All what happened in that crater, even the St. George thing, you'll be rid of all of it, gone. I was thinking, if you wanted, you could come back home, get the old place going, or anywhere else you fancied, there's enough land, take your pick. I put Noone away and we're free again, Tommy. Neither of us was to blame."

"We're as much to blame as anyone! You even more so!"

Billy waved a hand. "Ah, Jesus, can you not just let all that go?"

"Let it go? Have you heard yourself. Let it fucking go?"

"It was twenty-one years ago, we were children."

Tommy was shaking. "I still wake up in that crater sometimes. The noise of it, the smells. You talk like it's forgotten, like we did nothing wrong."

"We didn't. That's what I'm saying. Not compared to him. Noone used us, Tommy, you just said so yourself. Twisting everything, like he did with me and Drew Bennett, the man's a fucking snake in the grass. He ruined our lives, sending you off, splitting us up. Now's the chance to put it right."

"I don't want nothing from you. I'm happy. Don't go fucking that up."

"He's old now, Tommy," Billy said, smiling. "A

feeble old man, so I've heard. Got comfy in his mansion in Brisbane, sitting in lounges, smoking cigars."

"Leave it alone. For God's sake, Billy. Please."

"I can't."

"Why not?"

"It's not just for me I'm doing this. I've a family now."

"Exactly. And you know what he'll do. Who he'll go after next."

Billy stubbed out his cigarette. "After the inquest, after it all came out, me and Katherine have had no kind of marriage, she can't stand to look at me almost, told me so herself, and the children'll find out soon enough who their old man is, if they haven't already figured it out. I have to *do something*, Tommy. Before it's too late."

"It is too late. You already are whatever they think."

"I know that. Which is why I have to change it, confess."

Utter disbelief in Tommy's stare. "And what? Then they'll *forgive* you?"

"Aye, maybe."

"It isn't worth the risk."

Billy looked at him sadly. "You're still that scared of him, eh?"

"With good reason."

"Not anymore, mate. Not anymore. It's a whole different country out there. Look, I came down here to
see you, and tell you, not ask your permission about all
this. I've missed you, Tommy. Thought maybe you felt
the same. I suppose I was hoping you'd come home, get
Glendale going, be together again."

"Glendale's a *slaughterhouse*. How can you
even . . . ?"

Billy stared at him a long time, faint pity in his eyes.
Outside, through the rain patter, Tess barked then fell
silent and the horses nickered loudly in the barn. Billy
rose and gathered his cigarettes, shoved them into his
pocket, drained his tea.

"I'm glad I found you, anyhow. I was worried you
might be dead. If ever you want to visit, you know where
we are. Stay safe, little brother. Thanks for the tea."

"Wait," Tommy said, standing. "What you doing?"

"I didn't come all this way to lose you again. Not
like this."

"Hold up, now. Sit down."

"I know when I'm not welcome."

"'Course you bloody are."

A wan smile. "You know, I actually thought you'd
be all for it, me coming forward, saying what went on.
I know how cut up you always were."

Tommy had no answer for that. The idea of publicly

confessing had never occurred to him before. He asked, "When is this hearing anyhow?"

Billy waved a hand. "Not soon. Months, maybe, the deal needs arranging first. And Wells is on about visiting the crater. I wasn't expecting that."

"You've not been back?"

"What do you reckon?"

"You were so casual about it, Billy. Even after, it was like they were nothing."

Billy was silent a long time, a faraway look in his eyes. "I'm not proud of who I was back then. There's a lot I'm not proud of, even now."

His head hung, searching the floor. It was the first glimpse of contrition Tommy had ever seen from his brother, more than he could have imagined, and for a moment the admission hung like fire smoke, clogging the air in the room, clouding everything between them, until Billy jerked to life and snatched a breath as if it was forgotten, a gust of wind blowing the smoke clear.

"Right, well, I'd best be off."

"What time's the Melbourne train?"

"Next one's not till tomorrow. There a decent hotel in town?"

Tommy scoffed. "There's rooms at the pub but nothing decent about them. Stop for a bite at least, won't you? I could put some supper on?"

"You sure? A minute ago you seemed ready to throw me out the door."

"Mind, I've not got much food in and I'm no kind of a cook. Emily was meant to be bringing two pies up, and Rosie usually does the meals, so . . ."

"Two women now, is it? Ain't you a dark horse?"

"Rosie's Arthur's missus. They live in the house out back."

"Arthur? As in . . . ?"

Tommy nodded. "We split the land between us. Share it, I mean."

"Well, bugger me."

"Not sure how welcome you'd be at their place though."

Billy raised his hands in acceptance. "I'll take whatever you've got." He reached for his mug. "And maybe something stronger than tea?"

They took a bottle of whiskey out onto the front verandah and sat together on the bench, watching the gully through the curtain of the rainstorm, the daylight already fading, raising their voices over the din. Tommy lit the lanterns and sloshed a large measure of whiskey into their rinsed-out mugs; they touched, silently saluted, and sat there drinking contentedly, until Tommy said, "You really married Mrs. Sullivan?"

"I did," Billy said, laughing. "Luckiest bastard that

ever lived. Like I said, if it hadn't been for William coming it might not have happened—I missed you at the wedding, brother, stood up there on my own."

"In Bewley?"

"The little church. Same as always. Nothing much has changed."

"I saw the birth notice in *The Queenslander*. Suzanna. Four, it said?"

"I thought you didn't read the northern papers?" Billy said, glancing at him. Tommy shrugged. "Aye, two boys, two girls. The girls are angels. Isobel, the eldest's called. The boys . . . well, William's nothing like me, gave him my name but that's about it. Fucking useless around the station but good with his books, seems better suited to school. I tried teaching him but there's no point, too much of Katherine's side in his blood. But the other boy, Thomas—"

"You called your sons William and Thomas?"

"'Course I did, what else? Now, Thomas is a proper McBride: only eleven but there's a natural way with him, good on a horse, roping, all of it. Takes after his uncle, I reckon. Reminds me of us at that age."

Tommy drank, swallowing hard, pushing down the lump in his throat. To hear Billy speak of his children, of Tommy's nieces and nephews, of the boy Billy had named after him and who was skilled on a horse . . .

of a family, blood relations, still out there somewhere, after all this time. He said, "I had no idea, Billy."

"No, well, it's not always as perfect as it sounds. Nothing just landed in my lap. Most places up north folded in the drought—you must have heard how things was. It was close for a while there. I worked my arse off to keep us afloat. And our name's not done me any favors along the way, neither, I can guarantee you that."

"Aye, well, you and me both."

"Where did this Robert Thompson come from anyway?"

"Saw it on a gravestone, outside St. George."

"You nicked the name off a dead bloke?"

Tommy shrugged. "Figured he didn't need it no more."

Billy laughed, they both drank. "See, that's what I was thinking. It might be we can put all that into the deal, clear your name for good. Then you could properly be yourself again, move on."

"I know it might not seem much, but honestly, I'm happy here as I am."

"You belong up north, though, Tommy. This rain, the hills and valleys, it's all wrong. A tiny hut, no family to speak of, I mean your dog's nice enough but . . ."

Tommy leaned forward, glancing up and down the verandah.

"What you lost?" Billy said.

"She normally beats me round here. Reckon you must have scared her off."

"I have that effect on females. Even dogs."

Billy lit a cigarette, offered Tommy one. Another splash of whiskey in each mug. They drank and smoked in silence until Billy said, "So who's this Emily you were talking about? The one with the two lovely pies?"

Tommy smirked, took a drag of the cigarette, glanced at him sidelong. "She runs the little bakery in town."

"I saw her! Pretty blond thing? I saw her through the window this afternoon!"

"That's her. We've been off and on about a year now. Well, not off exactly, just . . . her husband died, we're taking it slow."

"For a year?"

"I've not always been well."

"As in sick?"

"I'm fine, we're fine. She would have been up here now if it wasn't for some suspect-looking bastard snooping around town. I told her to stay home."

"Hey now, don't blame me for your woman troubles, it ain't my fault you—"

Billy's head erupted in an explosion of blood and bone, smacked hard against the house wall then rebounded and came to rest hanging with his chin against his chest. The back of the head was missing, a smooth round hole at the front, a trickle of blood beginning to seep. His whiskey mug slid from his grip and thudded on the deck and turned a slow circle through the spillage; he was still somehow holding his cigarette. Aghast, Tommy stared at him, while in the distance, across the gully, through the rain, a single crack of gunfire reverberated in the hills.

Chapter 37
Tommy McBride

Billy's body slumped forward, arms hanging low. The cigarette finally fell. Half-lidded eyes, staring; the bullet hole in-between. A thin red bead ran along the bridge of his nose and dripped like sweat from the tip.

On the far bank of the gully, squatting drenched among the ferns and trees, Percy rodded another ball into that great Hawken rifle, and took aim again.

Tommy watched his brother tilting, the bead of blood hanging, the mug rocking lightly on the deck. Lost in a kind of reverie, numb, dimly registering the fading rifle report and the silence that followed in the hills. Then at the last a jolt of clarity, a premonition, and he hurled himself to the floor just as a second gunshot fizzed overhead and tore through the wall behind.

Percy tutted irritably. Tipped in a measure of powder. Dropped another ball in.

Around the bench Tommy scrambled, through the pool of spilled whiskey, past Billy's knees, legs, stockinged feet. He shouldered the door open and fell into the front room, and was showered in splinters as another shot hit. He kicked the door closed behind him, scrabbled on all fours for the kitchen archway, a cacophony of glass breaking as the front window was blown out.

Percy peppered the house, laughing. Like taking potshots at the fair.

Out of range around the archway, Tommy cowered with his back against the kitchen wall. Desperately scanning the room for a weapon, but there were only knives in the house. The nearest firearm was in the stables, the shotgun on the table, he'd seen it there earlier on. Idiot. Stupid to assume he was safe. But then he'd not counted on Billy, his arrogance, thinking he could come here, that Noone would not know, all the while leading him directly to Tommy's door.

Percy wiped the rain from the scope lens, then settled his sights again, smirking at Billy keeled over on the bench. "Chickenshit," he mumbled through his chewing tobacco, a wet brown squelch between his teeth. He roved the front of the house slowly. The other brother was hiding in the back. Meaning he'd either run for the stables or take off on foot over the fields. Percy knew which one he would wager. He placed his bets on the corner of the building and waited to see if he'd won.

At the back door Tommy paused and looked the room over, rain hammering the roof overhead. It was finished now, all this. The life he had found here, built here, was gone. He bowed his head, closed his eyes, then yanked open the door and stepped out. He pulled on his damp work boots and crept through the downpour, along the rear wall of the house, watching the yard in case of another intruder out back.

From the corner of the house he looked across a hundred-yard clearing to the stables, lantern light spilling through the open double doors. He didn't remember lighting one. The place shone like a parade. But the clearing was murky in the pelting rain, a no-man's-land between the house and the barn, and it felt like a muzzle-loader he was firing, given the gaps between rounds. Quick with it, though. An expert shot. Still, most likely that meant only one round, two at most, if he fired the very second Tommy ran. Shit, shit, shit. He had no choice. He needed a horse, needed to warn Arthur—if the shooter was mounted Tommy would never outrun him on foot. Then there was Emily, waiting in her apartment, sitting on her bed, her hands clasped in her lap. If he didn't get down there first there'd be a knock at the door and she would answer, her face crumpling in terror when she saw it was not him.

Tommy snatched a final breath, and ran.

A flash of movement breaking cover. "And here the boss reckons you're the clever one." Percy tracked the runner left to right in his scope, but the rain blurred his vision and it was dark between the buildings. Aim for the torso, in that case. A bigger target to hit. He adjusted the rifle a fraction, and fired.

Mad eyes bulging, teeth bared, boots slapping the waterlogged earth, Tommy fled for his life across the yard. Ahead the barn doors yawned in the dusk, seemingly coming no closer, if anything inching farther away. Leaden arms flailing, no strength left in his legs, but close enough now to see inside the stables, the shapes of the hanging saddles, the benches, the stalls, and lying in the aisle there were bundles of . . . lying in the aisle there were . . . lying in the aisle . . .

Missed him. Fucker slowed right at the last. Percy saw the shot kick harmlessly in the mud, cursed and quickly reloaded, raised the rifle again.

At the sound of the booming rifle report Tommy flung himself forward and rolled into the barn, landing hard on the straw-strewn ground. He lifted his head and looked at those bundles that had stalled him as he ran, and in the shadows from a distance had resembled heaped blankets or covered hay bales that he knew should not have been there, and that now, up close, were clearly nothing of the sort.

"*Good luck getting them saddles on,*" *Percy crowed, snatching up his rifle, carrying it by its forestock, skipping nimbly toward the house down the hill.*

The horses had had their throats slit, Tess's belly sawed open like a bean can. Tommy gripped his head and wrenched the skin taut, his eyes distended and red, death breaking over him in a wave. It was hopeless, he was doomed here, meaning so were Arthur and Rosie and Emily—no, not them. He staggered to the table, collected the shotgun, the box of shells. There was no way out but through him. No running away from this. Stepping over the animals and the pools of their mess, he made his way along the aisle to the barn's back door, sliding in two shells as he went. He forced the door open, stiff from under-use, then crept along the side of the building to the front corner facing the gully and fired a shot blindly into the rain.

Percy's feet went from under him at the sound of the shotgun blast. He slid in the wet scrub and scrambled behind a tree, squatting with his rifle clutched vertically between his legs. Waiting. He stuck his head around the tree then ducked back in at the sound of another blast, louder, coming closer. Silly boy.

Tommy fired the second cartridge as he sprinted across the track, buying time to find cover in the trees. He freewheeled down into the gully, slipping through the ferns and long grass and only just keeping his feet. He knew every path in this gully, every bush, every warren, every tree. Moving smoothly between them, reloading as he ran, all the way down to the creek, where he paused in a crouch, watching the foliage on the opposite bank. There was a crossing he had built a little way along, might make a good ambush point. He crept low, following the creek, until he reached it. A horse, soaked to the bone, its saddlebags laden, was tethered miserably to the nearside bridge post. It hadn't heard him coming. The rain was too loud. Tommy paused, like there might be an alternative, when he already knew there was not. Hidden behind a trunk, he raised the gun and shot the horse clean through its neck.

Another blast, but this time Percy was ready—he got a read on the position and set off after it, sidestepping down the hillside toward the creek. From a high vantage he followed its course until he caught a glimpse of the bridge. He halted. Shouldered the Hawken, used the scope. His horse lay on its side, its neck blown out, no sign of who had done it, no movement on the bank. Percy lowered the rifle. Fucker was really starting to piss him off now.

Tommy retreated from the crossing, backtracking into the trees, then with the shotgun raised waded into the creek to his waist. The water took his breath away. Shivering, he dragged himself into the root hollow of a fallen gray gum, reloaded with trembling fingers, steeled himself, and went on.

There. There he was, the cunt. Skulking up the hillside, shotgun in his hands, looked fucking petrified bless him, startled as a baby deer. Percy took up a shooting position. Adjusting his feet, shifting his weight. Rain bounced off the long barrel of the Hawken as he closed one eye and dipped the other to the scope. His finger slid to the trigger. Watching Tommy through the trees. There were too many of them. Trunk upon trunk, breaking his aim, and the Hawken wasn't good at close range. He lifted his head and very carefully laid the rifle on the ground, then reached for his belt and popped the clip on his knife sheath and drew out the long bowie blade, serrated on one side, curved on the other, still bloodstained from the barn. Noone's initials were engraved on the hilt. It was the finest gift Percy had ever received. Not once taking his eyes from Tommy, he felt around for a rock and threw it, and when Tommy jerked his shotgun to where it had landed, Percy crawled forward on his hands and knees.

Gripping tight to the shotgun, pushing through the

foliage, no sound now but the hissing rain. But he had heard it, a thud then faint rustling, like a footstep, a slip. He was out here, Tommy knew, he was close. Inching along the hillside, one reluctant step after the next; his heart pounded wildly, his whole body thrummed. In the presence of Death now, either his own or whoever had come. A familiar feeling. He'd met Him many times before. Walking toward the house with Billy, their parents lying dead inside; riding into the crater with Noone. Hell had its own sound, smell, taste, metallic and rancid, rising up in Tommy like he was already rotten inside; a concussive thud in his veins. His vision had contracted to a pinprick, homing in on that rustling he'd heard. He parted the ferns timidly. Like peeling a blanket from a sleeping child. But there was nothing. There was nobody. He looked about, lost, then realized: all there'd ever been was that one single sound.

Too late.

Tommy spun but Percy was on him, slashing at his throat with the knife. It caught him on the shoulder, a cut so deep and clean the blood was spilling in a torrent even before Tommy registered the pain. Howling, Percy swung again, a mad flurry, the knife so close to Tommy's face he could feel the rush in the air. Twice he fired the shotgun. The second caught Percy in the gut. He sprawled backward into the brush, his feet peddling, pawing desperately at his stomach with both hands. Tommy reloaded. He could hardly use his left arm. Blood soaked his shirtsleeve and hung like webbing from his hand. Once he had the cartridges in, he snapped the breechface closed and stood over the dying man, the shotgun raised to his face. He didn't recognize the ugly bastard, could have been anyone, but Tommy already knew why he had come.

"You're Noone's man, aren't you? Tell me—is this him?"

A stillness came over Percy. He looked up from his wound. When he smiled, his yellow teeth were swimming in tobacco-stained blood. He went to speak but coughed, and a thick gout spilled onto his chin.

"He'll kill you all," Percy said, laughing. "He'll fucking kill you all."

Tommy glanced across the gully, anguish in his eyes. "Arthur," he whispered, turning, before almost as an afterthought blowing a hole in Percy's chest.

Chapter 38
Tommy McBride

Across the fields he staggered: stumbling, falling, rising again. A ghostly presence in the twilight, clutching his wounded arm. Ahead, Arthur's house glowed warm against the darkness of the surrounding trees. Blurred lantern lights dancing, swimming in the rain, but there was no movement in the windows, no silhouettes in the rooms, the house as bereft as Glendale all those years ago, and now it was happening to him again. They were dead in there, Tommy knew. Noone's man had got to them first. He fell to his knees and cried out, lifted his face to the rain. Everything he'd ever loved, everyone—all had been taken from him, all were gone.

"Arthur!"

Eyes closed, body keening, voice echoing over the fields.

"*Arthur!*"

A figure stepped from behind the house, rifle raised, barely visible in the gloom: Arthur, peering through the downpour as Tommy pitched forward and lay motionless in the mud. Arthur tossed down his rifle, and ran.

They stood in a line at the graveside, Emily rubbing Tommy's back, Arthur and Rosie holding hands. Bright morning sunshine, birds chirruping, the field peaceful, the grass still glistening with rain. The shovel had gone in easily, the earth soft and damp; clean edges, clean walls, a mound of black soil alongside. Arthur had done most of the digging; Rosie and Emily helped. Tommy couldn't manage the shovel— his wound had been cleaned and stitched with catgut sutures and his arm hung limp in a sling. Nobody was talking. Not a word as they lowered Billy in. One on each wrist and ankle, his head tipped back, his white throat exposed, until he reached the bottom and lay there, waiting for the soil to fall. Tommy didn't offer a eulogy. He couldn't find anything good to say, Billy a stranger in all but name, save the boy he had been in childhood and the half hour they'd shared yesterday. Later, it would hit him. In the train carriage rattling north. A realization that with Billy's passing his whole family was gone, Tommy the last of them, and that after all these years spent blaming him, hating him, wondering about him, he still loved his brother just the same. He'd watch the moonlit fields through the carriage window, his reflection in the shuddering glass, and now and then catch a glimpse of Billy's face in his own. Haunting him. He'd spent the best part of twenty years in mourning. Now he was starting all over again.

Afterward, they went back to the house and sat around the kitchen table, waiting for Tommy to begin. He'd slept all through the night but this morning insisted he was well enough to put Billy in the ground; he'd explain things after, he'd said. So now he was going to tell them everything, the whole tortured bloody truth, and they weren't going to like what they heard. But he might as well be honest. He had so little left to lose. He loved them, all of them, and they were all in danger as a result of him. It seemed the very least they deserved.

"What are you talking about, Bobby?" Emily asked, reaching for his hand.

He shook his head sadly, found her eyes. "Well, I guess that's the start of the story. My name isn't really Bobby. It's Tommy—Tommy McBride."

They were silent while he told them. Tears stained Emily's cheeks. She rubbed his hand continually with her thumb and the rubbing never faltered, not once. But when he reached the part about the crater, he sensed the shift in Rosie, heard the gasp, saw the pinch in her eyes as she turned them away, and he knew she'd never be able to look at him with the same open affection again. Beside her, Arthur sullenly rubbed the table with his finger, as if he was also implicated, for of course he already knew.

Tommy left immediately after. Couldn't bear to stick around. He excused himself from the table and went into the bedroom, threw a few clothes and some money in a bag, and slipped out the front door without another word. He had Billy's travel tickets, and the lawyer's address: he would go to Brisbane and see him, he'd decided, finish what Billy had begun, take his place on the witness stand, there seemed no other way. *He'll kill you all*, the shooter had threatened, and he would, Tommy knew, one day Noone would come, unless he brought the cycle to an end. Let the truth out, tell the world, let that bastard drown in his own sins. Likewise Tommy. He'd take the consequences however they fell. After so long hiding, denying, burying his past way down, there was some comfort in the idea, some relief. For now he had a reason beyond his own guilt. Protecting them, all of them, then hoping, once it was over, if he survived, that they would be willing to take him back.

In town he asked the coachman to wait while he ducked into the startled notary's office, demanding he draw up a will: his house and his money he left to Emily; Arthur got the cattle and grazing land. He scribbled his signature and paid the man, then climbed into the coach outside. By that evening he had taken the district line to Melbourne, then, using Billy's ticket, traveling under his name, boarded the night train bound for Sydney, with connections through to Brisbane and the dark heart of central Queensland beyond.

After twenty-one years running, Tommy was going home.

Chapter 39
Magistrate MacIntyre

The houses sat on a quiet sandy lane, a handful of well-spaced properties built high on the bluff, overlooking grass-tufted dunes and a long golden beach and the shimmering two-tone waters of the South Coral Sea. Gentle surf rolled off the breakers, foam tide lines sank into the smooth wet sand. Gulls circled and strutted in the shallows; a lone fishing boat farther out, bobbing on the bay.

From one of these houses two elderly ladies emerged, sisters, shopping baskets in their hands. They navigated the front steps and made their way arm in arm along the lane, chatting, laughing, anticipating their trip into town. It was a twenty-minute walk along the coastal path and the highlight of both their days. A couple of hours spent shopping, a refreshment break in their favorite tearoom.

They might meet some friends there, exchange gossip, no doubt share the latest gripes about their respective husbands, for just like the aches and pains that afflicted them at this age, they all had their fair share.

Across the field from the house and the lane they now walked along was a little pine wood, where, leaning against one of the tree trunks, his folded jacket at his side, his shirtsleeves neatly rolled, Noone watched the sisters through his spyglass. He followed them as far as the end of the lane, where the hedgerows shielded them from view, then retracted the spyglass and took one last bite of the apple he'd been eating before tossing it behind him into the trees. He collected his jacket and draped it over his arm, and like a gentleman out for an easy sunshine stroll, ambled across the field, humming, trampling the wildflowers underfoot.

He climbed the fence easily, swung his leg over, hopped down. The track was quiet, the houses empty—most were used as holiday homes, he knew. He crossed to the house the two sisters had come from, mounted the stairs, and rang the handbell.

The front door had been left open. Only the fly screen was closed. Through the mesh was a hallway, sunlight dazzling the polished wood, and a man huffing his way along it, using a cane and rocking with each step. He looked up when he reached the fly screen, saw the tall frame silhouetted there, and even through the mesh Noone could sense his panic and fear. He struggled to compose himself. Chin wobbling with the strain. "My God—Edmund?" he managed to say.

"Hello, Spencer."

Noone pulled open the fly screen and the two men were face-to-face. Magistrate MacIntyre was now in his mid-sixties and his features bore every one of those long hard years. He had a beat-up look about him: wrinkled skin, sagging cheeks; dark and haunted eyes. "What the hell are you doing here?" he asked.

Noone smiled easily. "I was planning on asking you the same thing."

"How's that now?"

"I wouldn't have put you at the seaside after all those years inland."

"Doctor's orders. My lungs, apparently. Along with everything else."

"I have to say it suits you. You're looking remarkably well."

MacIntyre waved away the lie for what it was, and for a moment neither man moved, Noone smiling pleasantly, his jacket over his arm, until MacIntyre could no longer stand it, stepped back and said, "Come in, why don't you. The wife's gone out with her sister so I can't offer you anything to eat . . ."

"I've already eaten. Wouldn't want to put you out."

MacIntyre led him along the hallway, toward the back of the house, Noone glancing into the rooms as he passed. When they reached the kitchen MacIntyre mumbled, "There might be some cake if you're interested, but that's about all I can do. Don't know my arse from my elbow in there."

"I'm fine."

"Coffee? Tea? Something stronger?"

"Whatever you're having."

"All right. Head on out to the deck there, I'll fix us something up."

"I'll wait," Noone said.

MacIntyre's eyes pinched; he affected a little shrug. He leaned his cane against the wall and hobbled to the drinks cabinet in the living room, where he poured them each a brandy. He handed one to Noone and gestured to a pair of open French doors leading onto a raised deck. They stepped outside. A grand view over the beach and sea, the misty haze of the offing far away. Noone regarded it all expressionless. Might as well have been looking at a plain brick wall. MacIntyre pulled out a chair from the table and sat down heavily, wheezing with every breath. His lungs were the least of his worries, truthfully. His heart was failing him, as were his bowels; he struggled to walk more than fifty yards, given his knees. His mind slipped sometimes also. He forgot things. He blanked out. He tried covering these lapses with anger and bluster, but for a long time Margaret had known. His wife was in rude health, comparatively. She would outlast him by many years. When she'd first suggested moving here, she'd argued it would be good for him, but now he wasn't so sure. They lived next door to her sister, she'd made plenty of friends, while he was virtually housebound. She was setting herself up for afterward, he had realized, but then he'd have been like this anywhere, or worse, so what did it matter in the end?

And now Noone had visited. Sitting on the other side of the table, legs crossed, sipping his brandy, body angled toward the sea. MacIntyre took a drink, his hand trembling, though it did that anyway.

"What have you come for, Edmund?"

Noone drew a long breath and let it out in a sigh. "I have run into a spot of bother, Spencer, for which I'm afraid I need your help."

"Oh, aye?" MacIntyre said hopefully, straightening a little in his chair.

"It's that bloody McBride business, from Bewley, seems we aren't quite done with it yet. Honestly, of all the dispersals I led, all the work I did, those Kurrong bastards won't be silenced—it's like they don't know they're dead."

"Why, what's happened? What now?"

"You'll remember our mutual friend in Brisbane, the lawyer, Henry Wells? It seems he and Billy Mc-Bride are cooking up some plan to reopen the case, a Royal Commission or some such horseshit, I'm not entirely sure. They are coming for me, personally, Spencer. Me! The commissioner of police!"

"Some balls on the pair of them."

"Quite."

"You know, Billy's a rich man. Powerful friends."

"I'm sure he thinks so. But most rich men are fools."

"Aye, well, I'm sorry to hear it. I always thought Billy had more sense."

"Oh, he has no proof of anything, none of them do—it was twenty-one years ago, for God's sake. No, the risk for me lies in the reputational smear these rumors can bring. Times have changed after Federation. The past is an inconvenience people would rather forget. The origins of this country . . . they do not want to be reminded of what happened twenty, thirty, fifty years ago. Nobody cares. Would rather enjoy the spoils in peace. Which means, of course, that when weasels like Henry Wells start clamoring for justice, a sacrificial lamb must be found. Someone to blame so the rest of them can wash their hands of history and claim they have done nothing wrong."

"And this is you you're talking about? The lamb?"

"If Henry Wells had his way, yes."

"So, what are you going to do?"

Noone's gaze wandered to the ocean. He sipped his drink. "Billy McBride is dead. As is his little brother. As is Henry Wells."

MacIntyre spluttered laughter. "Bloody hell. That'll work."

Noone didn't say anything. His gaze on the ocean, steady and cold.

"I don't have much influence nowadays," MacIntyre said, such relief, such optimism in his voice, "but I can probably put a word in, help cover things up?"

"That won't be necessary."

"Do you need an alibi, maybe? I can say you were here the whole time?"

"No."

"Well then," he said, chuckling, "I don't much see how I can help you. Seems you've taken care of it all yourself."

Noone turned to look at him. The chair quietly creaked. "What I need for you to do, Spencer, is to die also. Today. This afternoon. Now. You are the very last of them, the people who know the truth. I cannot allow any witnesses. This Kurrong business risks becoming the thread that could unravel me. It is time to cut it off."

MacIntyre forced a nervous laugh that foundered as quickly as it began. "Hell, don't go making jokes like that to a man of my age."

"Your wife will be home later. I have chosen to spare her, you understand, since I assume she doesn't know. Or, we can wait for her return, and you can go together, whichever way you prefer."

"Christ, Edmund, after all I've done for you."

A twitch of a shrug as Noone saw off his drink.

"The reports I doctored, the crimes I overlooked—I fixed that bloody inquest for you, despite your own best efforts at buggering the whole thing up."

Noone checked the time on his pocket watch. "Is that your answer?"

"You know I'd never say anything! I've stayed quiet twenty years!"

"You are testing my patience here, Spencer. I am trying to be kind."

"Kind? You're on about killing me!" MacIntyre's eyes flicked to Noone's empty glass. "How about I get us another drink and we'll talk it over?"

Noone smirked. "Where is it?"

"Where's what?"

"The gun you are planning on fetching. The dining room, wall mounted, or do you keep one in the night-stand by your bed? Think about it, Spencer—how do you want to be found? Lying shot in a pool of your own shit, piss, and blood, or peacefully slumped in that chair there, your body having just . . . given up?"

MacIntyre flinched like the thing had burned him. "This chair right here?"

"The very same. Enjoying your idyllic view."

"You're a fucking monster."

Noone walked around the table, looming down upon MacIntyre, who watched him with bulging eyes. "If you make this difficult," Noone said, "Margaret will suffer. Look at it this way: after all your years of struggle, your time has simply come."

His gaze slid past Noone to the horizon, and when he spoke there was a crack in his voice: "The last thing I said to her was to remember my humbugs."

"Humbugs!" Noone roared. "What a wonderful final word!"

Down he lunged, clasping the back of MacIntyre's head with one hand, clamping the other over his mouth. The magistrate struggled pitifully; Noone knelt his weight upon him and the fight was soon done. With his thumb and forefinger, Noone pinched the judge's nose and cupped his palm to form a seal around his lips. A terrible empty sucking sound. MacIntyre's chest heaved up and down. In his bulbous eyes thin veins began appearing like the reveal of hidden ley lines.

The gasping faded. The eyes dulled. Noone brought his face so close they were almost nose to nose, and watched as the life snuffed out. He removed his hand. The lips were already blue. He eased himself off the chair and flicked a handkerchief from his pocket and wiped off the mucus and a trace of blood. He checked his skin for a break but found none. MacIntyre must have bitten his own tongue. Noone tilted the judge's head back, walked around the table and picked up his brandy glass, and checked the deck for anything else amiss. Only his jacket—he draped it over his arm and tucked in his chair and went into the kitchen to wash up the glass. He dried it and returned it to the drinks cabinet, aligning it neatly with the others. He paused in the hallway a moment. One last look over the house. Doilies on the surfaces, decorative china pots; it was a pathetic little life, no loss. Through the window MacIntyre sat with his head tipped backward, might have been fast asleep. "Humbugs," Noone said, chuckling, pushing open the fly-screen door. He closed it behind him and skipped down the steps, crossed the road and disappeared into the field, whistling.

Like he'd never been there at all.

Chapter 40
Tommy McBride

The train hissed to a standstill at Roma Street station in Brisbane and had disgorged most of its passengers and luggage before down from the first-class carriage limped a feverish Tommy McBride. He swayed on the platform, clutching his duffel bag. Sweat glazed his forehead and neck. He'd hardly slept at all during the journey: heavy eyes scanned the bustling station as if expecting trouble to come. It didn't. The odd frown at his appearance, the incongruity of him traveling first class, but nobody was waiting to accost him, there was no threat in their stares. Falteringly he began moving, unbalanced by the bag at his side. His left arm was in its sling still, but there was now a dark stain on his shirtsleeve—somewhere north of Sydney he'd peeled back the collar and been hit with a smell of rot. His catgut stitches were puckering. His wound was beginning to weep.

He pushed through the crowd on the concourse and winced into the sunshine outside, where the bustle and heat of Brisbane assaulted him from all sides. He hailed a cab. A struggle to clamber up. From his pocket he pulled the crumpled sheet of Bellevue notepaper he had found among Billy's things and gave the driver the address for this lawyer, Henry Wells.

Tommy collapsed against the backrest and watched the shops and pavements and pedestrians slide by, the buggy climbing up into the Valley until at the head of an alleyway the driver halted and announced, "Down there." Tommy paid him and got out and stood looking along a seedy side street as behind him the buggy clattered away. He walked forward, frowning. No place for a law office, this. There was shit on the pavement and litter blown into drifts, most windows were either papered or boarded up. A cat picking at a flattened bird carcass hissed at him, its hackles raised. A baby wailed high above. A man shouted. Glass smashed.

He almost missed the office at first, since it looked no different from the other shopfronts: the door graffitied, the window sloppily papered with pages from the *Brisbane Post*. But there was a little brass nameplate, the only one on the street; Tommy wiped the sweat from his eyes and found Henry Wells's name stenciled there. He dropped his bag and appraised the building anew. The red door had been scrawled with the word *fairy* in black paint, and it was the same headline on all the newspaper pages, he now realized, pasted in a repeating pattern over the entire windowpane. Tommy leaned closer to read it: DOUBLE JEOPARDY! TWO CITY LAWYERS FOUND DEAD! And with growing despair he scanned the story underneath: *perverted misadventure . . . fetish gone awry . . . fatal internal injuries to the disgraced barrister, Henry Wells . . . his lover, Jonathan Stevenson, solicitor in the attorney general's office . . . suicide with a bullet to the brain.*

Ha! Ha! had been daubed on the window, the paint running. *Ha! Ha!*

Reeling, Tommy turned away. So the lawyer was also dead. He clutched his head with a clawed hand and closed his eyes in despair. What was he even doing here? What did he think he could accomplish, going after a man like Noone? He'd told Billy, he'd warned him, he'd known what would happen, and it had. Wildly, Tommy lunged forward and kicked the defaced red door, planting his boot into the lower panel and swinging again and again, crying out and hammering the wood until it broke. He stepped back, panting. A ragged, frenzied stare. The door panel was hanging by only the thinnest of fibers; Tommy nudged it and it fell. He hesitated, knelt down, checked the alley in both directions then reached through and flicked the door latch. He stood, collected his duffel bag, turned the handle, and slipped inside, through a gloomy waiting area, the daylight shrouded by the papered windowpane, and into the back office beyond.

Tommy closed the door behind him, put down his bag, surveyed the ransacked room. Carefully he picked his way toward the desk, scanning the scattered piles of documents as he went, moved the chair aside and leafed through the papers strewn on top. Nothing. He didn't really know what he was looking for. Anything about Billy, the inquest, Noone. Anger flared in him. He tossed the papers aside. To think Billy had trusted this man with their secret, that he'd placed all their lives in his—

Tommy halted. There were two drawers in the desk stanchion, little brass handles, a keyhole in each, both locked. He sifted the desktop and found a letter opener under a stack of sealed deeds, slid it into the first drawer and prized it, pulling the handle gingerly with his left hand, until the lock popped and the drawer opened and Tommy peered inside. Again, nothing. Stationery, an address book, cigarettes, and a bottle of unlabeled liquor, for fuck's sake. He slammed the drawer closed, gave the bottom one a try, and found on top of a stack of notebooks a little black snub-nosed revolver and a box of cartridges, half-filled.

Tommy slid over the desk chair, flopped down, mopped his brow with his cuff, the leather cold on his clammy shirt-back, the fabric soaked through with sweat. It peeled from the chair as he leaned to the drawer, fished out the revolver and cartridges and placed them on the desk. The gun was already loaded. Not for protection, given the drawer was locked: the day when it all got too much.

Tommy pocketed the shells and sat looking at the chair opposite, across the littered desk. Billy must have sat there, maybe as recently as a few days ago. Cooking up their little scheme together, convincing each other they had a chance, Billy spilling all their secrets— Christ, had he told this lawyer where Tommy lived? Was that how Noone's man had known?

He wrenched open the top drawer again and snatched up Wells's address book. Flicking through one-handed until he reached the letter *M*, and sure enough there was an entry for McBride. But this was only Billy's address: *Broken Ridge Cattle Station, Bewley.* Tommy snorted and shook his head. He still wasn't used to it. This person Billy had become. Idly he flicked back and forth through the pages then froze with one half-turned. He opened it very slowly. Staring in disbelief at what he'd found. He smoothed down the spine and picked up the revolver, weighing it, toying with it in his hand, for the home address on the page before him belonged to Edmund Noone.

The sun was low and searing as he staggered along the road that wound sharply up the steep hillside, through a patchwork of enormous mansions and empty building lots, views of the city in the west, the bend of the river below. All a blur to Tommy, his eyes fixed on the road, his bag slapping hard against his calves, breath seething, a struggle planting one foot after the next. Sweat poured from his hairline and dripped off his jaw and a rusty stain bled through his sleeve.

Finally, a set of black double gates, the last house at the end of the street. Ivy covered the walls on either side of the gateposts, save a cutout for the brass nameplate: YARRAVILLE. Tommy dropped the duffel bag, grabbed a railing, hung his head. He couldn't get his balance; his heart pounded, his vision swam, like standing on that beach near Adelaide, seeing the sea for the very first time. He pressed his forehead against the railings and managed to focus on the house. It was grotesque. A sprawl of turrets and terraces, pavilions and verandahs and mismatched gable ends, a

Frankenstein of a building, experimental, obscene, surrounded by a shingle driveway lined with sapling trees, with a grand series of stepped and sun-bleached lawns sloping to the river below.

Tommy tried the gate but it was locked. Not too high, though, and neither were the walls, but he couldn't climb either in this state. He rattled the gate impotently and laughter sounded somewhere, like the house was mocking him, until across the lawns he noticed a group walking back up the hill: three women, a gaggle of children, servants carrying picnic things. The children were running and playing, falling over each other as they went; the women smiling and chatting beneath the brims of their sun hats.

Noone's family. Wife, daughters, grandchildren. All of them happy as larks.

One of the children noticed him. He pointed with an outstretched hand. Over marched a butler, striding between the saplings, shoes crunching the shingle stones, Tommy all the while simply standing there, waiting, no thought in his mind to run.

"Can I help you?" the man shouted as he neared.

"This Noone's house?"

"Police Commissioner Noone, yes."

"He here?"

Scowling, the butler approached the railings. "And you are?"

"I need to see him. Is he here or not?"

"No, he's—" Now the butler noticed the state of him. How he trembled, the untethered stare. "Are you unwell, sir? What are you doing here?"

"I just told you, I need to see him . . . when you expecting him back?"

"Well, that's hard to say. Particularly since—"

"He at work or something?"

"Particularly since you've not even given me a name."

The women were watching from the lawn, shielding their eyes, the children running about their legs. Tommy butted his head against the railing, his and the butler's faces only inches apart, and when Tommy looked at him again the butler asked, "Do you know the commissioner from his service days, perhaps?"

"From his service days?" Tommy pleaded, suddenly close to tears.

"Only I thought, a little like Sergeant Percy, you might have . . ."

Tommy was no longer listening. He reached behind him, into the damp waistband of his trousers, felt the warm metal of the revolver, its deadly weight. Visions of sliding it through these railings, the butler going down, the entire family lying slaughtered on the drive.

"I will kill the both of you and your families and anyone else you hold dear. There will be no warning. One day you will simply look upon my face and know what the other has done."

Noone. In the Broken Ridge atrium all those years ago. He had tried to turn Tommy into a monster back then, poisoning him, seducing him, recruiting him to the cause. Tommy let go of the revolver. Even now, he refused.

"If you'll just give me your name, sir, I will tell him that you called."

Woozily Tommy waved a hand and peeled away from the gates. He picked up his duffel bag, turned, managed a couple of teetering steps forward, then collapsed facedown in the road.

Chapter 41
Tommy McBride

B right white ceiling above him, bright white bed-sheets and walls; with a stab of horror Tommy woke in the featureless room and believed he was inside Noone's house. Silently panicking. Wide eyes darting about. The bed was iron-framed, with a hoodlike canopy blocking his view on either side; he was wearing somebody else's nightclothes. But on the opposite wall was another bed, empty, and there was a low hum of voices somewhere. Grimacing against the pain, Tommy levered himself onto an elbow and realized he was in a hospital ward.

Down he sank, onto his back. The last thing he remembered was speaking to that butler—he had no memory of falling, or of how he got here. He opened his nightshirt gingerly. Peeked at the wound on his arm. It had been cleaned, and resutured, and looked a lot healthier than before. He checked the bedside for his possessions but there was no sign.

"You're awake. Welcome back to the land of the living, Mr. McBride."

Footsteps coming closer, a brisk clip of heels. The nurse opened the canopy and put a hand on Tommy's forehead, nodded curtly, took his wrist and checked his pulse. She was older than him, perhaps mid-forties, with short graying hair and a kindly round face, and though she looked nothing like her, reminded Tommy of his mother somehow.

"How do you know my name?" he rasped. His throat was dry as hell.

"Your travel documents."

She arched her eyebrows knowingly, let go of his wrist, and from a trolley fetched a cup of water that she held to his lips. When he'd finished drinking, she dabbed his chin like an invalid; Tommy pushed her away and tried to rise.

"Where are my things?"

"In the back. Please, just relax."

"I need to go."

She eased him down by the shoulder. "Mr. McBride, you've had quite the fever. You've been very lucky, in fact. No sepsis or gangrene—you should be thankful you've still got the arm." Her eyes flicked to his missing fingers. "You'll just have to settle yourself. It's important you get some rest. I'll come back and check on you again in a little while. Perhaps see if you're up to some food."

"Please . . ." He reached up and touched her sleeve. No strength at all in his grip. "I can't stay here. Bring me my clothes, my tickets. I have to leave."

"Out of the question. Look at you. Still a little delusional, I would say."

"Please . . ."

She half-turned from the bedside. "I will let your friend know you are awake. Perhaps he can talk some sense into you."

The words came out strangled: "What friend?"

"Such a lovely man. What I would call a proper gent. Tall chap, very well-spoken, well-dressed. Sat by your bedside for hours this morning, talking to you quietly, he hardly ever stopped. I've never seen anything like it. He's very concerned about you, obviously. Said I was to call him the minute you came round."

Tommy lurched upward, fighting off the sheets. He swung out his legs and planted his bare feet on the cool floor tiles, the nurse fussing over him but he waved her away. He stood and swayed a moment, found his balance, found her eyes, and, jaw set, lips tight, told her, "Don't call that man. I'm as good as dead if you do."

She considered him carefully, her bluster gone, like she finally saw his fear for what it was. "What on earth do you mean?"

"He'll kill me—do you understand?"

"Are you sure we're talking about the same person?"

"Yes. Was it him that brought me in?"

"You came in a carriage. With a housekeeper, I think."

"But he was here this morning?"

"First thing. Has he threatened you? My goodness, it wasn't him who . . . ?"

She nodded to his wounded arm. Tommy said, "In a way."

"Well then we must call the police and report him. He would have signed in when he visited. I'm sure we have a name."

Tommy took hold of her shoulders with both hands, staring at her intently, his voice barely a whisper as he said, "Trust me, you don't want to get any more involved. Just . . . bring my things, let me leave. Give me an hour to get away, then call him, tell him I ran. Thank you for taking care of me, but it's best for everyone—you included—if I just go."

After a pause she nodded timidly, turned, and

walked away. Past the nurses' station at the entrance to the ward, a brief exchange with her colleague standing there. The other nurse left the station. Tommy sank onto the bed. He was both restless and exhausted, his heel tapping the tiles, his fingers drumming the bed-frame. Along the row an old man was staring at him, unblinking, with vacant glassy eyes—from the look of him, he might easily have already been dead.

The nurse brought his boots and duffel bag, placed the bag on the bed and told Tommy to hurry, her colleague would be back soon. Frantically, he dressed. She turned her back while he was stripping, scooped the nightclothes from the floor. Tommy shrugged on his jacket, pulled his boots on, no need for a sling. The shoulder felt far easier than it had done, stronger, more of an ache than that sharp flash of pain. He flicked through his travel papers and pocketed them, then went scrambling through his bag again. "Is this every-thing?" he said.

"Yes. Is something missing?"

The revolver, but he could hardly say it. "No, it's fine. What's your name?"

"Mary."

Tommy smiled. "My sister was Mary. She'd have been like you, I think."

"I'm far too old for flattery, Mr. McBride. And I

have the nagging feeling you're playing me for the fool here."

"It's not like that. Thank you."

"You do realize I could get into a lot of trouble for this?"

"Not as much as I'm in." He hoisted his bag onto his good shoulder. "An hour, then call him. Otherwise, stay away from that man."

There was a train leaving for Ipswich shortly after he arrived at the station: anything to get him out of Brisbane. From there, the guard told him, he could connect to Toowoomba, then pick up the Western Mail; barring anything unforeseen on the journey, he'd be in Charleville by tomorrow nightfall. Tommy thanked the man and, casting a hurried glance behind him, boarded the waiting train.

He didn't take his seat until the whistle had blown and with a judder the train began shunting on its way. Watching the platform through the window, and the carriage doors for any sign of Noone, then as the city receded Tommy flopped onto the cushioned bench and tipped back his head and let out a long, loud sigh.

He'd been an idiot yesterday. Could so easily have got himself killed.

He settled into the journey. The suburbs flashing by. Soon they were pulling into Ipswich, then after another leg Toowoomba, high in the Great Dividing Range. It still seemed incredible to him, traveling this way. Once, he had dreamed of small things, of seeing the ocean, or a city, never thought he would actually do it; now he hopped between cities like a bird. These mountains used to be impassable, a natural wall keeping people out—and in—yet here was a train line that carried you right through them like it was nothing at all, to a town built way up in the heavens, all shady streets and parkland, restaurants and hotels.

He had no time for sightseeing. He'd got lucky with the trains. At just before ten that evening the night service left Toowoomba for Roma with a free first-class berth that Tommy was all too happy to take. Stacking up the miles behind him. The sense of safety that they gave. Rattling over the immense plateau of the Darling Downs, its sea of crops and grazing pastures stitched together like a blanket, different tones of gray and black. Moonlit windmills broke the horizon, dotted shadows of cattle and sheep, the eerie symmetry of crop furrows ploughed in tight-knit rows. This was farming country, grazing country, not unlike the landscape of Barren Downs. A lifetime ago, but it all still echoed, his present only ever a reminder of something in his past. And now he was going back to it, to where that past began.

Still, it was beautiful country, Queensland. Despite itself. Despite him.

In his dream that night he was standing in the desert with Billy and Noone, calmly discussing the order in which they should each be killed. They had their revolvers drawn and pointed at one another's head, a triangular arrangement, links in a chain. It seemed to be understood that all of them would die here, but what they couldn't agree upon was the logistics, who would fire first, different arguments being advanced and rebutted like they were haggling the price of grain.

He woke with a start in his cabin, calmed when he realized he was alone. He rose from the bunk and worked out his shoulder—he'd slept fully clothed, boots on. He lifted the blind at the window. The view took his breath away. The open plains of his childhood, gum trees and grassland and the first amber soil he'd seen in years. It grew even darker after the change-over in Roma, where he boarded a mixed-use goods train pulled by a black locomotive with a cowcatcher plough, no first-class privileges here, the soil outside steadily turning that deep red color he'd been born to, as vital to Tommy as the blood in his veins. All day the train chugged across that endless nothingness, barren scrubland, empty sky, scorched by a brutal sunshine that boiled the carriage like a stew. Passengers stripped off their jackets and yanked off their ties and fanned themselves frantically with their hats, while Tommy simply gazed out of the window, expressionless, save the twinge of a smile, tight with trepidation, teasing the corners of his lips.

The train line ended in Charleville and with his duffel bag hooked on his shoulder Tommy slipped through the waiting crowd to the coach house, where he booked himself on the next coach heading north. But that wasn't until the following morning, meaning he would have to spend the night. He took a room at the hotel, ate a meal and drank at the bar, avoiding the gaze of curious locals and the assumptions that they knew him from somewhere—wasn't he somebody's brother, father, workmate, son?—with each confrontation a flutter in his stomach that here was another Alan Ames. It never was. Tommy shook his head and mumbled they were mistaken, then, once the bar had become rowdier, drunker, and the questions become more like threats—*Miserable bugger, ain't ya, I only asked yer bloody name*—turning and warning them outright to leave him the fuck alone.

The coach set out with six passengers crammed into

the carriage and two more riding on the roof, among a teetering pile of luggage and goods, all of which were gradually shed at the various towns and change stations they stopped at along the route. Now this was truly Tommy's country. Spinifex and clumps of scrub grass, termite mounds and boulder cairns, virgin soil that had never known a footprint, or the touch of rain. When there was only Tommy and one other passenger remaining, a white-bearded old man with mustaches waxed into points, the old-timer asked how far he was traveling, then after Tommy told him blew out his cheeks and shook his head.

"Arse-end of nowhere, Bewley. It's all blacks, thieves, and killers out there."

Tommy only stared at him. Another fucking echo. Would it ever end?

He was alone in the carriage by the time they arrived creaking into the little settlement, jerking upright in his seat as the desert suddenly ended and they passed a whitewashed barn with a cross mounted above its front door. The church looked no different from the last time Tommy had seen it, when he'd gone inside searching for his mother and been chased out by a vision of hanging men. He peered through the coach window. Watching the familiar buildings slide by. The coach halted in front of the post office and the coachman stiffly climbed down, red dust sliding off him like silt. He banged on the siding and Tommy started. "Here y'are, mate!" he yelled, wrenching open the door to find Tommy squatting petrified inside. He looked at his passenger queerly. He was holding Tommy's duffel bag. "Either you're getting out or stopping in but if y'are there'll be an extra fare."

Gingerly he climbed out, took the bag, the coachman frowning like he'd lost his mind. Tommy noticed the people watching, strangers all, though there was nothing to say they didn't recognize him. He doubted he had changed much. He felt like a boy again. Making his way warily along the main street, everything as he remembered it, save the odd little change: the general store whose signage no longer bore the name Spruhl; the courthouse with its flagpole, now missing its wooden stocks; the doctor's surgery, an older Dr. Shanklin at the desk, the man who was supposed to save Mary's life but never did; and at the end of the street Song's Hardware, where Tommy had once stolen a folding knife and briefly fallen for the owner's daughter, who'd done nothing more than talk to him, and delicately sweep the boards with her broom.

He crossed the street to the hardware store. It didn't seem possible she could still be here, but then time had so little meaning to Tommy that it felt just as likely she was. He came up the steps slowly, aware of the eyes on his back. The front door was open and a chair was outside and it was 1885 all over again. Mother was off buying groceries, Father was at the Lawton saleyards, Billy and Mary were waiting back at the house. There was still time to save them, to turn it all around, to change the course of every life he had lost.

"Help you?"

Tommy blinked, his eyes adjusting, peering into the dusty shop. The man was standing behind the counter, wiping his hands on a rag, loops of wire, rope, and rubber coiled on wall hooks behind. Tommy stepped forward, through the doorway, approached the counter. He lowered his bag. The shop hadn't changed. Finally he focused on the man again, his age or thereabouts, but good for it, a vitality to him, a freshness in his face.

"This still Song's Hardware?"

"That's what the sign says."

"You're Song?"

The man frowned. "Aye, Nathan Song—do I know you or something, mate?"

Tommy shook his head. "I was looking for Mia? Is she here?"

"Mia? What for?"

"Are you her husband?"

"Brother."

"You came back," Tommy said vaguely.

He spread his hands on the counter. Muscles roped his forearms. "What the hell's this about?"

"I knew her, your sister."

"Well, she's married now, moved away, so if you're some kind of old sweetheart you're about seven years too late."

"It's not like that. Look, sorry—I used to live round here, that's all."

"Oh, yeah? Got a name?"

"She was good to me once, but I did something, took something, so here . . ."

Tommy scrabbled in his pocket for his billfold, peeled off a note and stepped forward, the note quivering in his grip. Song only crossed his arms.

"What's that for?"

"A folding knife. I stole it. From that drawer there. Mia was sweeping. Your old man was asleep on the porch."

They both looked at the empty chair in the doorway. It was the exact same one. Nathan Song's eyes narrowed, as if seeing his late father sitting there, or seeing himself now in his place. Tommy lowered his hand.

"When was this?" Song asked.

"December of eighteen eighty-five."

The shopkeeper laughed. "You taking the piss?"

"Nope. I came in for rubber tubing. Was going to take that n'all."

"You stole some rubber tubing?"

He shook his head. "Mia put it in the book when no one else would."

"Well, that does sound like Mia."

"But she never knew about the knife. I need to set it right."

"Hell," Song said, laughing, "I think we can let that slide."

"I can't. Just . . . take it, please."

He dropped the note on the counter. Song was reckoning something. "You must have been only a boy."

"Fourteen. She was fifteen, she said."

"Eighteen eight-five. Me and our Peter were at the diggings."

"Yeah, she told me. Said you were coming back rich."

Song laughed, looked about, spread his arms. "Can't you tell?"

Tommy smirked. Song's face knotted into a frown. "So this pocketknife you stole has been eating you up all this time?"

"Among other things."

He nodded at the note. "And what, was it made of solid gold?"

"Call it interest."

"All right, suit yourself," Song said, sighing. He rang up the till, the drawer popped open, he slipped the note inside. "Though I'd feel better about it if you'd tell me your name."

"Do you ever hear from her? Mia?"

"She writes sometimes."

"Ask her, she might remember. Give her my best. Say thanks for the rubber tubing . . . and that I never did go to school."

Nathan Song looked at Tommy like he might as well have been speaking French. Tommy picked up his bag and left. A little lightness in him as he came down the steps; a tiny ghost laid to rest. In the street he paused and glanced along the track heading west out of town, the track that would eventually lead him to Glendale. He swallowed heavily. He wasn't ready for that yet, the ghosts were too big out there. He went to turn but glimpsed in the distance, trembling in the heat, the ramshackle buildings of the native camps. He hung his head. Some debts weren't so easily paid. He understood that now. He wasn't meant to forget, or bury it, as Arthur had once told him; it wasn't supposed to be as simple as moving on. What had happened to the

Kurrong, his role in it, what he'd done, was a part of him, a weight he would carry to the grave. And rightly so. It was the least he could do. Guilt was not a thing to be shed but a wound, a scar, a permanent reminder like the gash in his shoulder or the missing fingers of his hand. Maybe it would fade in time. As the years ticked over, maybe he would carry it a little easier, but he would carry it with him all the same.

Head lowered, he trudged through town to the stables, to see about hiring a horse.

Chapter 42
Katherine McBride

"My husband isn't here, Mr. Collins, as you've already been told."

"But . . . I've traveled all this way."

"Which is why you'll have to make do with me instead."

"No offense, miss, but it's business I'm here for, not a social call."

"I've not been a miss for over twenty years. Mrs. McBride, please."

"McBride, Sullivan . . . you're married so often it's hard to keep track."

His tongue slopped wantonly around his gums then he offered the same yellow, bucktoothed grin he'd worn when he first stepped through the office door. Now he sat across the desk from Katherine, sipping the bottom-shelf brandy she had offered him, while Katherine folded her hands on the desktop and returned his smile with one of her own.

"Yes, of course, do forgive me. Two names over two decades. Must be quite a challenge for you, I am sure."

He scowled at the insult, if that was what it was—she could almost see him calculating whether to take offense. A small man in a brown checked suit, blotchy-faced and sweating, he had a habit of dabbing himself with a handkerchief then sniffing it once he was done. He repeated the ritual and calmed a little, took a sip of his brandy, said, "Right, so when are you expecting him back?"

Days ago, thought Katherine; she had sent a telegram to the Bellevue Hotel and received a reply that Billy had checked out last week. She didn't know where he was. Beyond Brisbane, he'd not told her anything about his plans. But she held her smile and kept her shoulders pinned and replied, "As I said, he has gone to the city on business, which will take as long as it takes. Then there is the return journey. If you'd telegrammed beforehand, I'd have told you the same thing."

"Brave man, leaving his wife all the way out here, fending for herself."

Mischief in his eyes when he said it. Katherine knew that glint. "I'm hardly alone, Mr. Collins. And I'm more than capable of fending for myself."

He mulled it over for a moment. Another dab and sniff.

"It's the commission I'm getting," he said finally. "I need fifteen percent."

Katherine stifled a burst of laughter. "Fifteen percent?"

"Exactly."

"Up from five?"

"I know it's a jump, but costs are up, labor, everything's on the rise."

"Your costs aren't our concern, Mr. Collins."

"Well they should be. It's your cattle I'm putting through."

"Indeed. Quite a substantial number of them, as I recall."

"Still don't change the numbers. The business won't survive."

"How you run things at your end is not our problem."

"Will be if I go under. You could negotiate, at least."

She busied herself with a stack of papers awaiting signature on the desk, slid one across and considered it. "As I said, you really should have telegrammed first."

"Twelve and a half then. I could make do with twelve and a half."

She looked up at him. "You'll make do with five, like everyone else."

"Have a heart, Mrs. McBride. I've a family of my own to look after, so do my men. There's kiddies'll starve otherwise. You wouldn't want that, would you?"

Katherine put the papers aside again, leaned forward on the desk. "Well I'm pleased to see you've learned my name finally, but let me ask you this: If it were Billy sitting here instead of me, would you be asking for fifteen percent? Suggesting he *have a heart*, tossing out starving children like bait?"

"He's a reasonable man, your husband. Fair."

"You wouldn't still have your seat, Mr. Collins. You'd be out that door and down the front steps with his boot up your backside, or worse."

"It's only business, I don't mean nothing by it."

"Business. Exactly. So what makes you think my answer will be any different to his?"

"Ten, then. I could scrape by on ten percent."

"I'm sure you could. But you'll have to scrape by on five."

His stare hardened, a setting of the jaw. "You've a bloody nerve, sitting here in your mansion, telling me to scrape by. The hell do you know about any of it—you ain't never been nothing but a rich man's wife. A dozen years I've been your selling agent and I ain't asking for nothing except what's fair. Have Billy write when he's back from Brisbane. I ain't wasting any more of my time."

He went to stand but Katherine stopped him with a raised hand. "Mr. Collins, please, sit down. I think perhaps there's been a misunderstanding here."

A smirk teased his lips as he did so. Arms folded, head cocked, like he had her now. "All right, I'm listening," he said, nodding. "On you go."

"Thank you. You're very kind. And you are correct, of course, about the length of our association. Twelve years is a long time. Over the past decade we have, as you know, outlasted and outgrown almost every other cattle station in central Queensland. Nobody can match us, Mr. Collins. The competition has all but disappeared. Now, we are a fair employer. You can ask any of our men. But when it comes to commercial arrangements such as the one we have with you, there really is no question as to who holds the cards. We set the rates we trade at, we decide with whom to trade; it does not work the other way around." She paused and waited a beat before continuing: "Imagine a dingo, hunting out there in the scrubs, choosing which rabbit to go after—do you think the rabbits get any say? The best they can do to protect themselves, surely, is to keep their heads down, remain quiet, perhaps scurry into the long grass to hide. But now let us imagine that one particular rabbit begins jumping, screaming, provoking the dingo to its face—what do you think the dingo would do to it then?"

"Hold up now. I already said I never meant no offense."

"She would kill it, would she not? She would kill it and gut it and move on to the next. You are that rabbit, Mr. Collins. There are thousands of you out there. We can have ourselves another sales agent before you've even got back on your horse. But what would you be without us? Where's your next Broken Ridge?"

Shifting in the chair, dabbing himself furiously with his handkerchief, he stammered, "Look, all I'm doing is asking for fair compensation. Seven and a half, six even, anything just to—"

"I don't think you're listening to me."

"Fine. We'll stick at five. But I still want to talk to Billy about this."

"This is my station, not Billy's, and no, we will not stick at five. We are done, Mr. Collins. Our relationship is over. I will not have you come uninvited into

my home, insult me, patronize me, make demands
you would never dare make of a man, then expect us
to continue as before. We are finished—as, I would
wager, are you." She gestured to the door. "Now you
may leave. Hardy will show you out."

At the sound of his name Hardy opened the door
and stood waiting.

"But . . . we have a contract!" Collins spluttered.

"You'll receive a written termination. I'll get on
to it right away. The speed of the mail these days, I
daresay it will reach your office before you do. Or you
can wait in the atrium while I write it, however you
prefer."

"This is outrageous! You can't do this! Twelve
bloody years!"

"Don't make a scene, Mr. Collins. Good day."

Coldly she watched him snarl and bluster to his feet
then scurry like a scolded child from the room. Hardy
closed the door behind them and when she was sure
they were gone she let out a long breath and fell back
into her chair. She noticed his glass on the desktop,
the lip marks and fingerprints smeared on the side.
She cringed. A little laugh escaped. A giddiness at
what she'd just done. She regretted none of it. The
man deserved every word. She stood and went to the
cabinet and leafed through the papers until she found

the Collins contract, took it back to her desk, and readied her pen.

She had almost completed her paperwork when an hour later there came a knock on the door and Hardy announced that another rider was approaching on the track. Katherine laid down her pen and sighed. "Surely not Collins again?"

"I don't believe so, ma'am. In fact it looks a little like Mr. McBride."

She hurried outside and from the verandah railing watched him come. There was certainly a resemblance. Square shoulders, thick chest, a similar way of holding himself on the horse. But this wasn't Billy. The horse was too knackered, the clothes too unkempt, the rider leaner, trimmer, stronger, younger; hatless, with light fair hair. Trailing a hand along the railing she turned onto the stairs and came down very slowly, rocking slightly on her bad hip, not once breaking her stare. It might have been anyone, one of the men from the compound, a merchant up from town . . . so why this surge of excitement, this fluttering deep inside?

He beat her to the bottom of the staircase, dismounted and walked forward, lifting his gaze, those searching blue eyes, and with a gasp Katherine recognized him as the boy who had stood terrified with his brother in the bedroom just behind her, asking if their sister was still alive; the boy who'd never seen a Christmas tree until she showed him hers; the boy in whose saddlebag she'd hidden a packet of lemon lollies, before sending him off to a massacre; the boy who'd come back irrevocably changed.

She pulled up short on the final few steps. His expression had not changed since seeing her. Unsmiling, riven with deep unease. Gripping the banister she descended to the track, gravel crunching softly under her shoes.

"Tommy? Is that you?"

He nodded timidly. Running his thumb over his knuckles, wringing his dust-covered hands. And she knew then, with absolute certainty and a knifelike pain in her chest, that her fool of a husband had died. This scheme of his, this plan . . . he'd gone out there and got himself killed. She folded her arms defensively, tears brimming as she asked, "Is it Billy?" then dripping when Tommy's grimace confirmed that it was.

Her gaze slid over the sun-drenched hillside, the shadows gently lengthening, the daily sundial of the trees. It felt inevitable, really. In a way she had always expected this, that one day someone would ride up and tell her Billy was dead. A fall, a quarrel, a drunken brawl. He was never going to go nobly, or drift away in his bed at a grand old age. Roughly she swiped a tear from her cheek and asked Tommy, "How?"

He looked about uncertainly. "Here?"

"I want to know."

"All right." Awkwardly he shuffled foot to foot, then: "He found me, came to the house, only he was followed. It was one of Noone's men."

"Shot?"

"Long-range rifle. He never saw it coming. Went out happy in the end."

She scoffed—of course he bloody did. Oblivious even to his own death. But as the laughter faded she found that she was reeling, the ground lurching, nausea rising up; she reached for the banister behind her but missed it, stumbled, her heels struck the bottom step and she fell. Tommy lunged and caught her, helped her down, Katherine groping for the solidity of the staircase and sitting gratefully on the steps. She smoothed her skirt then went on rubbing it rhythmically back and forth, unable to fill a breath, the sun blinding suddenly, hot as a soldering iron, while her mind tumbled forward into her future like a bucket down an empty well. The children would grow up fatherless. She was a widow, again. Stuck out here, alone save the house staff; she would not remarry, she knew with startling clarity, not now she didn't have to, not now the only man she would love in her lifetime was dead.

Hesitantly Tommy sat down beside her, lowering himself stiffly onto the step, legs wide, elbows on his knees. His head was turned away from her, squinting off into the distance, to the compound and south to the land beyond.

"I want to know what happened. Don't spare me. Tell me everything."

She saw him nod and waited. He fished a cigarette tin from his pocket, offered one to Katherine. She didn't usually smoke but took one anyway; the tin looked like Billy's, she thought. Tommy lit the cigarette for her. The tip trembled terribly in the flame. He lit another for himself and for a moment they smoked in silence, Katherine's furtive little drags and exhalations, Tommy drawing the smoke all the way down to his boots.

"He said he'd been looking for me, for years maybe, some bloke of his finally tracked me down . . ."

Quietly she listened to the unraveling of Billy's life, and with it the children's, also hers. This folly he had embarked upon, the stranger at her birthday party, some misguided plan to go after Edmund Noone. Why? What was the point? Of course she could understand him wanting to find Tommy, but why couldn't that be enough? She already knew the answer. Because nothing ever was, for Billy. Not her, not their children, not the empire they had built . . . nothing was ever good enough.

"I think maybe he wanted to put things right about what happened," Tommy said. "Show you he was sorry for what we did."

"Billy isn't sorry. Surely you know him better than that."

"Well, that's what he told me anyhow."

Angrily, she tossed her cigarette. "Billy's only regret is that I found out the truth about him. Nothing more than that."

"He said he wanted you to be able to look him in the face again."

"More likely I'd have slapped him. He risked everything . . . and for what?"

"It ain't been easy, you know, living with what we did."

She looked at him sharply. "I'm sure it hasn't, for you. But Billy has slept like a baby every night of his life. I know you're only saying these things to be kind, Tommy, but don't. We both know what he is—was. Deep down Billy never cared about anyone but himself. He believed himself a victim too. Going out there to right the wrongs against him . . . in his own mind Billy was the hero of every story. It was always someone else to blame."

From her sleeve she pulled a handkerchief, dabbed her eyes, her nose, stuffed it back under the cuff and composed herself. "He would have taken us all down with him. You included. You're lucky you got out alive."

"Only barely."

"Do you have a family? Are they safe?"

"Of sorts. No children. I doubt he knows anything about them. Billy didn't."

"And what about you? Would Noone still come after you?"

Tommy shrugged. "I was lying in a hospital bed four days ago, he could have done anything to me then. Me and him, I don't know, I think he almost liked me in a way. It hardly seems worth his while bothering. What could I do?"

Hesitantly she reached for his hand and held it, the skin as rough as unplaned wood. "Thank you for coming all this way to tell me. I know it was a risk."

"You deserved to know."

"I suppose it makes this a little easier, hearing it from you."

She smiled at him, let go of his hand, watched him

take it back and cup it in his lap. He looked weak, she thought, compromised somehow. The stubs of his two missing fingers—she remembered him nursing the bandage, fourteen years old, right here on these same steps.

"Will you stay?" Katherine asked him. "Our eldest two are away at school, but Thomas and Suzanna would love to meet you I'm sure."

"It's their daddy they're waiting on, not me."

"They'd be grateful for it, Tommy. As would I."

He glanced at the house over his shoulder, a little fearfully Katherine thought. All the memories would be so raw for him, this the first time he'd been back. Watching him in profile, his worn and stubbled face, a faraway absence in his eyes. There was so much pain in him. All those awkward furtive glances and shrugs, the little tics, Tommy was a man literally crawling in his own skin. Obvious, now that she saw it, the effect his childhood still had. That same darkness she'd seen in Billy, but amplified, more raw, more real—he was not that naive little boy but a man, a stranger, truthfully she had no idea who he was.

"I was thinking I'd go down to the house while I'm here. Might be my only chance. Visit Mary too, if that's all right."

"Of course it is. Don't be silly. Take as long as you need."

"Will you manage, d'you think? After?"

She sat up tall and sighed. "I expect so. I'm used to being alone."

"What will you do?"

"Raise my children. Live my life. Carry on. Mourn him, obviously. When we were first together, Tommy . . ." She drifted into silence, shook her head. A quick burst of laughter as she said, "You know, he once just about threw my father down these steps. Kicked him out of the house, said he'd castrate him if he ever came back. I was horrified but delighted. That's the effect he had on me, the kind of man he was. Then, I don't know, status, money, secrets, lies—is it even possible for two people to love each other after such a length of time?"

"I wouldn't know about that."

She pulled herself up to her feet. "No, well, I'm not sure it is. Please consider staying, Tommy, even if it's just for one night. If you head down to Glendale now the sunset may catch you and you'll end up sleeping there, which is not the best idea. Besides, I'd welcome the company. I'd love to hear your stories— I've thought about you often, we both did, wondering where you'd got to, how you were. If it helps, I won't tell the children until after you're gone. That way you won't feel responsible, and it'll give me time to get used to the idea, not to mention figure out what on earth I'm going to say."

She walked back up the staircase, her shoes clipping softly on the wood. When she reached the top she turned and found that Tommy hadn't moved. Hunched forward, his head hanging, worrying his hands together, the wounded and the good, as if trying to rub them clean.

Chapter 43
Tommy McBride

The grave couldn't have been much longer than the shovel they'd dug it with. A five-foot plot with a low iron fence, and a white marble headstone bearing Mary's name and dates. No flowers, but that wasn't surprising. Flowers never lasted out here.

Tommy touched his fingers to his lips then rested them on the headstone, out of obligation more than anything, it had been so long ago. What was left in him now was not so much grief as the vivid memory of that grief, of standing hollowed-out at this graveside on the day they'd returned from the dispersal, only to learn that their sister was dead.

It had been Katherine who had told them. Funny how things come around. She had buried Mary while they were away to stop the body from rotting, and John

Sullivan had nearly shit himself that a McBride now lay in his land. Tommy smiled at that one. Glanced across the little cemetery to the mottled gray headstone that bore that fat fucker's name—who was buried on whose land now? For eternity Sullivan would lie there fuming in McBride soil; would have watched Billy take his station, marry his widow, raise their kids. Tommy didn't really believe in the afterlife, but it was nice to imagine sometimes.

On his way out of the cemetery, he spat on Sullivan's grave.

A boy was waiting for him when he reached the backyard gate. Tommy could guess who he was. Tall, dark-haired, his father's image, but there were parts of himself, or maybe his own father, in there too. Freckles on the kid's nose and cheekbones. A seriousness in his stare. He stood with his arms rigid at his sides, his fingers picking his trouser legs and itching his palms. Tommy came through the gate and the boy stepped determinedly forward with an outstretched hand.

"Glad to meet you, Uncle Tommy. My name's Thomas McBride."

It took him a moment to recover. Uncle Tommy— he'd never heard anything so strange. But he shook the boy's sweaty hand, an exaggerated flapping up and down, then swallowed and managed to reply, "Glad to meet you too, son."

"That's your sister buried up there," the boy told him, like this might be news.

"Aye, it is."

"Aunt Mary."

"*Aunt* Mary?" Tommy echoed, laughing.

He nodded. "She was the same age as me when she died."

"Which would make you eleven, I take it?"

"Yessir. I'll be twelve soon. Daddy says he'll take me mustering then."

Tommy winced. The laughter faded from his eyes. "I heard you liked cattle work. Skilled on a horse too, eh?"

"Daddy says I'm about as good as you were when you were a boy."

"Is that right now?"

"Yessir. Better than him even, and he's the best I've seen."

"Billy said that? That I was better than him?"

"Only with the horses. Not with nothing else."

Tommy smiled tightly. A short quick laugh through his nose. He looked at the boy standing earnestly before him and could feel the lump rising, a thickness in his throat. He reached out and scuffed his matted hair, warm and wiry in his hand, and at that moment the back door opened and Katherine was standing there, a girl peering past her, clinging to her waist. "Thomas," she scolded, her voice catching, her breathing ragged. She'd been crying. Tears stained her cheeks. "What did I tell you? I'm so sorry, Tommy—I warned him to leave you in peace."

"I'm glad to have met him at last. No wonder Billy's so proud."

He glanced again at Thomas, beaming at the praise, cupped his shoulder then turned to the girl hiding at Katherine's side. He stepped forward, crouching slightly, attempted a reassuring smile. "And you must be Suzanna?" he asked her. She gave a shy nod. Tommy knelt on the steps and touched her arm ever so gently with his left hand, the little girl watching his missing fingers like there might be magic there. "I read about you in a newspaper once," he told her. "Now look how big you've grown."

Katherine dismissed the kitchen staff early that evening, and she and Tommy sat around one end of the long rough-wood table, drinking wine and picking at cuts of bread, meat, and cheese, in the light of a single candle flame. Neither could stomach a formal supper. And Tommy held dark memories of that dining room. Dark memories of the whole house, in fact, but maybe these were the kind of memories he could manage to let go. Leave them all up here, where they belonged, find a way not to take them back home. Beginning, perhaps, in this kitchen, a room like any other, four walls, a table and chairs. There was no evil in here. Just him and Katherine, his sister-in-law, eating and drinking, sometimes laughing, swapping stories about Billy, remembering him, beginning to mourn.

"There was this one time," Katherine said, her hand whirling, loosened by the wine, "Billy got it in his head there was money to be made in camel breeding—did you ever come across a camel, Tommy?"

"Once or twice. Thought they were the strangest-looking horses I ever seen."

"Well, Billy bought a pair off this trader—I don't know where he met him, Billy met lots of men—and came back one day with the two of them plodding along behind, that funny walk they have, the bend in their knees. Anyway, I remember it, I was in the backyard, and I saw him lead these things into the old corral. Like Hannibal with his elephants, he was. Not sure I'd ever seen him so proud. 'What the hell are they for?' I asked him, and of course he says we're going to breed them, sell them, or even make use of them ourselves. Well, you can imagine my reaction, but there was no telling him sometimes, not when he'd got an idea in his head, and I thought if it made us a bit of money . . . this was during the drought, mind you, anything was worth a try. So, he starts up with these camels. Honestly, Tommy, I don't think I've ever laughed so hard. I'd stand out the back and watch him trying to train them, even better trying to get them to mate. You've heard of mules being stubborn, a camel wouldn't run if it didn't want to even if you set the thing on fire. Every day he'd be out there, getting bitten or stomped on or kicked. They destroyed the corral fences. Had to have a whole new one built. Billy would be trying to shove one onto the other, climbing up on the railings, dangling out food as bait. They just weren't interested. Didn't matter what he did. And the noise those creatures made! Have you heard them? Sometimes at night we'd hear them from the house, honking away like car horns! After about a week of this carry-on, Billy arranged for some vet to examine them, tell him what was going wrong. We all stood around the corral watching, me and Billy, a few of the men. The vet walked in, took one look at the camels, walked right out again. Didn't even inspect them. 'Well?' Billy asked him—you could see he wasn't pleased, he'd paid to have this bloke brought out here, he was some sort of expert, I think. And the vet looks him square in the eye, deadly serious, big beard and whiskers on him, asks, 'And you are hoping to breed these two camels, are you, Mr. McBride?' Billy looks about, confused, like this must be some sort of trick. 'I already told you that—what's wrong with them?' 'Nothing,' the old man answers. 'They're two perfectly healthy, if a little unhappy, examples of the species. Your problem is, they are both males.'"

Tommy burst out laughing. Katherine cupped her mouth with her hand, her eyes watering, she couldn't stop. She clutched her chest and fell back in the chair and dabbed her eyes with the back of her hand. "So what happened?" Tommy asked her finally. "What did he do with them?"

It took her a while to steady herself. She sniffed and sipped her wine. "He was furious! Didn't believe the vet at first. Asked him, 'You sure about that?' and the bloke offered to get both camels all excited just to prove it, though there'd be a hefty surcharge. Billy sent him packing. I don't know if he ever caught up with the trader in the end. The camels, I think he sold them. Knowing Billy he probably even made a profit, claimed they were thoroughbreds or something. The men joked about it for months afterward. I didn't dare. As you can imagine, Billy did *not* see the funny side, but it still tickles me to this day."

"Two males," Tommy said, shaking his head. "Didn't he notice?"

"You can't exactly see it on a camel. None of us thought to even check. This trader must have known, surely, but poor Billy just took him at his word."

They drifted into silence, lingering laughter at the tale. She sipped her wine and looked at him fondly. "I'm so glad you came, Tommy."

"I'm not staying."

"I know. But just having you here . . . Billy felt your absence, I'm sure he did, not that he ever told me how he felt about anything. He was a man of silence, mostly. Maybe you all are. But he missed you. There's no doubt about that."

"Aye, well."

"It's unfair, what happened to you both. You were so young."

"You weren't much older."

She shook her head. "No. And that wasn't fair either."

"I'll get off in the morning, I was thinking. It ain't good for me, being here. Head down to Glendale, then into town, see if I can pick up a coach."

"I can arrange one for you? A private carriage?"

"I'll be all right."

"Shall I come with you then? To the house?"

"What for?"

"Billy always struggled. Took him years before he went back. Probably you could count up all his visits on the fingers of just one hand."

"Yours or mine?" Tommy joked, weakly, but Katherine didn't laugh. He was ducking the question, doing his best to avoid her gaze.

"I mean it. Let me come with you. I've my own goodbyes to say down there."

He thought for a moment then shook his head. "I think I'd best do this alone."

That night he lay awake in one of the guest bedrooms, tracing tendrils of flowers on a section of wallpaper lit by a shaft of moonlight. Dog-tired from the journey but he couldn't sleep. He knew that wallpaper, this bedroom. The furniture was different—one big bed now, not two—but from the moment Katherine had stopped in the hallway, wished him good night outside the door, he had known.

This was the same room he and Billy had slept in, the night their parents were killed.

Chapter 44
Tommy McBride

Around the workers' compound, past the derelict watchman's hut, following the bridle path through sparse woodland and over lush grazing fields in the west, until he turned uphill onto a southern slope where the terrain was more barren, riddled with rock and scree, stubbled with spinifex and towering termite mounds, cathedrals of another world, and in the distance glimpsed the slender blue gum forest that had once marked the boundary between Broken Ridge station and his family's little cattle run.

Tommy could have ridden blindfolded, he'd done the journey so often in his dreams.

He dismounted in the trees and walked the horse through, the brush thicker than he remembered it, overgrown. On the other side he stood gazing over the sloping plains, ablaze in the morning sunshine, the land scrubby and perished, not a blade of decent feed. He took off the hat Katherine had given him— one of Billy's, she had said—and forlornly wafted the flies with his hand. The place was a wasteland. And to think it had once been his whole world.

He settled the hat back on his head; good fit, nice feel, pure rabbit felt. Something to remember us by, Katherine had said, as if he was likely to forget. The two of them standing on the verandah, a drawn-out goodbye, Katherine again offering to come with him, Tommy refusing, a shake of the head. She'd hugged him long and hard, made him promise to write, mumbling about arranging another visit sometime. The children would appreciate it, she had added, so he'd agreed. But he doubted he would ever see any of them again.

The horse trotted reluctantly over that hard, rubbled ground, hooves slipping, her gait wary, and still a long way to go. Tommy patted her neck sympathetically. He knew exactly how she felt. The sooner they got there, and got this over with, the sooner they'd both be gone.

They crested the final hillside and at last the little

homestead peeled into view, ringed by its molder-
ing outbuildings, ghostly and abandoned in that dust-
blown scrubland. Tommy pulled the horse up short
and sat staring. The place looked condemned. Holes
in the walls, holes in the sagging roof; one side of the
scullery had collapsed. The storage shed had been flattened, the stables looked burned-out, a carpet of weeds
covered the yard. He walked the horse slowly down the
hillside, struggling to understand the disrepair. Hadn't
Billy said he'd lived here? Hadn't he visited? Wasn't
this all part of the Broken Ridge estate?

Tommy tied off the horse at the cattle yards, the
railings dangling, the posts chewed by rot, and walked
carefully toward the house and main yard. Total silence
out here save the crunch of his footsteps. Deathly still.
No cattle, no insects, no birds. Ahead the house was
lit up in the sunshine and all the more decrepit for it,
the front door standing open, dark shadows inside . . .
Tommy looked away, to the bunkhouse, the remnants
of a firepit outside the entrance, the rusted frame of
a cot bed visible through the doors. He reached the
verandah and wavered. Breathing in staccato jags. He
could almost hear Mother sweeping, the swish of her
broom on the boards; he snatched free of the memory
and hurried around the back of the house.

Headstones, he'd expected. Marble, like Mary's,

something with their names. Instead he saw only thick scrub and bald soil patches, no grave markers of any kind, no sign that his parents, or anyone, had ever been buried here.

Bewildered, Tommy trudged through the weeds and clump grass, glancing back at the house to get a fix on where they'd dug the holes. He found them eventually. A pair of plain white wooden crosses lying discarded in the dirt, the surrounding scrub a little thinner, two rectangles, the vague outline of each plot.

Tommy knelt and snatched up the nearest cross and tried shoving it back in, but the earth was baked solid, no give beneath the dust. He heaved and heaved, jabbing at the ground, until the join between the arms splintered and the cross fell apart in his hands. He looked at the two halves despairingly, then screamed and launched them into the scrub, falling onto all fours and snatching up weeds with both fists. This was his mother's grave he was tending. He'd dug it out himself. Worrying he'd made it too big for her, lowering her in; now she lay here like she was nothing, had meant nothing, like she wasn't a mother at all. "Fuck, Billy!" Tommy yelled, panting, rearing back on his heels. His hat fell off. Hands cut and filthy, but his scrabbling had made no difference at all.

Up Tommy labored. He retrieved his hat and stood

over those two outlines and paid his respects with silence, the only way he knew. He wasn't one for praying, or talking to the dead, and anyway if they could hear him, he figured they already knew. He missed them, was the crux of it. And he was sorry as hell for how they'd gone. That day had punched a hole through Tommy that nothing had been able to fill. You never get over becoming an orphan. Not for all the Arthurs and Jack Kerrigans in this world. He hoped they would be proud of what he'd made of his life, what little he'd achieved, but deep down didn't see how they could.

He left the other cross lying in the long grass, left the graves unmarked. Fuck it—this land had defined his parents, sustained them, ruined them, it might as well swallow them now. It felt fitting, almost. They belonged here totally, in a way that for the first time Tommy was realizing he did not. This endless red flatland he'd always thought of as home . . . but it wasn't anymore, was it, all it ever brought him was pain. He felt no sense of belonging being back here. No, home for Tommy was Gippsland, with his cattle, his gully, his pastures, and with Emily, and Arthur, and Rosie; they were his family now.

But he had to go inside the house again. Had to lay

that ghost to rest. He walked around the front, beneath the rusted windmill, past the crumbling log pile and dried-up well, the little clearing where they'd found the dogs stabbed, and forced himself face-to-face with the old slab hut, planting his boots in the weed-strewn dirt directly in front of the steps, the open door yawning beyond. Dark in there, but not fully, the gloom leavened by shards of sunlight through the patchwork roof. He glimpsed the curtain to his old bedroom, swallowed and steeled himself. All he had to do was go inside. Then he could go home.

Slow boot tread on the steps then the verandah. A dark stain between the bench and the door. Tommy pictured Father slumped there, three holes in him, his rifle across his lap, and had to grab the doorframe for support. He took Billy's hat off. Dropped it on the cobwebbed bench. He exhaled shakily. Get in, get out, and he was done here. He'd never be back again.

Tommy stepped into the room and the gunshot flung him backward, a searing pain in his midriff, total incomprehension in his eyes. He slammed against the wall and slid to the floor, clutching his side; the hand came away soaked in blood. Desperately searching the shadows, broken by those dusty columns of light, until his gaze settled on the far corner of the room and the outline of a tall man, sitting at the head of the table, in Father's old chair.

A match flared in the darkness. Noone's hollow face in the flame.

"You took your time, Tommy," he said, drawing on his pipe stem, shaking the match dead. "I was expecting you yesterday."

Tommy groaned in anguish. Blood gushed through his fingers from the wound. His eyes closed then he opened them, fixed them again on Noone.

"You know, I did warn Percy that he should shoot you first, that you were the more dangerous of the pair. I suspect he just couldn't help himself, he and Billy had never got along. I am assuming you killed him for his troubles, the poor lad. I've not heard from him, so . . ."

Noone shrugged, like it was all the same to him. Tommy's legs were tingling. He shivered, suddenly cold. His gaze sliding aimlessly around this room that had once been the very center of his life, the safest place in the world. He could almost feel them with him, his family, gathered around the table, shuffling between the rooms. Noone like a specter in the shadows, the slender outline of his body, his crossed legs, his crooked arm, holding the pipe to his lips. The silver revolver was on the table beside him, among a small scattering of victuals and supplies.

"That could have been you, Tommy. I always said you'd have made a fine officer one day. And truly, I planned on leaving you alone, out there, living your life. You will notice that not once over the years have I attempted to track you down, when really it would have been no trouble at all. Even after you killed that headman, down in St. George. And remember, I was a serving police inspector at the time."

A draw on the pipe, a thick plume through the sunlight; Tommy's head rolled.

"Now, your brother on the other hand . . . the man always was a buffoon, though I thought we had an understanding, I must say. The problem is, you people just can't seem to forget me, it's like we are sweethearts, old flames." He chuckled, shook his head. "Whereas, truthfully, I have not given either you or Billy or the events that connect us even the slightest thought in all this time. It was nothing to me, what happened here. Nothing—do you understand? But then Billy goes running to some lawyer and I learn you brought a gun to my house. To my *house*, Tommy. I was very disappointed. I expected a great deal more from you."

Hopelessly Tommy was fixating on Noone's revolver, the same revolver with which he had once killed a man. Delirious thoughts of grabbing it, of doing the same to Noone, his mind lurching uncontrollably between imagined and real. There was a pistol in the room behind him, he was thinking. Mother kept one hidden under the bed. As if he was still living here. Fourteen again.

Noone leaned forward, into a bar of sunlight, his gaunt face looming, those terrible dead gray eyes. "Are you hearing me, Tommy? Are you still with us in there? I hope so, because I want you to know exactly what I plan on doing down in Gippsland once you are dead."

Tommy grunted nonsensically, spittle bubbling; a defiant, animalistic growl. Noone was still talking but he could hardly hear him, consumed by the pain and a futile urge to stand. If he could just get that revolver . . . if he could lay his hands on Noone . . .

In the corner of his eye Tommy glimpsed the doorway and stalled. Katherine stood there with a shotgun, barefoot in her housedress, framed by the sunlight outside. Visibly trembling. Pleading with her eyes. Tommy nodded as best he could manage, screaming internally, willing her on. Across the room Noone was now rising to his feet, dumping his dead tobacco, collecting his things, preparing to leave. Katherine wavered terribly. Tommy grunted but she still didn't move. And all the while Noone was saying,

"I have Drew Bennett to visit then this is over. Unless of course the widow is part of it too. My God, if I have to see to her and her children also . . . how far must this thing go?"

Katherine sprang forward and Noone went for the revolver but before he could reach it she unloaded the shotgun in a searing, deafening blast that tore his face in two. He staggered, still pawing for the revolver, his mouth hanging slackly, a lopsided palsied stare. Part of his jaw was missing, his cheek a bloodied, ragged pulp. He groped for the table edge but missed it and down he went, toppling the chair as he collapsed. Moaning horribly. A noise that was not of this world. Seething, Tommy forced himself upright as Katherine fumbled another cartridge, struggling to reload. Noone's legs, beneath the table, began to shiver and twitch. His hands were still moving, one clawing the air, the other drifting to the second revolver holstered on his belt, and with an immense effort Tommy flung himself forward and crawled across the floor. He reached Noone's boots and climbed up him: kneecaps, thighs, rib cage, the bones like fingerholds, until he was looking down into the voids of his eyes. Noone's neck and face had been lacerated, the artery punctured; blood pulsed in weak gouts. His eyes settled on Tommy and his mouth twisted oddly in what might have been an attempt at a smile. He said something. *Wait for you*, it sounded like. Tommy reared up and clasped both his hands around what remained of Noone's neck, and with everything he had left in him, everything he was, squeezed. Blood bubbled over his fingers. Noone slapped a limp hand puppetlike against Tommy's cheek. Tommy didn't falter. Didn't slacken his grip. He wrung the life from Noone's body until his final foul breath escaped. The hand slid from Tommy's cheek and the eyes clouded further still, yet Tommy went on throttling, tears falling, screaming, "Die, you fucking bastard! Die!"

A gentle hand on his shoulder. "Tommy, enough, it's done."

Slowly he came back to himself. His grip loosened, his body wilted; Katherine held his arm and helped him stand, and together they looked down at Noone. Tommy felt for the shotgun. He peeled it from her hands. She'd managed to get the second cartridge in. "I have to make sure," Tommy said. Katherine backed around the table but didn't avert her gaze, watching as Tommy rested the muzzle squarely on Noone's forehead, and blew it clean away.

The house went up like a bonfire, flames gorging the desiccated wood. In the yard Tommy leaned against Katherine, her arm around his waist, holding a rag to his side, watching his childhood burn. And all it held within it, all the memories, all the pain; Noone. There would be nothing left when the fire was finished, nobody would find the body, nobody would be looking for him out here. Another unseen killing, another hidden pyre. All across this vast country they were burning, as they had for a hundred years, all lit by men like Noone. So many dead in the ashes, thousands of them, scattered over the colonies, never to be found, the wind tossing their remains like a plaything, and teasing the dust off their bones.

Epilogue

1908
Gippsland, Victoria

He is pulling up carrots from the veggie patch when he hears singing from inside the house. He pauses, straightens, grimacing; his hand goes to his side. Barefoot and shirtless in the warm sunshine, wearing only a pair of ragged shorts, there is a star-shaped knot of scar tissue in his sunken midriff and a jagged white line high on his left arm. He stands listening. She must have been crying again. But Emily has the same way with their daughter as he's had with certain horses over the years. Just the sound of her voice soothes her. Soothes him too, in truth.

Carrots dangling in his hand, he walks back to the house, brushes off his feet on the porch. He opens the door, steps inside, puts the carrots on the kitchen bench. Arthur and Rosie will be over later. It's Tommy's turn to cook supper for once. Quietly he pads to the archway and listens, peeking around the wall. They are in the living room, the two of them, bathed in hazy sunlight through the window, Emily rocking the baby while she sings. Elizabeth, they have called her, after his mother; Lizzie is what she gets. Swaddled in a white blanket, her pink little face peering out, staring up at Emily with something close to awe. His wife and his baby—Tommy can scarcely believe that it's real. At a break in the song Emily nuzzles Lizzie playfully, and Tommy hears her giggle for the first time. He gasps and Emily catches it, turns to him and smiles. She beckons him forward. Tommy steps into the room. Emily hands him the baby and he takes her, clumsily, he still looks awkward as hell. He will get used to it, she has told him. If you don't practice you'll never learn. But he worries that he is hurting her, or will drop her; he worries about everything now. He cradles her against his sun-warmed chest and her heavy eyes seem to narrow into a frown. As if asking, who is this man, what is he to her, what will he become? Everything, if Tommy is able. He will give her everything he has, though nothing from before she was born: his past is not her weight to bear.

His daughter, his wife, himself even; if he can help it, they will know him only for the man he is now.

The baby's eyes close gradually. Tommy kisses the top of her head. She is so beautiful, he thinks, so peaceful. Lying there in her swaddling, the soft wash of her breathing, eyelids fluttering faintly, asleep in her father's arms.

Author's Note

The characters, events and some of the locations in this novel are fictitious, but all are rooted in historical fact. The Native Police operated in Queensland from the colony's formation in 1859 until the early years of the twentieth century, and is considered by some historians to have been one of the biggest single killers of Aboriginal people during that time. Knowledge of the force's crimes was widespread, but despite numerous coronial inquests no Native Police officer was ever criminally convicted over an Aboriginal death. For his comprehensive study of this subject, and all aspects of the force, I am again grateful for the work of Jonathan Richards, whose book *The Secret War: A True History of Queensland's Native Police*

(University of Queensland Press) has been a valuable resource throughout.

Billy McBride's line "You'll get nothing out of it" in chapter 21 echoes notorious Native Police Sub-Inspector Lyndon Poingdestre, who, at an inquest into Aboriginal killings at Kimberley, and aware the bodies had already been removed, reportedly mocked the presiding magistrate, "What's the use of the enquiry, you'll get nothing out of it." Sure enough, Poingdestre was only disciplined on a technicality; no criminal charges were brought. Mark Finnane and Jonathan Richards's paper "'You'll Get Nothing Out of It'? The Inquest, Police and Aboriginal Deaths in Colonial Queensland" (*Australian Historical Studies*, no. 123, April 2004), provided the quote and its context, along with a helpful overview of the futility of frontier inquests.

Evan McHugh's *The Drovers* (Viking) is both an entertaining read and a trove of firsthand tales from drovers who worked the central Australian stock routes in their heyday. The phrase "coochies and debil-debils" in chapter 18 appears in that book, quoting from George Farwell's *Land of Mirage* (HarperCollins), as do the stories of the ill-fated teacher walking to Birdsville and the friends on their way to a race meeting forced to drink their horses' blood.

David Hampton (Curator, Workshops Rail Museum,

Ipswich, Qld) and Jeff Powell (Curator, Cobb & Co Museum, Toowoomba, Qld) were generous with their time and expertise on period rail and coach travel, respectively—my thanks to both.

The epigraph is an abridged version of an article that appeared in *The Queenslander* on February 7, 1885, reporting the acquittal of Native Police Sub-Inspector William Nichols following charges relating to the murder of Aboriginals at Irvinebank by troopers under his command. The full article—and countless others like it—is available via Trove (http://nla.gov.au /nla.news-article19796331), a valuable online resource offered by the National Library of Australia.

Any historical errors or inaccuracies in the novel are my own.

Acknowledgments

Thanks to: my agent Lucy Luck and all at C&W; Anna Stein at ICM Partners; Luke Speed at Curtis Brown; my editors Terry Karten and Laura Macaulay, publicists Tracy Locke and Poppy Stimpson, and all at HarperCollins and Pushkin Press; the many reviewers, bloggers, booksellers, and authors who have supported my work; my family for their continued support and encouragement; my parents—to whom this book is dedicated—for giving me the courage to dream; and Sarah, for helping to make those dreams come true.

About the Author

PAUL HOWARTH is a British-Australian author and former lawyer who holds an MA in creative writing from the University of East Anglia, where he was awarded the Malcolm Bradbury Scholarship. In 2018, his debut novel, *Only Killers and Thieves*, was published to international acclaim, winning the Barnes & Noble Discover Award for fiction, and appearing on numerous other awards and books-of-the-year lists. He currently lives in Norwich, England, with his family.

Dust Off the Bones is his second novel.

HARPER LARGE PRINT

We hope you enjoyed reading
our new, comfortable print size and found it
an experience you would like to repeat.

Well – you're in luck!

Harper Large Print offers the finest in
fiction and nonfiction books in this same larger
print size and paperback format. Light and easy to read,
Harper Large Print paperbacks are for the book lovers
who want to see what they are reading without strain.

For a full listing of titles and
new releases to come, please visit our website:
www.hc.com

HARPER LARGE PRINT